THE COMPLETE STORIES

The Complete Stories

Anita Desai

Chatto & Windus

LONDON

1 3 5 7 9 10 8 6 4 2

Chatto & Windus, an imprint of Vintage,
20 Vauxhall Bridge Road,
London SW1V 2SA

Chatto & Windus is part of the Penguin Random House group of companies
whose addresses can be found at global.penguinrandomhouse.com.

Penguin
Random House
UK

First published in the UK by Chatto & Windus in 2017

penguin.co.uk/vintage

A CIP catalogue record for this book is available from the British Library

ISBN 9781784741891

Typeset in 11/14.173 pt Adobe Jenson Pro by Jouve (UK), Milton Keynes
Printed and bound by Clays Ltd, St Ives plc

Penguin Random House is committed to a sustainable future
for our business, our readers and our planet. This book is made from
Forest Stewardship Council® certified paper.

CONTENTS

Preface

I was always a scribbler. As soon as I was taught the alphabet I scribbled – even before I could spell so that I was always harassing everyone in the household (including the cook who knew no word of English) 'How do you spell "house"? How do you spell tree, fire, bird, fish . . . ?' (He responded by making me a magnificent gift on my birthday of an inkwell carved out of soft soapstone which I unfortunately ruined by pouring real ink into that delicate, decorative object.) I filled notebook after notebook seated on a cane stool at my round green table and was labelled, with an understandably resigned sigh, 'The Writer in the Family'.

What was I writing? Consciously, with awareness and intent, very little. I simply had an urge to put everything, everything that I saw, heard and experienced on paper, in ink. I had little awareness of categories – books were books to me, the imposing leather-bound books behind the glass on my parents' bookshelves, the worn, dog-eared paperbacks on my siblings' bookshelves and boxes, and the exciting, inviting ones in all their diversity in the bookshop where I spent my pocket money. I can't remember when I learnt to differentiate between the short story and the novel – no, actually I can: it was when I first decided to send a piece out to be published (publishing was important, I knew writing had to be in print if it was to earn its name) and it was of course of a short length to fit into a magazine or journal. But I was also always writing at length with the idea of a book, a proper book, in my mind, and a part of me believed short stories to be failed novels.

But a short story is not a failed novel any more than a novella is an extended short story. Each has an altogether different set of rules and effects. Length is one of them but lengths vary wildly. As Hortense Calisher said, 'How long should a short story be? As long as a piece of string. I mean – to tie up the parcel with.' I like her practical, workmanlike approach but there is in addition the element of chance. How did one piece I scribbled end up a short story, another extend, unwrap itself, wander, digress and venture onto a path, a road to a further destination – novella, or novel?

It is all a matter of instinct really, and exploration, a conviction that dawns upon one while one works that one has said what one set out to say, there is no need to go further. It may be just one small episode, stumbled upon unexpectedly, a glimpse out of a window, the fall of light on one object while bypassing another, that gives one pause and for some reason is not forgotten. Why has it stayed in the mind when so many other impressions, encounters and experiences have turned into a blur and disappeared? And when one has found the answer to that – the story is done. It can come to one quickly or it may take long, very long, to discover. In the short story it need not be pursued further. Many writers have commented on its identity being closer to a poem than a novel.

I have written only a few short stories that have provided me with that sensation that one craves: ah, I have done what I set out to do, no more is needed. The stories that constitute this collected edition are those that I ended upon that note. For the most part I have taken longer and watched the stone I'd flung into the pond create ripples that extend further, ripple on ripple, arc on arc, struggling to reach the far shore, and wondered: where will this go? How will it end? And that search has turned into a novel.

It is the latter mode that I have mostly chosen. It is the one that offers space both dangerous and forgiving, and lays one open to what may be years of discouragement, dejection, doubt and isolation while one considers options, takes one direction and then another, makes errors, corrects them, picks oneself up and struggles on, only gradually building up the momentum needed for narrative. But while involved in so much that is frustrating and exhausting, one may be granted – briefly and sporadically – that mysterious breath of air that comes up unexpectedly, creating a ripple, a stir, a tide that thrusts one forward and sends one soaring, sailing, flying through space and time.

It is the pursuit of that elusive and mysterious sensation that one undertakes in the short story, so different a form. Instead of those long stretches in which a novelist becomes stranded, the short-story writer must launch forth on what is a high-wire act, refusing to look back or down into the abyss, running the length of it at a sprint so as not to lose balance: quick, quick before you fall! You may go back and start all over again, or change sentences and scenes, but that initial urge must retain its urgency from beginning to end.

> Lightning that mocks the night,
> Brief even as bright.
> (Percy Bysshe Shelley)

In this the short story is the more challenging form – as I realized when I had the temerity to 'teach' the writing of it to students who came to the writing of fiction as complete novices, simply because it was easier to fit into the space of a class, a term – that 'length of string' again. But it was the very brevity and confinement of the form that demanded skill, learning and understanding to make it 'work', i.e. to create the desired effect.

But every once in a while, when completing that frantic dash of the short story, even after it is in print, one finds it won't let go of one. It pursues one – or, rather, one pursues it because there is more to be said, more to be delved into, discovered and exposed. So every once in a while I have found, years and years on in time, a short story written long ago insisting on becoming a novel.

It is the experience I had when I wrote the short story 'The Accompanist'. I felt then that I had put on paper all I knew – very little – about that minor figure of the musical world, the musician in the background, barely noticed, all attention being given to the maestro, the soloist. Was he content for it to be so?

Was he – or not? There was so much in the life and work of that overlooked artist, and I wrote the novel *In Custody* to give him his due although I changed the two characters into a poet and scholar. And again, later still, into the novella 'Translator Translated'. One of my earliest short stories, 'Scholar and Gypsy', eventually carried on a whole new life as the novel *Journey to Ithaca*, something I did not even know till a reader pointed out the development of the theme: the difference between the character who feels the world is all we need and the character for whom the world is limited, beyond it there surely lies more. The search for that other world – physical or spiritual – that compels them on their journeys, had carried on from the short story into the novel as a sketch might lead to a painting. This subterranean element rising to the surface surprised me, I had not been conscious of that development.

Each form requires a different set of abilities, even materials – as an artist might need pencil or pen and ink or water colours or paint for one work or another. Brevity and concision will do for one while the other requires doubt, mystery, mistake and stamina. If one writes both, which gives the greater satisfaction? Now one, now the other – that is the only answer.

Anita Desai
November, 2016

Games at Twilight

It was still too hot to play outdoors. They had had their tea, they had been washed and had their hair brushed, and after the long day of confinement in the house that was not cool but at least a protection from the sun, the children strained to get out. Their faces were red and bloated with the effort, but their mother would not open the door, everything was still curtained and shuttered in a way that stifled the children, made them feel that their lungs were stuffed with cotton wool and their noses with dust and if they didn't burst out into the light and see the sun and feel the air, they would choke.

'Please, Ma, please,' they begged. 'We'll play in the veranda and porch – we won't go a step out of the porch.' 'You will, I know you will, and then—'

'No – we won't, we won't,' they wailed so horrendously that she actually let down the bolt of the front door so that they burst out like seeds from a crackling, overripe pod into the veranda, with such wild, maniacal yells that she retreated to her bath and the shower of talcum powder and the fresh sari that were to help her face the summer evening.

They faced the afternoon. It was too hot. Too bright. The white walls of the veranda glared stridently in the sun. The bougainvillea hung about it, purple and magenta, in livid balloons. The garden outside was like a tray made of beaten brass, flattened out on the red gravel and the stony soil in all shades of metal – aluminium, tin, copper and brass. No life stirred at this arid time of day – the birds still drooped, like dead fruit, in the papery tents

1

of the trees; some squirrels lay limp on the wet earth under the garden tap. The outdoor dog lay stretched as if dead on the veranda mat, his paws and ears and tail all reaching out like dying travellers in search of water. He rolled his eyes at the children – two white marbles rolling in the purple sockets, begging for sympathy – and attempted to lift his tail in a wag but could not. It only twitched and lay still.

Then, perhaps roused by the shrieks of the children, a band of parrots suddenly fell out of the eucalyptus tree, tumbled frantically in the still, sizzling air, then sorted themselves out into battle formation and streaked away across the white sky.

The children, too, felt released. They too began tumbling, shoving, pushing against each other, frantic to start. Start what? Start their business. The business of the children's day which is – play.

'Let's play hide-and-seek.'

'Who'll be It?'

'You be It.'

'Why should I? You be—'

'You're the eldest—'

'That doesn't mean—'

The shoves became harder. Some kicked out. The motherly Mira intervened. She pulled the boys roughly apart. There was a tearing sound of cloth but it was lost in the heavy panting and angry grumbling and no one paid attention to the small sleeve hanging loosely off a shoulder.

'Make a circle, make a circle!' she shouted, firmly pulling and pushing till a kind of vague circle was formed. 'Now clap!' she roared and, clapping, they all chanted in melancholy unison: 'Dip, dip, dip – my blue ship—' and every now and then one or the other saw he was safe by the way his hands fell at the crucial moment – palm on palm, or back of hand on palm – and dropped out of the circle with a yell and a jump of relief and jubilation.

Raghu was It. He started to protest, to cry 'You cheated – Mira cheated – Anu cheated—' but it was too late, the others had all already streaked away. There was no one to hear when he called out, 'Only in the veranda – the porch – Ma said – Ma *said* to stay in the porch!' No one had stopped to listen, all he saw were their brown legs flashing through the dusty shrubs, scrambling up brick walls, leaping over compost heaps and hedges, and then the porch stood empty in the purple shade of the bougainvillea and the garden was as empty as before; even the limp squirrels had whisked away, leaving everything gleaming, brassy and bare.

Only small Manu suddenly reappeared, as if he had dropped out of an invisible cloud or from a bird's claws, and stood for a moment in the centre of the yellow lawn, chewing his finger and near to tears as he heard Raghu shouting, with his head pressed against the veranda wall, 'Eighty-three, eighty-five, eighty-nine, ninety . . .' and then made off in a panic, half of him wanting to fly north, the other half counselling south. Raghu turned just in time to see the flash of his white shorts and the uncertain skittering of his red sandals, and charged after him with such a bloodcurdling yell that Manu stumbled over the hosepipe, fell into its rubber coils and lay there weeping, 'I won't be It – you have to find them all – all – all!'

'I know I have to, idiot,' Raghu said, superciliously kicking him with his toe. 'You're dead,' he said with satisfaction, licking the beads of perspiration off his upper lip, and then stalked off in search of worthier prey, whistling spiritedly so that the hiders should hear and tremble.

Ravi heard the whistling and picked his nose in a panic, trying to find comfort by burrowing the finger deep-deep into that soft tunnel. He felt himself too exposed, sitting on an upturned flower pot behind the garage. Where could he burrow? He could run around the garage if he heard Raghu come – around and around and around – but he hadn't much faith in his short legs when matched against Raghu's long, hefty, hairy footballer legs. Ravi had a frightening glimpse of them as Raghu combed the

hedge of crotons and hibiscus, trampling delicate ferns underfoot as he did so. Ravi looked about him desperately, swallowing
a small ball of snot in his fear.

The garage was locked with a great heavy lock to which the
driver had the key in his room, hanging from a nail on the wall
under his work-shirt. Ravi had peeped in and seen him still
sprawling on his string-cot in his vest and striped underpants,
the hair on his chest and the hair in his nose shaking with the
vibrations of his phlegm-obstructed snores. Ravi had wished he
were tall enough, big enough to reach the key on the nail, but it
was impossible, beyond his reach for years to come. He had
sidled away and sat dejectedly on the flower pot. That at least was
cut to his own size.

But next to the garage was another shed with a big green
door. Also locked. No one even knew who had the key to the
lock. That shed wasn't opened more than once a year when Ma
turned out all the old broken bits of furniture and rolls of mat-
ting and leaking buckets, and the white ant hills were broken and
swept away and Flit sprayed into the spider webs and rat holes so
that the whole operation was like the looting of a poor, ruined
and conquered city. The green leaves of the door sagged. They
were nearly off their rusty hinges. The hinges were large and
made a small gap between the door and the walls – only just
large enough for rats, dogs and, possibly, Ravi to slip through.

Ravi had never cared to enter such a dark and depressing
mortuary of defunct household goods seething with such
unspeakable and alarming animal life but, as Raghu's whistling
grew angrier and sharper and his crashing and storming in the
hedge wilder, Ravi suddenly slipped off the flower pot and
through the crack and was gone. He chuckled aloud with astonishment at his own temerity so that Raghu came out of the
hedge, stood silent with his hands on his hips, listening, and
finally shouted 'I heard you! I'm coming! *Got* you—' and came
charging round the garage only to find the upturned flower pot,
the yellow dust, the crawling of white ants in a mud-hill against

the closed shed door – nothing. Snarling, he bent to pick up a stick and went off, whacking it against the garage and shed walls as if to beat out his prey.

Ravi shook, then shivered with delight, with self-congratulation. Also with fear. It was dark, spooky in the shed. It had a muffled smell, as of graves. Ravi had once got locked into the linen cupboard and sat there weeping for half an hour before he was rescued. But at least that had been a familiar place, and even smelt pleasantly of starch, laundry and, reassuringly, of his mother. But the shed smelt of rats, ant hills, dust and spider webs. Also of less definable, less recognizable horrors. And it was dark. Except for the white-hot cracks along the door, there was no light. The roof was very low. Although Ravi was small, he felt as if he could reach up and touch it with his finger tips. But he didn't stretch. He hunched himself into a ball so as not to bump into anything, touch or feel anything. What might there not be to touch him and feel him as he stood there, trying to see in the dark? Something cold, or slimy – like a snake. Snakes! He leapt up as Raghu whacked the wall with his stick – then, quickly realizing what it was, felt almost relieved to hear Raghu, hear his stick. It made him feel protected.

But Raghu soon moved away. There wasn't a sound once his footsteps had gone around the garage and disappeared. Ravi stood frozen inside the shed. Then he shivered all over. Something had tickled the back of his neck. It took him a while to pick up the courage to lift his hand and explore. It was an insect – perhaps a spider – exploring *him*. He squashed it and wondered how many more creatures were watching him, waiting to reach out and touch him, the stranger.

There was nothing now. After standing in that position – his hand still on his neck, feeling the wet splodge of the squashed spider gradually dry – for minutes, hours, his legs began to tremble with the effort, the inaction. By now he could see enough in the dark to make out the large solid shapes of old wardrobes, broken buckets and bedsteads piled on top of each other around him. He recognized an old bathtub – patches of enamel glimmered at him and at last he lowered himself onto its edge.

He contemplated slipping out of the shed and into the fray. He wondered if it would not be better to be captured by Raghu and be returned to the milling crowd as long as he could be in the sun, the light, the free spaces of the garden and the familiarity of his brothers, sisters and cousins. It would be evening soon. Their games would become legitimate. The parents would sit out on the lawn on cane basket chairs and watch them as they tore around the garden or gathered in knots to share a loot of mulberries or black, teeth-splitting jamun from the garden trees. The gardener would fix the hosepipe to the water tap and water would fall lavishly through the air to the ground, soaking the dry yellow grass and the red gravel and arousing the sweet, the intoxicating scent of water on dry earth – that loveliest scent in the world. Ravi sniffed for a whiff of it. He half-rose from the bathtub, then heard the despairing scream of one of the girls as Raghu bore down upon her. There was the sound of a crash, and of rolling about in the bushes, the shrubs, then screams and accusing sobs of, 'I touched the den' – 'You did not' – 'I did' – 'You liar, you did *not*' and then a fading away and silence again.

Ravi sat back on the harsh edge of the tub, deciding to hold out a bit longer. What fun if they were all found and caught – he alone left unconquered! He had never known that sensation. Nothing more wonderful had ever happened to him than being taken out by an uncle and bought a whole slab of chocolate all to himself, or being flung into the soda-man's pony cart and driven up to the gate by the friendly driver with the red beard and pointed ears. To defeat Raghu – that hirsute, hoarse-voiced football champion – and to be the winner in a circle of older, bigger, luckier children – that would be thrilling beyond imagination. He hugged his knees together and smiled to himself almost shyly at the thought of so much victory, such laurels.

*

There he sat smiling, knocking his heels against the bathtub, now and then getting up and going to the door to put his ear to the broad crack and listening for sounds of the game, the pursuer and the pursued, and then returning to his seat with the dogged determination of the true winner, a breaker of records, a champion.

It grew darker in the shed as the light at the door grew softer, fuzzier, turned to a kind of crumbling yellow pollen that turned to yellow fur, blue fur, grey fur. Evening. Twilight. The sound of water gushing, falling. The scent of earth receiving water, slaking its thirst in great gulps and releasing that green scent of freshness, coolness. Through the crack Ravi saw the long purple shadows of the shed and the garage lying still across the yard. Beyond that, the white walls of the house. The bougainvillea had lost its lividity, hung in dark bundles that quaked and twittered and seethed with masses of homing sparrows. The lawn was shut off from his view. Could he hear the children's voices? It seemed to him that he could. It seemed to him that he could hear them chanting, singing, laughing. But what about the game? What had happened? Could it be over? How could it when he was still not found?

It then occurred to him that he could have slipped out long ago, dashed across the yard to the veranda and touched the 'den'. It was necessary to do that to win. He had forgotten. He had only remembered the part of hiding and trying to elude the seeker. He had done that so successfully, his success had occupied him so wholly that he had quite forgotten that success had to be clinched by that final dash to victory and the ringing cry of 'Den!'

With a whimper he burst through the crack, fell on his knees, got up and stumbled on stiff, benumbed legs across the shadowy yard, crying heartily by the time he reached the veranda so that when he flung himself at the white pillar and bawled, 'Den! Den! Den!' his voice broke with rage and pity at the disgrace of it all and he felt himself flooded with tears and misery.

Out on the lawn, the children stopped chanting. They all turned to stare at him in amazement. Their faces were pale and triangular in the dusk. The trees and bushes around them stood inky and sepulchral, spilling long shadows across them. They stared, wondering at his reappearance, his passion, his wild animal howling. Their mother rose from her basket chair and came towards him, worried, annoyed, saying, 'Stop it, stop it, Ravi. Don't be a baby. Have you hurt yourself?' Seeing him attended to, the children went back to clasping their hands and chanting 'The grass is green, the rose is red . . .'

But Ravi would not let them. He tore himself out of his mother's grasp and pounded across the lawn into their midst, charging at them with his head lowered so that they scattered in surprise. 'I won, I won, I won,' he bawled, shaking his head so that the big tears flew. 'Raghu didn't find me. I won, I won—'

It took them a minute to grasp what he was saying, even who he was. They had quite forgotten him. Raghu had found all the others long ago. There had been a fight about who was to be It next. It had been so fierce that their mother had emerged from her bath and made them change to another game. Then they had played another and another. Broken mulberries from the tree and eaten them. Helped the driver wash the car when their father returned from work. Helped the gardener water the beds till he roared at them and swore he would complain to their parents. The parents had come out, taken up their positions on the cane chairs. They had begun to play again, sing and chant. All this time no one had remembered Ravi. Having disappeared from the scene, he had disappeared from their minds. Clean.

'Don't be a fool,' Raghu said roughly, pushing him aside, and even Mira said, 'Stop howling, Ravi. If you want to play, you can stand at the end of the line,' and she put him there very firmly.

The game proceeded. Two pairs of arms reached up and met in an arc. The children trooped under it again and again in a lugubrious circle, ducking their heads and intoning:

'The grass is green,
The rose is red;
Remember me
When I am dead, dead, dead, dead . . .'

And the arc of thin arms trembled in the twilight, and the heads
were bowed so sadly, and their feet tramped to that melancholy
refrain so mournfully, so helplessly, that Ravi could not bear it. He
would not follow them, he would not be included in this funereal
game. He had wanted victory and triumph – not a funeral. But he
had been forgotten, left out and he would not join them now. The
ignominy of being forgotten – how could he face it? He felt his
heart go heavy and ache inside him unbearably. He lay down full
length on the damp grass, crushing his face into it, no longer crying, silenced by a terrible sense of his insignificance.

Private Tuition by Mr Bose

Mr Bose gave his private tuition out on the balcony, in the evenings, in the belief that, since it faced south, the river Hooghly would send it a wavering breeze or two to drift over the rooftops, through the washing and the few pots of tulsi and marigold that his wife had placed precariously on the balcony rail, to cool him, fan him, soothe him. But there was no breeze: it was hot, the air hung upon them like a damp towel, gagging him and, speaking through this gag, he tiredly intoned the Sanskrit verses that should, he felt, have been roared out on a hilltop at sunrise.

Aum. Usa va asvasya medhyasya sirah . . .

It came out, of course, a mumble. Asked to translate, his pupil, too, scowled as he had done, thrust his fist through his hair and mumbled:

'Aum is the dawn and the head of a horse . . .'

Mr Bose protested in a low wail. 'What horse, my boy? What horse?'

The boy rolled his eyes sullenly. 'I don't know, sir, it doesn't say.'

Mr Bose looked at him in disbelief. He was the son of a Brahmin priest who himself instructed him in the Mahabharata all morning, turning him over to Mr Bose only in the evening when he set out to officiate at weddings, puja and other functions for which he was so much in demand on account of his stately bearing, his calm and inscrutable face and his sensuous voice that so suited the Sanskrit language in which he, almost always, discoursed. And this was his son – this Pritam with his red-veined eyes and oiled locks, his stumbling fingers and shuffling feet that betrayed his secret life, its scruffiness, its gutters and drains full of resentment and destruction. Mr Bose suddenly remembered how he had seen him, from the window of a bus that had come to a standstill on the street due to a fist fight between the conductor and a passenger, Pritam slipping up the stairs, through the door, into a neon-lit bar off Park Street.

'The sacrificial horse,' Mr Bose explained with forced patience. 'Have you heard of Asvamedha, Pritam, the royal horse that was let loose to run through the kingdom before it returned to the capital and was sacrificed by the king?'

The boy gave him a look of such malice that Mr Bose bit the end of his moustache and fell silent, shuffling through the pages. 'Read on, then,' he mumbled and listened, for a while, as Pritam blundered heavily through the Sanskrit verses that rolled off his father's experienced tongue, and even Mr Bose's shy one, with such rich felicity. When he could not bear it any longer, he turned his head, slightly, just enough to be able to look out of the corner of his eye through the open door, down the unlit passage at the end of which, in the small, dimly lit kitchen, his wife sat kneading dough for bread, their child at her side. Her head was bowed so that some of her hair had freed itself of the long steel pins he hated so much and hung about her pale, narrow face. The red border of her sari was the only stripe of colour in that smoky scene. The child beside her had his back turned to the door so that Mr Bose could see his little brown buttocks under the short white shirt, squashed firmly down upon the woven mat. Mr Bose wondered what it was that kept him so quiet – perhaps his mother had given him a lump of dough to mould into some thick and satisfying shape. Both of them seemed bound together and held down in some deeply absorbing act from which he was excluded. He would have liked to break in and join them.

Pritam stopped reading, maliciously staring at Mr Bose whose lips were wavering into a smile beneath the ragged moustache. The woman, disturbed by the break in the recitation on the balcony, looked up, past the child, down the passage and into Mr Bose's face. Mr Bose's moustache lifted up like a pair of wings and, beneath them, his smile lifted up and out with almost a laugh of tenderness and delight. Beginning to laugh herself, she quickly turned, pulled down the corners of her mouth with mock sternness, trying to recall him to the path of duty, and picking up a lump of sticky dough, handed it back to the child, softly urging him to be quiet and let his father finish the lesson.

Pritam, the scabby, oil-slick son of a Brahmin priest, coughed theatrically – a cough imitating that of a favourite screen actor, surely, it was so false and over-done and suggestive. Mr Bose swung around in dismay, crying 'Why have you stopped? Go on, go on.'

'You weren't listening, sir.'

Many words, many questions leapt to Mr Bose's lips, ready to pounce on this miserable boy whom he could hardly bear to see sitting beneath his wife's holy tulsi plant that she tended with prayers, water-can and oil-lamp every evening. Then, growing conscious of the way his moustache was agitating upon his upper lip, he said only, 'Read.'

'Ahar va asvam purustan mahima nvajagata . . .'

Across the road someone turned on a radio and a song filled with a pleasant, lilting *weltschmerz* twirled and sank, twirled and rose from that balcony to this. Pritam raised his voice, grinding through the Sanskrit consonants like some dying, diseased tram-car. From the kitchen only a murmur and the soft thumping of the dough in the pan could be heard – sounds as soft and comfortable as sleepy pigeons. Mr Bose longed passionately to listen to them, catch every faintest nuance of them, but to do this he would have to smash the radio, hurl the Brahmin's son down the iron stairs . . . He curled up his hands on his knees and drew his feet together under him, horrified at this welling up of violence inside him, under his pale pink bush-shirt, inside his thin, ridiculously heaving chest. As often as Mr Bose longed to alter the entire direction of the world's revolution, as often as he longed to break the world apart into two halves and shake out of them – what? Festival fireworks, a woman's soft hair, blood-stained feathers? – he would shudder and pale at the thought of his indiscretion, his violence, this secret force that now and then threatened, clamoured, so that he had quickly to still it, squash it. After all, he must continue with his private tuitions: that was what was important. The baby had to have his first pair of shoes and soon he would be needing oranges, biscuits, plastic toys. 'Read,' said Mr Bose, a little less sternly, a little more sadly.

But, 'It is seven, I can go home now,' said Pritam triumphantly, throwing his father's thick yellow Mahabharata into his bag, knocking the bag shut with one fist and preparing to fly. Where did he fly to? Mr Bose wondered if it would be the neon-lit bar off Park Street. Then, seeing the boy disappear down the black stairs – the bulb had fused again – he felt it didn't matter, didn't matter one bit since it left him alone to turn, plunge down the passage and fling himself at the doorposts of the kitchen, there to stand and gaze down at his wife, now rolling out puris with an exquisite, back-and-forth rolling motion of her hands, and his son, trying now to make a spoon stand on one end.

She only glanced at him, pretended not to care, pursed her lips to keep from giggling, flipped the puri over and rolled it finer and flatter still. He wanted so much to touch her hair, the strand that lay over her shoulder in a black loop, and did not know how to – she was so busy. 'Your hair is coming loose,' he said.

'Go, go,' she warned, 'I hear the next one coming.'

So did he, he heard the soft patting of sandals on the worn steps outside, so all he did was bend and touch the small curls of hair on his son's neck. They were so soft, they seemed hardly human and quite frightened him. When he took his hand away he felt the wisps might have come off onto his fingers and he rubbed the tips together wonderingly. The child let fall the spoon, with a magnificent ring, onto a brass dish and started at this discovery of percussion.

The light on the balcony was dimmed as his next pupil came to stand in the doorway. Quickly he pulled himself away from the doorpost and walked back to his station, tense with unspoken words and unexpressed emotion. He had quite forgotten that his next pupil, this Wednesday, was to be Upneet. Rather Pritam again than this once-a-week typhoon, Upneet of the flowered sari, ruby earrings and shaming laughter. Under this Upneet's gaze such ordinary functions of a tutor's life as sitting down at a table, sharpening a pencil and opening a book to the correct page became matters of farce, disaster and hilarity. His very bones sprang out of joint. He did not know where to look – everywhere were Upneet's flowers, Upneet's giggles. Immediately, at the very sight of the tip of her sandal peeping out beneath the flowered hem of her sari, he was a man broken to pieces, flung this way and that, rattling. Rattling.

Throwing away the Sanskrit books, bringing out volumes of Bengali poetry, opening to a poem by Jibanandan Das, he wondered ferociously: Why did she come? What use had she for Bengali poetry? Why did she come from that house across the road where the loud radio rollicked, to sit on his balcony, in view of his shy wife, making him read poetry to her? It was intolerable. Intolerable, all of it – except, only for the seventy-five rupees paid at the end of the month. Oranges, he thought grimly, and milk, medicines, clothes. And he read to her:

'Her hair was the dark night of Vidisha,
Her face the sculpture of Svarasti . . .'

Quite steadily he read, his tongue tamed and enthralled by the rhythm of the verse he had loved (copied on a sheet of blue paper, he had sent it to his wife one day when speech proved inadequate).

'"Where have you been so long?" she asked,
Lifting her bird's-nest eyes,
Banalata Sen of Natore.'

Pat-pat-pat. No, it was not the rhythm of the verse, he realized, but the tapping of her foot, green-sandalled, red-nailed, swinging and swinging to lift the hem of her sari up and up. His eyes slid off the book, watched the flowered hem swing out and up, out and up as the green-sandalled foot peeped out, then in, peeped out, then in. For a while his tongue ran on of its own volition:

'All birds come home, and all rivers,
Life's ledger is closed . . .'

But he could not continue – it was the foot, the sandal that carried on the rhythm exactly as if he were still reciting. Even the radio stopped its rollicking and, as a peremptory voice began to enumerate the day's disasters and achievements all over the world, Mr Bose heard more vigorous sounds from his kitchen as well. There too the lulling pigeon sounds had been crisply turned off and what he heard were bangs and rattles among the kitchen pots, a kettledrum of commands, he thought. The baby, letting out a wail of surprise, paused, heard the nervous commotion continue and intensify and launched himself on a series of wails.

Mr Bose looked up, aghast. He could not understand how these two halves of the difficult world that he had been holding so carefully together, sealing them with reams of poetry, reams of Sanskrit, had split apart into dissonance. He stared at his pupil's face, creamy, feline, satirical, and was forced to complete the poem in a stutter:

'Only darkness remains, to sit facing
Banalata Sen of Natore.'

But the darkness was filled with hideous sounds of business and anger and command. The radio news commentator barked, the baby wailed, the kitchen pots clashed. He even heard his wife's voice raised, angrily, at the child, like a threatening stick. Glancing again at his pupil whom he feared so much, he saw precisely that lift of the eyebrows and that twist of a smile that disjointed him, rattled him.

'Er – please read,' he tried to correct, to straighten that twist of eyebrows and lips. 'Please read.'

'But you have read it to me already,' she laughed, mocking him with her eyes and laugh.

'The next poem,' he cried, 'read the next poem,' and turned the page with fingers as clumsy as toes.

'It is much better when you read to me,' she complained impertinently, but read, keeping time to the rhythm with that restless foot which he watched as though it were a snake-charmer's pipe, swaying. He could hear her voice no more than the snake could the pipe's – it was drowned out by the baby's wails, swelling into roars of self-pity and indignation in this suddenly hard-edged world.

Mr Bose threw a piteous, begging look over his shoulder at the kitchen. Catching his eye, his wife glowered at him, tossed the hair out of her face and cried, 'Be quiet, be quiet, can't you see how busy your father is?' Red-eared, he turned to find Upneet looking curiously down the passage at this scene of domestic anarchy, and said, 'I'm sorry, sorry – please read.'

'I have read!' she exclaimed. 'Didn't you hear me?'

'So much noise – I'm sorry,' he gasped and rose to hurry down the passage and hiss, pressing his hands to his head as he did so, 'Keep him quiet, can't you? Just for half an hour!'

'He is hungry,' his wife said, as if she could do nothing about that.

'Feed him then,' he begged.

'It isn't time,' she said angrily.

'Never mind. Feed him, feed him.'

'Why? So that you can read poetry to that girl in peace?'

'Shh!' he hissed, shocked, alarmed that Upneet would hear. His chest filled with the injustice of it. But this was no time for pleas or reason. He gave another desperate look at the child who lay crouched on the kitchen floor, rolling with misery. When he turned to go back to his pupil who was watching them interestedly, he heard his wife snatch up the child and tell him, 'Have your food then, have it and eat it – don't you see how angry your father is?'

He spent the remaining half-hour with Upneet trying to distract her from observation of his domestic life. Why should it interest her? he thought angrily. She came here to study, not to mock, not to make trouble. He was her tutor, not her clown! Sternly, he gave her dictation but she was so hopeless – she learnt no Bengali at her convent school, found it hard even to form the letters of the Bengali alphabet – that he was left speechless. He crossed out her errors with his red pencil – grateful to be able to cancel out, so effectively, some of the ugliness of his life – till there was hardly a word left uncrossed and, looking up to see her reaction, found her far less perturbed than he. In fact, she looked quite mischievously pleased. Three months of Bengali lessons to end in this! She was as triumphant as he was horrified. He let fall the red pencil with a discouraged gesture. So, in complete discord, the lesson broke apart, they all broke apart and for a while Mr Bose was alone on the balcony, clutching at the rails, thinking that these bars of cooled iron were all that were left for him to hold. Inside all was a conflict of shame and despair, in garbled grammar.

But, gradually, the grammar rearranged itself according to rule, corrected itself. The composition into quiet made quite clear the exhaustion of the child, asleep or nearly so. The sounds of dinner being prepared were calm, decorative even. Once more the radio was tuned to music, sympathetically sad. When his wife called him in to eat, he turned to go with his shoulders beaten, sagging, an attitude repeated by his moustache.

'He is asleep,' she said, glancing at him with a rather ashamed face, conciliatory.

He nodded and sat down before his brass tray. She straightened it nervously, waved a hand over it as if to drive away a fly he could not see, and turned to the fire to fry hot puris for him, one by one, turning quickly to heap them on his tray so fast that he begged her to stop.

'Eat more,' she coaxed. 'One more' – as though the extra puri were a peace offering following her rebellion of half an hour ago.

He took it with reluctant fingers but his moustache began to quiver on his lip as if beginning to wake up. 'And you?' he asked. 'Won't you eat now?'

About her mouth, too, some quivers began to rise and move. She pursed her lips, nodded and began to fill her tray, piling up the puris in a low stack.

'One more,' he told her, 'just one more,' he teased, and they laughed.

Studies in the Park

— Turn it off, turn it off, turn it off! First he listens to the news in Hindi. Directly after, in English. Broom – brroom – brrroom – the voice of doom roars. Next, in Tamil. Then in Punjabi. In Gujarati. What next, my God, what next? Turn it off before I smash it onto his head, fling it out of the window, do nothing of the sort of course, nothing of the sort.

— And my mother. She cuts and fries, cuts and fries. All day I hear her chopping and slicing and the pan of oil hissing. What all does she find to fry and feed us on, for God's sake? Eggplants, potatoes, spinach, shoe soles, newspapers, finally she'll slice me and feed me to my brothers and sisters. Ah, now she's turned on the tap. It's roaring and pouring, pouring and roaring into a bucket without a bottom.

— The bell rings. Voices clash, clatter and break. The tin-and-bottle man? The neighbours? The police? The Help-the-Blind man? Thieves and burglars? All of them, all of them, ten or twenty or a hundred of them, marching up the stairs, hammering at the door, breaking in and climbing over me – ten, twenty or a hundred of them.

— Then, worst of all, the milk arrives. In the tallest glass in the house. 'Suno, drink your milk. Good for you, Suno. You need it. Now, before the exams. Must have it, Suno. Drink.' The voice wheedles its way into my ear like a worm. I shudder. The table tips over. The milk runs. The tumbler clangs on the floor. 'Suno, Suno, how will you do your exams?'

— That is precisely what I ask myself. All very well to give me a room – Uncle's been pushed off on a pilgrimage to Hardwar to clear a room for me – and to bring me milk and say, 'Study, Suno, study for your exams.' What about the uproar around me? These people don't know the meaning of the word Quiet. When my mother fills buckets, sloshes the kitchen floor, fries and sizzles things in the pan, she thinks she is being Quiet. The children have never even heard the word, it amazes and puzzles them. On their way back from school they fling their satchels in at my door, then tear in to snatch them back before I tear them to bits. Bawl when I pull their ears, screech when Mother whacks them. Stuff themselves with her fries and then smear the grease on my books.

So I raced out of my room, with my fingers in my ears, to scream till the roof fell down about their ears. But the radio suddenly went off, the door to my parents' room suddenly opened and my father appeared, bathed and shaven, stuffed and set up with the news of the world in six different languages—his white dhoti blazing, his white shirt crackling, his patent leather pumps glittering. He stopped in the doorway and I stopped on the balls of my feet and wavered. My fingers came out of my ears, my hair came down over my eyes. Then he looked away from me, took his watch out of his pocket and enquired, 'Is the food ready?' in a voice that came out of his nose like the whistle of a punctual train. He skated off towards his meal, I turned and slouched back to my room. On his way to work, he looked in to say, 'Remember, Suno, I expect good results from you. Study hard, Suno.' Just behind him, I saw all the rest of them standing, peering in, silently. All of them stared at me, at the exam I was to take. At the degree I was to get. Or not get. Horrifying thought. Oh study, study, study, they all breathed at me while my father's footsteps went down the stairs, crushing each underfoot in turn. I felt their eyes on me, goggling, and their breath on me, hot with earnestness. I looked back at them, into their open mouths and staring eyes.

'Study,' I said, and found I croaked. 'I know I ought to study. And how do you expect me to study – in this madhouse? You

run wild, *wild*. I'm getting out,' I screamed, leaping up and grabbing my books, 'I'm going to study outside. Even the street is
quieter,' I screeched and threw myself past them and down the
stairs that my father had just cowed and subjugated so that
they still lay quivering, and paid no attention to the howls that
broke out behind me of 'Suno, Suno, listen. Your milk – your
studies – your exams, Suno!'

At first I tried the tea shop at the corner. In my reading I had
often come across men who wrote at café tables – letters, verse,
whole novels – over a cup of coffee or a glass of absinthe. I
thought it would be simple to read a chapter of history over a cup
of tea. There was no crowd in the mornings, none of my friends
would be there. But the proprietor would not leave me alone.
Bored, picking his nose, he wandered down from behind the
counter to my table by the weighing machine and tried to pass
the time of day by complaining about his piles, the new waiter
and the high prices. 'And sugar,' he whined. 'How can I give you
anything to put in your tea with sugar at four rupees a kilo?
There's rationed sugar, I know, at two rupees, but that's not
enough to feed even an ant. And the way you all sugar your tea –
hai, hai,' he sighed, worse than my mother. I didn't answer. I
frowned at my book and looked stubborn. But when I got rid of
him, the waiter arrived. 'Have a biscuit?' he murmured, flicking at
my table and chair with his filthy duster. 'A bun? Fritters? Make
you some hot fritters?' I snarled at him but he only smiled, determined to be friendly. Just a boy, really, in a pink shirt with purple
circles stamped all over it – he thought he looked so smart. He
was growing sideburns, he kept fingering them. 'I'm a student,
too,' he said, 'sixth class, fail. My mother wanted me to go back
and try again, but I didn't like the teacher – he beat me. So I came
here to look for a job. Lalaji had just thrown out a boy called Hari
for selling lottery tickets to the clients so he took me on. I can
make out a bill . . .' He would have babbled on if Lalaji had not
come and shoved him into the kitchen with an oath. So it went

on. I didn't read more than half a chapter that whole morning. I didn't want to go home either. I walked along the street, staring at my shoes, with my shoulders slumped in the way that makes my father scream, 'What's the matter? Haven't you bones? A spine?' I kicked some rubble along the pavement, down the drain, then stopped at the iron gates of King Edward's Park.

'Exam troubles?' asked a gram vendor who sat outside it, in a friendly voice. Not insinuating, but low, pleasant. 'The park's full of boys like you,' he continued in that sympathetic voice. 'I see them walk up and down, up and down with their books, like mad poets. Then I'm glad I was never sent to school,' and he began to whistle, not impertinently but so cheerfully that I stopped and stared at him. He had a crippled arm that hung out of his shirt sleeve like a leg of mutton dangling on a hook. His face was scarred as though he had been dragged out of some terrible accident. But he was shuffling hot gram into paper cones with his one hand and whistling like a bird, whistling the tune of, 'We are the bulbuls of our land, our land is Paradise.' Nodding at the greenery beyond the gates, he said, 'The park's a good place to study in,' and, taking his hint, I went in.

I wonder how it is I never thought of the park before. It isn't far from our house and I sometimes went there as a boy, if I managed to run away from school, to lie on a bench, eat peanuts, shy stones at the chipmunks that came for the shells, and drink from the fountain. But then it was not as exciting as playing marbles in the street or stoning rats with my school friends in the vacant lot behind the cinema. It had straight paths, beds of flapping red flowers – cannas, I think – rows of palm trees like limp flags, a dry fountain and some green benches. Old men sat on them with their legs far apart, heads drooping over the tops of sticks, mumbling through their dentures or cackling with that mad, ripping laughter that makes children think of old men as wizards and bogey-men. Bag-like women in grey and fawn saris or black burkhas screamed, just as grey and fawn and black birds do, at children falling into the fountain or racing on rickety legs after the chipmunks and pigeons. A madman or two, prancing around in paper caps and bits of rags, munching banana peels and scratching like monkeys. Corners behind hibiscus bushes stinking of piss. Iron rails with rows of beggars contentedly dozing, scratching, gambling, with their sackcloth backs to the rails. A city park.

What I hadn't noticed, or thought of, were all the students who escaped from their city flats and families like mine to come and study here. Now, walking down a path with my history book tucked under my arm, I felt like a gatecrasher at a party or a visitor to a public library trying to control a sneeze. They all seemed to belong here, to be at home here. Dressed in loose pyjamas, they strolled up and down under the palms, books open in their hands, heads lowered into them. Or they sat in twos and threes on the grass, reading aloud in turns. Or lay full length under the trees, books spread out across their faces – sleeping, or else imbibing information through the subconscious. Opening out my book, I too strolled up and down, reading to myself in a low murmur.

In the beginning, when I first started studying in the park, I couldn't concentrate on my studies. I'd keep looking up at the boy strolling in front of me, reciting poetry in a kind of thundering whisper, waving his arms about and running his bony fingers through his hair till it stood up like a thorn bush. Or at the chipmunks that fought and played and chased each other all over the park, now and then joining forces against the sparrows over a nest or a paper cone of gram. Or at the madman going through the rubble at the bottom of the dry fountain and coming up with a rubber shoe, a banana peel or a piece of glittering tin that he appreciated so much that he put it in his mouth and chewed it till blood ran in strings from his mouth.

It took me time to get accustomed to the ways of the park. I went there daily, for the whole day, and soon I got to know it as well as my own room at home and found I could study there, or sleep, or daydream, as I chose. Then I fell into its routine, its rhythm, and my time moved in accordance with its time. We were like a house-owner and his house, or a turtle and its shell, or a river and its bank – so close. I resented everyone else who came to the park – I thought they couldn't possibly share my feeling for it. Except, perhaps, the students.

The park was like an hotel, or an hospital, belonging to the city but with its own order and routine, enclosed by iron rails, laid out according to prescription in rows of palms, benches and paths. If I went there very early in the morning, I'd come upon a yoga class. It consisted of young bodybuilders rippling their muscles like snakes as well as old crack-pots determined to keep up with the youngest and fittest, all sitting crosslegged on the grass and displaying hus-mukh to the sun just rising over the palms: the Laughing Face pose it was called, but they looked like gargoyles with their mouths torn open and their thick, discoloured tongues sticking out. If I were the sun, I'd feel so disgusted by such a reception I'd just turn around and go back. And that was the simplest of their poses – after that they'd go into contortions that would embarrass an ape. Once their leader, a black and hirsute man like an aborigine, saw me watching and called me to join them. I shook my head and ducked behind an oleander. You won't catch me making an ass of myself in public. And I despise all that body-beautiful worship anyway. What's the body compared to the soul, the mind?

I'd stroll under the palms, breathing in the cool of the early morning, feeling it drive out, or wash clean, the stifling dark of the night, and try to avoid bumping into all the other early morning visitors to the park – mostly aged men sent by their wives to fetch the milk from the government dairy booth just outside the gates. Their bottles clinking in green cloth bags and newspapers rolled up and tucked under their arms, they strutted along like stiff puppets and mostly they would be discussing philosophy. 'Ah but in Vedanta it is a different matter,' one would say, his eyes gleaming fanatically, and another would announce, 'The sage

Shanakaracharya showed the way,' and some would refer to the Upanishads or the Bhagavad Puranas, but in such argumentative, hacking tones that you could see they were quite capable of coming to blows over some theological argument. Certainly it was the mind above the body for these old coots but I found nothing to admire in them either. I particularly resented it when one of them disengaged himself from the discussion long enough to notice me and throw me a gentle look of commiseration. As if he'd been through exams, too, long long ago, and knew all about them. So what?

Worst of all were the athletes, wrestlers, Mr Indias and others who lay on their backs and were massaged with oil till every muscle shone and glittered. The men who massaged them huffed and puffed and cursed as they climbed up and down the supine bodies, pounding and pummelling the men who lay there wearing nothing but little greasy clouts, groaning and panting in a way I found obscene and disgusting. They never looked up at me or at anyone. They lived in a meaty, sweating world of their own – massages, oils, the body, a match to be fought and won – I kicked up dust in their direction but never went too close.

The afternoons would be quiet, almost empty. I would sit under a tree and read, stroll and study, doze too. Then, in the evening, as the sky softened from its blank white glare and took on shades of pink and orange and the palm trees rustled a little in an invisible breeze, the crowds would begin to pour out of Darya Ganj, Mori Gate, Chandni Chowk and the Jama Masjid bazaars and slums. Large families would come to sit about on the grass, eating peanuts and listening to a transistor radio placed in the centre of the circle. Mothers would sit together in flocks like screeching birds while children jumped into the dry fountains, broke flowers and terrorized each other. There would be a few young men moaning at the corners, waiting for a girl to roll her hips and dart her fish eyes in their direction, and then start the exciting adventure of pursuit. The children's cries would grow more piercing with the dark; frightened, shrill and exalted with mystery and farewell. I would wander back to the flat.

The exams drew nearer. Not three, not two, but only one month to go. I had to stop daydreaming and set myself tasks for every day and remind myself constantly to complete them. It grew so hot I had to give up strolling on the paths and staked out a private place for myself under a tree. I noticed the tension tightening the eyes and mouths of other students – they applied themselves more diligently to their books, talked less, slept less. Everyone looked a little demented from lack of sleep. Our books seemed attached to our hands as though by roots, they were a part of us, they lived because we fed them. They were parasites and, like parasites, were sucking us dry. We mumbled to ourselves, not always consciously. Chipmunks jumped over our feet, mocking us. The gram seller down at the gate whistled softly 'I'm glad I never went to school, I am a bulbul, I live in Paradise . . .'

My brains began to jam up. I could feel it happening, slowly. As if the oil were all used up. As if everything was getting locked together, rusted. The white cells, the grey matter, the springs and nuts and bolts. I yelled at my mother – I think it was my mother – 'What do you think I am? What do you want of me?' and crushed a glass of milk between my hands. It was sticky. She had put sugar in my milk. As if I were a baby. I wanted to cry. They wouldn't let me sleep, they wanted to see my light on all night, they made sure I never stopped studying. Then they brought me milk and sugar and made clicking sounds with their tongues. I raced out to the park. I think I sobbed as I paced up and down, up and down, in the corner that stank of piss. My head ached worse than ever. I slept all day under the tree and had to work all night.

My father laid his hand on my shoulder. I knew I was not to fling it off. So I sat still, slouching, ready to spring aside if he lifted it only slightly. 'You must get a first, Suno,' he said through his nose, 'must get a first, or else you won't get a job. Must get a job, Suno,' he sighed and wiped his nose and went off, his patent leather pumps squealing like mice. I flung myself back in my chair and howled. Get a first, get a first, get a first – like a railway engine, it went charging over me, grinding me down, and left me dead and mangled on the tracks.

Everything hung still and yellow in the park. I lay sluggishly on a heap of waste paper under my tree and read without seeing, slept without sleeping. Sometimes I went to the water tap that leaked and drank the leak. It tasted of brass. I spat out a mouthful. It nearly went over the feet of the student waiting for his turn at that dripping tap. I stepped aside for him. He swilled the water around his mouth and spat, too, carefully missing my feet. Wiping his mouth, he asked, 'BA?'

'No, Inter.'

'Hu,' he burped. 'Wait till you do your BA. Then you'll get to know.' His face was like a grey bone. It was not unkind, it simply had no expression. 'Another two weeks,' he sighed and slouched off to his own lair.

I touched my face. I thought it would be all bone, like his. I was surprised to find a bit of skin still covering it. I felt as if we were all dying in the park, that when we entered the examination hall it would be to be declared officially dead. That's what the degree was about. What else was it all about? Why were we creeping around here, hiding from the city, from teachers and parents, pretending to study and prepare? Prepare for what? We hadn't been told. Inter, they said, or BA, or MA. These were like official stamps – they would declare us dead. Ready for a dead world. A world in which ghosts went about, squeaking or whining, rattling or rustling. Slowly, slowly we were killing ourselves in order to join them. The ball-point pen in my pocket was the only thing that still lived, that still worked. I didn't work myself any more – I mean physically, my body no longer functioned. I was constipated, I was dying. I was lying under a yellow tree, feeling the dust sift through the leaves to cover me. It was filling my eyes, my throat. I could barely walk. I never strolled.

Only on the way out of the park, late in the evening, I crept down the path under the palms, past the benches.

Then I saw the scene that stopped it all, stopped me just before I died.

Hidden behind an oleander was a bench. A woman lay on it, stretched out. She was a Muslim, wrapped in a black burkha. I hesitated when I saw this straight, still figure in black on the bench. Just then she lifted a pale, thin hand and lifted her veil. I saw her face. It lay bared, in the black folds of her burkha, like a flower, wax-white and composed, like a Persian lily or a tobacco flower at night. She was young. Very young, very pale, beautiful with a beauty I had never come across even in a dream. It caught me and held me tight, tight till I couldn't breathe and couldn't move. She was so white, so still, I saw she was very ill – with anaemia, perhaps, or TB. Too pale, too white – I could see she was dying. Her head – so still and white it might have been carved if it weren't for this softness, this softness of a flower at night – lay in the lap of a very old man. Very much older than her. With spectacles and a long grey beard like a goat's, or a scholar's. He was looking down at her and caressing her face – so tenderly, so tenderly, I had never seen a hand move so gently and tenderly. Beside them, on the ground, two little girls were playing. Round little girls, rather dirty, drawing lines in the gravel. They stared at me but the man and the woman did not notice me. They never looked at anyone else, only at each other, with an expression that halted me. It was tender, loving, yes, but in an inhuman way, so intense. Divine, I felt, or insane. I stood, half-hidden by the bush, holding my book, and wondered at them. She was ill, I could see, dying. Perhaps she had only a short time to live. Why didn't he take her to the Victoria Zenana Hospital, so close to the park? Who was this man – her husband, her father, a lover? I couldn't make out although I watched them without moving, without breathing. I felt not as if I were staring rudely at strangers, but as if I were gazing at a painting or a sculpture, some work of art. Or seeing a vision. They were still and I stood still and the children stared. Then she lifted her arms above her head and laughed. Very quietly.

I broke away and hurried down the path, in order to leave them alone, in privacy. They weren't a work of art, or a vision, but real, human and alive as no one else in my life had been real and alive. I had only that glimpse of them. But I felt I could never open my books and study or take degrees after that. They belonged to the dead, and now I had seen what being alive meant. The vision burnt the surfaces of my eyes so that they watered as I groped my way up the stairs to the flat. I could hardly find my way to the bed.

It was not just the examination but everything else had suddenly withered and died, gone lifeless and purposeless when compared with this vision. My studies, my family, my life – they all belonged to the dead and only what I had seen in the park had any meaning.

Since I did not know how to span the distance between that beautiful ideal and my stupid, dull existence, I simply lay still and shut my eyes. I kept them shut so as not to see all the puzzled, pleading, indignant faces of my family around me, but I could not shut out their voices.

'Suno, Suno,' I heard them croon and coax and mourn. 'Suno, drink milk.'

'Suno, study.'

'Suno, take the exam.'

And when they tired of being so patient with me and I still would not get up, they began to crackle and spit and storm.

'Get up, Suno.'

'Study, Suno.'

'At once, Suno.'

Only my mother became resigned and gentle. She must have seen something quite out of the ordinary on my face to make her so. I felt her hand on my forehead and heard her say, 'Leave him alone. Let him sleep tonight. He is tired out, that is what it is – he has driven himself too much and now he must sleep.'

Then I heard all of them leave the room. Her hand stayed on my forehead, wet and smelling of onions, and after a bit my tears began to flow from under my lids.

'Poor Suno, sleep,' she murmured.

I went back to the park of course. But now I was changed. I had stopped being a student – I was a 'professional'. My life was dictated by the rules and routine of the park. I still had my book open on the palms of my hands as I strolled but now my eyes strayed without guilt, darting at the young girls walking in pairs, their arms linked, giggling and bumping into each other. Sometimes I stopped to rest on a bench and conversed with one of the old men, told him who my father was and what examination I was preparing for, and allowing him to tell me about his youth, his politics, his philosophy, his youth and again his youth. Or I joked with the other students, sitting on the grass and throwing peanut shells at the chipmunks, and shocking them, I could see, with my irreverence and cynicism about the school, the exam, the system. Once I even nodded at the yoga teacher and exchanged a few words with him. He suggested I join his class and I nodded vaguely and said I would think it over. It might help. My father says I need help. He says I am hopeless but that I need help. I just laugh but I know that he knows I will never appear for the examination, I will never come up to that hurdle or cross it – life has taken a different path for me, in the form of a search, not a race as it is for him, for them.

Yes, it is a search, a kind of perpetual search for me and now that I have accepted it and don't struggle, I find it satisfies me entirely, and I wander about the park as freely as a prince in his palace garden. I look over the benches, I glance behind the bushes, and wonder if I shall ever get another glimpse of that strange vision that set me free. I never have but I keep hoping, wishing.

Surface Textures

It was all her own fault, she later knew – but how could she have helped it? When she stood, puckering her lips, before the fruit barrow in the market and, after sullen consideration, at last plucked a rather small but nicely ripened melon out of a heap on display, her only thought had been Is it worth a rupee and fifty paise? The lichees looked more poetic, in large clusters like some prickly grapes of a charming rose colour, their long stalks and stiff grey leaves tied in a bunch above them – but were expensive. Mangoes were what the children were eagerly waiting for – the boys, she knew, were raiding the mango trees in the school compound daily and their stomach-aches were a result, she told them, of the unripe mangoes they ate and for which they carried paper packets of salt to school in their pockets instead of handkerchiefs – but, leave alone the expense, the ones the fruiterer held up to her enticingly were bound to be sharp and sour for all their parakeet shades of rose and saffron; it was still too early for mangoes. So she put the melon in her string bag, rather angrily – paid the man his one rupee and fifty paise which altered his expression from one of promise and enticement to that of disappointment and contempt, and trailed off towards the vegetable barrow.

That, she later saw, was the beginning of it all, for if the melon seemed puny to her and boring to the children, from the start her husband regarded it with eyes that seemed newly opened. One would have thought he had never seen a melon before. All through the meal his eyes remained fixed on the plate in the centre of the table with its big button of a yellow melon. He left most of his rice and pulses on his plate, to her

31

indignation. While she scolded, he reached out to touch the melon that so captivated him. With one finger he stroked the coarse grain of its rind, rough with the upraised criss-cross of pale veins. Then he ran his fingers up and down the green streaks that divided it into even quarters as by green silk threads, so tenderly. She was clearing away the plates and did not notice till she came back from the kitchen.

'Aren't you going to cut it for us?' she asked, pushing the knife across to him.

He gave her a reproachful look as he picked up the knife and went about dividing the melon into quarter-moon portions with sighs that showed how it pained him.

'Come on, come on,' she said, roughly, 'the boys have to get back to school.'

He handed them their portions and watched them scoop out the icy orange flesh with a fearful expression on his face – as though he were observing cannibals at a feast. She had not the time to pay any attention to it then but later described it as horror. And he did not eat his own slice. When the boys rushed away, he bowed his head over his plate and regarded it.

'Are you going to fall asleep?' she cried, a little frightened.

'Oh no,' he said, in that low mumble that always exasperated her – it seemed a sign to her of evasiveness and pusillanimity, this mumble – 'Oh no, no.' Yet he did not object when she seized the plate and carried it off to the kitchen, merely picked up the knife that was left behind and, picking a flat melon seed off its edge where it had remained stuck, he held it between two fingers, fondling it delicately. Continuing to do this, he left the house.

The melon might have been the apple of knowledge for Harish – so deadly its poison that he did not even need to bite into it to imbibe it: that long, devoted look had been enough. As he walked back to his office which issued ration cards to the population of their town, he looked about him vaguely but with hunger, his eyes resting not on the things on which people's eyes normally rest – signboards, the traffic, the number of an approaching bus – but on such things, normally considered non-descript and unimportant, as the paving stones on which their feet momentarily pressed, the length of wire in a railing at the side of the road, a pattern of grime on the windowpane of a disused printing press . . . Amongst such things his eyes roved and hunted and, when he was seated at his desk in the office, his eyes continued to slide about – that was Sheila's phrase later: 'slide about' – in a musing, calculating way, over the surface of the crowded desk, about the corners of the room, even across the ceiling. He seemed unable to focus them on a file or a card long enough to put to them his signature – they lay unsigned and the people in the queue outside went for another day without rice and sugar and kerosene for their lamps and Janta cookers. Harish searched – slid about, hunted, gazed – and at last found sufficiently interesting a thick book of rules that lay beneath a stack of files. Then his hand reached out – not to pull the book to him or open it, but to run the ball of his thumb across the edge of the pages. In their large number and irregular cut, so closely laid out like some crisp palimpsest, his eyes seemed to find something of riveting interest and his thumb of tactile wonder. All afternoon he massaged the cut edges of the book's seven hundred-odd pages – tenderly, wonderingly. All afternoon his eyes gazed upon them with strange devotion. At five o'clock, punctually, the office shut and the queue disintegrated into vociferous grumbles and threats as people went home instead of to the ration shops, empty-handed instead of loaded with those necessary but, to Harish, so dull comestibles.

Although government service is as hard to depart from as to enter – so many letters to be written, forms to be filled, files to be circulated, petitions to be made that it hardly seems worthwhile – Harish was, after some time, dismissed – time he happily spent judging the difference between white blotting paper and pink (pink is flatter, denser, white spongier) and the texture of blotting paper stained with ink and that which is fresh, that which has been put to melt in a saucer of cold tea and that which has been doused in a pot of ink. Harish was dismissed.

The first few days Sheila stormed and screamed like some shrill, wet hurricane about the house. 'How am I to go to market and buy vegetables for dinner? I don't even have enough for that. What am I to feed the boys tonight? No more milk for them. The washerwoman is asking for her bill to be paid. Do you *hear*? Do you hear? And we shall have to leave this flat. Where shall we go?' He listened – or didn't – sitting on a cushion before her mirror, fingering the small silver box in which she kept the red kumkum that daily cut a gash from one end of her scalp to the other after her toilet. It was of dark, almost blackened silver, with a whole forest embossed on it – banana groves, elephants, peacocks and jackals. He rubbed his thumb over its cold, raised surface.

After that, she wept. She lay on her bed in a bath of tears and perspiration, and it was only because of the kindness of their neighbours that they did not starve to death the very first week, for even those who most disliked and distrusted Harish – 'Always said he looks like a hungry hyena,' said Mr Bhatia who lived below their flat, 'not human at all, but like a hungry, hunch-backed hyena hunting along the road' – felt for the distraught wife and the hungry children (who did not really mind as long as there were sour green mangoes to steal and devour) and looked to them. Such delicacies as Harish's family had never known before arrived in stainless-steel and brass dishes, with delicate unobtrusiveness. For a while wife and children gorged on sweet-meats made with fresh buffalo milk, on pulses cooked according to grandmother's recipes, on stuffed bread and the first pome-granates of the season. But, although delicious, these offerings came in small quantities and irregularly and soon they were really starving.

'I suppose you want me to take the boys home to my parents,' said Sheila bitterly, getting up from the bed. 'Any other man would regard that as the worst disgrace of all – but not you.

What is my shame to you? I will have to hang my head and crawl home and beg my father to look after us since you won't,' and that was what she did. He was sorry, very sorry to see her pack the little silver kumkum box in her black trunk and carry it away.

Soon after, officials of the Ministry of Works, Housing and Land Development came and turned Harish out, cleaned and painted the flat and let in the new tenants who could hardly believe their luck – they had been told so often they couldn't expect a flat in that locality for at least another two years.

The neighbours lost sight of Harish. Once some children reported they had seen him lying under the pipal tree at the corner of their school compound, staring fixedly at the red gashes cut into the papery bark and, later, a boy who commuted to school on a suburban train claimed to have seen him on the railway platform, sitting against a railing like some tattered beggar, staring across the criss-cross of shining rails. But next day, when the boy got off the train, he did not see Harish again.

Harish had gone hunting. His slow, silent walk gave him the appearance of sliding rather than walking over the surface of the roads and fields, rather like a snail except that his movement was not as smooth as a snail's but stumbling as if he had only recently become one and was still unused to the pace. Not only his eyes and his hands but even his bare feet seemed to be feeling the earth carefully, in search of an interesting surface. Once he found it, he would pause, his whole body would gently collapse across it and hours – perhaps days – would be devoted to its investigation and worship. Outside the town the land was rocky and bare and this was Harish's especial paradise, each rock having a surface of such exquisite roughness, of such perfection in shape and design, as to keep him occupied and ecstatic for weeks together. Then the river beyond the rock quarries drew him away and there he discovered the joy of fingering silk-smooth stalks and reeds, stems and leaves.

Shepherd children, seeing him stumble about the reeds, plunging thigh-deep into the water in order to pull out a water lily with its cool, sinuous stem, fled screaming, not certain whether this was a man or a hairy water snake. Their mothers came, some with stones and some with canes at the ready, but when they saw Harish, his skin parched to a violet shade, sitting on the bank and gazing at the transparent stem of the lotus, they fell back, crying, 'Wah!', gathered closer together, advanced, dropped their canes and stones, held their children still by their hair and shoulders, and came to bow to him. Then they hurried back to the village, chattering. They had never had a Swami to themselves, in these arid parts. Nor had they seen a Swami who looked holier, more inhuman than Harish with his matted hair, his blue, starved skin and single-focused eyes. So, in the evening, one brought him a brass vessel of milk, another a little rice. They pushed their children before them and made them drop flowers at his feet. When Harish stooped and felt among the offerings for something his fingers could respond to, they were pleased, they felt accepted. 'Swamiji,' they whispered, 'speak.'

Harish did not speak and his silence made him still holier, safer. So they worshipped him, fed and watched over him, interpreting his moves in their own fashion, and Harish, in turn, watched over their offerings and worshipped.

Sale

There they are, at the door now, banging. They had met him, written a note and made an appointment – and here they are, as a direct result of it all, rattling. He stands on the other side of the door, in the dusk-mottled room, fingering an unshaven chin and dropping cigarette butts on the floor which is already littered with them. There is a pause in the knocking. He hears their voices – querulous, impatient. He turns and silently goes towards the inner door that opens onto a passage. He pushes it ajar, quietly, holding his breath. At the end of the passage another door stands open: it is like a window or an alcove illuminated by the deep glow of the fire. There his wife sits, kneading dough in a brass bowl, with her head bowed so that her long hair broods down to her shoulders on either side of her heavy, troubled face. The red border of her sari cuts a bright gash through the still tableau. The child sits on the mat beside her, silent, absorbed in the mysteries of a long-handled spoon which he turns over with soft, wavering fingers that are unaccustomed to the unsympathetic steel. His head, too, is bowed so that his father, behind him, can see the small wisps of hair on the back of his neck. He looks at them, holding his breath till it begins to hurt his chest. Then the knocking is resumed and his wife, hearing it, raises her head. She sees him then, at the door, like a dog hanging about, wanting something, and immediately her nostrils flare. 'Can't you answer the door?' she cries. 'What's the matter with you? It must be them – this is your chance.' Startled, the child drops the spoon with a clatter. Quickly he shuts the door. Then he goes and opens the front door and lets them in.

'We were about to give up,' one man cries, laughing, and brings in his friend and also a woman, seeing whom the artist, who is not expecting her, finds himself dismayed and confused. A woman – therefore someone in league with his wife, he thinks, and stares at her lush, unreluctant face and the bright enamelled earrings that frame it. He is silent. The two men stare at him.

'You *were* expecting us, weren't you?' enquires the jovial man whom he had liked, once. 'We wrote—'

'Yes,' he murmurs. 'Oh yes, yes,' and stands there, on the threshold, with an empty match box in his hand, his face looking like a house from which ghosts had driven away all inhabitants.

Then the man introduces his wife. 'She also paints,' he says, 'and was so interested in seeing your pictures, I brought her along. You don't mind, do you?'

'No,' he says, gathering himself together with a laboured effort, and steps aside to let them in. Then it is they who are silent, staring in dismay at the shambles about them. There are pictures to look at, yes, but one lies on the floor with a bundle of rags and some cigarette stubs on it, another is propped up on a shelf with bottles of hair oil, clay toys and calendars before it, and others have drifted off the wooden divan into corners of the room, peering out from under old newspapers and dirty clothes. The artist watches them, wondering at the imbecility of their appearance as they huddle together and gape. 'Oh,' he says, recovering, 'the light,' and switches it on. It is unshaded and hangs low over the flat table at which he paints so that they are illuminated weirdly from the waist downwards, leaving their faces more confused with shadows than before. The woman is quickest to relax, to make herself known, to become acquainted. 'Ah,' she cries, hurrying to the shelf to pull out a picture. 'What are they?' she asks him, gazing first at the flowers that blaze across the dirty paper, then at him, coaxing him for their secret with an avidly enquiring look. 'Not cannas, not lotuses – what can they be?'

He smiles at her curiosity. 'Nothing,' he says. 'Not real flowers – just anything at all.'

'Really!' she exclaims, shaking her enamelled earrings. 'How wonderful to be able to imagine such forms, such colours. Look, Ram, aren't they pretty?' The two men become infected by her exaggerated attitude of relaxation. They begin to prowl about the room, now showing amusement at the litter which is, after all, only to be expected in an artist's studio, then crinkling their noses for, one has to admit, it *does* smell, and then showing surprised interest in the pictures of which they have come to select one for their home which is newly built and now to be furnished. What with the enthusiasm and thoroughness they bring to their task, the rags and grime of the studio are soon almost obliterated by the fanfare of colour that spills forth, a crazy whorl of them, unknown colours that cannot be named, spilling out of forms that cannot be identified. One cannot pinpoint any school, any technique, any style – one can only admit oneself in the presence of a continuous and inspired act of creation: so they tell themselves. The woman gives cry upon cry of excitement and turns again and again to the artist who stands watching them thoughtfully. But how did you get this colour? You must tell me because I paint – and I could never get anything like this. What is it?'

'Ahh, Naples Yellow,' he says, as if making a guess. 'No, but there is some orange in it too.'

'Ah yes, a little orange also.'

'And green?'

'Yes, a little perhaps.'

'No, but that special tinge – how did you get it? A little bit of white – or flesh pink? What is it? Ram, Ram, just look, isn't it pretty – this weird bird? I don't suppose it has a name?'

'No, no, it is not real. I am a city man, I know nothing about birds.'

'But you know everything about birds! And flowers. I suppose they *are* birds and flowers, all these marvellous things. And your paintings are full of them. How can it possibly be that you have never seen them?'

He has to laugh then – she is so artless, so completely without any vestige of imagination, and so completely unlike his wife. 'Look,' he says, suddenly buoyant, and points to the window. She has to stand on her toes to look out of the small aperture, through the bars, and then she gazes out with all the intentness she feels he expects of her, at the deep, smoke-ridden twilight wound around the ill-lit slum, the smoking heaps of dung-fires and the dark figures that sit and stand in it hopelessly. Like fog-horns, conch shells begin to blow as tired housewives summon up their flagging spirits for the always lovely, always comforting ritual of evening prayers. She tries to pierce the scene with her sharp eyes, trying to see what he sees in it, till she hears him laughing behind her with a cracked kind of hilarity. 'There you see – my birds and my flowers,' he tells her, clapping his hands as though enjoying a practical joke he has played on her. 'I see a tram – and that is my mountain. I see a letter-box – and that is my tree. Listen! Do you hear my birds?' He raises his hand and, with its gesture, ushers in the evening voices of children uttering those cries and calls peculiar to the time of parting, the time of relinquishing their games, before they enter their homes and disappear into sleep – voices filled with an ecstasy of knowledge, of sensation drawn to an apex, brought on by the realization of imminent departure and farewell: voices panicky with love, with lament, with fear and sacrifice.

The artist watches the three visitors and finds them attentive, puzzled. 'There,' he says, dropping his hand. 'There are my birds. I don't see them – but I hear them and imagine how they look. It is easy, no, when you can hear them so clearly?'

'You are a magician,' says the quiet man, shaking his head and turning to a crayon drawing of pale birds delicately stalking the shallows of a brooding sea. 'Look at these – I can't believe you haven't actually painted them on the spot.'

'No, I have not, but I do know the sea. You know, I am a fisherman! I should have been – my people are. How do you like this one of fishing boats? I used to see them coming in like this, in the evening, with the catch. And then my mother would cook one large one for dinner – oh, it was good, good!'

They all stand around him, smiling at this unexpected burst of childish exuberance. 'You paint from memory then?' enquires one, but the woman cries, 'You like fish? You must come and eat it at our house one day – I cook fish very well.'

'I will, I will,' he cries, scurrying about as though he were looking for something he had suddenly remembered he needed, hunting out seascapes for them to see, and more of the successful flowers. 'Oh, I will love that – to see this new house of yours and eat a meal cooked by you. Yes, I will come. Here, look, another one – a canal scene. Do you like it? That is paddy growing there – it is so green . . .' Now he wants to turn out the entire studio for them, bring out his best. He chatters, they laugh. Pictures fall to the floor. Crayons are smeared, oils are smudged – but he does not mind. He does not even sign his pictures. When the woman pauses over a pastel that is blurred by some stroke of carelessness, he says, 'Oh that is nothing, I can touch it up. Do you see the blue? Do you like it? Yes, I will see your paintings and I will tell you plainly what I like and what I don't like, and you will appreciate anyway. Oh, I love fish . . .' Only now and then he grows aware of his wife, breathing heavily because of the weight of the child asleep on her arm, straining to hear at the door, frowning because she cannot understand, is not certain, is worried, worried to death . . . and then he draws down the corners of his mouth and is silent. But when a picture of curled flowers is brought to him, he stares at it till it comes into proper focus and explains it to them. 'Ah,' he says, 'I painted that long ago – for my son, when he was born. I wanted him to have flowers, flowers all about his bed, under his head, at his feet, everywhere. And I did not have any. I did not know of a garden from where I could get some. So I painted them. That is one of them. Ah yes, yes,' he smiles, and the three who watch him grow tender, sympathetic. The woman says, '*This* one? It is your son's? How lovely – how lucky.'

'No,' he cries loudly. 'I mean, you can have it. Do you like it? It is what you want for your new house?'

'Oh no,' she says softly and puts it away. 'You painted it for your child. I can't take it from him.'

The artist finds himself sweating and exhausted – he had not realized how he was straining himself. He has had nothing but tea and cigarettes since early that morning and there is no breath of air coming through the barred window. He wipes his face with his hand and blotches another crayon with his wet fingers as he picks it up and flings it away. 'Then what do you want?' he asks in a flat voice. 'What do you like? What do you want to have – a flower picture or a landscape?'

'Perhaps figures – people always make a room seem bright.'

'I don't paint figures,' he says shortly. 'You told me you wanted a landscape. Here they are – all sizes, big, small, medium; hills, seas, rivers; green, blue, yellow. Is there nothing you like?'

'Yes, yes,' they all assure him together, upset by his change of tone, and one holds up a picture at arm's length to admire it lavishly, another bends to shuffle through the pile on the table. But there are so many, they say, it is hard to choose. That is nothing, he says, *he* will choose for them. Oh no, they laugh, glancing to see if he is serious, for they have something very special in mind – something that will light up their whole house, become its focal point, radiate and give their home a tone, an atmosphere. No, not this one, not *quite* – it is lovely, but . . . Before he knows it, they are at the door, descending the stairs with one backward look at all the heroic mass of colour inside, saying goodbye. He rushes down the stairs after them, spreading out his arms. Their car stands under the lamp-post. He flings himself at the door, hangs on to it.

'There is not one you liked? I thought you had come to buy – you said—'

'Yes, we wanted to,' says the man whom he had liked, once. 'But not one of these. You see, we have something very special in mind, something quite extraordinary—'

'But – not one of those I showed you? I thought you liked them – you said—'

'I did, I did,' chirps the woman from the soft recesses of the back seat. 'Oh and those lovely flowers you painted for your son – *lucky* child!'

'You liked them? I will paint you another like it, just like it—'

'But we wanted a landscape really,' says the man. 'Something in those cool greys and whites. Perhaps a snow scene – now *that* would be something different.'

'Snow?' shouts the artist. 'I will paint snow. I will paint the Himalayas for you. How big do you want it? So big? So?'

'No, no,' they laugh. 'Not so big. That would be too expensive.'

'All right, smaller. I will paint it. By the end of the week you will have it.'

They laugh at his haste, his trembling, shrill excitement. 'But, my friend, have you ever seen snow?' enquires the jovial one, patting his arm.

'Ah!' he gives such a cry that it halts them in their movements of departure, to turn and see him spread out his arms till his fingers reach out of the smoke of the dung-fires and the dust of the unlit lanes, to reach out to the balm of ice and snow and isolation. 'I will paint such snow for you as you have never seen, as no one has ever painted. I can see it all, here,' and he taps his forehead with such emphasis that they smile – he is quite a comic. Or even a bit crazy. Drunk?

'Now, now, my friend,' says the man, patting his arm again. 'Don't be in a hurry about it. You paint it when you are in the mood. Then it will be good.'

'I am in the mood now,' he cries. 'I am always in the mood, don't you see? Tomorrow, tomorrow I will have it ready. I will bring it to your house. Give me the address!'

They laugh. The engine stutters to life and there is a metallic finality in the sound of the doors being shut. But he clings to the handle, thrusts his head in, his eyes blazing. 'And will you give me an advance?' he asks tensely. 'I need money, my friend. Can you give me an advance?'

The woman creeps away into a corner, wrapping herself closely in a white shawl. One man, in embarrassment, falls silent. The other laughs and puts his hands in his pockets, then draws them out to show they are empty. 'Brother, if I had some with me, I would give it to you – all of it – but since we only came to see, I didn't bring any. I'm sorry.'

'I need it.'

'Listen, when you bring the picture, I will give you something, even if I don't want it, I will give you something – in advance, for the one we will buy. But today, just now, I have nothing.'

The artist steps back to let them go. As they drive out of the lane and the smoke smudges and obscures the tail-lights, he hears his wife come out on the stairs behind him.

Pineapple Cake

Victor was a nervous rather than rebellious child. But it made no difference to his mother: she had the same way of dealing with nerves and rebels.

'You like pineapple cake, don't you? Well, come along, get dressed quickly – yes, yes, the velvet shorts – the new shoes, yes – hurry – pineapple cake for good boys . . .'

So it had gone all afternoon and, by holding out the bait of pineapple cake, his favourite, Mrs Fernandez had the boy dressed in his new frilled shirt and purple velvet shorts and new shoes that bit his toes and had him sitting quietly in church right through the long ceremony. Or so she thought, her faith in pineapple cake being matched only by her faith in Our Lady of Mount Mary, Bandra Hill, Bombay. Looking at Victor, trying hard to keep his loud breathing bottled inside his chest and leaning down to see what made his shoes so vicious, you might have thought she had been successful, but success never satisfies and Mrs Fernandez sighed to think how much easier it would have been if she had had a daughter instead. Little girls love weddings, little girls play at weddings, little girls can be dressed in can-can petticoats and frocks like crêpe-paper bells of pink and orange, their oiled and ringleted hair crowned with rustling wreaths of paper flowers. She glanced around her rather tiredly to hear the church rustling and crepitating with excited little girls, dim and dusty as it was, lit here and there by a blazing afternoon window of red and blue glass, a flare of candles or a silver bell breathless in the turgid air. This reminded her how she had come to this church to pray and light candles to Our Lady when she was expecting Victor, and it made her glance down at him and wonder why he was perspiring so. Yes, the collar of the frilled shirt was a bit tight and the church was airless and stuffy but it wasn't very refined of him to sweat so. Of course all the little boys in her row seemed to be in the same state – each one threatened or bribed into docility, their silence straining in their chests, soundlessly clamouring. Their eyes were the eyes of prisoners, dark and blazing at the ignominy and boredom and injustice of it all. When they shut their eyes and bowed their heads in prayer, it was as if half the candles in church had gone out, and it was darker.

Relenting, Mrs Fernandez whispered, under cover of the sonorous prayer led by the grey padre in faded purple, 'Nearly over now, Victor. In a little while we'll be going to tea – pineapple cake for you.'

Victor hadn't much faith in his mother's promises. They had a way of getting postponed or cancelled on account of some small accidental lapse on his part. He might tear a hole in his sleeve – no pocket money. Or stare a minute too long at Uncle Arthur who was down on a visit from Goa and had a wen on the back of his bald head – no caramel custard for pudding. So he would not exchange looks with her but stared stolidly down at his polished shoes, licked his dry lips and wondered if there would be Fanta or Coca-Cola at tea.

Then the ceremony came to an end. How or why, he could not tell, sunk so far below eye-level in that lake of breathless witnesses to the marriage of Carmen Maria Braganza of Goa and George de Mello of Byculla, Bombay. He had seen nothing of it, only followed, disconsolately and confusedly, the smells and sounds of it, like some underground creature, an infant mole, trying to make out what went on outside its burrow, and whether it was alarming or enticing. Now it was over and his mother was digging him in the ribs, shoving him out, hurrying him by running into his heels, and now they were streaming out with the tide. At the door he made out the purple of the padre's robes, he was handed a pink paper flower by a little girl who held a silver basket full of them and whose face gleamed with fanatic self-importance, and then he was swept down the stairs, held onto by his elbow and, once on ground level, his mother was making a din about finding a vehicle to take them to the reception at Green's. 'The tea will be at Green's, you know,' she had been saying several times a day for weeks now. 'Those de Mellos must have money – they can't be so badly off – tea at Green's, after all.'

It was no easy matter, she found, to be taken care of, for although there was a whole line of cabs at the kerb, they all belonged to the more important members of the de Mello and Braganza families. When Mrs Fernandez realized this, she set her lips together and looked dangerously wrathful, and the party atmosphere began quickly to dissolve in the acid of bad temper and the threat to her dignity. Victor stupidly began a fantasy of slipping out of her hold and breaking into a toy shop for skates and speeding ahead of the whole caravan on a magic pair, to arrive at Green's before the bride, losing his mother on the way . . . But she found two seats, in the nick of time, in a taxi that already contained a short, broad woman in a purple net frock and a long thin man with an Adam's apple that struggled to rise above his polka-dotted bow tie and then slipped down again with an audible croak. The four of them sat squeezed together and the women made little remarks about how beautiful Carmen Maria had looked and how the de Mellos couldn't be badly off, tea at Green's, after all. 'Green's,' the woman in the purple net frock yelled into the taxi driver's ear and gave her bottom an important shake that knocked Victor against the door. He felt that he was being shoved out, he was not wanted, he had no place here. This must have made him look piqued for his mother squeezed his hand and whispered, 'You've been a good boy – pineapple cake for you.' Victor sat still, not breathing. The man with the Adam's apple stretched his neck longer and longer, swivelled his head about on the top of it and said nothing, but the frog in his throat gurgled to itself.

Let out of the taxi, Victor looked about him at the wonders of Bombay harbour while the elders tried to be polite and yet not pay the taxi. Had his father brought him here on a Sunday outing, with a ferry boat ride and a fresh coconut drink for treats, he would have enjoyed the Arab dhows with their muddy sails, the ships and tankers and seagulls and the Gateway of India like a coloured version of the photograph in his history book, but it was too unexpected. He had been promised pineapple cake at Green's, sufficiently overwhelming in itself – he hadn't the wherewithal to cope with the Gateway of India as well.

Instinctively he put out his hand to find his mother's and received another shock – she had slipped on a pair of gloves, dreadfully new ones of crackling nylon lace, like fresh bandages on her purple hands. She squeezed his hand, saying, 'If you want to do soo-soo, tell me, I'll find the toilet. Don't you go and wet your pants, man.' Horrified, he pulled away but she caught him by the collar and led him into the hotel and up the stairs to the tea room where refreshments were to be served in celebration of Carmen Maria's and George de Mello's wedding. The band was still playing 'Here Comes the Bride' when Victor and his mother entered.

Here there was a repetition of the scene over the taxi: this time it was seats at a suitable table that Mrs Fernandez demanded, could not find, then spotted, was turned away from and, finally, led to two others by a slippery-smooth waiter used to such scenes. The tables had been arranged in the form of the letter E, and covered with white cloths. Little vases marched up the centres of the tables, sprouting stiff zinnias and limp periwinkles. The guests, chief and otherwise, seemed flustered by the arrangements, rustled about, making adjustments and readjustments, but the staff showed no such hesitations over protocol. They seated the party masterfully, had the tables laid out impeccably and, when the band swung into the 'Do Re Mi' song from *The Sound of Music*, brought in the wedding cake. Everyone craned to see Carmen Maria cut it, and Victor's mother gave him a pinch that made him half-rise from his chair, whispering, 'Stand up if you can't see, man, stand up to see Carmen Maria cut the cake.' There was a burst of laughter, applause and raucous congratulation with an undertone of ribaldry that unnerved Victor and made him sink down on his chair, already a bit sick.

The band was playing a lively version of 'I am Sixteen, Going on Seventeen' when Victor heard a curious sound, as of a choked drain being forced. Others heard it too for suddenly chairs were being scraped back, people were standing up, some of them stepped backwards and nearly fell on top of Victor who hastily got off his chair. The mother of the bride, in her pink and silver gauzes, ran up, crying 'Oh no, oh no, no, no!'

Two seats down sat the man with the long, thin neck in which an Adam's apple rose and fell so lugubriously. Only he was no longer sitting. He was sprawled over his chair, his head hanging over the back in a curiously unhinged way, as though dangling at the end of a rope. The woman in the purple net dress was leaning over him and screaming, 'Aub, Aub, my darling Aubrey! Help my darling Aubrey!' Victor gave a shiver and stepped back and back till someone caught and held him.

Someone ran past – perhaps one of those confident young waiters who knew all there was to know – shouting 'Phone for a doctor, quick! Call Dr Patel,' and then there was a long, ripping groan all the way down the tables which seemed to come from the woman in the purple net dress or perhaps from the bride's mother, Victor could not tell – 'Oh, why did it have to happen *today?* Couldn't he have gone into another day?' Carmen Maria, the bride, began to sob frightenedly. After that someone grasped the long-necked old man by his knees and armpits and carried him away, his head and his shoes dangling like stuffed paper bags. The knot of guests around him loosened and came apart to make way for what was obviously a corpse.

Dimly, Victor realized this. The screams and sobs of the party-dressed women underlined it. So did the slow, stunned way in which people rose from the table, scraped back their chairs and

49

retreated to the balcony, shaking their heads and muttering, 'An omen, I tell you, it must be an omen.' Victor made a hesitant move towards the balcony – perhaps he would see the hearse arrive.

But Victor's mother was holding him by the arm and she gave it an excited tug. 'Sit *down*, man,' she whispered furtively, 'here comes the pineapple cake,' and, to his amazement, a plate of pastries was actually on the table now – iced, coloured and gay. 'Take it, take the pineapple cake,' she urged him, pushing him towards the plate, and when the boy didn't move but stared down at the pastry dish as though it were the corpse on the red Rexine sofa, her mouth gave an impatient twitch and she reached out to fork the pineapple cake onto her own plate. She ate it quickly. Wiping her mouth primly, she said, 'I think we'd better go now.'

The Accompanist

It was only on the night of the concert, when we assembled on-stage behind drawn curtains, that he gave me the notes to be played. I always hoped he would bring himself to do this earlier and I hovered around him all evening, tuning his sitar and preparing his betel leaves, but he would not speak to me at all. There were always many others around him – his hosts and the organizers of the concert, his friends and well-wishers and disciples – and he spoke and laughed with all of them, but always turned his head away when I came near. I was not hurt: this was his way with me, I was used to it. Only I wished he would tell me what he planned to play before the concert began so that I could prepare myself. I found it difficult to plunge immediately, like lightning, without pause or preparation, into the music, as he did. But I had to learn how to make myself do this, and did. In everything, he led me, I followed.

For fifteen years now, this has been our way of life. It began the day when I was fifteen years old and took a new tanpura, made by my father who was a maker of musical instruments and also played several of them with talent and distinction, to a concert hall where Ustad Rahim Khan was to play that night. He had ordered a new tanpura from my father who was known to all musicians for the fine quality of the instruments he made for them, with love as well as a deep knowledge of music. When I arrived at the hall, I looked around for someone to give the tanpura to but the hall was in darkness as the management would not allow the musicians to use the lights before the show and only onstage was a single bulb lit, lighting up the little knot of musicians and surrounding them with elongated, restless and, somehow, ominous shadows. The Ustad was tuning his sitar, pausing to laugh and talk to his companions every now and then. They were all talking and no one saw me. I stood for a long time in the doorway, gazing at the famous Ustad of whom my father had spoken with such reverence. 'Do not mention the matter of payment,' he had warned me. 'He is doing us an honour by ordering a tanpura from us.' This had impressed me and, as I gazed at him, I knew my father had been truthful about him. He was only tuning his sitar, casually and haphazardly, but his fingers were the fingers of a god, absolutely in control of his instrument and I knew nothing but perfection could come of such a relationship between a musician and his instrument.

So I slowly walked up the aisle, bearing the new tanpura in my arms and all the time gazing at the man in the centre of that restless, chattering group, himself absolutely in repose, controlled and purposeful. As I came closer to the stage, I could see his face beneath the long locks of hair, and the face, too, was that of a god: it was large, perhaps heavy about the jaws, but balanced by a wide forehead and with blazing black eyes that were widely spaced. His nostrils and his mouth, too, were large, royal, but intelligent, controlled. And as I looked into his face, telling myself of all the impressive points it contained, he looked down at me. I do not know what he saw, what he could see in the darkness and shadows of the unlit hall, but he smiled with sweet gentleness and beckoned to me. 'What do you have there?' he called.

Then I had the courage to run up the steps at the side of the stage and straight to him. I did not look at anyone else. I did not even notice the others or care for their reaction to me. I went straight to him who was the centre of the gathering, of the stage and thereafter of my entire life, and presented the tanpura to him.

'Ah, the new tanpura. From Mishraji in the music lane? You have come from Mishraji?'

'He is my father,' I whispered, kneeling before him and still looking into his face, unable to look away from it, it drew me so to him, close to him.

'Mishraji's son?' he said, with a deep, friendly laugh. After running his fingers over the tanpura strings, he put it down on the carpet and suddenly stretched out his hand so that the fine white muslin sleeve of his kurta fell back and bared his arm, strong and muscular as an athlete's, with veins finely marked upon the taut skin, and fondled my chin. 'Do you play?' he asked. 'My tanpura player has not arrived. Where is he?' he called over his shoulder. 'Why isn't he here?'

All his friends and followers began to babble. Some said he was ill, in the hotel, some that he had met friends and gone with them. No one really knew. The Ustad shook his head thoughtfully, then said, 'He is probably in his cups again, the old drunkard. I won't have him play for me any more. Let the child play,' and immediately he picked up his sitar and began to play, bowing his head over the instrument, a kind of veil of thoughtfulness and concentration falling across his face so that I knew I could not interrupt with the questions I wished to ask. He glanced at me, once, briefly, and beckoned to me to pick up the tanpura and play. '"Raga Dipak,"' he said, and told me the notes to be played in such a quick undertone that I would not have heard him had I not been so acutely attentive to him. And I sat down behind him, on the bare floor, picked up the new tanpura my father had made, and began to play the three notes he gave me – the central one, its octave and quintet – over and over again, creating the discreet background web of sound upon which he improvized and embroidered his raga.

And so I became the tanpura player for Ustad Rahim Khan's group. I have played for him since then, for no one else. I have done nothing else. It is my entire life. I am thirty years old now and my Ustad has begun to turn grey, and often he interrupts a concert with that hacking cough that troubles him, and he takes more opium than he should to quieten it – I give it to him myself for he always asks me to prepare it. We have travelled all over

India and played in every city, at every season. It is his life, and mine. We share this life, this music, this following. What else can there possibly be for me in this world? Some have tried to tempt me from his side, but I have stayed with him, not wishing for anything else, anything more.

Ours is a world formed and defined and enclosed not so much by music, however, as by a human relationship on solid ground level – the relationship of love. Not an abstract quality, like music, or an intellectual one, like art, but a common human quality lived on an everyday level of reality – the quality of love. So I believe. What else is it that weaves us together as we play, so that I know every movement he will make before he himself does, and he can count on me to be always where he wants me? We never diverge: we leave and we arrive together. Is this not love? No marriage was closer.

When I was a boy many other things existed on earth for me. Of course music was always important, the chief household deity of a family musical by tradition. The central hall of our house was given over to the making of musical instruments for which my father and his father before him were famous. From it rose sounds not only of the craft involved – the knocking, tapping, planing and tuning – but also of music. Music vibrated there constantly, sometimes harmoniously and sometimes discordantly, a quality of the very air of our house: dense, shaped by infinite variation, and never still. I was only a child, perhaps four years old, when my father began waking me at four o'clock every morning to go down to the hall with him and take lessons from him on the tanpura, the harmonium, the sitar and even the tabla. He could play them all and wished to see for which I had an aptitude. Music being literally the air we breathed in that tall, narrow house in the lane that had belonged for generations to the makers of musical instruments in that city, that I would display an aptitude was never in question. I sat crosslegged on the mat before him and played, gradually stirring to life as I did so, and finally sleep would lift from me like a covering, a smothering that had belonged to the night, till the inner core of my being stood forth and my father could see it clearly – I was a musician, not a maker, but a performer of music, that is what he saw. He taught me all the ragas, the raginis, and tested my knowledge with rapid, persistent questioning in his unmusical, grating voice. He was unlike my Ustad in every way, for he spat betel juice all down his ragged white beard, he seemed to be aware of everything I did and frequently his hand shot out to grab my ears and pull till I yelped. From such lessons I had a need to escape and, being a small, wily boy, managed this several times a day, slipping through my elders' fingers and hurtling down the steep stairs into the lane where I played gulli danda and kho and marbles with the luckier, more idle and less supervized boys of the mohalla.

There was a time when I cared more passionately for marbles than for music, particularly a dark crimson, almost black one in which white lines writhed like weeds, or roots, that helped me to win every match I played till the pockets of my kurta bulged and tore with the weight of the marbles I won.

How I loved my mother's sweetmeats, too – rather more, I'm sure, than I did the nondescript, mumbling, bald woman who made them. She never came to life for me, she lived some obscure, indoor life, unhealthy and curtained, undemanding and uninviting. But what halwa she made, what jalebis. I ate them so hot that I burnt the skin off my tongue. I stole my brothers' and sisters' share and was beaten and cursed by the whole family.

Then, when I was older, there was a time when only the cinema mattered. I saw four, five, as many as six cinema shows a week, creeping out of my room at night barefoot, for silence, with money stolen from my father, or mother, or anyone, clutched in my hand, then racing through the night-wild bazaar in time for the last show. Meena Kumari and Nargis were to me the queens of heaven, I put myself in the place of their screen lovers and felt myself grow great, hirsute, active and aggressive as I sat on the straw-stuffed seat, my feet tucked up under me, a cone of salted gram in my hand, uneaten, as I stared at these glistening, sequined queens with my mouth open. Their attractions, their graces filled up the empty spaces of my life and gave it new colours, new rhythms. So then I became aware of the women of our mohalla as women: ripe matrons who stood in their doorways, hands on hips, in that hour of the afternoon when life paused and presented possibilities before evening duties choked them off, and the younger girls, always moving, never still, eluding touch. They were like reeds in dirty water for however shabby they were, however unlike the screen heroines, they never quite lacked the enticements of subtle smiles, sly glances and bits of gold braid and lace. Some answered the look in my eyes, promised me what I wanted, later perhaps, after the late show, not now.

But all fell away from me, all disappeared in the shadows, on the side, when I met my Ustad and began to play for him. He took the place of my mother's sweet halwa, the cinema heroines, the street beauties, marbles and stolen money, all the pleasures and riches I had so far contrived to extract from the hard stones of existence in my father's house in the music lane. I did not need such toys any more, such toys and dreams. I had found my purpose in life and, by following it without hesitation and without holding back any part of myself, I found such satisfaction that I no longer wished for anything else.

It is true I made a little money on these concert tours of ours, enough to take care of my father during his last years and his illness. I even married. That is, my mother managed to marry me off to some neighbour's daughter of whom she was fond. The girl lived with her. I seldom visited her. I can barely remember her name, her face. She is safe with my mother and does not bother me. I remain free to follow my Ustad and play for him.

I believe he has the same attitude to his family and the rest of the world. At all events I have not seen him show the faintest interest in anything but our music, our concerts. Perhaps he is married. I have heard something of the sort but not seen his wife or known him to visit her. Perhaps he has children and one day a son will appear onstage and be taught to accompany his father.

So far it has not happened. It is true that in between tours we do occasionally go home for a few days of rest. Inevitably the Ustad and I both cut short these 'holidays' and return to his house in the city for practice. When I return, he does not question or even talk to me. But when he hears my step, he recognizes it, I know, for he smiles a half-smile, as if mocking himself and me, then he rolls back his muslin sleeve, lifts his sitar and nods in my direction. 'The Raga Desh,' he may announce, or 'Malhar,' or 'Megh', and I sit down behind him, on the bare floor, and play for him the notes he needs for the construction of the raga.

You may think I exaggerate our relationship, his need of me, his reliance on my tanpura. You may point out that there are other members of his band who play more important roles. And I will confess you may be right, but only in a very superficial way. It is quite obvious that the tabla player who accompanies him plays an 'important' role – a very loud and aggressive, at times thunderous one. But what is this 'importance' of his? It is not indispensable. As even the foremost critics agree, my Ustad is at his best when he is playing the introductory passage, the unaccompanied alap. This he plays slowly, thoughtfully, with such purity and sensibility that I can never hear it without tears coming to my eyes. But once Ram Nath has joined in with a tap and a run of his fingers on the tablas, the music becomes quick, bold and competitive and, not only in my opinion but also in that of many critics, of diminished value. The audience certainly enjoys the gat more than the quiet alap, and it pays more attention to Ram Nath than to me. At times he even draws applause for his performance, during a particularly brilliant passage when he manages to match or even outshine my Ustad. Then my Ustad will turn to him and smile, faintly, in approval, or even nod silently for he is so greathearted and generous, my Ustad. He never does this to me. I sit at the back, almost concealed behind my master and his accompanist. I have no solo passage to play. I neither follow my Ustad's raga nor enter into any kind of competition. Throughout the playing of the raga I run my fingers over the three strings of my tanpura, again and again, merely producing a kind of drone to fill up any interval in sound, to form a kind of road, or track, for my Ustad to keep to so he may not stray from the basic notes of the raga by which I hold him. Since I never compete, never ask for attention to be diverted from him to me, never try to rival him in his play, I maintain I am his true accompanist, certainly his truer friend. He may never smile and nod in approval of me. But he cannot do without me. This is all the reward I need to keep me with him like a shadow. It does not bother me at all when Ram Nath, who is coarse and hairy and scratches his big stomach under his shirt and wears gold rings in his ears like a washerman, puts out his foot and trips me as I am getting onto the stage, or when I see him helping himself to all the pulao on the table and leave me only some cold, unleavened bread. I know his true worth, or lack of it, and merely give him a look that will convey this to him.

Only once was I shaken out of my contentment, my complacency. I am ashamed to reveal it to you, it was so foolish of me. It only lasted a very little while but I still feel embarrassed and stupid when I think of it. It was of course those empty-headed, marble-playing friends of my childhood who led me into it. Once I had put them behind me, I should never have looked back. But they came up to me, after a rehearsal in our home city, a few hours before the concert. They had stolen into the dark hall and sat in the back row, smoking and cracking jokes and laughing in a secret, muffled way which nevertheless drifted up to the stage, distracting those who were not sufficiently immersed in the music to be unaware of the outside world. Of course the Ustad and I never allowed our attention to stray and continued to attend to the music. Our ability to simply shut out all distraction from our minds when we play is a similarity between us of which I am very proud.

As I was leaving the hall I saw they were still standing in the doorway, a jumbled stack of coloured shirts and oiled locks and garish shoes. They clustered around me and it was only because of the things they said, referring to our boyhood games in the alley, that I recognized them. In every other matter they differed totally from me, it was plain to see we had travelled in opposite directions. The colours of their cheap bush-shirts and their loud voices immediately gave me a headache and I found it hard to keep smiling although I knew I ought to be modest and affectionate to them as my art and my position called for such behaviour from me. I let them take me to the tea shop adjoining the concert hall and order tea for me. For a while we spoke of home, of games, of our families and friends. Then one of them – Ajit, I think – said, 'Bhai, you used to play so well. Your father was so proud of you, he thought you would be a great Ustad. He used to tell us what a great musician you would be one day. What are you doing, sitting at the back of the stage, and playing the tanpura for Rahim Khan?'

No one had ever spoken to me in this manner, in this voice, since my father died. I spilt tea down my lap. My head gave an uncontrolled jerk, I was so shocked. I half-stood up and thought I would catch him by his throat and press till all those ugly words and ugly thoughts of his were choked, bled, white and incapable of moving again. Only I am not that sort of a man. I know myself to be weak, very weak. I only brushed the tea from my clothes and stood there, staring at my feet. I stared at my broken old sandals, streaked with tea, at my loose clothes of white homespun. I told myself I lived so differently from them, my aim and purpose in life were so different from anything those gaudy street vagabonds could comprehend that I should not be surprised or take it ill if there were such a lack of understanding between us.

'What sort of instrument is the tanpura?' Ajit was saying, still loudly. 'Not even an accompaniment. It is nothing. Anyone could play it. Just three notes, over and over again. Even I could play it,' he ended with a shout, making the others clap his back and lean forwards in laughter at his wit.

Then Bhola leant towards me. He was the quietest of them,

although he wore a shirt of purple and white flowers and had dyed his moustache ginger. I knew he had been to jail twice already for housebreaking and theft. Yet he dared to lean close to me, almost touching me, and to say, 'Bhai, go back to the sitar. You even know how to play the sarod and the vina. You could be a great Ustad yourself, with some practice. We are telling you this for your own good. When you become famous and go to America, you will thank us for this advice. Why do you spend your life sitting at the back of the stage and playing that idiot tanpura while someone else takes all the fame and all the money from you?'

It was as if they had decided to assault me. I felt as if they were climbing on top of me, choking me, grabbing me by my hair and dragging me down. Their words were blows, the idea they were throwing at me an assault. I felt beaten, destroyed, and with my last bit of strength shook them off, threw them off and, pushing aside the table and cups and plates, ran out of the tea shop. I think they followed me because I could hear voices calling me as I went running down the street, pushing against people and only just escaping from under the rickshaws, tongas and buses. It was afternoon, there were crowds on the street, dust and smoke blotted out the natural light of day. I saw everything as vile, as debased, as something amoral and ugly, and pushed it aside, pushed through as I ran.

And all the time I thought, Are they right? Could I have played the sitar myself? Or the sarod, or the vina? And become an Ustad myself? This had never before occurred to me. My father had taught me to play all these instruments and disciplined me severely, but he had never praised me or suggested I could become a front-rank musician. I had learnt to play these instruments as the son of a carpenter would naturally have learnt to make beds and tables and shelves, or the son of a shopkeeper learnt to weigh grain and sell and make money. But I had practised on these instruments and played the ragas he taught me to play without thinking of it as an art or of myself as artist. Perhaps I was a stupid, backward boy. My father always said so. Now these boys, who had heard me play in the dark hall of our house in the music lane, told me I could have been an Ustad myself, sat in the centre of the stage, played for great audiences and been applauded for my performance. Were they right? Was this true? Had I wasted my life?

As I ran and pushed, half-crying, I thought these things for the first time in my life, and they were frightening thoughts – large, heavy, dark ones that threatened to crush and destroy me. I found myself pushed up against an iron railing. Holding onto its bars, looking through tears at the beds of flowering cannas and rows of imperial palms of a dusty city park, I hung against those railings, sobbing, till I heard someone address me – possibly a policeman, or a beggar, or perhaps just a kindly passer-by. 'In trouble?' he asked me. 'Got into trouble, boy?' I did not want to speak to anyone and shook him off without looking at him and found the gate and went into the park, trying to control myself and order my thoughts.

I found a path between some tall bushes, and walked up and down here, alone, trying to think. Having cried, I felt calmer now. I had a bad headache but I was calmer. I talked to myself.

When I first met my Ustad, I was a boy of fifteen – a stupid, backward boy as my father had often told me I was. When I walked up to the stage to give him the tanpura he had ordered from my father, I saw greatness in his face, the calm and wisdom and kindness of a true leader. Immediately I wished to deliver not only my tanpura but my whole life into his hands. Take me, I wanted to say, take me and lead me. Show me how to live. Let me live with you, by you, and help me, be kind to me. Of course I did not say these words. He took the tanpura from me and asked me to play it for him. This was his answer to the words I had not spoken but which he had nevertheless heard. 'Play for me' – and with these words he created me, created my life, gave it form and distinction and purpose. It was the moment of my birth and he was both my father and my mother to me. He gave birth to me – Bhaiyya, the tanpura player.

Before that I had no life. I was nothing: a dirty, hungry street urchin, knocking about in the lane with other idlers and vagrants. I had played music only because my father made me, teaching me by striking me across the knuckles and pulling my ears for every mistake I made. I had stolen money and sweets from my mother. I was nothing. And no one cared that I was nothing. It was Ustad Rahim Khan who saw me, hiding awkwardly in the shadows of an empty hall with a tanpura in my hands, and called me to come to him and showed me what to do with my life. I owe everything to him, my very life to him.

Yes, it was my destiny to play the tanpura for a great Ustad, to sit behind him where he cannot even see me, and play the notes he needs so that he may not stray from the bounds of his composition when gripped by inspiration. I give him, quietly and unobtrusively, the materials upon which he works, with which he constructs the great music for which the whole world loves him. Yes, anyone could play the tanpura for him, do what I do. But he did not take anyone else, he chose *me*. He gave me my destiny, my life. Could I have refused him? Does a mortal refuse God?

It made me smile to think anyone could be such a fool. Even I, Bhaiyya, had known when the hour of my destiny had struck. Even a backward, feckless boy from the streets had recognized his god when he met him. I could not have refused. I took up the tanpura and played for my Ustad, and I have played for him since. I could not have wished for a finer destiny.

Leaving the park, I hailed a tonga and ordered the driver to take me to my Ustad. Never in my life had I spoken so loudly, as surely as I did then. You should have heard me. I wish my Ustad had heard me.

A Devoted Son

When the results appeared in the morning papers, Rakesh scanned them, barefoot and in his pyjamas, at the garden gate, then went up the steps to the veranda where his father sat sipping his morning tea and bowed down to touch his feet.

'A first division, son?' his father asked, beaming, reaching for the papers.

'At the top of the list, Papa,' Rakesh murmured, as if awed. 'First in the country.'

Bedlam broke loose then. The family whooped and danced. The whole day long visitors streamed into the small yellow house at the end of the road, to congratulate the parents of this wunderkind, to slap Rakesh on the back and fill the house and garden with the sounds and colours of a festival. There were garlands and halwa, party clothes and gifts (enough fountain pens to last years, even a watch or two), nerves and temper and joy, all in a multicoloured whirl of pride and great shining vistas newly opened: Rakesh was the first son in the family to receive an education, so much had been sacrificed in order to send him to school and then medical college, and at last the fruits of their sacrifice had arrived, golden and glorious.

To everyone who came to him to say, 'Mubarak, Varmaji, your son has brought you glory,' the father said, 'Yes, and do you know what is the first thing he did when he saw the results this morning? He came and touched my feet. He bowed down and touched my feet.' This moved many of the women in the crowd so much that they were seen to raise the ends of their saris and dab at their tears while the men reached out for the betel leaves and sweetmeats that were offered around on trays and shook their heads in wonder and approval of such exemplary filial behaviour. 'One does not often see such behaviour in sons any more,' they all agreed, a little enviously perhaps. Leaving the house, some of the women said, sniffing, 'At least on such an occasion they might have served pure ghee sweets,' and some of the men said, 'Don't you think old Varma was giving himself airs? He needn't think we don't remember that he comes from the vegetable market himself, his father used to sell vegetables, and he has never seen the inside of a school.' But there was more envy than rancour in their voices and it was, of course, inevitable – not every son in that shabby little colony at the edge of the city was destined to shine as Rakesh shone, and who knew that better than the parents themselves?

And that was only the beginning, the first step in a great, sweeping ascent to the radiant heights of fame and fortune. The thesis he wrote for his MD brought Rakesh still greater glory, if only in select medical circles. He won a scholarship. He went to the USA (that was what his father learnt to call it and taught the whole family to say – not America, which was what the ignorant neighbours called it, but, with a grand familiarity, 'the USA') where he pursued his career in the most prestigious of all hospitals and won encomiums from his American colleagues which were relayed to his admiring and glowing family. What was more, he came *back*, he actually returned to that small yellow house in the once-new but increasingly shabby colony, right at the end of the road where the rubbish vans tipped out their stinking contents for pigs to nose in and rag-pickers to build their shacks on, all steaming and smoking just outside the neat wire fences and well-tended gardens. To this Rakesh returned and the first thing he did on entering the house was to slip out of the embraces of his sisters and brothers and bow down and touch his father's feet.

As for his mother, she gloated chiefly over the strange fact that he had not married in America, had not brought home a foreign wife as all her neighbours had warned her he would, for wasn't that what all Indian boys went abroad for? Instead he agreed, almost without argument, to marry a girl she had picked out for him in her own village, the daughter of a childhood friend, a plump and uneducated girl, it was true, but so old-fashioned, so placid, so complaisant that she slipped into the household and settled in like a charm, seemingly too lazy and too good-natured to even try and make Rakesh leave home and set up independently, as any other girl might have done. What was more, she was pretty – really pretty, in a plump, pudding way that only gave way to fat – soft, spreading fat, like warm wax – after the birth of their first baby, a son, and then what did it matter?

For some years Rakesh worked in the city hospital, quickly rising to the top of the administrative organization, and was made a director before he left to set up his own clinic. He took his parents in his car – a new, sky-blue Ambassador with a rear window full of stickers and charms revolving on strings – to see the clinic when it was built, and the large sign-board over the door on which his name was printed in letters of red, with a row of degrees and qualifications to follow it like so many little black slaves of the regent. Thereafter his fame seemed to grow just a little dimmer – or maybe it was only that everyone in town had grown accustomed to it at last – but it was also the beginning of his fortune for he now became known not only as the best but also the richest doctor in town.

However, all this was not accomplished in the wink of an eye. Naturally not. It was the achievement of a lifetime and it took up Rakesh's whole life. At the time he set up his clinic his father had grown into an old man and retired from his post at the kerosene dealer's depot at which he had worked for forty years, and his mother died soon after, giving up the ghost with a sigh that sounded positively happy, for it was her own son who ministered to her in her last illness and who sat pressing her feet at the last moment – such a son as few women had borne.

For it had to be admitted – and the most unsuccessful and most rancorous of neighbours eventually did so – that Rakesh was not only a devoted son and a miraculously good-natured man who contrived somehow to obey his parents and humour his wife and show concern equally for his children and his patients, but there was actually a brain inside this beautifully polished and formed body of good manners and kind nature and, in between ministering to his family and playing host to many friends and coaxing them all into feeling happy and grateful and content, he had actually trained his hands as well and emerged an excellent doctor, a really fine surgeon. How one man – and a man born to illiterate parents, his father having worked for a kerosene dealer and his mother having spent her life in a kitchen – had achieved, combined and conducted such a medley of virtues, no one could fathom, but all acknowledged his talent and skill.

It was a strange fact, however, that talent and skill, if displayed for too long, cease to dazzle. It came to pass that the most admiring of all eyes eventually faded and no longer blinked at his glory. Having retired from work and having lost his wife, the old father very quickly went to pieces, as they say. He developed so many complaints and fell ill so frequently and with such mysterious diseases that even his son could no longer make out when it was something of significance and when it was merely a peevish whim. He sat huddled on his string-bed most of the day and developed an exasperating habit of stretching-out suddenly and lying absolutely still, allowing the whole family to fly around him in a flap, wailing and weeping, and then suddenly sitting up, stiff and gaunt, and spitting out a big gob of betel juice as if to mock their behaviour.

He did this once too often: there had been a big party in the house, a birthday party for the youngest son, and the celebrations had to be suddenly hushed, covered up and hustled out of the way when the daughter-in-law discovered, or thought she discovered, that the old man, stretched out from end to end of his string-bed, had lost his pulse; the party broke up, dissolved, even turned into a band of mourners, when the old man sat up and the distraught daughter-in-law received a gob of red spittle right on the hem of her new organza sari. After that no one much cared if he sat up crosslegged on his bed, hawking and spitting, or lay down flat and turned grey as a corpse. Except, of course, for that pearl amongst pearls, his son Rakesh.

It was Rakesh who brought him his morning tea, not in one of the china cups from which the rest of the family drank, but in the old man's favourite brass tumbler, and sat at the edge of his bed, comfortable and relaxed with the string of his pyjamas dangling out from under his fine lawn night-shirt, and discussed or, rather, read out the morning news to his father. It made no difference to him that his father made no response apart from spitting. It was Rakesh, too, who, on returning from the clinic in the evening, persuaded the old man to come out of his room, as bare and desolate as a cell, and take the evening air out in the garden, beautifully arranging the pillows and bolsters on the divan in the corner of the open veranda. On summer nights he saw to it that the servants carried out the old man's bed onto the lawn and himself helped his father down the steps and onto the bed, soothing him and settling him down for a night under the stars.

All this was very gratifying for the old man. What was not so gratifying was that he even undertook to supervise his father's diet. One day when the father was really sick, having ordered his daughter-in-law to make him a dish of sooji halwa and eaten it with a saucerful of cream, Rakesh marched into the room, not with his usual respectful step but with the confident and rather contemptuous stride of the famous doctor, and declared, 'No more halwa for you, Papa. We must be sensible, at your age. If you must have something sweet, Veena will cook you a little kheer, that's light, just a little rice and milk. But nothing fried, nothing rich. We can't have this happening again.'

The old man who had been lying stretched out on his bed, weak and feeble after a day's illness, gave a start at the very sound, the tone of these words. He opened his eyes – rather, they fell open with shock – and he stared at his son with disbelief that darkened quickly to reproach. A son who actually refused his father the food he craved? No, it was unheard of, it was incredible. But Rakesh had turned his back to him and was cleaning up the litter of bottles and packets on the medicine shelf and did not notice while Veena slipped silently out of the room with a little smirk that only the old man saw, and hated.

Halwa was only the first item to be crossed off the old man's diet. One delicacy after the other went – everything fried to begin with, then everything sweet, and eventually everything, everything that the old man enjoyed. The meals that arrived for him on the shining stainless-steel tray twice a day were frugal to say the least – dry bread, boiled lentils, boiled vegetables and, if there were a bit of chicken or fish, that was boiled too. If he called for another helping – in a cracked voice that quavered theatrically – Rakesh himself would come to the door, gaze at him sadly and shake his head, saying, 'Now, Papa, we must be careful, we can't risk another illness, you know,' and although the daughter-in-law kept tactfully out of the way, the old man could just see her smirk sliding merrily through the air. He tried to bribe his grandchildren into buying him sweets (and how he missed his wife now, that generous, indulgent and illiterate cook), whispering, 'Here's fifty paise' as he stuffed the coins into a tight, hot fist. 'Run down to the shop at the crossroads and buy me thirty paise worth of jalebis, and you can spend the remaining twenty paise on yourself. Eh? Understand? Will you do that?' He got away with it once or twice but then was found out, the conspirator was scolded by his father and smacked by his mother and Rakesh came storming into the room, almost tearing his hair as he shouted through compressed lips, 'Now Papa, are you trying to turn my little son into a liar? Quite apart from spoiling your own stomach, you are spoiling him as well – you are encouraging him to lie to his own parents. You should have heard the lies he told his mother when she saw him bringing back those jalebis wrapped up in filthy newspaper. I don't allow anyone in my house to buy sweets in the bazaar, Papa, surely you know that. There's cholera in the city, typhoid, gastroenteritis – I see these cases daily in the hospital, how can I allow my own family to run such risks?' The old man sighed and lay down in the corpse position. But that worried no one any longer.

There was only one pleasure left the old man now (his son's early morning visits and readings from the newspaper could no longer be called that) and those were visits from elderly neighbours. These were not frequent as his contemporaries were mostly as decrepit and helpless as he and few could walk the length of the road to visit him any more. Old Bhatia, next door, however, who was still spry enough to refuse, adamantly, to bathe in the tiled bathroom indoors and to insist on carrying out his brass mug and towel, in all seasons and usually at impossible hours, into the yard and bathe noisily under the garden tap, would look over the hedge to see if Varma were out on his veranda and would call to him and talk while he wrapped his dhoti about him and dried the sparse hair on his head, shivering with enjoyable exaggeration. Of course these conversations, bawled across the hedge by two rather deaf old men conscious of having their entire households overhearing them, were not very satisfactory but Bhatia occasionally came out of his yard, walked down the bit of road and came in at Varma's gate to collapse onto the stone plinth built under the temple tree. If Rakesh were at home he would help his father down the steps into the garden and arrange him on his night bed under the tree and leave the two old men to chew betel leaves and discuss the ills of their individual bodies with combined passion.

'At least you have a doctor in the house to look after you,' sighed Bhatia, having vividly described his martyrdom to piles.

'Look after me?' cried Varma, his voice cracking like an ancient clay jar. 'He – he does not even give me enough to eat.'

'What?' said Bhatia, the white hairs in his ears twitching. 'Doesn't give you enough to eat? Your own son?'

'My own son. If I ask him for one more piece of bread, he says no, Papa, I weighed out the aata myself and I can't allow you to have more than two hundred grammes of cereal a day. He *weighs* the food he gives me, Bhatia – he has scales to weigh it on. That is what it has come to.'

'Never,' murmured Bhatia in disbelief. 'Is it possible, even in this evil age, for a son to refuse his father food?'

'Let me tell you,' Varma whispered eagerly. 'Today the family was having fried fish – I could smell it. I called to my daughter-in-law to bring me a piece. She came to the door and said No . . .'

'Said No?' It was Bhatia's voice that cracked. A drongo shot out of the tree and sped away. '*No?*'

'No, she said no, Rakesh has ordered her to give me nothing fried. No butter, he says, no oil—'

'No butter? No oil? How does he expect his father to *live?*'

Old Varma nodded with melancholy triumph. 'That is how he treats me – after I have brought him up, given him an education, made him a great doctor. Great doctor! This is the way great doctors treat their fathers, Bhatia,' for the son's sterling personality and character now underwent a curious sea change. Outwardly all might be the same but the interpretation had altered: his masterly efficiency was nothing but cold heartlessness, his authority was only tyranny in disguise.

There was cold comfort in complaining to neighbours and, on such a miserable diet, Varma found himself slipping, weakening and soon becoming a genuinely sick man. Powders and pills and mixtures were not only brought in when dealing with a crisis like an upset stomach but became a regular part of his diet – became his diet, complained Varma, supplanting the natural foods he craved. There were pills to regulate his bowel movements, pills to bring down his blood pressure, pills to deal with his arthritis and, eventually, pills to keep his heart beating. In between there were panicky rushes to the hospital, some humiliating experiences with the stomach pump and enema, which left him frightened and helpless. He cried easily, shrivelling up on his bed, but if he complained of a pain or even a vague, grey fear in the night, Rakesh would simply open another bottle of pills and force him to take one. 'I have my duty to you, Papa,' he said when his father begged to be let off.

'Let me be,' Varma begged, turning his face away from the pills on the outstretched hand. 'Let me die. It would be better. I do not want to live only to eat your medicines.'

'Papa, be reasonable.'

'I leave that to you,' the father cried with sudden spirit. 'Let me alone, let me die now, I cannot live like this.'

'Lying all day on his pillows, fed every few hours by his daughter-in-law's own hands, visited by every member of his family daily – and then he says he does not want to live "like this",' Rakesh was heard to say, laughing, to someone outside the door.

'Deprived of food,' screamed the old man on the bed, 'his wishes ignored, taunted by his daughter-in-law, laughed at by his grandchildren – *that* is how I live.' But he was very old and weak and all anyone heard was an incoherent croak, some expressive grunts and cries of genuine pain. Only once, when old Bhatia had come to see him and they sat together under the temple tree, they heard him cry, 'God is calling me – and they won't let me go.'

The quantities of vitamins and tonics he was made to take were not altogether useless. They kept him alive and even gave him a kind of strength that made him hang on long after he ceased to wish to hang on. It was as though he were straining at a rope, trying to break it, and it would not break, it was still strong. He only hurt himself, trying.

In the evening, that summer, the servants would come into his cell, grip his bed, one at each end, and carry it out to the veranda, there setting it down with a thump that jarred every tooth in his head. In answer to his agonized complaints they said the Doctor Sahib had told them he must take the evening air and the evening air they would make him take – thump. Then Veena, that smiling, hypocritical pudding in a rustling sari, would appear and pile up the pillows under his head till he was propped up stiffly into a sitting position that made his head swim and his back ache. 'Let me lie down,' he begged. 'I can't sit up any more.'

'Try, Papa, Rakesh said you can if you try,' she said, and drifted away to the other end of the veranda where her transistor radio vibrated to the lovesick tunes from the cinema that she listened to all day.

So there he sat, like some stiff corpse, terrified, gazing out on the lawn where his grandsons played cricket, in danger of getting one of their hard-spun balls in his eye, and at the gate that opened onto the dusty and rubbish-heaped lane but still bore, proudly, a newly touched-up signboard that bore his son's name and qualifications, his own name having vanished from the gate long ago.

At last the sky-blue Ambassador arrived, the cricket game broke up in haste, the car drove in smartly and the doctor, the great doctor, all in white, stepped out. Someone ran up to take his bag from him, others to escort him up the steps. 'Will you have tea?' his wife called, turning down the transistor set, 'or a Coca-Cola? Shall I fry you some samosas?' But he did not reply or even glance in her direction. Ever a devoted son, he went first to the corner where his father sat gazing, stricken, at some undefined spot in the dusty yellow air that swam before him. He did not turn his head to look at his son. But he stopped gobbling air with his uncontrolled lips and set his jaw as hard as a sick and very old man could set it.

'Papa,' his son said, tenderly, sitting down on the edge of the bed and reaching out to press his feet.

Old Varma tucked his feet under him, out of the way, and continued to gaze stubbornly into the yellow air of the summer evening.

'Papa, I'm home.'

Varma's hand jerked suddenly, in a sharp, derisive movement, but he did not speak.

'How are you feeling, Papa?'

Then Varma turned and looked at his son. His face was so out of control and all in pieces, that the multitude of expressions that crossed it could not make up a whole and convey to the famous man exactly what his father thought of him, his skill, his art.

'I'm dying,' he croaked. 'Let me die, I tell you.'

'Papa, you're joking,' his son smiled at him, lovingly. 'I've brought you a new tonic to make you feel better. You must take it, it will make you feel stronger again. Here it is. Promise me you will take it regularly, Papa.'

Varma's mouth worked as hard as though he still had a gob of betel in it (his supply of betel had been cut off years ago). Then he spat out some words, as sharp and bitter as poison, into his son's face. 'Keep your tonic – I want none – I want none – I won't take any more of – of your medicines. None. Never,' and he swept the bottle out of his son's hand with a wave of his own, suddenly grand, suddenly effective.

His son jumped, for the bottle was smashed and thick brown syrup had splashed up, staining his white trousers. His wife let out a cry and came running. All around the old man was hubbub once again, noise, attention.

He gave one push to the pillows at his back and dislodged them so he could sink down on his back, quite flat again. He closed his eyes and pointed his chin at the ceiling, like some dire prophet, groaning, 'God is calling me – now let me go.'

The Farewell Party

Before the party she had made a list, faintheartedly, and marked off the items as they were dealt with, inexorably – cigarettes, soft drinks, ice, kebabs and so on. But she had forgotten to provide lights. The party was to be held on the lawn: on these dry summer nights one could plan a lawn party weeks in advance and be certain of fine weather, and she had thought happily of how the roses would be in bloom and of the stars and perhaps even fireflies, so decorative and discreet, all gracefully underlining her unsuspected talent as a hostess. But she had not realized that there would be no moon and therefore it would be very dark on the lawn. All the lights on the veranda, in the portico and indoors were on, like so many lanterns, richly copper and glowing, with extraordinary beauty as though aware that the house would soon be empty and these were the last few days of illumination and family life, but they did very little to light the lawn which was vast, a still lake of inky grass.

Wandering about with a glass in one hand and a plate of cheese biscuits in another, she gave a start now and then to see an acquaintance emerge from the darkness which had the gloss, the sheen, the coolness but not the weight of water, and present her with a face, vague and without outlines but eventually recognizable. 'Oh,' she cried several times that evening, 'I didn't know you had arrived. I've been looking for you,' she would add with unaccustomed intimacy (was it because of the gin and lime, her second, or because such warmth could safely be held to lead to nothing now that they were leaving town?). The guest, also having had several drinks between beds of flowering balsam and torenias before launching out onto the lawn, responded with an equal vivacity. Sometimes she had her arm squeezed or a hand slid down the bareness of her back – which was athletic: she had once played tennis, rather well – and once someone said, 'I've been hiding in this corner, watching you,' while another went so far as to say, 'Is it true you are leaving us, Bina? How can you be so cruel?' And if it were a woman guest, the words were that much more effusive. It was all heady, astonishing.

It was astonishing because Bina was a frigid and friendless woman. She was thirty-five. For fifteen years she had been bringing up her children and, in particular, nursing the eldest who was severely spastic. This had involved her deeply in the workings of the local hospital and with its many departments and doctors, but her care for this child was so intense and so desperate that her relationship with them was purely professional. Outside this circle of family and hospital – ringed, as it were, with barbed wire and lit with one single floodlight – Bina had no life. The town had scarcely come to know her for its life turned in the more jovial circles of mah-jong, bridge, coffee parties, club evenings and, occasionally, a charity show in aid of the Red Cross. For these Bina had a kind of sad contempt and certainly no time. A tall, pale woman, heavy-boned and sallow, she had a certain presence, a certain dignity, and people, having heard of the spastic child, liked and admired her, but she had not thought she had friends. Yet tonight they were coming forth from the darkness in waves that quite overwhelmed.

Now here was Mrs Ray, the Commissioner's wife, chirping inside a nest of rustling embroidered organza. 'Why are you leaving us so soon, Mrs Raman? You've only been here – two years, is it?'

'Five,' exclaimed Bina, widening her eyes, herself surprised at such a length of time. Although time dragged heavily in their household, agonizingly slow, and the five years had been so hard that sometimes, at night, she did not know how she had crawled through the day and if she would crawl through another, her back almost literally broken by the weight of the totally depend-ent child and of the three smaller ones who seemed perpetually to clamour for their share of attention, which they felt they never got. Yet now these five years had telescoped. They were over. The Raman family was moving and their time here was spent. There had been the hospital, the girls' school, the boys' school, picnics, monsoons, birthday parties and measles. Crushed together into a handful. She gazed down at her hands, tightened around glass and plate. 'Time has flown,' she murmured incredulously.

'Oh, I wish you were staying, Mrs Raman,' cried the Com-missioner's wife and, as she squeezed Bina's arm, her fragrant talcum powder seemed to lift off her chalky shoulders and some of it settled on Bina who sneezed. 'It's been so nice to have a fam-ily like yours here. It's a small town, so little to do, at least one must have good friends . . .'

Bina blinked at such words of affection from a woman she had met twice, perhaps thrice before. Bina and her husband did not go in for society. The shock of their first child's birth had made them both fanatic parents. But she knew that not everyone considered this vital factor in their lives, and spoke of 'social duties' in a somehow reproving tone. The Commissioner's wife had been annoyed, she always felt, by her refusal to help out at the Red Cross fair. The hurt silence with which her refusal had been accepted had implied the importance of these 'social duties' of which Bina remained so stubbornly unaware.

However, this one evening, this last party, was certainly given over to their recognition and celebration. 'Oh, everyone, every-one is here,' rejoiced the Commissioner's wife, her eyes snapping from face to face in that crowded aquarium, and, at a higher pitch, cried, 'Renu, why weren't you at the mah-jong party this morning?' and moved off into another powdery organza embrace that rose to meet her from the night like a moth and then was submerged again in the shadows of the lawn. Bina gave one of those smiles that easily-frightened people found mocking, a shade too superior, somewhat scornful. Looking down into her glass of gin and lime, she moved on and in a minute found herself brought up short against the quite regal although overweight figure, in raw silk and homespun and the somewhat saturnine air of underpaid culture, of Bose, an employee of the local museum whom she had met once or twice at the art competitions and exhibitions to which she was fond of hauling her children, whether reluctant or enthusiastic, because 'it made a change,' she said.

'Mrs Raman,' he said in the fruity tones of the culture-bent Bengali, 'how we'll miss you at the next children's art competitions. You used to be my chief inspiration—'

'Inspiration?' she laughed, incredulously, spilling some of her drink and proffering the plate of cheese biscuits from which he helped himself, half-bowing as though it were gold she offered, gems.

'Yes, yes, inspiration,' he went on, even more fruitily now that his mouth was full. 'Think of me – alone, the hapless organizer – surrounded by mammas, by primary school teachers, by three, four, five hundred children. And the judges – they are always the most trouble, those judges. And then I look at you – so cool, controlling your children, handling them so wonderfully and with such superb results – my inspiration!'

She was flustered by this unaccustomed vision of herself and half-turned her face away from Bose the better to contemplate it, but could find no reflection of it in the ghostly white bush of the Queen of the Night, and listened to him murmur on about her unkindness in deserting him in this cultural backwater to that darkest of dooms – guardian of a provincial museum – where he saw no one but school teachers herding children through his halls or, worse, government officials who periodically and inexplicably stirred to create trouble for him and made their official presences felt amongst the copies of the Ajanta frescoes (in which even the mouldy and peeled-off portions were carefully reproduced) and the cupboards of Indus Valley seals. Murmuring commiseration, she left him to a gloomy young professor of history who was languishing at another of the institutions of provincial backwaters that they so deplored and whose wife was always having a baby, and slipped away, still feeling an unease at Bose's unexpected vision of her which did not tally with the cruder reality, into the less equivocal company provided by a ring of twittering 'company wives'.

These women she had always encountered in just such a ring as they formed now, the kind that garden babblers form under a hedge where they sit gabbling and whirring with social bitchiness, and she had always stood outside it, smiling stiffly, not wanting to join and refusing their effusively nodded invitation. They were the wives of men who represented various mercantile companies in the town – Imperial Tobacco, Brooke Bond, Esso and so on – and although they might seem exactly alike to one who did not belong to this circle, inside it were subtle gradations of importance according to the particular company for which each one's husband worked and of these only they themselves were initiates. Bina was, however unwillingly, an initiate. Her husband worked for one of these companies but she had always stiffly refused to recognize these gradations, or consider them. They noted the rather set sulkiness of her silence when amongst them and privately labelled her queer, proud, boring and difficult. Also, they felt she belonged to their circle whether she liked it or not.

Now she entered this circle with diffidence, wishing she had stayed with the more congenial Bose (why hadn't she? What was it in her that made her retreat from anything like a friendly approach?) and was taken aback to find their circle parting to admit her and hear their cries of welcome and affection that did not, however, lose the stridency and harshness of garden babblers' voices.

'Bina, how do you like the idea of going back to Bombay?'

'Have you started packing, Bina? Poor you. Oh, are you having packers over from Delhi? Oh well then it's not so bad.'

Never had they been so vociferous in her company, so easy, so warm. They were women to whom the most awful thing that had ever happened was the screw of a golden earring disappearing down the bathroom sink or a mother-in-law's visit or an ayah deserting just before the arrival of guests: what could they know of Bina's life, Bina's ordeal? She cast her glance at the drinks they held – but they were mostly of orange squash. Only the Esso wife, who participated in amateur dramatics and ran a boutique and was rather taller and bolder than the rest, held a whisky and soda. So much affection generated by just orange squash? Impossible. Rather tentatively, she offered them the remains of the cheese biscuits, found herself chirping replies, deploring the nuisance of having packing crates all over the house, talking of the flat they would move into in Bombay, and then, sweating unobtrusively with the strain, saw another recognizable fish swim towards her from the edge of the liquescent lawn, and swung away in relief, saying, 'Mrs D'Souza! How late you are, but I'm so glad—' for she really was.

Mrs D'Souza was her daughter's teacher at the convent school and had clearly never been to a cocktail party before so that all Bina's compassion was aroused by those school-scuffed shoes and her tea-party best – quite apart from the simple truth that she found in her an honest individuality that all those beautifully dressed and poised babblers lacked, being stamped all over by the plain rubber stamps of their husbands' companies – and she hurried off to find Mrs D'Souza something suitable to drink. 'Sherry? Why yes, I think I'll be able to find you some,' she said, a bit flabbergasted at such an unexpected fancy of the pepper-haired schoolteacher, 'and I'll see if Tara's around – she'll want to see you,' she added, vaguely and fraudulently, wondering why she had asked Mrs D'Souza to a cocktail party, only to see, as she skirted the rose bed, the admirable Bose appear at her side and envelop her in this strange intimacy that marked the whole evening, and went off, light-hearted, towards the table where her husband was trying, with the help of some hired waiters in soggy white uniforms with the name of the restaurant from which they were hired embroidered in red across their pockets, to cope with the flood of drinks this party atmosphere had called for and released.

Harassed, perspiring, his feet burning, Raman was nevertheless pleased to be so obviously employed and be saved the strain of having to converse with his motley assembly of guests: he had no more gift for society than his wife had. Ice cubes were melting on the tablecloth in sopping puddles and he had trouble in keeping track of his bottles: they were, besides the newly bought dozens of beer bottles and Black Knight whisky, the remains of their five years in this town that he now wished to bring to their end – bottles brought by friends from trips abroad, bottles bought cheap through 'contacts' in the army or air force, some gems, extravaganzas bought for anniversaries such as a nearly full bottle of Vat 69, a bottle with a bit of creme de menthe growing sticky at the bottom, some brown sherry with a great deal of rusty sediment, a red Golconda wine from Hyderabad, and a bottle of Remy Martin that he was keeping guiltily to himself, pouring small quantities into a whisky glass at his elbow and gulping it down in between mixing some very weird cocktails for his guests. There was no one at the party he liked well enough to share it with. Oh, one of the doctors perhaps, but where were they? Submerged in grass, in dark, in night and chatter, clatter of ice in glass, teeth on biscuit, teeth on teeth. Enamel and gold. Crumbs and dregs. All awash, all soaked in night. Watery sound of speech, liquid sound of drink. Water and ice and night. It occurred to him that everyone had forgotten him, the host, that it was a mistake to have stationed himself amongst the waiters, that he ought to move out, mingle with the guests. But he felt himself drowned, helplessly and quite delightfully, in Remy Martin, in grass, in a border of purple torenias.

Then he was discovered by his son who galloped through the ranks of guests and waiters to fling himself at his father and ask if he could play the new Beatles record, his friends had asked to hear it.

Raman considered, taking the opportunity to pour out and

gulp down some more of the precious Remy Martin. 'All right,' he said, after a judicious minute or two, 'but keep it low, everyone won't want to hear it,' not adding that he himself didn't, for his taste in music ran to slow and melancholy, folk at its most frivolous. Still, he glanced into the lighted room where his children and the children of neighbours and guests had collected, making themselves tipsy on Fanta and Coca-Cola, the girls giggling in a multicoloured huddle and the boys swaggering around the record-player with a kind of lounging strut, holding bottles in their hands with a sophisticated ease, exactly like experienced cocktail party guests, so that he smiled and wished he had a ticket, a passport that would make it possible to break into that party within a party. It was chillingly obvious to him that he hadn't one. He also saw that a good deal of their riotousness was due to the fact that they were raiding the snack trays that the waiters carried through the room to the lawn, and that they were seeing to it that the trays emerged half-empty. He knew he ought to go in and see about it but he hadn't the heart, or the nerve. He couldn't join that party but he wouldn't wreck it either so he only caught hold of one of the waiters and suggested that the snack trays be carried out from the kitchen straight onto the lawn, not by way of the drawing room, and led him towards a group that seemed to be without snacks and saw too late that it was a group of the company executives that he loathed most. He half-groaned, then hiccuped at his mistake, but it was too late to alter course now. He told himself that he ought to see to it that the snacks were offered around without snag or error.

Poor Raman was placed in one of the lower ranks of the companies' hierarchy. That is, he did not belong to a British concern, or even to an American-collaboration one, but merely to an Indian one. Oh, a long-established, prosperous and solid one but, still, only Indian. Those cigarettes that he passed around were made by his own company. Somehow it struck a note of bad taste amongst these fastidious men who played golf, danced at the club on Independence Eve and New Year's Eve, invited at least one foreign couple to every party and called their decorative wives 'darling' when in public. Poor Raman never had belonged. It was so obvious to everyone, even to himself, as he passed around those awful cigarettes that sold so well in the market. It had been obvious since their first disastrous dinner party for this very ring of jocular gentlemen, five years ago: Nono had cried right through the party, Bina had spent the evening racing upstairs to see to the babies' baths and bedtime and then crawling reluctantly down, the hired cook had got drunk and stolen two of the chickens so that there was not enough on the table, no one had relaxed for a minute or enjoyed a second — it had been too sad and harrowing even to make a good story or a funny anecdote. They had all let it sink by mutual consent and the invitations to play a round of golf on Saturday afternoon or a rubber of bridge on Sunday morning had been issued and refused with conspiratorial smoothness. Then there was that distressing hobby of Raman's: his impossibly long walks on which he picked up bits of wood and took them home to sandpaper and chisel and then call wood sculpture. What could one do with a chap who did that? He himself wasn't sure if he pursued such odd tastes because he was a social pariah or if he was one on account of this oddity. Not to speak of the spastic child. Now that didn't even bear thinking of, and so it was no wonder that Raman swayed towards them so hesitantly, as though he were wading through water instead of over clipped grass, and handed his cigarettes around with such an apologetic air.

But, after all, hesitation and apology proved unnecessary. One of them — was he Polson's Coffee or Brooke Bond Tea? — clasped Raman about the shoulders as proper men do on meeting, and hearty voices rose together, congratulating him on his promotion (it wasn't one, merely a transfer, and they knew it), envying him his move to the metropolis. They talked as if they had known each other for years, shared all kinds of public school-boy fun. One — was he Voltas or Ciba? — talked of golf matches at the Willingdon as though he had often played there with

Raman, another spoke of kebabs eaten on the roadside after a party as though Raman had been one of the gang. Amazed and grateful as a schoolboy admitted to a closed society, Raman nodded and put in a few cautious words, put away his cigarettes, called a waiter to refill their glasses and broke away before the clock struck twelve and the golden carriage turned into a pumpkin, he himself into a mouse. He hated mice.

Walking backwards, he walked straight into the soft barrier of Miss Dutta's ample back wrapped and bound in rich Madras silk.

'Sorry, sorry, Miss Dutta, I'm clumsy as a bear,' he apologized, but here, too, there was no call for apology for Miss Dutta was obviously delighted at having been bumped into.

'My dear Mr Raman, what can you expect if you invite the whole town to your party?' she asked in that piercing voice that invariably made her companions drop theirs self-consciously. 'You and Bina have been so popular – what are we going to do without you?'

He stood pressing his glass with white-tipped fingers and tried to think what he or Bina had provided her with that she could possibly miss. In any case, Miss Dutta could always manage, and did manage, everything single-handedly. She was the town busy-body, secretary and chairman of more committees than he could count: they ranged from the Film Society to the Blood Bank, from the Red Cross to the Friends of the Museum, for Miss Dutta was nothing if not versatile. 'We hardly ever saw you at our film shows of course,' her voice rang out, making him glance furtively over his shoulder to see if anyone were listening, 'but it was so nice *knowing* you were in town and that I could count on you. So few people here *care*, you know,' she went on, and affectionately bumped her comfortable middle-aged body into his as someone squeezed by, making him remember that he had once heard her called a man-eater, and wonder which man she had eaten and even consider, for a moment, if there were not, after all, some charm in those powdered creases of her creamy arms, equalling if not surpassing that of his worn and harassed wife's bony angles. Why did suffering make for angularity? he even asked himself with uncharacteristic unkindness. But when Miss Dutta laid an arm on top of his glass-holding one and raised herself on her toes to bray something into his ear, he loyally decided that he was too accustomed to sharp angles to change them for such unashamed luxuriance, and, contriving to remove her arm by grasping her elbow – how one's fingers sank into the stuff! – he steered her towards his wife who was standing at the table and inefficiently pouring herself another gin and lime.

'This is my third,' she confessed hurriedly, 'and I can't tell you how gay it makes me feel. I giggle at everything everyone says.'

'Good,' he pronounced, feeling inside a warm expansion of relief at seeing her lose, for the moment, her tension and anxiety. 'Let's hear you giggle,' he said, sloshing some more gin into her glass.

'Look at those children,' she exclaimed, and they stood in a bed of balsam, irredeemably crushed, and looked into the lighted drawing room where their daughter was at the moment the cynosure of all juvenile eyes, having thrown herself with abandon into a dance of monkey-like movements. 'What is it, Miss Dutta?' the awed mother enquired. 'You're more up in the latest fashions than I am – is it the twist, the rock or the jungle?' and all three watched, enthralled, till Tara began to totter and, losing her simian grace, collapsed against some wildly shrieking girl friends.

A bit embarrassed by their daughter's reckless abandon, the parents discussed with Miss Dutta whose finger, by her own admission, was placed squarely on the pulse of youth, the latest trends in juvenile culture on which Miss Dutta gave a neat sociological discourse (all the neater for having been given earlier that day at the convocation of the Home Science College) and Raman wondered uneasily at this opening of flood-gates in his own family – his wife grown giggly with gin, his daughter performing wildly to a Chubby Checker record – how had it all come about? Was it the darkness all about them, dense as the heavy curtains about a stage, that made them act, for an hour or so, on the tiny lighted stage of brief intimacy with such a lack of inhibition? Was it the drink, so freely sloshing from end to end of the house and lawn on account of his determination to clear out his 'cellar' (actually one-half of the sideboard and the top shelf of the wardrobe in his dressing-room) and his muddling and mixing them, making up untried and experimental cocktails and lavishly pouring out the whisky without a measure? But these were solid and everyday explanations and there was about this party something out of the ordinary and everyday – at least to the Ramans, normally so austere and unpopular. He knew the real reason too – it was all because the party had been labelled a 'farewell party', everyone knew it was the last one, that the Ramans were leaving and they would not meet up again. There was about it exactly that kind of sentimental euphoria that is generated at a ship-board party, the one given on the last night before the end of the voyage. Everyone draws together with an intimacy, a lack of inhibition not displayed or guessed at before, knowing this is the last time, tomorrow they will be dispersed, it will be over. They will not meet, be reminded of it or be required to repeat it.

As if to underline this new and Cinderella's ball-like atmosphere of friendliness and gaiety, three pairs of neighbours now swept in (and three kochias lay down and died under their feet, to the gardener's rage and sorrow): the couple who lived to the Ramans' left, the couple who lived to their right, and the couple from across the road, all crying, 'So sorry to be late, but you know what a long way we had to come,' making everyone laugh identically at the identical joke. Despite the disparity in their looks and ages – one couple was very young, another middle-aged, the third grandparents – they were, in a sense, as alike as the company executives and their wives, for they too bore a label if a less alarming one: Neighbours, it said. Because they were neighbours, and although they had never been more than nodded to over the hedge, waved to in passing cars or spoken to about anything other than their children, dogs, flowers and gardens, their talk had a vivid immediacy that went straight to the heart.

'Diamond's going to miss you so – he'll be heartbroken,' moaned the grandparents who lived alone in their spotless house with a black Labrador who had made a habit of visiting the Ramans whenever he wanted young company, a romp on the lawn or an illicit biscuit.

'I don't know what my son will do without Diamond,' reciprocated Bina with her new and sympathetic warmth. 'He'll force me to get a dog of his own, I know, and how will I ever keep one in a flat in Bombay?'

'When are you going to throw out those rascals?' demanded a father of Raman, pointing at the juvenile revellers indoors. 'My boy has an exam tomorrow, you know, but he said he couldn't be bothered about it – he had to go to the Ramans' farewell party.'

One mother confided to Bina, winning her heart forever, 'Now that you are leaving, I can talk to you about it at last: did you know my Vinod is sweet on your Tara? Last night when I was putting him to bed, he said, "Mama, when I grow up I will marry Tara. I will sit on a white horse and wear a turban and carry a sword in my belt and I will go and marry Tara." What shall we do about that, eh? Only a ten-year difference in age, isn't there – or twelve?' and both women rocked with laughter.

The party had reached its crest, like a festive ship, loud and illuminated for that last party before the journey's end, perched on the dizzy top of the dark wave. It could do nothing now but descend and dissolve. As if by simultaneous and unanimous consent, the guests began to leave (in the wake of the Commissioner and his wife who left first, like royalty), streaming towards the drive where cars stood bumper to bumper – more than had visited the Ramans' house in the previous five years put together. The light in the portico fell on Bina's pride and joy, a Chinese orange tree, lighting its miniature globes of fruit like golden lanterns. There was a babble, an uproar of leavetaking (the smaller children, already in pyjamas, watched open-mouthed from a dark window upstairs). Esso and Caltex left together, arms about each other and smoking cigars, like figures in a comic act. Miss Dutta held firmly to Bose's arm as they dipped, bowed, swayed and tripped on their way out. Bina was clasped, kissed – earrings grazed her cheek, talcum powder tickled her nose. Raman had his back slapped till he thrummed and vibrated like a beaten gong.

It seemed as if Bina and Raman were to be left alone at last, left to pack up and leave – now the goodbyes had been said, there was nothing else they could possibly do – but no, out popped the good doctors from the hospital who had held themselves back in the darkest corners and made themselves inconspicuous throughout the party, and now, in the manner in which they clasped the host by the shoulders and the hostess by her hands, and said, 'Ah *now* we have a chance to be with you at last, now we can begin *our* party,' revealed that although this was the first time they had come to the Ramans' house on any but professional visits, they were not merely friends – they were almost a part of that self-defensive family, the closest to them in sympathy. Raman and Bina both felt a warm, moist expansion of tenderness inside themselves, the tenderness they had till today restricted to the limits of their family, no farther, as though they feared it had not an unlimited capacity. Now its close horizons stepped backwards, with some surprise.

And it was as the doctors said – the party now truly began. Cane chairs were dragged out of the veranda onto the lawn, placed in a ring next to the flowering Queen of the Night which shook out flounces and frills of white scent with every rustle of night breeze. Bina could give in now to her two most urgent needs and dash indoors to smear her mosquito-bitten arms and feet with citronella and fetch Nono to sit on her lap, to let Nono have a share, too, in the party. The good doctors and their wives leant forward and gave Nono the attention that made the parents' throats tighten with gratitude. Raman insisted on their each having a glass of Remy Martin – they must finish it tonight, he said, and would not let the waiters clear away the ice or glasses yet. So they sat on the veranda steps, smoking and yawning.

Now it turned out that Dr Bannerji's wife, the lady in the Dacca sari and the steel-rimmed spectacles, had studied in Shan-tiniketan, and she sang, at her husband's and his colleagues' urging, Tagore's sweetest, saddest songs. When she sang, in heartbroken tones that seemed to come from some distance away, from the damp corners of the darkness where the fireflies flitted,

'Father, the boat is carrying me away,
Father, it is carrying me away from home,'

the eyes of her listeners, sitting tensely in that grassy, inky dark, glazed with tears that were compounded equally of drink, relief and regret.

Pigeons at Daybreak

One of his worst afflictions, Mr Basu thought, was not to be able to read the newspaper himself. To have them read to him by his wife. He watched with fiercely controlled irritation that made the corners of his mouth jerk suddenly upwards and outwards, as she searched for her spectacles through the flat. By the time she found them – on the ledge above the bathing place in the bathroom, of all places: what did she want with her spectacles in *there?* – she had lost the newspaper. When she found it, it was spotted all over with grease for she had left it beside the stove on which the fish was frying. This reminded her to see to the fish before it was over-done. 'You don't want charred fish for your lunch, do you?' she shouted back when he called. He sat back then, in his tall-backed cane chair, folded his hands over his stomach and knew that if he were to open his mouth now, even a slit, it would be to let out a scream of abuse. So he kept it tightly shut.

When she had finally come to the end of that round of bumbling activity, moving from stove to bucket, shelf to table, cupboard to kitchen, she came out on the balcony again, triumphantly carrying with her the newspaper as well as the spectacles. 'So,' she said, 'are you ready to listen to the news now?'

'Now,' he said, parting his lips with the sound of tearing paper, 'I'm ready.'

But Otima Basu never heard such sounds, such ironies or distresses. Quite pleased with all she had accomplished, and at having half an hour in which to sit down comfortably, she settled herself on top of a cane stool like a large soft cushion of white cotton, oiled hair and gold bangles. Humming a little air from the last Hindi film she had seen, she opened out the newspaper on her soft, doughy lap and began to hum out the headlines. In spite of himself, Amul Basu leant forward, strained his eyes to catch an interesting headline for he simply couldn't believe this was all the papers had to offer.

'"Rice smugglers caught",' she read out, but immediately ran along a train of thought of her own. 'What can they expect? Everyone knows there is enough rice in the land, it's the hoarders and black-marketeers who keep it from us, naturally people will break the law and take to smuggling.'

'What else? What else?' Mr Basu snapped at her. 'Nothing else in the papers?'

'Ah – ah – hmm,' she muttered as her eyes roved up and down the columns, looking very round and glassy behind the steel-rimmed spectacles. '"Blue bull menace in Delhi airport can be solved by narcotic drug—"'

'Blue bulls? Blue bulls?' snorted Mr Basu, almost tipping out of his chair. 'How do you mean, "blue bulls"? What's a blue bull? You can't be reading right.'

'I am reading right,' she protested. 'Think I can't read? Did my B.A., helped two children through school and college, and you think I can't read? Blue bulls it says here, blue bulls it is.'

'Can't be,' he grumbled, but retreated into his chair from her unexpectedly spirited defence. 'Must be a printing mistake. There are bulls, buffaloes, bullocks, and bulbuls, but whoever heard of a blue bull? Nilgai, do they mean? But that creature is nearly extinct. How can there be any at the airport? It's all rot, somebody's fantasy—'

'All right, I'll stop reading, if you'd rather. I have enough to do in the kitchen, you know,' she threatened him, but he pressed his lips together and, with a little stab of his hand, beckoned her to pick up the papers and continue.

'Ah – ah – hmm. What pictures are on this week, I wonder?' she continued, partly because that was a subject of consuming interest to her, and partly because she thought it a safe subject to move on to. '*Teri Meri Kismet* – "the heartwarming saga of an unhappy wife". No, no, no. *Do Dost* – winner of three Filmfare awards – ahh . . .'

'Please, please, Otima, the news,' Mr Basu reminded her.

'Nothing to interest you,' she said but tore herself away from the entertainments column for his sake. '"Anti-arthritis drug" – not your problem. "Betel leaves cause cancer." Hmph. I know at least a hundred people who chew betel leaves and are as fit—'

'All right. All right. What else?'

'What news are you interested in then?' she flared up, but immediately subsided and browsed on, comfortably scratching the sole of her foot as she did so. '"Floods in Assam." "Drought in Maharashtra." When is there not? "Two hundred cholera deaths." "A woman and child have a miraculous escape when their house collapses." "Husband held for murder of wife." See?' she cried excitedly. 'Once more. How often does this happen? "Husband and mother-in-law have been arrested on charge of pouring kerosene on Kantibai's clothes and setting her on fire while she slept." Yes, that is how they always do it. Why? Probably the dowry didn't satisfy them, they must have hoped to get one more . . .'

He groaned and sank back in his chair. He knew there was no stopping her now. Except for stories of grotesque births like those of two-headed children or five-legged calves, there was nothing she loved as dearly as tales of murder and atrocity, and short of his having a stroke or the fish-seller arriving at the door, nothing could distract her now. He even heaved himself out of his chair and shuffled off to the other end of the balcony to feed the parrot in its cage a green chilli or two without her so much as noticing his departure. But when she had read to the end of that fascinating item, she ran into another that she read out in a voice like a law-maker's, and he heard it without wishing to: '"Electricity will be switched off as urgent repairs to power lines must be made, in Darya Ganj and Kashmere Gate area, from 8 p.m. to 6 a.m. on the twenty-first of May." My God, that is today.'

'Today? Tonight? No electricity?' he echoed, letting the green chilli fall to the floor of the cage where other offered and refused chillies lay in a rotting heap. 'How will I sleep then?' he gasped fearfully, 'without a fan? In this heat?' and already his diaphragm seemed to cave in, his chest to rise and fall as he panted for breath. Clutching his throat, he groped his way back to the cane chair. 'Otima, Otima, I can't breathe,' he moaned.

She put the papers away and rose with a sigh of irritation and anxiety, the kind a sickly child arouses in its tired mother. She herself, at fifty-six, had not a wrinkle on her oiled face, scarcely a grey hair on her head. As smooth as butter, as round as a cake, life might still have been delectable to her if it had not been for the asthma that afflicted her husband and made him seem, at sixty-one, almost decrepit.

'I'll bring you your inhaler. Don't get worried, just don't get worried,' she told him and bustled off to find his inhaler and cortisone. When she held them out to him, he lowered his head into the inhaler like a dying man at the one straw left. He grasped it with frantic hands, almost clawing her. She shook her head, watching him. 'Why do you let yourself get so upset?' she asked, cursing herself for having read out that particular piece of news to him. 'It won't be so bad. Many people in the city sleep without electric fans – most do. We'll manage—'

'*You'll* manage,' he spat at her, 'but I?'

There was no soothing him now. She knew how rapidly he would advance from imagined breathlessness into the first frightening stage of a full-blown attack of asthma. His chest was already heaving, he imagined there was no oxygen left for him to breathe, that his lungs had collapsed and could not take in any air. He stared up at the strings of washing that hung from end to end of the balcony, the overflow of furniture that cluttered it, the listless parrot in its cage, the view of all the other crowded, washing-hung balconies up and down the length of the road, and felt there was no oxygen left in the air.

'Stay out here on the balcony, it's a little cooler than inside,' his wife said calmly and left him to go about her work. But she did it absently. Normally she would have relished bargaining with the fish-seller who came to the door with a beckti, some whiskered black river fish and a little squirming hill of pale pink prawns in his flat basket. But today she made her purchases and paid him off rather quickly – she was in a hurry to return to the balcony. 'All right?' she asked, looking down at her husband sunk into a heap on his chair, shaking with the effort to suck in air. His lips tightened and whitened in silent reply. She sighed and went away to sort out spices in the kitchen, to pour them out of large containers into small containers, to fill those that were empty and empty those that were full, giving everything that came her way a little loving polish with the end of her sari for it was something she loved to do, but she did not stay very long. She worried about her husband. Foolish and unreasonable as he seemed to her in his sickness, she could not quite leave him to his agony, whether real or imagined. When the postman brought them a letter from their son in Bhilai, she read out to him the boy's report on his work in the steel mills. The father said nothing but seemed calmer and she was able, after that, to make him eat a little rice and fish jhol, very lightly prepared, just as the doctor prescribed. 'Lie down now,' she said, sucking at a fish bone as she removed the dishes from the table. 'It's too hot out on the balcony. Take some rest.'

'Rest?' he snapped at her, but shuffled off into the bedroom and allowed her to make up his bed with all the pillows and bolsters that kept him in an almost sitting position on the flat wooden bed. He shifted and groaned as she heaped up a bolster here, flattened a cushion there, and said he could not possibly sleep, but she thought he did for she kept an eye on him while she leafed through a heap of film and women's magazines on her side of the bed, and thought his eyes were closed genuinely in sleep and that his breathing was almost as regular as the slow circling of the electric fan above them. The fan needed oiling, it made a disturbing clicking sound with every revolution, but who was there to climb up to it and do the oiling and cleaning? Not so easy to get these things done when one's husband is old and ill, she thought. She yawned. She rolled over.

When she brought him his afternoon tea, she asked 'Had a good sleep?' which annoyed him. 'Never slept at all,' he snapped, taking the cup from her hands and spilling some tea. 'How can one sleep if one can't breathe?' he growled, and she turned away with a little smile at his stubbornness. But later that evening he was genuinely ill, choked, in a panic at his inability to breathe as well as at the prospect of a hot night without a fan. 'What will I do?' he kept moaning in between violent struggles for air that shook his body and left it limp. 'What will I do?'

'I'll tell you,' she suddenly answered, and wiped the perspiration from her face in relief. 'I'll have your bed taken up on the terrace. I can call Bulu from next door to do it – you can sleep out in the open air tonight, eh? That'll be nice, won't it? That will do you good.' She brightened both at the thought of a night spent in the open air on the terrace, just as they had done when they were younger and climbing up and down stairs was nothing to them, and at the thought of having an excuse to visit the neighbours and having a little chat while getting them to come and carry up a string-bed for them. Of course old Basu made a protest and a great fuss and coughed and spat and shook and said he could not possibly move in this condition, or be moved by anyone, but she insisted and, ignoring him, went out to make the arrangements.

Basu had not been on the terrace for years. While his wife and Bulu led him up the stairs, hauling him up and propping him upright by their shoulders as though he were some lifeless bag containing something fragile and valuable, he tried to think when he had last attempted or achieved what now seemed a tortuous struggle up the steep concrete steps to the warped green door at the top.

They had given up sleeping there on summer nights long ago, not so much on account of old age or weak knees, really, but because of their perpetual quarrels with the neighbours on the next terrace, separated from theirs by only a broken wooden trellis. Noisy, inconsiderate people, addicted to the radio turned on full blast. At times the man had been drunk and troubled and abused his wife who gave as good as she got. It had been intolerable. Otima had urged her husband, night after night, to protest. When he did, they had almost killed him. At least they would have had they managed to cross over to the Basus' terrace which they were physically prevented from doing by their sons and daughters. The next night they had been even more offensive. Finally the Basus had been forced to give in and retreat down the stairs to sleep in their closed, airless room under the relentlessly ticking ceiling fan. At least it was private there. After the first few restless nights they wondered how they had ever put up with the public sleeping outdoors and its disturbances – its 'nuisance', as Otima called it in English, thinking it an effective word.

That had not – he groaned aloud as they led him up over the last step to the green door – been the last visit he had paid to the rooftop. As Bulu kicked open the door – half-witted he may be, but he was burly too, and good-natured, like so many half-wits – and the city sky revealed itself, in its dirt-swept greys and mauves, on the same level with them, Basu recalled how, not so many years ago, he had taken his daughter Charu's son by the hand to show him the pigeon roosts on so many of the Darya Ganj rooftops, and pointed out to him a flock of collector's pigeons like so many silk and ivory fans flirting in the sky. The boy had watched in silence, holding onto his grandfather's thumb with tense delight. The memory of it silenced his groans as they lowered him onto the bed they had earlier carried up and spread with his many pillows and bolsters. He sat there, getting back his breath, and thinking of Nikhil. When would he see Nikhil again? What would he not give to have that child hold his thumb again and go for a walk with him!

Punctually at eight o'clock the electricity was switched off, immediately sucking up Darya Ganj into a box of shadows, so that the distant glow of Cannaught Place, still lit up, was emphasized. The horizon was illuminated as by a fire, roasted red. The traffic made long stripes of light up and down the streets below them. Lying back, Basu saw the dome of the sky as absolutely impenetrable, shrouded with summer dust, and it seemed to him as airless as the room below. Nikhil, Nikhil, he wept, as though the child might have helped.

Nor could he find any ease, any comfort on that unaccustomed string-bed (the wooden pallet in their room was of course too heavy to carry up, even for Bulu). He complained that his heavy body sank into it as into a hammock, that the strings cut into him, that he could not turn on that wobbling net in which he was caught like some dying fish, gasping for air. It was no cooler than it had been indoors, he complained – there was not the slightest breeze, and the dust was stifling.

Otima soon lost the lightheartedness that had come to her with this unaccustomed change of scene. She tired of dragging around the pillows and piling up the bolsters, helping him into a sitting position and then lowering him into a horizontal one, bringing him his medicines, fanning him with a palm leaf and eventually of his groans and sobs as well. Finally she gave up and collapsed onto her own string-bed, lying there exhausted and sleepless, too distracted by the sound of traffic to sleep. All through the night her husband moaned and gasped for air. Towards dawn it was so bad that she had to get up and massage his chest. When done long and patiently enough, it seemed to relieve him.

'Now lie down for a while. I'll go and get some iced water for your head,' she said, lowering him onto the bed, and went tiredly down the stairs like some bundle of damp washing slowly falling. Her eyes drooped, heavy bags held the tiredness under them.

To her surprise, there was a light on in their flat. Then she heard the ticking of the fan. She had forgotten to turn it off when they went up to the terrace and it seemed the electricity had been switched on again, earlier than they had expected. The relief of it brought her energy back in a bound. She bustled up the stairs. I'll bring him down – he'll get some hours of sleep after all, she told herself.

'It's all right,' she called out as she went up to the terrace again. 'The electricity is on again. Come, I'll help you down – you'll get some sleep in your own bed after all.'

'Leave me alone,' he replied, quite gently.

'Why? Why?' she cried. 'I'll help you. You can get into your own bed, you'll be quite comfortable—'

'Leave me alone,' he said again in that still voice. 'It is cool now.'

It was. Morning had stirred up some breeze off the sluggish river Jumna beneath the city walls, and it was carried over the rooftops of the stifled city, pale and fresh and delicate. It brought with it the morning light, as delicate and sweet as the breeze itself, a pure pallor unlike the livid glow of artificial lights. This lifted higher and higher into the dome of the sky, diluting the darkness there till it, too, grew pale and gradually shades of blue and mauve tinted it lightly.

The old man lay flat and still, gazing up, his mouth hanging open as if to let it pour into him, as cool and fresh as water.

Then, with a swirl and flutter of feathers, a flock of pigeons hurtled upwards and spread out against the dome of the sky – opalescent, sunlit, like small pearls. They caught the light as they rose, turned brighter till they turned at last into crystals, into prisms of light. Then they disappeared into the soft, deep blue of the morning.

Scholar and Gypsy

Her first day in Bombay wilted her. If she stepped out of the air-conditioned hotel room, she drooped, her head hung, her eyes glazed, she felt faint. Once she was back in it, she fell across her bed as though she had been struck by calamity, was extinguished, and could barely bring herself to believe that she had, after all, survived. Sweating, it seemed to her that life, energy, hope were all seeping out of her, flowing down a drain, gurgling ironically.

'But you knew it would be hot,' David said, not being able to help a sense of disappointment in her. He had bought himself crisp bush-shirts of Madras cotton and open Kolhapur sandals. He was drinking more than was his habit, it was true, but it did not seem to redden and coarsen him as it did her. He looked so right, so fitting on the Bombay streets, striding over the coconut shells and betel-stained papers and the fish scales and lepers' stumps. 'You could hardly come to India and expect it to be cool, Pat.'

'Hot, yes,' she moaned, 'but not – not *killing*. Not so like death. I feel half dead, David, sometimes *quite* dead.'

'Shall we go and have a gin-and-lime in the bar?'

She tried that since it seemed to do him so much good. But the bar in the hotel was so crowded, the people there were so large and vital and forceful in their brilliant clothes and with their metallic voices and their eyes that flashed over her like barbers' shears, cutting and exposing, that she felt crushed rather than revived.

David attracted people like a magnet – with his charm, his nonchalance, his grace, he did it so well, so smoothly, his qualities

98

worked more efficiently than any visiting card system – and they started going to parties. It began to seem to her that this was the chief occupation of people in Bombay – going to parties. She was always on the point of collapse when she arrived at one: the taxi invariably stank, the driver's hair dripped oil, and then the sights and scenes they passed on the streets, the congestion and racket of the varied traffic, the virulent cinema posters, the blazing colours of women's clothing, the profusion of toys and decorations of coloured paper and tinsel, the radios and loudspeakers never tuned to less than top volume, and amongst them flower sellers, pilgrims, dancing monkeys and performing bears . . . that there should be such poverty, such disease, such filth, and that out of it boiled so much vitality, such irrepressible life, seemed to her unnatural and sinister – it was as if chaos and evil triumphed over reason and order. Then the parties they went to were all very large ones. The guests all wore brilliant clothes and jewellery, and their eyes and teeth flashed with such primitive lust as they eyed her slim, white-sheathed blonde self, that the sensation of being caught up and crushed, crowded in and choked sent her into corners where their knees pushed into her, their hands slid over her back, their voices bored into her, so that when she got back to the hotel, on David's arm, she was more like a corpse than an American globetrotter.

Folding her arms about her, she muttered at the window, 'I never expected them to be so primitive. I thought it would all be modern, up-to-date. Not this – this wild jungle stuff.'

He was pouring himself a night-cap and splashed it in genuine surprise. 'What do you mean? We've only been seeing the modern and up-to-date. These people would be at home at any New York cocktail party—'

'No,' she burst out, hugging herself tightly. 'No, they would *not*. They haven't the polish, the smoothness, the softness. David, they're *not* civilized. They're still a primitive people. When I see their eyes I see how primitive they are. When they touch me, I feel frightened – I feel I'm in danger.'

He looked at her with apprehension. They had drunk till it was too late to eat and now he was hungry, tired. He found her exhausting. He would have liked to sit back comfortably in that air-conditioned cool, to go over the party, to discuss the people they had met, to share his views with her. But she seemed launched in some other direction, she was going alone and he did not want to be drawn into her deep wake. 'You're very imaginative tonight,' he said lightly, playing with the bottle-opener and not looking at her. 'Here was I, disappointed at finding them so westernized. I would have liked them a bit more primitive – at least for the sake of my thesis. Now look at the Gidwanis. Did you ever think an Indian wife would be anything like Gidwani's wife – what was her name?'

'Oh, she was terrible, terrible,' Pat whispered, shuddering, as she thought of the vermilion sari tied below the navel, of the uneven chocolate-smooth expanse of belly and the belt of little silver bells around it. She didn't care to remember the dance she had danced with David on the floor of the nightclub. She had never even looked at the woman's face, she had kept her eyes lowered and not been able to go any further than that black navel. If that was not primitive, what could David, a sociology student, mean by the word?

It was at the Gidwanis' dinner later that week that she collapsed. She had begun to feel threatened, menaced, the moment they entered that flat. Leaving behind them the betel-stained walls of the elevator shaft, the servant boys asleep on mats in the passage, the cluster of watchmen and chauffeurs playing cards under the unshaded bulb in the lobby, they had stepped onto a black marble floor that glittered like a mirror and reflected the priceless statuary that sailed on its surface like ships of stone. Scarlet and vermilion ixora in pots. Menservants in stiffly starched uniform. Jewels, enamel, brocade and gold. Gidwani with a face like an amiable baboon's, immediately sliding a soft hand across her back. His wife's chocolate pudding belly with the sari slipping suggestively about her hips. Pat shrank and shrank. Her lips felt very dry and she licked and licked them, nervously. She lost David's arm. Her feet in their sandals seemed to swell grotesquely. She sat at the table, her head slanting. She saw David looking at her concernedly. The manservant's stomach pushed against her shoulder as he lowered the dishes for her. The dishes smelt, she wondered of what – oil, was it, or goat's meat? It was not conducive to appetite. Her fork slipped. The table slipped. She had fainted. They were all crying, shoving, crowding. She pushed at them with her hands in panic.

'David, get me out, get me out,' she blubbered, trying to free herself of them.

Later, sitting at the foot of her bed, 'We'd better leave,' he said sadly. Was it Gidwani's wife's belly that saddened him, she wondered. It was not a sight that one could forget, or discard, or deny. 'Delhi's said to be dryer,' he said, 'not so humid. It'll be better for you.'

'But your thesis, David?' she wept, repentantly. 'Will you be able to work on it there?'

'I suppose so,' he said gloomily, looking down at her, shrunk into something small on the bed, paler and fainter each day that she spent in the wild jungles of the city of Bombay.

Delhi was dryer. It was dry as a skeleton. Yellow sand seethed and stormed, then settled on wood, stone, flesh and skin, brittle and gritty as powdered bone. Trees stood leafless. Red flowers blazed on their black branches, golden and purple ones burgeoned. Beggars drowsed in their shade, stretched unrecognizable limbs at her. I will pull myself together, Pat said, walking determinedly through the piled yellow dust, I must pull myself together. Her body no longer melted, it did not ooze and seep out of her grasp any more. It was dry, she would hold herself upright, she would look into people's eyes when they spoke to her and smile pleasantly – like David, she thought. But the dust inside her sandals made her feet drag. If she no longer melted, she burnt. She felt the heat strike through to her bones. Even her eyes, protected by giant glare glasses, seemed on fire. She thought she would shrivel up like a piece of paper under a magnifying glass held to reflect the sun. Rubbing her fingers together, she made a scraping, papery sound. Her hair was full of sand.

'But you can't let climate get you down, dear,' David said softly, in order to express tenderness that he hardly felt any longer, seeing her suffer so unbeautifully, her feet dusty, her hair stringy, her face thin and appalled. 'Climate isn't *important*, Pat – rise above it, there's so much else. Try to concentrate on *that*.' He wanted to help her. It made things so difficult for him if she wouldn't come along but kept drifting off loosely in some other direction, obliging him to drop things and go after her since she seemed so uncontrolled, dangerously so. He couldn't meet people, work on his thesis, do anything. He had never imagined she could be a burden – not the companion and fellow gypsy she had so fairly promised to be. She came of plain, strong farmer stock – she ought to have some of that blood in her, strong, simple and capable. Why wasn't she capable? He held his hand to her temple – it throbbed hard. They sat sipping iced coffee in a very small, very dark restaurant that smelt, somehow, of railway soot.

'I must try,' she said, flatly and without conviction.

That afternoon she went round the antique shops of New Delhi, determined to take an interest in Indian art and culture. She left the shopping arcade after an hour, horror rising in her throat like vomit. She felt pursued by the primitive, the elemental and barbaric, and kept rubbing her fingers together nervously, recalling those great heavy bosoms of bronze and stone, the hips rounded and full as water pots, the flirtatious little bells on ankles and bellies, the long, sly eyes that curved out of the voluptuous stone faces, not unlike those of the shopkeepers themselves with their sibilant, inviting voices. Then the gods they showed her, named for her, with their flurry of arms, their stamping feet, their blazing, angered eyes and flying locks, all thunder and lightning, revenge and menace. Scraping the papery tips of her fingers together, she hurried through the dust back to the hotel.

Back on her bed, she wept into her pillow for the lost home, for apple trees and cows, for red barns and swallows, for ice-cream sodas and drive-in movies, all that was innocent and sweet and lost, lost, lost.

'I'm just not sophisticated enough for you,' she gulped over the iced lemon tea David brought her. It was the first time she mentioned the disparity in their backgrounds – it had never seemed to matter before. Laying it bare now was like digging the first rift between them, the first division of raw, red clay. It frightened them both. 'I expect you knew about such things – you must have learnt them in college. You know I only went to high school and stayed home after that—'

'Darling,' he said, with genuine pain and tenderness, and could not go on. His tastes would not allow him to, or his scruples: the vulgarity appalled him as much as the pain. 'Do take a shower and have a shampoo, Pat. We're going out—'

'No, no, no,' she moaned in anguish, putting away the iced tea and falling onto her pillow.

'But to quite different people this time, Pat. To see a social worker – I mean, Sharma's wife is a social worker. She'll show you something quite different. I know it'll interest you.'

'I couldn't bear it,' she wept, playing with the buttons of her dress like a child.

But they did prove different. The Delhi intellectual was poorer than the Bombay intellectual, for one thing. He lived in a small, airless flat with whitewashed walls and a divan and bits of folk art. He served dinner in cheap, bright ceramic ware. Of course there was the inevitable long-haired intellectual – either journalist or professor – who sat crosslegged on the floor and held forth, abusively, on the crassness of the Americans, to David's delight and Pat's embarrassment. But Sharma's wife was actually a new type, to Pat. She was a genuine social worker, trained, and next morning, having neatly tucked the night before under the divan, she took Pat out to see a milk centre, a creche, a nursery school, clinics and dispensaries, some housed in cow sheds, others in ruined tombs. Pat saw workers' babies asleep like cocoons in hammocks slung from tin sheds on building sites; she saw children with kohl-rimmed eyes solemnly eating their free lunches out of brass containers, and schools where children wrote painstakingly on wooden boards with reed pens and the teacher sneezed brown snuff sneezes at her. It was different in content. It was the same in effect. Her feet dragged, dustier by the hour. Her hair was like string on her shoulders. When she met David in the evening, at the hotel, he was red from the sun, like a well-ripened tomato, longing to talk, to tell, to ask and question, while she drooped tired, dusty, stringy, dry, trying to revive herself, for his sake, with little sips of some iced drink but feeling quite surely that life was shrivelling up inside her. She never spoke of apple trees or barns, of popcorn or drug stores, but he saw them in her eyes, more remote and faint every day. Her eyes had been so blue, now they were fading, as if the memory, the feel of apple trees and apples were fading from her. He panicked.

'We'd better go to the hills for a while,' he said: he did not want murder on his hands. 'Sharma said June is bad, very bad, in Delhi. He says everyone who can goes to the hills. Well, we can. Let's go, Pat.'

She looked at him dumbly with her fading eyes, and tried to smile. She thought of the way the child at the hospital had smiled after the doctor had finished painting her burns with gentian violet and given her a plastic doll. It had been a cheap, cracked pink plastic doll and the child had smiled at it through the gentian violet, its smile stamped in, or cut out, in that face still taut with pain, as by a machine. Pat had known that face would always be in pain, and the smile would always be cut out as by the machine of charity, mechanically. The plastic doll and the gentian violet had been incidental.

At the airlines office, the man could only find them seats on the plane to Manali, in the Kulu Valley. To Manali they went.

*

Not, however, by plane, for there were such fierce sandstorms sweeping through Delhi that day that no planes took off, and they went the three hundred miles by bus instead. The sandstorm did not spare the highway or the bus – it tore through the cracked windows and buried passengers and seats under the yellow sand of the Rajasthan desert. The sun burnt up the tin body of the bus till it was a great deal hotter inside than out in the sun. Pat sat stone-still, as though she had been beaten unconscious, groping with her eyes only for a glimpse of a mango grove or an avenue of banyans, instinctively believing she would survive only if she could find and drink in their dark, damp shade. David kept his eyes tightly shut behind his glare glasses. Perspiration poured from under his hair down his face, cutting rivers through the map of dust. The woman in the seat behind his was sick all the way up the low hills to Bilaspur. In front of him a small child wailed without stop while its mother ate peanuts and jovially threw the shells over her shoulder into his lap. The bus crackled with sand, peanut shells and explosive sounds from the protesting engine. There was a stench of diesel oil, of vomit, of perspiration and stale food such as he had never believed could exist – it was so thick. The bus was long past its prime but rattled, roared, shook and vibrated all the way through the desert, the plains, the hills, to Mandi where it stopped for a tea break in a rest house under some eucalyptus trees in which cicadas trilled hoarsely. Then it plunged, bent on suicide, into the Beas river gorge.

After one look down the vertical cliff-side of slipping, crumbling slate ending in the wild river tearing through the narrow gorge in a torrent of ice-green and white spray, David's head fell back against the seat, lolled there loosely, and he muttered, 'This is the end, Pat, my girl, I'm afraid it's the end.'

'But it's cooler,' fluted a youthful voice in a rising inflection, and David's head jerked with foolish surprise. Who had spoken? He turned to his wife and found her leaning out of the window, her strings of hair flying back at him in the breeze. She turned to him her excited face – dust-grimed and wan but with its eyes alive and observant. 'I can feel the spray – cold spray, David. It's better than a shower or air-conditioning or even a drink. Do just feel it.'

But he was too baffled and stunned and slain to feel anything at all. He sat slumped, not daring to watch the bus take the curves of that precarious path hewn through cliffs of slate, poised above the river that hurtled and roared over the black rocks and dashed itself against the mountainside. He was not certain what exactly would happen – whether the overhanging slate would come crashing down upon them, burying them alive, or if they would lurch headlong into the Beas and be dashed to bits on the rocks – but he had no doubt that it would be one or the other. In the face of this certainty, Pat's untimely revival seemed no more than a pathetic footnote.

To Pat, being fanned to life by that spray-spotted breeze, no such possibility occurred. She was watching the white spray rise and spin over the ice-green river and break upon the gleaming rocks, looking out for small sandy coves where pink oleanders bloomed and banana trees hung their limp green flags, exclaiming with delight at the small birds that skimmed the river like foam – feeling curiosity, pleasure and amusement stir in her for the first time since she had landed in India. She no longer heard the retching of the woman behind them or the faint mewing of the exhausted child in front. Peanut shells slipped into her shoes and out of them. The stench of fifty perspiring passengers was lost in the freshness of the mountains. Up on the ridge, if she craned her neck, she could see the bunched needles of pine trees flashing.

When they emerged from the gorge into the sunlight, apricot-warm and mild, of the Kulu Valley, she sat back with a contented sigh and let the bus carry them alongside the now calm and wide river Beas, through orchards in which little apples knobbled the trees, past flocks of royal mountain goats and their blanketed shepherds striding ahead with the mountaineer's swing, up into the hills of Manali, its deodar forests indigo in the evening air and the snow-streaked rocks of the Rohtang Pass hovering above them, an incredible distance away.

Then they were disgorged, broken sandals, shells, hair, rags, children and food containers, into the Manali bazaar, and the bus conductor swung himself onto the roof of the bus and hurled down their bags and boxes. David was on his knees, picking up the pieces of his broken suitcase and holding them together. The crying child was fed hot fritters his father had fetched from a wayside food stall. The vomiting woman squatted, holding her head in her hands, and a pai dog sniffed at her in curiosity and consolation. A big handsome man with a pigtail and a long turquoise earring came up to Pat with an armful of red puppies, his teeth flashing in a cajoling smile. 'Fifty rupees,' he murmured, and raised it to 'Eighty' as soon as Pat reached out to fondle the smallest of them. Touts and pimps, ubiquitously small and greasy, piped around David 'Moonlight Hotel, plumbing and flush toilet,' and 'Hotel Paradise, non-vegetarian and best view, sir.'

David, holding his suitcase in his arms, looked over the top of their heads and at the mountain peaks, as if for succour. Then his face tilted down at them palely and he shook his head, his eyes quite empty. 'Let's go, Pat,' he sighed, and she followed him up through the bazaar for he had, of course, made bookings and they had rooms at what had been described to them as an 'English boarding house'.

It was on the hillside, set in a sea of apple trees, and they had to walk through the bazaar to it, nudging past puppy-sellers, women who had spread amber and coral and bronze prayer bells on the pavement, stalls in which huge pans of milk boiled and steamed and fritters jumped up and hissed, and holiday crowds that stood about eating, talking and eyeing the newcomers.

'Jesus,' David said in alarm, 'the place is full of hippies.' Pat looked at the faces they passed then and saw that the crowd outside the baker's was indeed one of fair men and women, even if they seemed to be beggars. Some were dressed like Indian gurus, in loincloths or saffron robes, with beads around their necks, others as gypsies in pantaloons or spangled skirts, some in plain rags and tatters. All were barefoot and had packs on their backs, and one or two had silent, stupefied babies astride their hips. 'Why,' she said, watching one woman with a child approach an Indian couple with her empty hand outstretched, 'they might be Americans!' David shuddered and turned up a dusty path that went between the deodar trees to the red-roofed building of the boarding house. But several hippies were climbing the same path, not to the boarding house but vanishing into the forest, or crossing the wooden bridge over the river into the meadows beyond. Americans, Europeans, here in Manali, at the end of the world – what were they doing? she wondered. Well, what was she doing? Ah, she'd come to try and live again. She threw back her shoulders and took in lungfuls of the clear, cold air and it washed through her like water, cleansing and pure. Someone in a red cap was sawing wood outside the boarding house, she saw, and blue smoke curled out of its chimney as in a Grandma Moses painting. There was a sound of a rushing stream below. A cuckoo called. Above the tips of the immense deodars the sky was a clear turquoise, an evening colour, without heat although still distilled with sunlight. Dog roses bloomed open and white on the hillside. She tried to clasp David's arm with joy but he was holding onto the suitcase which had broken its locks and burst open and he could not spare her a finger.

'But David,' she coaxed, 'it's going to be lovely.'

'I'm glad,' he said, white-lipped, and pitched the suitcase onto the wooden veranda at the feet of the proprietor who sat benignly as a Buddha on a wooden upright chair, in a white pullover and string cap, gazing down at them with an expression of pity under his bland welcome.

The room was clean, although bare but for two white iron bedsteads and a dressing table with a small yellow mirror. Its window overlooked a yard in which brown hens pecked and climbed onto overturned buckets and wood piles, and wild daisies bloomed, as white and yellow as fresh bread and butter, around a water pump. The bathroom had no tub but a very well-polished brass bucket, a green plastic mug and, holy of holies, a flush toilet that worked, however reluctantly and complainingly. The proprietor, apple-cheeked and woolly – was he an Anglo-Indian, European or Indian? Pat could not tell – sent them tea and Glaxo biscuits on a tin tray. They sat on the bed and drank the black, bitter tea, sighing 'Well, it's *hot*.'

But Pat could not stay still. Once she had examined the drawers of the dressing table and read scraps from the old newspaper with which they were lined, turned on the taps in the bathroom and washed, changed into her Delhi slippers and drunk her tea, she wanted to go out and 'Explore!' David looked longingly at the clean white, although thin and darned, sheets stretched on the beds and the hairy brown blanket so competently tucked in, but she was adamant.

'We can't waste a minute,' she said urgently, for some unknown reason. 'We mustn't waste this lovely evening.'

He did not see how it would be wasted if they were to lie down on their clean beds, wait for hot water to be brought for their baths and then sleep, but realized it would be somehow craven and feeble for him to say so when she stood at the window with something strong and active in the swing of her hips and a fervour in her newly pink and washed face that he had almost forgotten was once her natural expression – in a different era, a different land.

'We're surrounded by apple trees,' she enticed him, 'and I think, I think I heard a cuckoo.'

'Why not?' he grumbled, and followed her out onto the wooden veranda where the proprietor continued to look comfortable on that upright chair, and down the garden path to the road that took them into the forest.

It was a deodar forest. The trees were so immensely old and

tall that while the lower boughs already dipped their feet into the evening, the tops still brushed the late sunlight, and woolly yellow beams slanted through the black trunks as through the pillars of a shadowy cathedral. The turf was soft and uneven under their feet, wild iris bloomed in clumps and ferns surrounded rocks that were conspicuously stranded here and there. Pat fell upon the wild strawberries that grew with a careless luxuriance – small, seed-ridden ones she found sweet. The few people they passed, village men and women wrapped in white Kulu blankets with handsome stripes, had faces that were brown and russet, calm and pleasant, although they neither smiled nor greeted Pat and David, merely observed them in passing. Pat liked them for that – for not whining or wheedling or begging or sneering as the crowds in Bombay and Delhi had done – but simply conferring on them a status not unlike their own. 'Such independence,' she glowed, 'so self-contained. True mountain people, you know.'

David looked at her a little fearfully, not having noted such a surge of Vermont pride in his country wife before. 'Do you feel one of them yourself?' he asked, a little tentatively.

He was startled by the positive quality of the laugh that rang out of her, by the way she threw out her arms in an open embrace. 'Why, *sure*,' she cried, explosively, and sprang over a small stream that ran over the moss like a trickle of mercury. 'Look, here's dear old Jack in the pulpit,' she cried, darting at some ferns from which protruded that rather sinister gentleman, striped and hooded, David thought, like a silent cobra. She plucked it and strode on, her hair no longer like string but like drawn toffee, now catching fire in the sunbeams, now darkening in the shade. After a while, she remarked, 'It isn't much like the friendly Vermont woods, really. It's more like a grand medieval cathedral, isn't it?'

'An observation several before you have made on forests,' he remarked, a trifle drily. 'Is one permitted to sit in your cathedral or can one only kneel?' he asked, lowering himself onto a rock. 'Jesus, is my bottom sore from that bus ride.'

She laughed, threw the Jack in the pulpit into his lap and flung herself on the grass at his feet. And so they might have stopped and talked and laughed a bit before going back to an English supper and their fresh, clean beds but, swinging homewards hand-in-hand, they came suddenly upon a strange edifice on a slope in the forest, like a great pagoda built of wood, heavy and dark timber, rough-hewn and sculpted as a stone temple might be, with trees rearing about it in the twilight, shaggy and dark, like Himalayan bears.

'Could it be a temple?' Pat wondered, for the temples she had so far seen had been bursting at the seams with loud pilgrims and busy beggars and priests, affairs of garish paint and plaster, clatter of bells and malodorous marigolds. A still temple in a silent forest – she had quite lost hope of finding such a thing in this overpopulated land.

'We might go in,' David said since she was straining at his hand and, after hovering at the threshold for a bit, they slipped off their sandals and crossed its high wooden plinth.

It was very much darker inside, like a cave scooped out of a tree trunk. The floor, however, was of clay, hard-packed and silky. A shelf of rock projected from the dark wall and a lamp hung from it with a few flowers bright around its wick. It had that minute been blown out by a tall woman with an appropriately wooden face who wore her hair in a tight plait around her head. She lifted her hand, swung only once but vigorously a large bell, and left with a quick stride, barely glancing at them as she went. They bent to study the stone slab beneath the gently smoking lamp and could only just make out the outline of a giant footprint on it. That was all by way of an image and there were neither offerings nor money-box, neither priest nor pilgrim around.

They came out in silence and walked away slowly, as though afraid something would jump out at them from it, or from the forest – they were so much a part of each other, that forest and its temple.

Finally they emerged from the trees and were within sight of the red roof and chimney pot of the English boarding house amongst its apple trees, far below the snow-streaked black ridges of the mountain pass, still pale and luminous against the darkening sky, at once threatening and protective in its attitude, like an Indian god.

'I'm sure I've never seen anything like that before,' Pat murmured then.

'What, not even in Vermont?' he teased, but received no answer.

They ate their dinner in silence, Pat hugely although reflectively, while David sipped a cup of soup and felt as peevish as a neglected invalid.

Perhaps it was only the smallness of Manali – barely a town, merely an overgrown village, a place for shepherds to halt on their way up to the Pass and over it to Lahaul, and apple growers to load their fruit onto lorries bound for the plains, suddenly struck and swollen by a seasonal avalanche of tourists and their vehicles – that led Pat so quickly to know it and feel it as home. It presented no difficulty, as other Indian towns of her acquaintance had, it was innocent and open and if it did not clamorously and cravenly invite, it did not shut its doors either – it had none to shut. It lay in the cup of the valley, the river and forest to one side, bright paddy fields and apple orchards to the other, open and sunlit, small and easy.

She bought herself a cloth bag to sling over her shoulder and with it strode down the single street of Manali in her friendlily squeaking sandals. She stopped at the baker's for ginger biscuits and to smile, somewhat tentatively, at the hippies who stood barefoot at the door, begging for loaves of bread from Indian tourists who seemed as embarrassed as stupefied to discover that it was not only Indians who could beg, and always gave them far more than they did to poorer Indian beggars. She eyed the vegetable stalls and the baskets of ripe fruit on the pavements with envy, wishing she could set up house and do her own marketing. This walk through the bazaar invariably took her to the Tibetan quarter, a smelly lane that took off to one side. Pat could not explain why she had to visit it daily. David refused to accompany her after one visit. He could not face the open drain that one had to jump over in order to enter one of its shops. He could not face the yellow pai dogs and the abjectly filthy children one had to pass, nor the extraordinary odour of the shops in which sweaty castaway woollens discarded by returning mountaineers and impecunious hippies made soft furry mountains along with Tibetan rugs, exquisitely chased silver candlesticks and bronze icons that democratically lived together with tawdry plastic and glass jewellery, all presided over by stolid women with faces carved intricately out of hard wood. So David thought them. To Pat they were wise and inscrutable old ladies who parted with objects of great value at pathetically low prices. Pushing through old dresses and woollen pullovers that hung from the rafters, she knelt on worn rugs and shuffled through the baubles and beads in order to pick out a lama carved in wood with the elegance of extreme simplicity, bits of turquoise, a ball of amber like solidified honey, a string of prayer beads as cool as river pebbles between her fingers . . .

'Junk, junk, junk,' David groaned as she spread them out on the bed for him to see. 'Couldn't you walk in some other direction? Must it be that bloody bazaar every day?'

'It isn't,' she protested. 'I walk all over. Just come with me and I'll show you,' she offered, but rather indifferently, and he saw that she did not care at all if he came with her or not, while in Bombay or Delhi she would have cared passionately. This needled him into closing his typewriter, laying his papers in the dressing-table drawer and coming with her for once, stepping gingerly over the goat droppings and puddles in the yard, out onto the dusty road.

He found she did know, as she had claimed to, every path and stream and orchard in the place for miles, and was determined to prove it to him. To his horror, she even waved and beamed at the drug-struck, meditative hippies as they swung past the Happy Café where they invariably gathered to eat, talk, play on flutes and gaze into space in that dim, dusty interior where a chart hung on the wall offering the table d'hôte: daily it was Brown Rice, Beans and Custard. What hippy had carried his macroculture to Manali, David wondered, pinning it to the wall above the counter where flies circled plates of yellow sweetmeats and Britannia Biscuit packets? The faces of the pale Europeans who gathered there seemed to him distressingly vacant, their postures defeated and vague, but when he mentioned this to Pat, she was scornful.

'You're just making up your mind about them without really looking,' she claimed. 'Now look at that man in white robes – doesn't he look like Christ? And it isn't just the bone structure. And see that young man who's always laughing? That's his pet loris on his shoulder. There's another I see in that bazaar sometimes, who has a pet eagle, but he lives way off in the mountains. It's true they don't talk much – but you often see them laugh. Or else they just sit and think. Isn't that beautiful, to be able to do that? I think it's beautiful.'

'I think they're stoned,' he said, happy to leave the Happy Café to its shadowy, macrocultural bliss and climb the steep hill into the deodar forest. 'Lord, must we go to the temple *again?*' he moaned, as she led him forward, having already seen it till he could no longer keep his yawns from cracking his jaws apart while he had again to sit outside, on some excruciating roots, and wait for his wife to pay it a ritual visit. He was not really sure what she did in there, nor did he wish to know. Surely she didn't pray? No, she came out looking much too jolly for that.

But no, today she was taking him for a walk and for a walk she would take him, she said, with that new positivism in her jaw-line and swing of her arms that he rather feared. She led him along a stream in which a man and a woman in gypsy dress – and bald patch, and red curls, respectively – were scrubbing some incredibly blackened pots and pans, like children at play – 'Aren't they charming?' Pat enquired, as if of a painted landscape tastefully peopled with just a few rural figures, and David retorted 'Damn vagabonds' – and down lanes that wound through orchards overhung with apricot trees from which fruit dropped ripe and soft onto the stones under their feet, past farm houses screened by daisies and day lilies from which issued bursts, sometimes of tubercular coughing and sometimes of abstract, atonal music, both curiously foreign, and then uphill, beside a stream that leapt over the rocks like a startled hare, white and flashing between ferns and boulders, to a village of large, square stone and wood houses – the ground floors smaller, built solidly of square blocks of stone, the upper floors larger, their elaborately carved wooden balconies overhanging the courtyards in which cows ate the apricots swept up in hills for them, and children climbed crackling haystacks. Apricot trees festooned with unhealthy-looking mistletoe shaded that village and Pat stopped to ask an old man in a blue cap if he had some to sell. They waited in his courtyard, amongst dung pats and milk pails, standing close to the stone wall to let a herd of mountain goats go by, silk-shawled, tip-tapping and bleat-voiced as a party of tipsy ladies, while the man climbed his tree and plucked them a capful. Eating them out of their pockets – they proved not quite ripe and not as sweet as those sold in the bazaar, but Pat wouldn't say so and David did – they continued uphill, out of the village (David glimpsed a lissome brunette in purple robes and biblical sandals climbing down to the stream but averted his eyes) into the deodar forest again. David was so grateful for its blue shade, and so overfull with bucolic scenes and apricots, that he was ready to sprawl. His wife sprang on ahead, calling, and then he saw her destination. Another temple. He might have known.

Catching up with her, he found Pat fondling the ears of a big tawny dog that had come barking out of the temple courtyard, with familiarity and a wag of its royal tail. 'We can't go in, it's shut,' she reassured him, 'but do see,' she coaxed, and led him through the courtyard and eventually he had to admit that even as Kulu temples went, this one in Nasogi was a pearl. It was no larger than Hansel and Gretel's hut, its roof sloping steeply to the ground, edged with carved icicles of wood. Its doors and beams were massive, but every bit was elegantly carved and fitted. There was a paved courtyard opening into others, all open and inviting, possibly for pilgrims, and around it a grandeur of trees. David lowered himself onto a root, put his arms around his knees, tilted his head to one side and said, 'Well yes, you have something here, Pat, I'll give that to you.'

She glowed. 'I think it's the most magical spot on earth, if you'd like to know.'

'Aren't you funny?' he commented. 'I take you the length and breadth of India, I show you palaces and museums, jewels and tiger skins – and all the time you were hankering after a forest and an orchard and a village. Little Gretchen you, little Martha, hmm?'

'Do you think that's all I see in it?' she enquired, and he did not quite like, quite trust her sudden gravity that had something too set about it, too extreme, like that of a fanatic. But what was she being so fanatical about – the country life? A mountain idyll? Surely that was obtainable and possible without fanaticism.

She gave only a hint – it was obvious she had thought nothing out yet, however much she had felt. 'This isn't like the rest of India, Dave. It's come to me as a relief, as an escape from India. You know, down in those horrible cities, I'd gotten to think of India as one horrible temple, bursting, *crawling* with people – people on their knees, *hopeless* people – and those horrible idols towering over them with their hundred legs and hundred heads – all *horrible* . . .' (David, tiring of that one adjective, clicked his tongue like an impatient pedagogue, making her veer, only slightly, then return to her track, sifting dry deodar needles

through nervous brown fingers) . . . 'and then, to walk through
the forest and come upon this – this little shrine – it's like escaping from all those Hindu horrors – it's like coming out into the
open and breathing naturally again, without fear. That's what I
feel here, you know,' she said with a renewed burst of confidence,
'– without *fear*. And you can see that's something I share with, or
perhaps have just learnt from, the mountain people here. That's
what I admire so in them, in the Tibetans. I don't mean the
ones down in the bazaar – those are just like the greasy Indian
masses, whining and cajoling and sneering – oh, *horrible* – but
the ones one sees on the mountain roads. They're upright, they're
honest, independent. They have such a strong swing and a stride
to their walk – they walk like gods amongst those crawling,
cringing masses. And they haven't those furtive Indian faces
either – eyes sliding this way and that, expressions showing and
then closing up – *their* faces are all open, and they laugh and sing.
All they have is a black old kettle and a pack of wood on their
backs, rope sandals and a few sheep, but they laugh and sing and
go striding up the mountains like – like lords. I watch them all
the time, I admire them, you know, and I got to thinking what
makes them so different? I wondered if it was their religion. I
feel, being Buddhists, they're different from the Hindus, and it
must be something in their belief that gives them this – this fear-
lessness. When I come to this shrine and sit and think things
out quietly, I can see where they get their strength from, and
their joy . . .'

But here he could stand it no longer. 'Pat, Pat,' he cried, jump-
ing up and striking his sides. 'You're all confused, Pat, you're so
muddled, so hopelessly muddled! My dear, addled wife, Pat!'

She frowned and squinted, her fist closed on a handful of needles, ceased to sift them. 'What do you mean?' she asked, in a
tight, closed voice.

'What do I mean? Don't you know? You're sitting outside a
Hindu shrine, this is a Hindu temple, and you're making it out to
be a source of Buddhist strength and serenity! Don't you even

know that the Kulu Valley has a Hindu population, and the shrines you see here are Hindu shrines?' He whooped with laughter, he pulled her to her feet and dragged her homeward, laughing so much that every time she opened her mouth to protest, he drowned her out with his roars of derision. In the end, that laughter gave him a headache.

He tired of his thesis – the notes he had collected while in Bombay and Delhi and the typescript he was now preparing – long before it was done. The whole job had begun to seem totally irrelevant. Ramming the cover onto the little flat Olivetti, he pushed his legs out so that the waste-paper basket went sprawling, and yawned angrily. The cock on the woodpile at the window caught his eye and gave a wicked wink, but David looked away almost without registering it. Where was Pat?

That was the perennial question these days. Pat was never there. What was more, he no longer asked her where she had been when she appeared for meals or to throw herself down on the bed for the night, her feet raw and dirty from walking in sandals, her cloth bag flung onto the floor. (Once he saw a ragged copy of the Dhammapada slip out of it and hastily looked away: the idea of his poor, addled wife poring over ancient Buddhist texts embarrassed him acutely.) He merely eyed her with accusation and with distaste: she was playing a role he had not engaged her to play, she was making a fool of herself, she was embarrassing him, she was absolutely outrageous. As she grew browner from the outdoor life and her limbs sturdier from the exercise, it seemed to him she was losing the fragility, the gentleness that he had loved in her, that she was growing into some tough, sharp countrywoman who might very well carry loads, chop wood, haul water and harvest, but was scarcely fit to be his wife – his, David's, the charming and socially graceful young David of Long Island upbringing – and her movements were marked by rough angles that jarred on him, her voice, when she bothered at all to reply to his vague questions, was brusque and abrupt. It was clear there was no meeting point between them any more – he would have considered it lowering in status to make a move towards her and she clearly had no interest in meeting him halfway, or anywhere.

He had not cared for the answers she had given him when he had first, mistakenly, asked. On coming upon her one morning, while slouching through the bazaar to post a packet of letters, in, of all places, the Happy Café, round-shouldered on a bench, drinking something cloudy out of a thick glass, in the company of those ragged pilgrims with the incongruously fair heads, he had questioned her with some heat.

'Yes, they're friends of mine,' she shrugged, standing with her new stolidity in the centre of the room to which he had insisted on taking her back. 'I could have told you about them earlier if you'd asked. There's no need for you to spy.'

'Don't be ridiculous,' he snapped. 'Spy on *you*? What for? Why should it interest me what you do with yourself while I'm slogging away in here—'

'Then why ask?' she snapped back.

His curiosity was larger than his distaste in the beginning. Over dinner he asked her the questions he had earlier resolved not to ask and, pleased with the big plateful of food before her, she had talked pleasantly about the Californian couple she had taken up with, and told him the story of their erratic and precipitous voyage from the forests of Big Sur to those of the Kulu Valley, via Afghanistan and Nepal, in search of a guru they had indeed found but now discarded in favour of communal life, vegetarianism and bhang which seemed to them a smooth and gentle path to earthly nirvana.

'Nirvana on earth!' he snorted. 'That's a contradiction in terms, don't you know?' Then, seeing her nostrils flare dangerously, went on hastily, but no more wisely, 'Is that what you were drinking down there in that joint, Pat?'

She gave a whoop of delight on seeing the pudding – caramel custard – and buried her nose in a plateful with greed. 'Gee, all this walking makes me hungry,' she apologized, 'and sleepy. Jesus, *how* sleepy.' She went straight to bed.

On another and even more uncomfortable occasion, he had found her while out taking the air after a particularly dull and boring day at the typewriter, in the park in front of the Moonlight Hotel and Rama's Bakery where the hippies were wont to gather, some even to sleep at night, rolled in their blankets on the grass. One of the Indian gurus who held court there was seated, lotus style, under a sun-dressed lime tree, with an admiring crowd of fair and tattered hippies about him, his wife Pat as crosslegged, as smiling and as tattered as the rest. He was too far away to hear what they were saying but it seemed more as if they were bandying jokes – what jokes could East and West possibly share? – than meditating or discoursing on theology. What particularly anguished him was the sight of the Indian tourists who had made an outer circle around this central core of seekers of nirvana and bliss-through-bhang, as if this were one of the sights of the Kulu Valley that they had paid to see. They stood about with incredulous faces, smiling uneasily, exchanging whispered asides with one another, exactly as if they were watching some disquieting although amusing play. There was condescension and, in some cases, pity in their expressions and attitudes that he could not bear to see directed at his fellow fair-heads, much less at his own wife. He turned and almost raced back to the boarding house.

That evening he had tried to question her again but she was tired, vague, merely brushed the hair from her face and murmured 'Yes, that's Guru Dina Nath. He's so sweet – so gay – so—' and went up to bed. He sniffed the air in the room suspiciously. Was it bhang? But he wouldn't know what it smelt like if it were. He imagined it would be sweetish and the air in their room was sour, acid. He wrenched the window open, with violence, hoping to wake her. It did not.

The day he gave up questioning her or pursuing her was when she came in, almost prancing, he thought, like some silly mare, burbling, 'Do you remember Nasogi, David? That darling village where we ate apricots? You remember its temple like a little doll's house? Well, I met some folks who live in a commune right next to it – a big attic over a cowshed actually, but it overlooks the temple and has an orchard all around it, so it's real nice. Edith – she's from Harlem – took me across, and I had coffee with some of them—'

'Sure it was coffee?' he snarled and, turning his back, hurled himself at the typewriter with such frenzy that she could not make herself heard. She sat on her bed, chewing her lip for a while, then got up and went out again. What she had planned to say to him was put away, like an unsuccessful gift.

She kept out of his way after that, and made no further attempts to take him along with her on the way to nirvana. When, at breakfast, he told her, 'It's time I got back to Delhi. I've got more material to research down there and I can't sit here in your valley and contemplate the mountains any more. I plan to book some seats on that plane for Delhi.'

She was shocked, although she made a stout attempt to disguise it, and he was gratified to see this. 'When d'you want to leave?' she asked, spitting a plum seed into her fist.

'Next Monday, I think,' he said.

She said nothing and disappeared for the rest of the day. She was out again before he'd emerged from his bath next morning, and he had to go down to the bus depot by himself, hating every squalid step of the way: the rag market where Tibetans sold stained and soiled imported clothes to avid Indian tourists and played dice in the dust while waiting for customers, the street where snot-gobbed urchins raced and made puppies scream, only just managing to escape from under roaring lorries and stinking buses. He directed looks of fury at the old beggar without a nose or fingers who solicited him for alms and at the pig-tailed Tibetan with one turquoise earring who tried to sell him a mangey pup. 'We're going to get out of here,' he ground out at them through

121

his teeth, and they smiled at him with every encouragement. The booking office was, however, not yet open for business and he was obliged to wait outside the bus depot which was the filthiest spot in the whole bazaar. He stood slouching against a wooden pillar, watching a half-empty bus push through a herd of worriedly bleating sheep and then come up, boiling and steaming, its green-painted, rose-wreathed sides almost falling apart with the effort. It groaned the last few yards of the way and expired at his feet, with a hiss of steam that made its bonnet rise inches into the air.

The driver, a wiry young Sikh who had hung his turban on a peg by the seat and wore only a purple handkerchief over his top-knot, leapt out and raced around to fling open the bonnet before the contraption exploded. His assistant, who had jumped down from the back door and vanished into the nearest shop, a gro-cer's, now came running out with an enamel jug of water which the driver grabbed from his hands and, before David's incredu-lous eyes, threw onto the radiator.

The next thing that David knew was that an explosion of steam and boiling water had hit him, hit the driver, the assistant and he didn't know how many bystanders – he couldn't see, he flung his hands to his face, but too late, he was on fire, he was howling – everyone was howling. Someone grabbed his shoul-ders, someone shouted 'Sir, sir, are you blind? Are you blind?' and he roared 'Yes, damn you, I'm blind, *blind*.' And where was Pat, his bloody useless wife, where was *she*? Here was he, blinded, scalded, being dragged through the streets by strangers, mad-men, all trying to carry him, all babbling as at a universal holocaust.

'There, try opening your eyes now. I think you can, son, just try it,' a blessedly American voice spoke, and prised away his hands from his face. In his desperation to see the owner of this blessed voice, David allowed his hands to be loosed from his face and actually opened his eyes – an act he had never thought to perform again – and gazed upon the American doctor with the auburn sideburns and the shirt of blue and brown checked wool as at a vision of St Michael at the golden gates. 'That's wonderful, just wonderful,' beamed the gorgeous man, solid and middle-aged and wondrously square. 'You haven't lost your eyes, see. Now let me just paint those burns for you and you'll leave here as fit as a fiddle, see if you don't . . .' So he burbled on, in that rich, heavy voice from the Middle West, and David sat back as helpless as a baby, and felt those large dry hands with their strong growth of ginger hair gently dab at his face, bringing peace and blessing in their wake. He was the American mission hospital doctor but to David he was God himself on an inspection visit mercifully timed to coincide with David's accident.

It was David's accident. He quite forgot to ask about the driver or his brainless help or the hapless bystanders who had been standing too close to the boiling radiator. He merely sat there, limp and helpless, feeling the doctor's voice flow over him like a stream of American milk. And then he was actually handed a glass of milk – Horlicks, the doctor called it, sweet and hot – and he sipped it with bowed head like a child, afraid he would cry now that the agony was over and the convalescence so sweetly begun.

'It's the shock,' the doctor was saying kindly. 'Your eyes are quite safe, son, and the burns are superficial – luckily – it's just the shock,' and he patted David on the back with those ginger-tufted hands that were so square and sure. 'We see all kinds of accidents up here, you know. Yesterday it was one of those crazy hippies who had to be brought in on a stretcher. He'd fallen off a mountain. Now can you credit that? A grown man just going and falling off a mountain like he was a kid? He'd broken both legs, see. I had to send my assistant with him to Delhi. They'll have quite a time getting him on his feet again but the Holy Family Hospital tries its best. Still,' he added, in the considerate manner of one who knows how to deal with a patient, 'yours sure is the most *unnecessary* accident we've had, I'll say that,' he declared, filling David with sweet pride. Bowing his head, he sipped his milk and drank in the doctor's kindly gossip. He tried to say, 'Yeah, those hippies – they shouldn't be allowed – I don't see how they're allowed—' but his voice died away and the doctor shrugged tolerantly and laughed. 'It takes all kinds, you know, but they really are kids, they shouldn't be allowed out of their mamma's sight. How about another drink of Horlicks? You think you can walk home now? Feel OK, son?' David would have given a great deal to say he was not OK at all, that he couldn't possibly walk home, that he wanted to stay and tell the doctor all about Pat, how she had practically deserted him, and about the unsavoury friends she had made here. He wanted to ask him to speak to Pat, reason with her, return his wife to him, return his former life to him. It made him weep, almost, to think that he was expected to get up and walk out. He threw a look of anguish at the doctor as he was seen down the rickety stairs to the bus depot, and did not realize that no one could make out his expression through that coating of gentian violet that coloured his entire face, neck and ears with an extraordinary neon glow.

'My God, what's up with *you?*' screamed Pat when she came in, hours later, and was struck still by shock.

He glared at her, exulting at having elicited such a response from her. But a minute later he saw that she had collapsed against the door frame, not with shock, but with laughter.

'What have you *done*, Dave?' she squealed. 'What made you do *that?*'

Harsh words were exchanged then. David, having lost his tight-lipped control (that morning's sweet Horlicks had washed it away) demanded roughly where she had been when he was standing in the sun to buy tickets and getting scalded and very nearly blinded in the process. Didn't she care about him, he wanted to know, and what *did* she care about at all now? And she, revolted, she said, by his egoism and conceit that didn't allow him to see beyond the tip of his nose – what was wrong with him that he couldn't move out of the way of a bus, for Christ's sake, didn't it just show that he saw nothing, noticed nothing outside him-self? – told him what she cared about. She had found a place for herself in the commune at Nasogi. It was what she was meant for, she realized – not going to parties with David, but to live with other men and women who shared her beliefs. They were going to live the simple life, wash themselves and their dishes in a stream, cook brown rice and lentils, pray and meditate in the forest and, at the end, perhaps, become Buddhists – 'A Buddhist, you crackpot? In a Hindu temple?' he spluttered – but she con-tinued calmly that she was sure to find, in the end, something that could not be found on the cocktail rounds of Delhi, Bombay or even, for that matter, Long Island, but that she was positive existed here, in the forest, on the mountains.

'What cocktail rounds? Are you trying to imply I'm a social gadabout, not a serious student of sociology, working on a thesis on which my entire career is based?'

'Working on a thesis?' she screeched derisively. 'Sociology? The idea of you, Dave, when you've never so much as looked, I mean really looked, into the soul, the prana, of the next man – is just too—' she spluttered to a stop, wildly threw her hair about her face and burst out, 'You, you don't even know it's possible to find Buddha in a Hindu temple. Why, you can find him in a church, a forest, anywhere. Do you think he's as narrow-minded as *you?*' she flung at him, and the explosiveness with which this burst from her showed how his derision had cut into her, how it had festered in her.

The English boarding house was treated to much more hurling of American abuse that night, to throwing around of suitcases, to sounds of packing and dramatic partings and exits, and many heads leant out of the windows into the chalky moonlight to see Pat set off, striding through the daisy-spattered yard in her newly acquired hippy rags that whipped against her legs as she marched off, bag and prayer beads in hand, with never a backward look. There was no one, however, but the pro-prietor, bland and inscrutable as ever, to see David off next morning making a quieter, neater and sadder departure for Delhi, unconventional only on account of the brilliant purple hue of his face.

If the truth were to be told, he felt greater regret at having to arrive in Delhi with a face like a painted baboon's than to arrive without his wife.

Royalty

All was prepared for the summer exodus: the trunks packed, the household wound down, wound up, ready to be abandoned to three months of withering heat and engulfing dust while its owners withdrew to their retreat in the mountains. The last few days were a little uncomfortable – so many of their clothes already packed away, so many of their books and papers bundled up and ready for the move. The house looked stark, with the silver put away, the vases emptied of flowers, the rugs and carpets rolled up; it was difficult to get through this stretch, delayed by one thing or another – a final visit to the dentist, last instructions to the stockbrokers, a nephew to be entertained on his way to Oxford. It was only the prospect of escape from the blinding heat that already hammered at the closed doors and windows, poured down on the roof and verandas, and withdrawal to the freshness and cool of the mountains which helped them to bear it. Sinking down on veranda chairs to sip lemonade from tall glasses, they sighed, 'Well, we'll soon be out of it.'

In that uncomfortable interlude, a postcard arrived – a cheap, yellow printed postcard that for some reason to do with his age, his generation, Raja still used. Sarla's hands began to tremble: news from Raja. In a quivering voice she asked for her spectacles. Ravi passed them to her and she peered through them to decipher the words as if they were a flight of migrating birds in the distance: Raja was in India, at his ashram in the south, Raja was going to be in Delhi next week, Raja expected to find her there. She *would* be there, wouldn't she? 'You won't desert me?'

After Ravi had made several appeals to her for information,

127

for a sharing of the news, she lifted her face to him, grey and mottled, and said in a broken voice, 'Oh Ravi, Raja has come. He is in the south. He wants to visit us – next week.'

It was only to be expected that Ravi's hands would fall upon the table, fall onto china and silverware, with a crash, making all rattle and jar. Raja was coming! Raja was to be amongst them again!

A great shiver ran through the house like a wind blowing that was not a wind so much as a stream of shining light, shimmering and undulating through the still, shadowy house, a radiant serpent, not without menace, some threat of danger. Whether it liked it or not, the house became the one chosen by Raja for a visitation, a house in waiting.

With her sari wrapped around her shoulders tightly, as if she were cold, Sarla went about unlocking cupboards, taking out sheets, silver, table linen. Her own trunks, and Ravi's, had to be thrown open. What had been put away was taken out again. Ravi sat uncomfortably in the darkened drawing room, watching her go back and forth, his lips thin and tight, but his expression one of helplessness. Sometimes he dared to make things difficult for her, demanding a book or a file he knew was at the very bottom of the trunk, pretending that it was indispensable, but when she performed the difficult task with every expression of weary martyrdom, he relented and asked, 'Are you all right? Sarla?' She refused to answer, her face was clenched in a tightly contained storm of emotion. Despondently, he groaned, 'Oh, aren't we too old—?' Then she turned to look at him, and even spoke: 'What do you mean?' Ravi shook his head helplessly. Was there any need to explain?

Raja arrived on an early morning train. Another sign of his generation: he did not fly when he was in India. Perhaps he had not taken in the fact that one could fly in India too, or else he preferred the trains, no matter how long they took, crawling over the endless, arid plains in the parched heat before the rains. At dawn, no sun yet visible, the sky was already white with heat; crows rose from the dust-laden trees, cawing, then dropped to the ground, sun-struck. Sweepers with great brooms made desultory swipes at the streets, their mouths covered with a strip of turban, or sari, against the dust they raised. Motor rickshaws and taxis were being washed, lovingly, tenderly, by drivers in striped underpants. The city stank of somnolence, of dejection, like sweat-stained clothes. Sarla and Ravi stood on the railway platform, waiting, and when Sarla seemed to waver, Ravi put out a gentlemanly hand to steady her. When she turned her face to him in something like gratitude or pleading, a look passed between them as can only pass between two people married to each other through the droughts and hurricanes of thirty years. Then the train arrived, with a great blowing of triumphant whistles: it had completed its long journey from the south, it had achieved its destination, hadn't it *said* it would? Magnificently, it was a promise kept. Immediately, coolies in red shirts and turbans, with legs like ancient tree roots, sprang at the compartments, leaping onto the steps before the train had even halted or its doors opened, and the families and friends waiting on the platform began to run with the train, waving, calling to the passengers who leaned out of the windows. Sarla and Ravi stood rooted to one place, clinging to each other in order not to be torn apart or pushed aside by the crowd in its excitement.

The pandemonium only grew worse when the doors were unlatched and the passengers began to dismount at the same time as the coolies forced their way in, creating human gridlock. Sighting their friends and relatives, the crowds on the platform began to wave and scream. Till coolies were matched with baggage, passengers with reception parties, utter chaos ruled. Sarla and Ravi peered through it, turning their heads in apprehension. Where was Raja? Only after the united families began to leave, exhorting coolies to bring up the rear with assorted trunks, bedding rolls and baskets balanced on their heads and held against their hips, and the railway platform had emerged from the scramble, did they hear the high-pitched, wavering warble of the voice they recognized: 'Sar-la! Ra-vi! My dears, how *good* of you to come! How *good* to see you! If you only knew what I've beeen through, about the man who insisted on telling me about his *alligator* farm, describing at such length how they are turned into *handbags*, as though I were a *leather merchant* . . .' and they turned to see Raja stepping out of one of the coaches, clutching his silk dhoti with one hand, waving elegantly with the other, a silver lock of his hair rising from his wide forehead as he landed on the platform in his slippered feet. And then the three of them were embracing each other, all at once, and it might have been Oxford, it might have been thirty years ago, it might even have been that lustrous morning in May emerging from dew-drenched meadows and the boat-crowded Isis, with ringing out of the skies and towers above them – bells, bells, bells, bells . . .

'And then there was *another* extraordinary passenger, a young man with hair like a nest of serpents, you know, and when he understood I would *not* eat a "two-egg mamlet" offered to me by this *incredibly* ragged and *totally* sooty little urchin with a tin tray under his arm, nor even a *"one*-egg mamlet" to please him or anyone, this marvellous person leapt down from the bunk above my head, and shot out of the door – oh, I assure you we were at a standstill, in the most *desolate* little station imaginable, for no reason I could see or guess at if I cudgelled my brains ever so *ferociously* – and then he returned with a basket *overflowing* with fruit, a positive *cornucopia*. Sarla, you'd have *fainted* with bliss! Never did you see such fruit; oh, nowhere, nowhere on those mythical farms of California, certainly, worked on by those armies of the exploited from the sad lands to the south, I assure you, Ravi, such fruit as seemed a reincarnation of the fruit one ate as a child, *stolen*, you know, from the neighbour's orchard, fruit one ate hidden in the *darkest* recesses of one's compound, surreptitiously, one's tongue absolutely *shrivelled* by the *piercing* sweetness of the mangoes, the *cruel* tartness of unripe guavas, the unripe pulp of the plantains. Oh, Sarla, such joys! And I sat peeling a *tiny* banana and eating it – it was no bigger than my little finger and contained the flavour of the ripest, sweetest, best banana any-where on earth within its cunning little yellow speckled jacket – I asked, naturally, what I owed him. But that incredible young man, who looked something like a cornucopia *himself,* with that abundant hair – it had such a quality of *liveliness* about it, every strand almost *electric* with energy – he merely folded his hands and said he would not take one paisa from me, not *one. Well,* of course I pushed away the basket and said I could not possibly accept it, totally against my principles, etcetera, and he gave me this tender, tender smile, quite unspeakably loving, and said he could take nothing from me because in a previous incarnation I had been his grandfather: he recognized me. "What?" said I, "*what?* What makes you say so? How *can* you say so?"'

'Watch out!' Ravi shouted at the driver who overtook a bull-ock cart so closely he almost ran into its great creaking wheels and overturned it.

'And he merely smiled, this sweet, *ineffably* sweet smile of his, and assured me I was no other than this esteemed ancestor of his who had left his home and family at the age of fifty and gone off into the Himalayas to live as a hermit and meditate. "Well," said I—'

'Slow down,' Ravi ordered the driver curtly.

'"Well," said I, "I *assure* you I have never been in the Himala-yas – although it is *indeed* my life's ambition to do so, and therefore I could not have returned from there." By the way, I began to won-der if it was *altogether* flattering to be called Grandfather by a man by no means in the first flush of youth, more like the becalmed middle years, whereupon he told me – imagine, Sarla, imagine, Ravi – he told me his grandfather had *died* there, in Rishikesh, on the banks of the Ganga, many years ago. His family had all trav-elled up from Madras to witness the cremation and carry the ashes to Benares, but *now,* in the railway carriage, that little tin box *bak-ing* in the sun as we crossed the red earth and ravines of Central India, he claimed he'd seen his reincarnation. He was as *certain* of it as the banana in my hand was a banana! He would not tell me *why*, or *how*, but he was clearly a clairvoyant. And isn't that a *superb* combination: clearly clairvoyant! Or do you think it a touch *de trop*? Hmm, Ravi, Sarla?'

The car lurched around one of the countless circles set within the radiating avenues of New Delhi, now steadily filling with traffic that streamed towards the city's business and government centres, far from this region of immense jamun trees, large low villas, smooth hedges, closed gates, sentries in sentry boxes, and parakeets in flamboyant trees.

'But that is the kind of experience, the kind of encounter that India bestows on one like a *gift*, a *jewel*,' Raja was fluting as the car drew up at one of the closed gates. The driver honked the horn discreetly, the watchman came hurrying to unlock it, and they swept in and up the drive to the porch that stood loaded with the weight of magenta bougainvillea. 'And,' Raja continued as he let the driver help him out of the car, 'I was so *delighted*, so *overjoyed* to find it still so, Ravi, in spite of that frightful man you have installed as the head of your government – an *economist*, is he not? – yes, please, I shall need that bag almost *immediately*, and the other too, if I am to bathe and refresh myself, but,' he concluded, triumphantly, 'what further refreshment can one *possibly* require after one has already been blessed with such, such *enchanting* acceptance, not, not physical, but positively, positively . . .'

'Spiritual?' Ravi ventured, smiling, as he helped Raja up the stairs into the shaded cool of the veranda with its pots of flowers and ferns, a slowly revolving electric fan and an arrangement of wicker furniture where he lowered Raja into an armchair with a flowered cushion.

It was not that Raja was any more elderly than they. They had all been contemporaries at Oxford, and Raja may even have been a year or two younger. Sarla had complained that his southern ancestry had given Raja an unfair advantage over their northern genes which seemed to produce businessmen and shopkeepers more readily than mathematicians or philosophers. Yet there was about him an air of fragility, of some precious commodity that they had been called upon to cherish. At Oxford Ravi had found himself taking Raja's laundry to be done while Raja, who had neglected to attend to it till he had absolutely nothing left to wear, had stayed in bed under his blankets till Ravi returned with fresh clothes. He was wryly amused as well as a little annoyed to find that he still fell into the trap.

Sarla was hurrying into the house, to make sure Raja's luggage was carried carefully into the room prepared for him – the bedroom at the back of the house, which Raja loved because it looked onto a garden full of lemon trees and jasmine vines that he said he dreamt about during that part of the year that he spent in Los Angeles – and against Raja's wishes to order breakfast, because, after all, she and Ravi had not benefited from the generosity of the young man with hair like a serpent's nest in the railway carriage, she said a little acidly.

Why her words sounded acid, she could not say. It was all she could do not to go down on her knees and remove Raja's slippers from his feet, or to bring water in a basin and wash them. She had to sharpen her faculties to fight that urge. But she brought out the coffee pot herself – she had taken the silver coffee service out of storage for Raja's visit – and poured him a cup with all the grace that she had acquired in her years as a diplomat's wife in the embassies and High Commissions where Ravi had 'served', she 'presided'. She could scarcely restrain herself, only tremblingly managed to restrain herself from mentioning that last day in May, that last embrace – oh, it would be so unsuitable, so unsuitable—

And then a second car came sweeping up the drive, parked beside theirs – an identical car, a silver-grey Ambassador with tinted glass and window curtains – and her sister tumbled out of the driver's seat, a woman almost identical to Sarla, and in an equal state of excitement and agitation. And then they were all embracing each other, after all, successively, simultaneously.

Maya had not been with them on the bank of the festive, the bacchanalian Isis that May morning; she had not fetched Raja's laundry or cooked him rice on a gas ring on foggy winter nights when he could not walk to the Indian restaurant in the cold, not with his asthmatic condition: Maya had been at the London School of Economics a few years later. Maya had also met her husband at university, but his path had been different from Ravi's. 'No bloody Civil Service for me; I've always thought it most *uncivil*,' Pravin had declared when Maya suggested it, 'and at this stage of history can you really contemplate anything so reactionary? Are we not moving into the future, *free* of colonial institutions?' So it had been a political career for Pravin, not the dirty politics of people Raja had just referred to so disparagingly, but politics as practised by the press, idealistically, morally, scrupulously (even if only on paper). And so, when Maya embraced Raja, it was with vigour, with her head tossed back with pride so that her now grey hair hung from her shoulders with as carefree an air as a young girl might toss her darker, glossier locks, and with a laugh that rang out resonantly. 'What, you've travelled by train in a silk dhoti? Oh Raja, must you go to such *extremes* when you play the southern gentleman visiting the barbarians of the north?' and Raja hung upon her shoulder and shook his finger at her, fluting at a higher pitch than ever before, 'Is that husband of yours still playing the patriot while dressed in Harris tweeds, and does he still wear that mouldy felt hat when following the elections amongst the cow-dung patties and buffalo sheds of Bihar?' and Sarla was retreating to the wicker sofa with the coffee tray, glowering, turning ashen and tight-lipped once more. But her occupation of the sofa was strategic – now Maya and Raja could not sit upon it, side by side: it belonged to her, and she could preside, icily, silver coffee pot in hand, looking upon the two as if they were somewhat trying children, and Ravi would give her a look – of sympathy, or pity? – from the stool on which he perched, waiting patiently to be passed a cup.

She passed it, then said, interrupting Maya who was giving a humorous account of the last election campaign Pravin had covered, 'If to go to the Himalayas is your life's ambition, Raja, then that can easily be achieved. Won't you consider driving up with us when we go for the summer to *Winhaven?*'

'Winhaven? Winhaven?' Raja twisted around to her. 'Oh, Sarla, Sarla, the very word, the very name – it recalls – how does it go—

'I have desired to go
Where springs not fail—

'and then? And then? How does it go—

'And I have asked to be
Where no storms come
Where the green swell is in the heaven's dumb,
And out of the swing of the sea—

'remember? remember?'

Who did not? Who did not, Sarla would have liked to know, but suddenly Simba was upon them, bursting out of the house, his great tail thumping, his claws slithering across the veranda tiles in his excitement as he dashed at Maya, then at Ravi, finally at Raja and, to Sarla's horror, Raja was pushed back into his chair by Simba's vigorous attention, but Raja was pushing back at him, laughing, 'Oh, Simba, Simba of the Kenyan highlands! You remember me, do you?' and Sarla, cupping her chin in her hand, leaving her coffee untouched, watched as Raja, suddenly as sprightly as a boy, the boy who had bicycled helter-skelter down the streets of Oxford, dark hair rising up from his great brow and falling into the luminous eyes, now ran down the stairs with Simba into the garden, then bent to pick up a stick and send it flying up at the morning sun for the pleasure of having Simba leap for it. Old Simba, usually so gloomy, so lethargic, was now spring-ing up on his hindlegs to catch the falling toy and run with it into the shade of the flamboyant tree, Raja following him, his pale silk dhoti floating about him, his white hair glistening, making the startled parakeets fly out of the clusters of scarlet flowers with screams.

Then both Sarla and Maya released small sighs. Ravi watched their expressions from the stool on which he was perched, and finally asked, diffidently, 'May I have a lump of sugar and a little milk, please?'

In spite of his poetic response to Sarla's suggestion that he accompany them to the mountains, Raja continually postponed the journey. No, he had come to Delhi, all the way to Delhi in the heat of June, to see them, to relive the remembered joys of their beautiful home. How could he cut short his time here? And there was so much for him to see, to do, to catch up on. He wanted Sarla to drive him to the silver market in Chandni Chowk so he could gaze upon the magnificent craftsmanship on display there, perhaps even purchase a piece to take back with him to California where the natives had never seen such art bestowed upon craft, and then if Maya were to accompany him to the Cottage Industries emporium, and help him select a pashmina shawl, then he could be happy even on those chill, rainy days that he was forced to endure. What, didn't they *know*, California had such weather? Had they been deceived by posters of palm trees and golden beaches? Didn't they know the *fraudulence* inherent in the very notion and practice of tourism, that abominable habit of the Western world? Tourism! Now, when *he* returned to India, it was not to see the sights, he already knew them – they were imprinted upon his heart – but to imbibe them, savour them, nourish himself upon them. And so when Sarla and Ravi took him to Nizamuddin and beside the saint's tomb they heard a blind beggar play his lute and sing in a voice so soulful that it melted one's very being,

When I was born
I was my mother's prince.
When I married

Royalty

I became my wife's king.
But you have reduced me
To being a beggar, Lord,
Come begging for alms
With my hands outstretched—

it was as if the thirst of Raja's pilgrim soul was being slaked, and
never had thirst been slaked by music so sublime as made by this
ancient beggar in his rags, a tin can at his knee for alms – and of
course he must have whatever was in Raja's purse, every last coin,
alas that they were so few. Now if this beggar were performing in
the West, the great theatres of every metropolis would throw
open their doors to him. He would perform under floodlights,
his name would be on posters, in the papers, on everyone's lips.
Gold would pile up at his feet – but then, would he be such a
singer as he was now, a pilgrim soul content to sit in the shade of
the great saint Nizamuddin's little fretted marble tomb, and
dedicate his song to him as homage?

Raja, leaving his slippers at the gateway to the courtyard,
approached the tomb with such ecstasy etched upon his noble
features that Sarla, and Ravi too, found themselves gazing at him
rather than about them – Sarla's bare and Ravi's stockinged feet
on the stones, braving the dirt and flies and garbage that had first
made them shrink and half turn away. Sarla had held her sari to
her nose as they passed a row of butchers' shops on their way to
the tomb, buffalo's innards had hung like curtains in the small
booths, and the air was rife with raw blood and the thrum of
flies, and she asked Raja, in the car, 'How is it that you, a vegetar-
ian, a Brahmin, walked in there and never even twitched your
nose?' He cast his eyes upon her briefly – and they were still those
narrow, horizontal pools of darkness she remembered – and
sighed, 'My dear, true souls do not turn away from humanity or,
if they do, it is only to meditate and pray, then come back, forti-
fied, to embrace it – beggars, thieves, lepers, whoever – their
sores, their rags. They do not flinch from them, for they know

these are only the covering, the concealing robes of the soul, don't you know?' and Sarla, and Ravi, seated on either side of Raja on the comfortably upholstered back seat of the air-conditioned Ambassador, now speeding past the Lodi Gardens to their own green enclave, wondered if Raja was referring to himself or the sufi.

That afternoon, as they sat on the veranda, sipping tea and nibbling at the biscuits the cook had sent up in a temper (he was supposed to be on leave, he was not going to bake fancy cakes at a time when he was rightfully to have had his summer vacation, and so the sahibs could do with biscuits bought in the bazaar), Raja, a little melancholy, a little subdued – which Sarla and Ravi put down to the impression left on him by their visit to the sufi's tomb – piped up in a beseeching voice, 'Sarla, Ravi, where are those ravishing friends of yours I met when you were at the High Commission in London? The Dutta-Rays, was it not? You must know who I mean – you told me how they'd returned to Delhi and built this absolutely fabulous hacienda in Vasant Vihar. Isn't that quite close by?'

'It is,' Ravi admitted.

Like a persistent child, Raja continued, 'Then *why* don't we have them over? This evening? I remember she sang like a nightingale – those melancholy, funereal songs of Tagore's. Wouldn't they be perfect on an evening like this which simply hangs suspended in time, don't you know, as if the dust and heat were holding it in their *cruel* grasp? Oh, Sarla, do telephone, do send for her – tell her I *pine* to hear the sound of her avian voice. Just for that, I'm even willing to put up with her husband who I remember finding – how shall I put it – a *trifle* wanting?'

Sarla found herself quite unwilling. Truth be told, the morning's expedition had left her with a splitting headache; she was not in the habit of walking around in the midday sun, leave that to mad dogs and – she'd always said. Even now, her temples throbbed and perspiration trickled discreetly down the back of her knees, invisible under the fresh cotton sari she'd donned for tea. But Raja would not hear of a refusal, or accept any excuse. If she thought the Dutta-Rays had left for Kashmir, why did she not ring and find out? Oh, there was no need to get up and *go* to the telephone – 'In this land of fantasies fulfilled, isn't there always a willing hand-maid, so to speak, to bring the mountain to Mohammed?' and Sarla had to send for the telephone to be brought out to the veranda, the servant Balu unwinding the telephone line all the way, and she was forced to speak into it and verify that the Dutta-Rays were indeed still in Delhi, held up by a visit from a former colleague at India House, but were going out that evening to that party – didn't Sarla and Ravi know of it? 'We're supposed to be *away*,' Sarla said stiffly into the telephone. 'Everyone thinks we are in the *hills* by now. We usually are.' Well, the Dutta-Rays would drop in on their way – and so they did, she a vision of grace in her finely embroidered Lucknow sari, pale green on white, to Raja's great delight, and only too willing to sing for his delectation, only not tonight since they were already late.

So Sarla and Ravi found themselves throwing a party – a party that was to be the setting for a recital given by Ila Dutta-Ray, a woman neither of them had any warm feelings for, remembering how unhelpful she had been when they had first arrived in London and so badly needed help in finding a flat, engaging servants, placing their children in school, all so long ago of course. Instead of *helping*, she had sent them her old cook, declaring he was the best, but really saving herself the air fare back to India because he proved good for nothing but superannuation. They rang up whoever of their circle of friends remained in Delhi to invite them for the occasion. It was quite extraordinary how many friends Raja remembered and managed to trace, and also how many who were on the point of going away, changed their plans on hearing his name and assured Sarla and Ravi they would come.

Then there occurred a dreadful incident: Sarla was choosing from amongst her saris one cool enough for the evening ahead, which was, of course, one of the summer's worst, that kind of still, yellow, lurid evening that it inflicted when one thought one could bear no more, and meant that the recital would be held not in the garden after all but in the air-conditioned drawing room instead, when a terrible thought struck her: she had forgotten to invite Maya! Maya and her husband Pravin! How could she have? It was true Maya had told her Pravin was very preoccupied with a special issue his paper was bringing out on the rise of Hindu fundamentalism but that was no reason to assume they might not be free. Sarla stood in front of the mirror that was attached to one leaf of the armoire, and clasped her hand over her mouth with a look so stricken that Ravi, coming in to ask what glasses should be taken out for the evening, wondered if she had a sudden toothache. 'Ravi! Oh, Ravi,' she wailed.

The telephone was brought to her – Balu unwinding the coils of an endless wire – and the number dialled for her. Then Sarla spoke into it in gasps, but unfortunately she had not taken the time to collect her wits and phrase her invitation with more tact. Maya's sharp ears picked up every indication that her sister had been unforgivably remiss, and coldly rejected the insulting last-minute invitation, insisting proudly that Pravin was working late and she could not possibly leave his side, he never wrote a line without consulting her.

As if that was not agony enough, Sarla had to undergo the further humiliation of Raja piping up in the middle of the party – just as Ila Dutta-Ray was tuning her tanpura and about to open her mouth and utter the first note of her song – 'But Sarla, where is Maya, that aficionado of Tagore's music? *Surely* we should wait for her? *Why* is she so late?' An awful hush fell – and Sarla again assumed her stricken look. What was she to say, how was she to explain? She found herself stumbling over Maya's insincere excuse, but of course everyone guessed. Frowning in disapproval, Ila Dutta-Ray began her song on a very low, very deep and hoarse note.

*

In retaliation, Maya and Pravin threw a party as soon as Pravin's column had been written and the special issue had gone to press, and *their* party was in honour of the Minister of Human Resources, whose wife was such an admirer of Raja's, had read every word he had written and wanted so much to meet him – 'in an intimate setting'. Since she had made this special request, they had felt obliged to cut down their guest list – and were sure Sarla and Ravi would not mind since they had the pleasure of Raja's company every day. But when Ravi stoically offered to drive Raja across to their house, he found the whole road lined with cars, many of them chauffeur-driven and with government number plates, and had the humiliation of backing out of it after dropping Raja at the gate, then returning to Sarla who had given way to a fierce migraine and was insisting that they book seats on a train to the hills as soon as possible.

'But don't we need to wait till Raja is gone?'

'Raja is incapable of making decisions – we'll have to make his for him,' she snapped, waving at Balu who was slouching in the doorway, waiting to take away the remains of their meagre supper from the dining table.

She was still agonized enough the following morning – digging violently into half a ripe papaya in the blazing light that spilt over the veranda even at that early hour – actually to ask Raja, 'How can you bear this heat? Do you really not mind it? I feel I'm going to collapse—'

Raja, who had a look of sleepy contentment on his face – he had already meditated for an hour in the garden, done his yoga exercises, bathed, drunk his tea and had every reason to look forward to another day – did not seem to catch her meaning at all. Reaching out to stroke her hand, he said, 'I know what you need, my dear – a walk in the sublime Lodi Gardens when the sun is setting and Venus appears in the sky so *silently*—' and went on to describe the ruins, their patina of lichen, their tiles of Persian blue, the echoes that rang beneath their domes, in such terms that Sarla sank back in her chair, sighing, agreeing.

What she did not know was that he had already arranged to

walk there with Maya, Ila Dutta-Ray, and the wife of the Minister of Human Resources who, it turned out, had read that book of verses he had written when in Oxford and had published by a small press in London, long expired, so that copies were now collectors' pieces. All three women owned such copies. And Sarla found herself trailing behind them while Raja pranced, actually pranced with delight, with enthusiasm, in their company. At their suggestion he recited those verses:

> The lamp of heaven is hung upon the citrus bough,
> The nightingale falls silent.
> All is waiting,
> For a royal visit by night's own queen—

and then burst into mocking, self-deprecating laughter, waving away their protests to say, 'Oh, those adolescent excesses! What was I *thinking* of, in Oxford, in the fog and the smog and the cold I suffered from perpetually! Well, you know, I was thinking of – *this*,' and he waved at the walled rose garden and beyond it the pond and beyond that the tombs of the Lodi emperors surrounded by neem trees, and they all gazed with him. Eventually the Minister's wife sighed, 'You make us all see it with new eyes, as if we had never seen it before.'

Sarla, who had hung back, and was standing by a rose bush, fingering the fine petals of one flower pensively, realized that this was so exactly true: it was Raja who opened their eyes, who made them see it as they never saw it themselves, as a place of magic, enchantment, of pleasure so immense and rich that it could never be exhausted. She gazed at his back, his noble head, the silvery hair, the gracefully gesturing arm in its white muslin sleeve, there in the shade of the neem tree, totally disregarding the dust, the smouldering heat at the summer day's end, and seeing it all as romantic, paradisaical – and she clasped her hands together, pressing a petal between them, grateful for knowing him.

*

That evening she tried again. 'Raja, I *know* you would love Win-haven,' she told him, interrupting the Vedic hymn he was reciting to prove to Ravi that his Sanskrit was still fluent – hadn't he taught it to the golden youth of Berkeley, of Stanford, of the universities in Los Angeles and San Francisco, for all these years of his exile? 'And I would love to see you in the Himalayas,' she went on, raising her voice, 'because they would make the most perfect setting for you. Perhaps you would begin to write again over there—'

'But darling Sarla,' Raja beamed at her, showing both the pleasure he took in her suggestion and his determination not to be swept away by it, 'Maya tells me there is to be a lecture at India International Centre next week on the Himalayas as an inspiration for Indian poets through the centuries, and I would *hate* to miss it. It's to be given by Professor Dandavate, that old bore – d'you remember him? What a *dreary* young man he was at Oxford! I can quite imagine how much drearier he is now – and I can't resist the opportunity to pick holes in all he says, and in public too—'

'But next week?' Sarla enquired helplessly. 'It'll – it'll be even hotter.'

'Sarla, don't you *ever* think of anything else?' he reproved her gently, although with a little twitch of impatience about his eyes. 'Now I don't *ever* notice the heat. Drink the delicious fresh lemonades your marvellous cook makes, rest in the afternoons, and there's no reason why you shouldn't *enjoy* the summer. Oh, think of the fruit alone that summer brings us—'

But it was the marvellous cook himself who brought an end to Raja's idyll in Sarla and Ravi's gracious home: that very day he took off his apron, laid down his egg whisk and his market bag, declared that enough was enough, that he was needed in his village to bring in the harvest before the monsoon arrived. He was already late and had received a postcard from his son to say they could not delay it by another day. He demanded his salary and caught his train.

Sarla was sufficiently outraged by his treachery to make the afternoon tea herself, braving the inferno of the kitchen where she seldom had need to venture, and was rewarded by Raja's happy and Ravi's proud beam as she brought out the tea tray to the veranda. But dinner proved something else altogether. Balu showed not the slightest inclination that he meant to help: he kept to the pantry with grim determination, giving the glasses and silver another polishing rather than take a step into the kitchen. Sarla had a whispered consultation with Ravi, suggesting they take Raja out to India International Centre or the Gymkhana Club for dinner, but Ravi reminded her that the car had gone for servicing and they could go nowhere tonight. Sarla, her sari end tucked in at her waist, wiping the perspiration from her face with her elbow, went back into the kitchen and peered into its recesses to see if the cook had not repented and left some cooked food for them after all, but she found little that she could put together even if she knew how. At one point, she even telephoned Maya to see if her sister would not come to her aid – Maya was known for her superb culinary skill – but there was no answer: Maya and Pravin were out. It was to an embarrassingly inadequate repast of sliced cucumber, yoghurt and bread that the three finally sat down – Balu looking as if it were far beneath his dignity to serve such an excuse for a meal, Sarla tight-lipped with anger with herself for failing so blatantly, Ravi trying, with embarrassed sincerity, to thank her for her brave effort, and Raja saying nothing at all, but quietly crumbling the bread beside his plate till he confessed a wish to go to bed early.

But this meant that he was up earlier than ever next morning, and by the time Sarla rose and went wearily kitchenwards to make him tea, he had been awake for hours, performed his yoga and meditation, walked Simba round the garden several times, and was waiting querulously for it. Balu was nowhere to be seen. When Sarla went in search of him – surely he should have been able to make their guest a cup of tea? – she found the door to his room shut, coloured cutouts from film magazines of starlets in swimsuits stuck all over it, and when she called out his name, heard only a groan in reply. In agitation, she hurried to find Ravi and send him to find out what was wrong. Ravi went in reluctantly, his face bearing an expression of martyrdom, and reappeared to inform her that Balu was suffering from a stomach ache and needed to be taken to a doctor. '*You* do that,' she snapped at him, hardly able to believe this terrible turn in their fortunes.

By lunchtime, Raja had made a series of phone calls and discovered that the Dutta-Rays were leaving for Kashmir next day and would be only too delighted to have him accompany them. Sarla stood in the doorway, watching him pack his little bag with beautifully laundered underwear, and wailed, 'But Raja, if you had wanted to go to the hills, we could have gone to Winhaven ages ago! I *asked* you, you remember?'

Raja gave her a look that said, 'Winhaven? With you? When I can be on a houseboat in Kashmir with Ila instead?' But of course, what he really did was blow her a kiss across the room and whisper conspiratorially, 'Darling, think of the *stories* I'll come back with to entertain you,' and snapped shut the lock on his bag with a satisfied click.

'Simba! Simba!' Ravi put his hands around his mouth and called after the dog who had loped away up to the top of the hill and vanished. Then he turned around to look for Sarla. He could see neither his dog nor his wife – one had gone too far ahead, the other lagged too far behind. He lowered himself onto a rock to catch his breath and picked up a pine cone to toss from hand to hand while he waited, whistling a little tune.

Evening light flooded down from the vast sky, spilling over the pine needles and stones of the hillside. Everything seemed to be bathed in its pale saffron glow. An eagle drifted through the ravine below. He could hear the wind in its feathers, a melancholy whistle.

'Sarla?' he called out finally, and just then saw her come into sight on a turn of the path below him, amongst a mass of black-berry bushes. She seemed to be dragging herself along, her sari trailing in the white dust, her head bowed over the walking stick she held in a slightly trembling hand.

At his voice she looked up and her face was haggard. He stared in surprise: he had not considered this such a difficult climb, or so long a walk. It was where they had always come, to watch the sunset. He himself could still spring up it with no more than a little panting. 'Sarla?' he asked questioningly. 'Want some help, old girl?'

'Coming, coming,' she grumbled, toiling on, 'can't you see I'm coming?'

When she reached the rock where he was waiting, she sank down onto it and wiped her face with the corner of her sari. 'I can't do these climbs any more,' she admitted, with a wince. 'You had better do them alone.'

'Oh, Sarla,' he said, catching up her hand in his, 'I would never want to come up here without you, you know.' They sat there a while, breathing deeply. Beside them a small cricket began to chirp and chirp, and after some time it was no longer light that came spilling down the hill, but shadows.

Winterscape

She stands with the baby in her arms in front of the refrigerator, and points at the pictures she has taped on its white enamel surface, each in turn, calling out the names of the people in the photographs. It is a game they play often to pass the time, the great stretches of time they spend alone together. The baby jabs his short pink finger at a photograph, and the mother cries, 'That's Daddy, in his new car!' or 'Susan and cousin Ted, on his first birthday!' and 'Grandma by the Christmas tree!' All these pictures are as bright and festive as bits of tinsel or confetti. Everyone is smiling in them, and there are birthday cakes and Christmas trees, the shining chrome of new cars, bright green lawns and white houses. 'Da-dee!' the baby shouts. 'Soo-sun!' The bright colours make the baby smile. The mother is happy to play the game, and laughs: her baby is learning the names of all the members of the family; he is becoming a part of the family.

Then the baby reaches out and waves an ineffectual hand at a photograph that is almost entirely white, only a few shades of grey to bring out the shapes and figures in it. There are two, and both are draped in snow-white clothes which cover their shoulders, exposing only the backs of their heads which are white too, and they are standing beside the very same white refrigerator in the same white-painted kitchen, in front of a white-framed window. They are looking out of it, not at the camera but at the snow that is falling past the windowpanes, covering the leafless tree and the wooden fence and the ground outside, providing them with a white snowscape into which they seem nearly to have merged. Nearly.

The baby's pink finger jabs at the white photograph. The mother says nothing immediately: she seems silenced, as if she too has joined the two figures at the window and with them is looking out of the white kitchen into a white world. The photograph somehow calls for silence, creates silence, like snow.

The baby too drops his hand, lowers his head on his mother's shoulder, and yawns. Snow, silence, and sleep: the white picture has filled him with sleep, he is overcome by it. His mother holds him and rocks him, swaying on her feet. She loves the feel of the baby's head on her shoulder; she tucks it under her chin protectively. She swivels around to the window as if she sees the two white figures there now, vanishing into the green dusk of a summer evening. She sings softly into the baby's dark hair: 'Ma and Masi – Ma and Masi together.'

'*Two?*' Beth turned her head on the pillow and stared at him over the top of her glasses, lowering the book she was reading to the rounded dome of her belly under the blue coverlet. '*Two* tickets? For *whom?*' because she knew Rakesh did not have a father, that his mother was a widow.

'For my mother and my aunt,' he said, in a low, almost sullen voice, sitting on the edge of the bed in his pyjamas and twisting his fingers together. His back was turned to her, his shoulders stooped. Because of the time difference, he had had to place the call to the village in India in the middle of the night.

'Your *aunt?*' Beth heard her own voice escalate. 'Why do we have to pay for your aunt to visit us? Why does *she* have to visit us when the baby is born? I can't have so many guests in the house, Rakesh!'

He turned around towards her slowly, and she saw dark circles under his eyes. Another time they might have caused her to put her finger out to touch those big, bluish pouches, like bruises, but now she felt herself tense at the thought of not just one, but two strangers, foreigners, part of Rakesh's past, invading their house. She had already wished she had not allowed Rakesh to send for his mother to attend to the birth of their child. It had seemed an outlandish, archaic idea even when it was first suggested; now it was positively bizarre. 'Why both of them? We only asked your mother,' she insisted.

Rakesh was normally quick with his smile, his reassuring words, soft and comforting murmurs. He had seemed nervous ever since she became pregnant, more inclined to worry about what she took as a natural process. But she could see it was not that, it was something else that made him brood, silently, on the edge of the bed, the blue pouches hanging under his eyes, and his hands twisted.

'What's the matter?' she said sharply, and took off her glasses and turned over her book. 'What's wrong?'

He roused himself to shake his head, attempted to smile, and failed. Then he lifted up his legs and lay down on the bed, beside her, turning to her with that same brooding expression, not really seeing her. He put out his hand and tried to stroke the hair at her temple. It annoyed her: he was so clearly about to make a request, a difficult request. She tensed, ready to refuse. He ought not to be asking anything of her in her condition. Two guests, two foreigners – at such a time. 'Tell me,' she demanded.

So he began to tell her. 'They are both my mothers, Beth,' he said. 'I have two mothers.'

There were three years between them and those seemed to have made all the difference. Asha was the first child in the family. So delighted was her father that it never crossed his mind she should have been a son. He tossed her up and caught her in his arms and put his face into her neck to make growling sounds that sent her into squeals of laughter. That she was fair-skinned, plump and had curly hair and bright black eyes all pleased him. He liked his wife to dress the child in frilly, flounced, flowered dresses and put ribbons in her hair. She was glad and relieved he was so pleased with his daughter: it could have been otherwise, but he said, 'A pretty daughter is an ornament to the home.'

So Asha grew up knowing she was an ornament, and a joy. She had no hesitation ever in asking for a toy or a sweet, in climbing onto her parents' laps or standing in the centre of a circle to sing or skip.

When Anu was born, three years later, it was different. Although her father bent over her and fondled her head and said nothing to express disappointment, disappointment was in the air. It swaddled baby Anu (no one even remembered her full name, the more majestic Annapurna), and among the first things she heard were the mutterings of the older people in the family who had no compunction about pronouncing their disappointment. And while her mother held her close and defended her against them, baby Anu knew she was in a weak position. So one might have thought, watching her grow. Although she stayed close to her elder sister, clinging to the hem of her dress, shadowing her, and Asha was pleased to have someone so entirely under her control, there remained something hesitant, nervous and tentative about Anu's steps, her movements and speech. Everything about her expressed diffidence.

While Asha proved a natural housekeeper and joined, with gusto, in the cooking, the washing, the sweeping, all those household tasks shared between the women, pinning her chunni back behind her ears, rolling up the sleeves of her kameez, and settling down to kneading the dough, or pounding spices, or rolling out chapatis with a fine vigour, Anu proved sadly incompetent. She managed to get her hand burnt when frying pakoras, took so long to grind chillies that her mother grew impatient and pushed her out of the way, and was too weak to haul up a full bucket of water from the well, needing to do it half a bucket at a time. When visitors filled the house and everything was in an uproar, Anu would try to slip away and make herself invisible and only return when summoned – to be scolded soundly for shirking work. 'Look at your sister,' she was always counselled, and she did, raising her eyes with timid admiration. Asha, used to her sister's ways, gave her a wink and slipped her one of the snacks or sweets she had missed. An understanding grew between them, strengthened by strand upon strand upon strand of complicity.

Later, sons were born to their parents, and the pressure, the tension in their relationships with their daughters was relieved. Good-naturedly, the father allowed both of them to go to school. 'What is the harm?' he asked the elderly critics of this unusual move. 'These days it is good for girls to be educated. One day, who knows, they may work in an office – or a bank!'

That certainly did not happen. Another generation would be born and raised before any girl in that Punjab village became an office clerk or a bank teller. Asha and Anu had a few years in the local government school where they wore blue cotton kameezes with white chunnis, and white gym shoes, and sat on benches learning the Punjabi alphabet and their numbers. Here the scales may well have tipped the other way, because Asha found the work ferociously difficult and grew hot and bothered as she tried to work out problems in addition and subtraction or to read her lessons from the tattered, illustrated textbooks, while Anu discovered an unexpected nimbleness of mind that skipped about the numbers with the agility of a young goat, and scampered through the letters quite friskily. Asha threw her sister exasperated looks but did not mind so much when Anu took over her homework and did it for her in her beautiful hand. Anu drew praise when she wrote essays on 'The Cow' and 'My Favourite Festival' – but, alas, the latter proved to be her swan song because at this point Asha turned fifteen and the family found her a bridegroom and married her off and Anu had to stay home from then on to help her mother.

Asha's bridegroom was a large man, not so young, but it did not matter because he owned so much land and cattle. He had a great handlebar moustache and a turban and Anu was terrified for Asha when she first saw him, but was later to find no cause for terror: he was a kindly, good-natured man who clearly adored his bright-eyed, quick-tongued, lively young wife and was generous to her and to her entire family. His voice was unexpectedly soft and melodious, and he often regaled his visitors, or a gathering in the village, with his songs. Asha – who had plenty of talents but not artistic ones – looked at him with admiration then, sitting back on her haunches and cupping her chin in her hands which were bedecked with the rings and bracelets he had given her.

They often asked Anu to come and stay with them. Asha found she was so accustomed to having her younger sister at her heels, she really could not do without her. She might have done, had she had children, but, though many were born to her, they were either stillborn or died soon after birth, none living for more than a few days. This created an emptiness in the big house so full of goods and comforts, and Asha grew querulous and plaintive, a kind of bitterness informing her every gesture and expression, while her husband became prone to depression which no one would have predicted earlier. Anu often came upon him seated in an armchair at the end of the veranda, or up on the flat roof of the house in the cool evenings, looking out with an expression of deep melancholy across his fields to the horizon where the white spire and the golden dome of the Sikh temple stood against the sky. He left the work on the farm to a trusted headman to supervise and became idle himself, exasperating Asha who tended to throw herself into every possible activity with determined vigour and thought a man should too.

After yet another miscarriage, Asha roused herself with a grim wilfulness to join in the preparation for Anu's wedding, arranged by the parents to a clerk in a neighbouring town, a sullen, silent young man with large teeth and large hands that he rubbed together all the time. Anu kept her face and her tears hidden throughout the wedding, as brides did, and Asha was both consoling and encouraging, as women were.

Unexpectedly, that unpromising young man, who blinked through his spectacles and could scarcely croak one sentence at a time, showed no hesitation whatsoever when it came to fathering a child. Nor did Anu, who was so slight of frame and mousy in manner, seem to be in any way handicapped as a woman or mother – her child was born easily, and it was a son. A round, black-haired, red-cheeked boy who roared lustily for his milk and thrashed out with his legs and grabbed with his hands, clearly meant for survival and success.

If Anu and her husband were astonished by him, it could scarcely have matched Asha and her husband's wonder. They were enthralled by the boy: he was the child of their dreams, their thwarted hopes and desires. Anu lay back and watched how Asha scooped Rakesh up into her large, soft arms, how she cradled and kissed him, then how her husband took him from her, wrapped in the candy pink wool shawl knitted by Asha, and crooned over him. She was touched and grateful for Asha's competence, as adept at handling the baby as in churning butter or making sweets. Anu stayed in bed, letting her sister fuss over both her and the baby – making Anu special milk and almond and jaggery drinks in tall metal tumblers, keeping the baby happy and content, massaging him with mustard oil, feeding him sips of sweetened milk from a silver shell, tickling him till he smiled.

Anu's husband looked on, awkwardly, too nervous to hold his own child: small creatures made him afraid; he never failed to kick a puppy or a kitten out of his way, fiercely. Anu rose from her bed occasionally to make a few tentative gestures of motherhood but soon relinquished them, one by one, first letting Asha feed the baby and dress him, then giving up attempts to nurse the boy and letting Asha take over the feeding.

At the first hint of illness – actually, the baby was teething which caused a tummy upset – Asha bundled him up in his blanket and took him home, promising, 'I'll bring him back as soon as he is well. Now you go and rest, Anu, you haven't slept and you look sick yourself.'

When Anu went to fetch him after a week, she came upon Asha's husband, sitting on that upright chair of his on the veranda, but now transformed. He had the baby on his knee and was hopping him up and down while singing a rhyme, and his eyes sparkled as vivaciously as the child's. Instead of taking her son from him, Anu held back, enjoying the scene. Noticing her at last, the large man in the turban beamed at her. 'A prince!' he said, 'and one day he will have all my fields, my cattle, the dairy, the cane-crushing factory, everything. He will grow up to be a prince!'

Rakesh's first birthday was to be celebrated at Asha's house – 'We will do it in style,' she said, revealing how little she thought Anu and her husband were capable of achieving it. Preparations went on for weeks beforehand. There was to be a feast for the whole village. A goat was to be slaughtered and roasted, and the women in the family were busy making sweets and delicacies with no expense spared: Asha's husband was seeing to that. He himself went out to shoot partridges for the festive dinner, setting out before dawn into the rippling grainfields and calling back to the women to have the fire ready for his return.

Those were his last words – to have the fire ready. 'As if he knew', wept Asha's mother, 'that it was the funeral pyre we would light.' Apparently there had been an accident with the gun. It had gone off unexpectedly and the bullet had pierced his shoulder and a lung: he had bled to death. There were no birthday festivities for one-year-old Rakesh.

Knowing that the one thing that could comfort Asha was the presence of the baby in her arms, Anu refrained from suggesting she take him home. At first, she had planned to leave the boy with her widowed sister for the first month of mourning, then drew it out to two and even three months. When her husband, taunted by his own family for his failure to establish himself as head of his household, ordered her to bring their son home, Anu surprised herself by answering, 'Let him be. Asha needs him. We can have more sons for ourselves.' Their house was empty and melancholy – it had always been a mean place, a narrow set of rooms in the bazaar, with no sunlight or air – but she sat in its gloom, stitching clothes for her rapidly growing son, a chunni drawn over her head, a picture of acceptance that her husband was not able to disturb, except briefly, with fits of violence.

After one of these, they would go and visit the boy, with gifts, and Rakesh came to look upon his parents as a visiting aunt and uncle, who offered him sweets and toys with a dumbly appeasing, appealing air. No one remembered when he started calling them Masi and Masa. Asha he already addressed as Ma: it was so clearly her role.

Anu had been confident other children would follow. She hoped for a daughter next time, somehow feeling a daughter might be more like her, and more likely to stay with her. But Rakesh had his second and third birthday in Asha's house, and there was no other child. Anu's husband looked discouraged now, and resentful, his own family turning into a chorus of mocking voices. He stayed away at work for long hours; there were rumours – quickly brought to Anu's attention – that he had taken to gambling, and drugs, and some even hinted at having seen him in quarters of the town where respectable people did not go. She was not too perturbed: their relationship was a furtive, nocturnal thing that never survived daylight. She was concerned, of course, when he began to look ill, to break out in boils and rashes, and come down with frequent fevers, and she nursed him in her usual bungling, tentative way. His family came to take over, criticizing her sharply for her failings as a nurse, but he only seemed to grow worse, and died shortly before Rakesh's fifth birthday. His family set up a loud lament and clearly blamed her for the way he had dwindled away in spite of their care. She packed her belongings – in the same tin trunk in which she had brought them as a bride, having added nothing more to them – and went to live with Asha – and the child.

In the dark, Beth found it was she who was stroking the hair at Rakesh's temple now, and he who lay stretched out with his hands folded on his chest and his eyes staring at the ceiling.

'Then the woman you call Ma – she is really your aunt?' Beth queried.

Rakesh gave a long sigh. 'I always knew her as my mother.'

'And your aunt is your real mother? When did they tell you?'

'I don't know,' he admitted. 'I grew up knowing it – perhaps people spoke of it in the village, but when you are small you don't question. You just accept.'

'But didn't your *real* mother ever tell you, or try to take you away?'

'No!' he exclaimed. 'That's just it, Beth. She never did – she had given me to her sister, out of love, out of sympathy when her husband died. She never tried to break up the relationship I had with her. It was out of love.' He tried to explain again, 'The love sisters feel.'

Beth, unlike Rakesh, had a sister. Susan. She thought of her now, living with her jobless, worthless husband in a trailer somewhere in Manitoba with a string of children. The thought of handing over her child to her was so bizarre that it made her snort. 'I know I couldn't give my baby to Susan for anything,' she declared, removing her hand from his temple and placing it on her belly.

'You don't know, you can't say – what may happen, what things one may do—'

'*Of course* I know,' she said, more loudly. 'Nothing, no one, could make me do that. Give my baby away?' Her voice became shrill and he turned on his side, closing his eyes to show her he did not wish to continue the conversation.

She understood that gesture but she persisted. 'But didn't they ever fight? Or disagree about the way you were brought up? Didn't they have different ideas of how to do that? You know, I've told Susan—'

He sighed again. 'It was not like that. They understood each other. Ma looked after me – she cooked for me and fed me, made me sit down on a mat and sat in front of me and fed me with her own hands. And what a cook she is! Beth, you'll love—' he broke off, knowing he was going too far, growing foolish now. 'And Masi,' he recovered himself, 'she took me by the hand to school. In the evening, she lit the lamp and made me show her my books. She helped me with my lessons – and I think learned with me. She is a reader, Beth, like you,' he was able to say with greater confidence.

'But weren't they jealous of each other – of one for cooking for you and feeding you, and the other for sharing your lessons? Each was doing what the other didn't, after all.'

He caught her hand, on the coverlet, to stop her talking. 'It wasn't like that,' he said again, and wished she would be silent so he could remember for himself that brick-walled courtyard in the village, the pump gushing out the sweet water from the tube well, the sounds of cattle stirring in the sheaves of fodder in the sheds, the can of frothing milk the dairyman brought to the door, the low earthen stove over which his mother – his aunt – stirred a pan in the smoky dimness of dawn, making him tea. The pigeons in the rafters, cooing, a feather drifting down –

'Well, I suppose I'll be seeing them both, then – and I'll find out for myself,' Beth said, a bit grimly, and snapped off the light.

'Never heard of anything so daft,' pronounced her mother, pouring out a cup of coffee for Beth who sat at her kitchen table with her elbows on its plastic cover and her chin cupped in her hands. Doris was still in her housecoat and slippers, going about her morning in the sunlit kitchen. Beth had come early.

When Beth did not reply, Doris planted her hands on the table and stared into her brooding face. 'Well, isn't it?' she demanded. 'Whoever heard of such a thing? Rakesh having two mothers! Why ever didn't he tell us before?'

'He told me about them both of course,' Beth flared up, and began to stir her coffee. 'He talked of them as his mother and aunt. I knew they were both widows, lived together, that's all.'

Doris looked as if she had plenty more to say on the subject than that. She tightened the belt around her red-striped housecoat and sat down squarely across from Beth. 'Looks as if he never told you who his mother was though, or his father. The real ones, I mean. I call that peculiar, Beth, pec-u-liar!'

Beth stirred resentfully. 'I s'pose he hardly thinks of it that way – he was a baby when it happened. He says he grew up just accepting it. They *love* each other, he said.'

Doris scratched at her head with one hand, rattled the coffee cup in its saucer with the other. 'Two sisters loving each other – that much? That's what's so daft – who in her right mind would give away her baby to her sister just like that? I mean, would you hand yours over to Susan? And would Susan take it? I mean, as if it were a birthday present!'

'Oh, Mum!'

'Now you've spilt your coffee! Wait, I'll get a sponge. Don't get up. You're getting big, girl. You OK? You mustn't mind me.'

'I'm OK, Mum, but now I'm going to have two women visiting. Rakesh's mum would be one thing, but two of 'em together – I don't know.'

'That's what I say,' Doris added quickly. 'And all that expense – why's he sending them tickets? I thought they had money: he keeps talking about that farm as if they were landlords—'

'Oh, that's where he grew up, Mum. They sold it long ago – that's what paid for his education at McGill, you know. That costs.'

'What – it cost them the whole farm? He's always talking about how big it was—'

'They sold it a bit at a time. They helped pay for our house, too, and then set up his practice.'

'Hmm,' said Doris, as she shook a cigarette out of a packet and put it in her mouth.

'Oh, Mum, I can't stand smoke now! It makes me nauseous – you know that—' Beth protested.

'Sorry, love,' Doris said, and laid down the matchbox she had picked up but with the cigarette still between her lips. 'I'm just worried about you – dealing with two Indian women – in your condition—'

'I guess they know about babies,' Beth said hopefully.

'But do they know about Canada?' Doris came back smartly, as one who had learnt. 'And about the Canadian *winter*?'

They thought they did – from Rakesh's dutiful, although not very informative, letters over the years. After Rakesh had graduated from the local college, it was Asha who insisted he go abroad 'for further studies'. Anu would not have had the courage to suggest it, and had no money of her own to spend, but here was another instance of her sister's courage and boldness. Asha had seen all the bright young people of the village leave and told Anu, 'He' – meaning her late husband – 'wanted Rakesh to study abroad. "We will give him the best education," he had said, so I am only doing what he told me to.' She tucked her widow's white chunni behind her ears and lifted her chin, looking proud. When Anu raised the matter of expense, she waved her hand – so competent at raising the boy, at running the farm, and now at handling the accounts. 'We will sell some of the land. Where is the need for so much? Rakesh will never be a farmer,' she said. So Rakesh began to apply to foreign universities, and although his two mothers felt tightness in their chests at the prospect of his leaving them, they also swelled with pride to think he might do so, the first in the family to leave the country 'for further studies'. When he had completed his studies – the two women selling off bits and pieces of the land to pay for them till there was nothing left but the old farmhouse – he wrote to tell them he had been offered jobs by several firms. They wiped their eyes with the corners of their chunnis, weeping for joy at his success and the sorrowful knowledge that he would not come back. Instead, they received letters about his achievements: his salary, his promotion, and with it the apartment in the city, then his own office and practice, photographs accompanying each as proof.

Then, one day, the photograph that left them speechless: it showed him standing with his arm around a girl, a blonde girl, at an office party. She was smiling. She had fair hair cut short and wore a green hairband and a green dress. Rakesh was beaming.

He had grown rather fat, his stomach bulging out of a striped shirt, above a leather belt with a big buckle. He was also rather bald. The girl looked small and slim and young beside him. Rakesh did not tell them how old she was, what family she came from, what schooling she had had, when was the wedding, should they come, and other such particulars of importance to them. Rakesh, when he wrote, managed to avoid almost all such particulars, mentioning only that the wedding would be small, merely an official matter of registration at the town hall, they need not trouble to come – as they had ventured to suggest.

They were hurt. They tried to hide it from their neighbours as they went around with boxes of tinsel-spread sweets as gifts to celebrate the far-off occasion. So when the letter arrived announcing Beth's punctual pregnancy and the impending birth, they did not again make the mistake of tactful enquiries: Anu's letter stated with unaccustomed boldness their intention to travel to Canada and see their grandchild for themselves. That was her term – 'our grandchild'.

Yet it was with the greatest trepidation that they set out on this adventure. Everyone in the village was encouraging and supportive. Many of them had flown to the US, to Canada, to England, to visit their children abroad. It had become almost commonplace for the families to travel to New Delhi, catch a plane and fly off to some distant continent, bearing bundles and boxes full of the favourite pickles, chutneys and sweets of their far-flung progeny. Stories abounded of these goodies being confiscated on arrival at the airports, taken away by indignant customs officers to be burnt: 'He asked me, "What is *this*? What is *this*?" He had never seen mango pickle before, can you believe?' 'He didn't know what is betel nut! "Beetle? You are bringing in an insect?" he asked!' – and of being stranded at airports by great blizzards or lightning strikes by airline staff – 'We were lucky we had taken our bedroll and could spread out on the floor and sleep' – and of course they vied with each other with reports of their sons' and daughters' palatial mansions, immense cars, stocked refrigerators, prodigies of shopping in the most extensive of department stores. They brought back with them electrical appliances, cosmetics, watches, these symbols of what was 'foreign'.

The two mothers had taken no part in this, saying, 'We can get those here too,' and contenting themselves by passing around the latest photographs of Rakesh and his wife and their home in Toronto. Now that they too were to join this great adventure, they became nervous – even Asha did. Young, travelled daughters and granddaughters of old friends came around to reassure them: 'Auntie, it is not difficult at all! Just buy a ticket at the booth, put it in the slot, and step into the subway. It will take you where you like,' or 'Over there you won't need kerosene or coal for the stove, Auntie. You have only to switch on the stove, it will light by itself,' or 'You won't need to wash your clothes, Auntie. They have machines, you put everything in, with soap, it washes by itself.' The two women wondered if these self-confident youngsters were pulling their legs: they were not reassured. Every piece of information, meant to help, threw them into greater agitation. They were convinced they would be swallowed up by the subway if they went out, or electrocuted at home if they stayed in. By the time the day of their departure came around, they were feverish with anxiety and sleeplessness. Anu would gladly have abandoned the plan – but Asha reminded her that Rakesh had sent them tickets, his first present to them after leaving home, how could they refuse?

It was ten years since Rakesh had seen his mothers, and he had forgotten how thinly they tended to dress, how unequipped they might be. Beth's first impression of them as they came out of the immigration control area, wheeling a trolley between them with their luggage precariously balanced on it, was of their wisps of widows' white clothing – muslin, clearly – and slippers flapping at their feet. Rakesh was embarrassed by their skimpy apparel, Beth unexpectedly moved. She had always thought of them as having so much; now her reaction was: they have so little!

She took them to the stores at once to fit them out with over-coats, gloves, mufflers – and woollen socks. They drew the line at shoes: they had never worn shoes, could not fit their feet into them, insisting on wearing their sandals with thick socks instead. She brought them back barely able to totter out of the car and up the drive, weighed down as they were by great duffel coats that kept their arms lifted from their sides, with their hands fitted into huge gloves, and with their heads almost invisible under the wrappings of woollen mufflers. Under it all, their white cotton kameezes hung out like rags of their past, sadly.

When Doris came around to visit them, she brought along all the spare blankets she had in her apartment, presciently. 'Thought you'd be cold,' she told them. 'I went through the war in England, and I know what that's like, I can tell you. And it isn't half cold yet. Wait till it starts to snow.' They smiled eagerly, in polite anticipation.

While Beth and Doris bustled about, 'settling them in', Rakesh stood around, unexpectedly awkward and ill at ease. After the first ecstatic embrace and the deep breath of their lingering odour of the barnyard and woodsmoke and the old soft muslin of their clothing, their sparse hair, he felt himself in their way and didn't know quite what to do with himself or with them. It was Beth who made them tea and tested their English while Rakesh sat with his feet apart, cracking his knuckles and smiling somewhat vacantly.

At the table, it was different: his mothers unpacked all the foods they had brought along, tied up in small bundles or packed in small boxes, and coaxed him to eat, laughing as they remembered how he had pestered them for these as a child. To them, he was still that: a child, and now he ate, and a glistening look of remembrance covered his face like a film of oil on his fingers, but he also glanced sideways at Beth, guiltily, afraid of betraying any disloyalty to her. She wrinkled her nose slightly, put her hand on her belly and excused herself from eating on account of her pregnancy. They nodded sympathetically and promised to make special preparations for her.

On weekends, Beth insisted he take them out and show them the sights, and they dutifully allowed themselves to be led into his car, and then around museums, up radio towers and into department stores – but they tended to become carsick on these excursions, foot-weary in museums and confused in stores. They clearly preferred to stay in. That was painful, and the only way out of the boredom was to bring home videos and put them on. Then everyone could put their heads back and sleep, or pretend to sleep.

On weekdays, in desperation, Beth too took to switching on the television set, tuned to programmes she surmised were blandly innocent, and imagined they would sit together on the sofa and find amusement in the nature, travel and cooking programmes. Unfortunately, these had a way of changing when her back was turned and she would return to find them in a state of shock from watching a torrid sex scene or violent battle taking place before their affronted and disbelieving eyes. They sat side by side with their feet dangling and their eyes screwed up, munching on their dentures with fear at the popping of guns, the exploding of bombs and grunting of naked bodies. Their relief when she suggested a break for tea was palpable. Once in the kitchen, the kettle whistling shrilly, cups standing ready with the threads of tea bags dangling out of them, they seemed reluctant to leave the sanctuary. The kitchen was their great joy, once they had got used to the shiny enamel and chrome and up-to-date gadgetry. They became expert at punching the buttons of the microwave although they never learnt what items could and what could not be placed in it. To Rakesh's surprise it was Anu who seemed to comprehend the rules better, she who peered at any scrap of writing, trying to decipher some meaning. Together the two would open the refrigerator twenty times in one morning, never able to resist looking in at its crowded, illuminated shelves; that reassurance of food seemed to satisfy them on some deep level – their eyes gleamed and they closed the door on it gently, with a dreamy expression.

Still, the resources of the kitchen were not limitless. Beth found they had soon run through them, and the hours dragged for her, in the company of the two mothers. There were just so many times she could ask Doris to come over and relieve her, and just so many times she could invent errands that would allow them all to escape from the house so crowded with their hopes, expectations, confusion and disappointments. She knew Rakesh disappointed them. She watched them trying to recreate what he had always described to her as his most warmly close and intimate relationship, and invariably failing. The only way they knew to do this was to cook him the foods of his childhood – as best they could reproduce these in this strange land – or retail the gossip of the village, not realising he had forgotten the people they spoke of, had not the slightest interest in who had married whom, or sold land or bought cattle. He would give embarrassed laughs, glance at Beth in appeal, and find reasons to stay late at work. She was exasperated by his failure but also secretly relieved to see how completely he had transformed himself into a husband, a Canadian, and, guiltily, she too dragged out her increasingly frequent escapes – spending the afternoon at her mother's house, describing to a fascinated Doris the village ways of these foreign mothers, or meeting girlfriends for coffee, going to the library to read child-rearing manuals – then returning in a rush of concern for the two imprisoned women at home.

She had spent one afternoon at the library, deep in an old stuffed chair in an undisturbed corner she knew, reading – something she found she could not do at home where the two mothers would watch her as she read, intently, as if waiting to see where it would take her and when she would be done – when she became aware of the light fading, darkness filling the tall window under which she sat. When she looked up, she was startled to see flakes of snow drifting through the dark, minute as tiny bees flying in excited hordes. They flew faster and faster as she watched, and in no time they would grow larger, she knew. She closed the magazine hastily, replaced it on the rack, put on her beret and gloves, picked up her bag and went out to the car. She opened the door and got in clumsily; she was so large now it was difficult to fit behind the steering wheel.

The streets were very full, everyone hurrying home before the snowfall became heavier. Her windscreen wiper going furiously, Beth drove home carefully. The first snowfall generally had its element of surprise; something childish in her responded with excitement. But this time she could only think of how surprised the two mothers would be, how much more intense their confinement.

When she let herself into the house with her key, she could look straight down the hall to the kitchen, and there she saw them standing, at the window, looking out to see the snow collect on the twigs and branches of the bare cherry tree and the tiles of the garden shed and the top of the wooden fence outside. Their white cotton saris were wrapped about them like shawls, their two heads leant against each other as they peered out, speechlessly.

They did not hear her, they were so absorbed in the falling of the snow and the whitening of the stark scene on the other side of the glass pane. She shut the door silently, slipped into her bedroom and fetched the camera from where it lay on the closet shelf. Then she came out into the hall again and, standing there, took a photograph.

Later, when it was developed – together with the first pictures of the baby – she showed the mothers the print, and they put their hands to their mouths in astonishment. 'Why didn't you tell us?' they said. 'We didn't know – our backs were turned.' Beth wanted to tell them it didn't matter, it was their postures that expressed everything, but then they would have wanted to know what 'everything' was, and she found she did not want to explain, she did not want words to break the silent completeness of that small, still scene. It was as complete, and as fragile, after all, as a snow crystal.

*

The birth of the baby broke through it, of course. The sisters revived as if he were a reincarnation of Rakesh. They wanted to hold him, flat on the palms of their hands, or sit crosslegged on the sofa and rock him by pumping one knee up and down, and could not at all understand why Beth insisted they place him in his cot in a darkened bedroom instead. 'He has to learn to go to sleep by himself,' she told them when he cried and cried in protest and she refused to give them permission to snatch him up to their flat bosoms and console him.

They could not understand the rituals of baby care that Beth imposed – the regular feeding and sleeping times, the boiling and sterilizing of bottles and teats, the cans of formula and the use of disposable diapers. The first euphoria and excitement soon led to little nervous dissensions and explosions, then to dejection. Beth was too absorbed in her child to care.

The winter proved too hard, too long for the visitors. They began to fall ill, to grow listless, to show signs of depression and restlessness. Rakesh either did not notice or pretended not to, so that when Beth spoke of it one night in their bedroom, he asked if she were not 'overreacting', one of his favourite terms. 'Ask them, just ask them,' she retorted. 'How can I?' he replied. 'Can I say to them "D'you want to go home?" They'll think I want them to.' She flung her arms over her head in exasperation. 'Why can't you just talk to each other?' she asked.

She was restless too, eager to bring to an end a visit that had gone on too long. The two little old women were in her way, underfoot, as she hurried between cot and kitchen. She tried to throw them sympathetic smiles but knew they were more like grimaces. She often thought about the inexplicable relationship of these two women, how Masi, small, mousy Masi, had borne Rakesh and then given him over to Ma, her sister. What could have made her do that? How could she have? Thinking of her own baby, the way he filled her arms and fitted against her breast, Beth could not help but direct a piercing, perplexed stare at them. She knew she would not give up her baby for anything, anyone, certainly not to her sister Susan who was hardly capable of bringing up her own, and yet these two had lived their lives ruled by that one impulse, totally unnatural to her. They looked back at her, questioningly, sensing her hostility.

And eventually they asked Rakesh – very hesitantly, delicately, but clearly after having discussed the matter between themselves and having come to a joint decision. They wanted to go home. The baby had arrived safely, and Beth was on her feet again, very much so. And it was too much for her, they said, a strain. No, no, she had not said a thing, of course not, nothing like that, and nor had he, even inadvertently. They were happy – they had been happy – but now – and they coughed and coughed, in embarrassment as much as on account of the cold. And out of pity he cut short their fumbling explanations, and agreed to book their seats on a flight home. Yes, he and Beth would come and visit them, with the baby, as soon as he was old enough to travel.

This was the right thing to say. Their creased faces lifted up to him in gratitude. He might have spilt some water on wilting plants: they revived; they smiled; they began to shop for presents for everyone at home. They began to think of those at home, laugh in anticipation of seeing home again.

At the farewell in the airport – he took them there while Beth stayed at home with the baby, who had a cold – they cast their tender, grateful looks upon him again, then turned to wheel their trolley with its boxes and trunks away, full of gifts for family and neighbours. He watched as their shoulders, swathed in their white chunnis, and their bent white heads, turned away from him and disappeared. He lifted a fist to his eyes in an automatic gesture, then sighed with relief and headed for his car waiting in the grey snow.

At home, Beth had put the baby to sleep in his cot. She had cooked dinner, and on hearing Rakesh enter, she lit candles on the table, as though it were a celebration. He looked at her questioningly but she only smiled. She had cooked his favourite pasta.

He sat at the table and lifted his fork, trying to eat. Why, what was she celebrating? He found a small, annoying knot of resentment fastened onto the fork at her evident pleasure at being alone with him and her baby again. He kept the fork suspended to look at her, to demand if this were so, and then saw, over her shoulder, the refrigerator with its array of the photographs and memos she liked to tape to its white enamel surface. What caught his eye was the photograph she had newly taped to it – with the view of the white window, and the two widows in white, and the whirling snow.

He put down his forkful of pasta. 'Rakesh? Rakesh?' Beth asked a few times, then turned to look herself. Together they stared at the winterscape.

'Why?' he asked.

Beth shrugged. 'Let it be,' she said.

Diamond Dust:

A Tragedy

'That dog will kill me, kill me one day!' Mrs Das moaned, her hand pressed to her large, soft, deep bosom when Diamond leapt at the chop she had cooked and set on the table for Mr Das; or when Diamond dashed past her, bumping against her knees and making her collapse against the door when she was going to receive a parcel from the postman who stood there, shaking, as he fended off the black lightning hurled at him. 'Diamond! Why did you call him Diamond? He is Satan, a shaitan, a devil. Call him Devil instead,' Mrs Das cried as she washed and bandaged the ankle of a grandchild who had only run after a ball and had that shaitan snap his teeth over his small foot.

But to Mr Das, he was Diamond and had been Diamond ever since he had bought him, as a puppy of an indecipherable breed, blunt-faced, with his wet nose gleaming and paws flailing for action. Mr Das could not explain how he had come upon that name. Feebly, he would laugh when questioned by friends he met in the park at five o'clock in the morning when he took Diamond for a walk before leaving for the office, and say, 'Yes, yes, black diamond, you see, black diamond.' But when C. P. Biswas, baring his terribly stained yellow teeth in an unpleasant laugh, said, 'Ah, coal – then call him that, my dear fellow, coal, koyla – and we would all understand.'

Never. Never would Mr Das do such a thing to his Diamond. If his family and friends only knew what names he thought up for the puppy, for the dog, in secret, in private – he did not exactly blush but he did laugh to himself, a little sheepishly. And yet his eyes shone when he saw how Diamond's coat gleamed as he streaked across the park after a chipmunk, or when he greeted the dog on his return from work before greeting Mrs Das, his grandchildren, or anyone at all, with the joyful cry, 'Diamond, my friend!'

Mrs Das had had a premonition – had she not known Mr Das since she had been a fourteen-year-old bride, he a nineteen-year-old bridegroom? – when she saw him bring that puppy home, cuddling it in his old brown jumper, lowering his voice to a whisper and his step to a tiptoe, as if afraid of alarming the sleeping creature. 'Get some warm milk – don't heat it too much – just warm it a little – and get some cotton wool.' She had stared at him. 'Not even about our own children, not even your firstborn son, or your grandchildren, have you made so much of as of that dog,' she had told him then.

She repeated it, not once, or twice, or thrice, but at regular intervals throughout that shining stretch of Mr Das's life when Diamond evolved from a round, glossy cocoon into a trembling, faltering fat puppy that bent its weak legs and left puddles all over Mrs Das's clean, fresh floors, and then into an awkwardly – so lovably awkwardly – lumbering young dog that Mr Das led around on a leash across the dusty maidan of Bharti Nagar, delighting in the children who came up to admire the creature but politely fearful of those who begged, 'Uncle, let me hold him! Let me take him for a walk, Uncle!' Only in the Lodi Gardens did he dare slip Diamond off his leash for the joy of seeing him race across that lawn after chipmunks that scurried up trees, furiously chattering and whisking their tails in indignation while Diamond sat at the foot of the tree, whining, his eyes lustrous with desire. 'Diamond, Diamond,' Mr Das would call, and lumbering up to him, would fondle his head, his ears and murmur words of love to entice him away from the scolding creatures in the leaves.

But there were times when Mr Das went beyond that, times

that his friends and colleagues whom he met daily on their morning walks were astounded, if not scandalized, to witness, so much so that they could hardly speak of it to each other. Mr Das had so clearly taken leave of his senses, and it made them worry: how could a reputable government servant, a colleague, fall so low? They had caught him, as portly and stiff as any of them, romping ridiculously in a rose garden enclosed by crumbling, half-ruined walls that he had imagined hid him from view, chasing or letting himself be chased around the rose beds by a wild-with-excitement dog whose barks rent the peace of the morning park. They hardly knew how to tell him he was making a fool of himself. Instead, settling down on a bench in the shade of a neem tree and with a view of the Lodi tombs, watching parrots emerge from the alcoves and shoot up into the brilliant summer air, they discussed it between themselves gravely, and with distaste, as became their age and station – the decent, elderly civil servants with a life of service and sobriety behind them.

'There was that time Raman Kutty's grandchild was visiting him from Madras, and he would bring her to the park. He would even push the pram, like an ayah. During that visit, he couldn't speak of anything, or say anything but "Look, she has a new tooth," or "See her sucking her toe, so sweet." And that child, with its crossed eyes—'

'Tch, tch,' another reproved him for his ill-mannered outburst.

But the outburst was really occasioned by Mr Das, and the sight they had all had of him kicking up his heels like a frolicking goat in the rose garden, oblivious of the gardeners who sat on their haunches in the shade, smoking and keeping a vigilant eye on their rose beds.

'Look, here he comes with that wretched beast,' C. P. Biswas cried out. He was never in very good humour in the mornings; they all knew it had to do with his digestive system and its discomforts: they had often come upon him seated in the waiting room of the homeopath's clinic which was open to the marketplace and in full view of those who shopped there for their eggs and vegetables. 'I think he should be told. What do you say, should we tell him?'

'Tell him what, C. P.?' asked the mild-mannered A. P. Bose.

'That such behaviour is not at all becoming!' exclaimed C. P. Biswas. 'After all, a civil servant – serving in the Department of Mines and Minerals – what will people say?'

'Who?'

'Who? Look, there is the Under Secretary walking over there with his wife. What if he sees? Or the retired Joint Secretary who is doing his yoga exercises over there by the tank. You think they don't know him? He has to be told – we are here to remind him.'

Unfortunately Mr Das chose not to join them that morning. He walked smartly past them, hanging onto Diamond's leash and allowing Diamond to drag him forward at a pace more suited to a youth of twenty, and an athletic one at that. He merely waved at his friends, seeing them arranged in a row on the bench, and, clearly not intending to join their sedate company, disappeared behind a magnificent grove of bamboos that twittered madly with mynah birds.

C. P. Biswas was beginning to rumble and threaten to explode but A. P. Bose drew out the morning newspaper from his briefcase, unclasped the pen from his pocket and tactfully asked for help in completing the day's crossword puzzle.

Of course their disapproval was as nothing compared to that of Mrs Das who did not merely observe Mr Das's passion from a distance but was obliged to live with it. It was she who had to mop up the puddles from her gleaming floors when Diamond was a puppy, she who had to put up with the reek of dog in a home that had so far been aired and cleaned and sunned and swept and dusted till one could actually see the walls and floors thinning from the treatment to which they had been subjected. Her groans and exclamations as she swept up (or, rather, had the little servant girl sweep up) tufts of dog's hair from her rugs – and sometimes even her sofas and armchairs – were loud and rang with lament. Of course she refused to go to the butcher's shop for buffalo meat for the dog – she would not go near that stinking hellhole on the outskirts of the marketplace, and Mr Das had to brave its bloody, reeking, fly-coated territory himself, clutching a striped plastic bag close to him with one hand and pressing a thickly folded handkerchief to his nose with the other – but, still, she had to sacrifice one of her cooking pots to it, and tolerate the bubbling and frothing of the meat stew on the back burner of her stove. During the hour that it took, she would retreat to the veranda and sit there in a wicker chair, fanning herself with melodramatic flair.

'But do you want the dog to starve? Do you think a dog such as Diamond can be brought up on bread and milk?' Mr Das pleaded. 'How would he grow? How would he live?'

'Why not? I have heard even of tigers being fed on milk. It is true. Absolutely. Don't give me those looks, D. P. There was a yogi in Jubbulpore when I was a girl, he lived in a cave outside the city, with a pet tiger, and it was said he fed it only on milk. He brought it to town on festival days, I saw it with my own eyes. It was healthy, that milk-fed tiger, and as harmless as a kitten.'

'But I am not a yogi and Diamond is not a yogi's pet. What about that cat you had? Did it not kill sparrows and eat fish?'

'*My* cat was the cleanest creature this earth has ever known!' Mrs Das cried, holding the fan to her breast for a moment, in tribute to the deceased pet. 'Yes, she enjoyed a little fish from my plate – but she ate so neatly, so cleanly—'

'But fish, wasn't it? And sparrows? You see, an animal's nature cannot be changed simply because it is domesticated, Sheila. That tiger you speak of, it is quite possible that one day it turned upon the yogi and made a meal of him—'

'What are you saying?' Mrs Das cried, and began to flutter her fan again. 'That yogi lived to be a hundred years old!' And Mr Das went off, muttering disbelievingly, to dish out the meat stew for Diamond in an earthenware bowl in the courtyard and then carefully shut the kitchen door behind him so Diamond could not drag one of the bones into the house to chew on a rug as he very much liked to do and would do if not prevented.

The children of the neighbourhood were more appreciative, and properly admiring, than his wife, Mr Das felt as he walked Diamond past the small stucco villas set in their gardens of mango trees and oleander hedges, attracting flocks of them as he went. But he was not so besotted or blinded as to ignore the need always to have Diamond firmly secured on his leash when children were around. He was not unaware that once he had turned his back, or if they had come upon Diamond when he was not around, they were quite capable of arousing the dog to a frenzy by teasing him. 'We were only playing, Uncle!' they would cry reproachfully after Diamond had broken loose and chased them until they fell sprawling in the dust, or even nipped at their heels as they ran. 'That is *not* how to play with a dog,' he reproved them severely. 'You must *not* wave a stick at him. You must *not* pick up a stone. You must *not* run—'

'If we don't run, he'll bite, Uncle! See, he bit Ranu on her heel—'

'Nonsense,' he retorted, 'that's only a scratch,' and Mr Das walked quickly away, Diamond held closely, protectively, at his side.

That was in the days of Diamond's innocent youth. Diamond was only in training then for what was to come – his career as a full-fledged badmash, the terror of the neighbourhood. There followed a period when Diamond became the subject of scandal: the postman made a complaint. He had only to appear and Diamond would rear up on his hind legs, bellowing for blood. Nor was it just an empty threat, that bellowing: he had chased the poor man right across the maidan, making him drop his bag filled with mail as he raced for shelter from Diamond's slavering jaws and snapping teeth. The dog had actually torn a strip off his trouser leg, the trousers the postal service had given him for a uniform. How was he to explain it? Who was going to replace it? he demanded furiously, standing on the Das's veranda and displaying the tattered garment as proof.

Mr Das paid up. But even so, their mail was no longer inserted in the mailbox nailed to the door but flung into their hedge from afar. 'The dog is locked up, what harm can he do you through the door?' Mr Das pleaded after Mrs Das complained that she had found a letter from her daughter lying in the road outside, and only by luck had her eye caught Chini's handwriting. It was the letter that informed them of their son-in-law's recent promotion and transfer, too; what if it had been lost? 'That dog of yours,' said the postman, 'his voice heard through the door alone is enough to finish off a man,' and continued to use the hedge as a mailbox. Who knew how many more of Chini's delightful and comforting letters to her mother were lost and abandoned because of this? 'Is he a man or a mouse?' Mr Das fumed.

It was not only the postman Diamond detested and chased off his territory: it was anyone at all in uniform – officials of the board of electricity come to check the meter, telephone lines repairmen come to restore the line after a dust storm had disrupted it; even the garbage could not be collected from the Das's compound because it drove Diamond absolutely insane with rage to see the men in their khaki uniforms leap down from the truck and reach through the back gate for the garbage can to carry its contents off to their truck; he behaved as if the men were bandits, as if the family treasure was being looted. Charging at the gate, he would hurl himself against it, then rear up on his hind legs so he could look over it and bark at them with such hysteria that the noise rang through the entire neighbourhood. It was small comfort that 'No thief dare approach our house,' as Mr Das said proudly when anyone remarked on his dog's temper; they looked at him as if to say, 'Why talk of thieves, why not of innocent people doing their jobs who are being threatened by that beast?' Of course Mrs Das did say it.

Later, disgracefully, Diamond's phobia went so far as to cause him to chase children in their neat grey shorts and white shirts, their white frocks and red ties and white gym shoes as they made their way to school. That was the worst of all for Mr Das – the parents who climbed the steps to the Das's veranda, quivering with indignation, to report Diamond's attacks upon their young and tender offspring, so traumatized now by the dog that they feared to cross the maidan to the school bus stop without adult protection, and even had to be fetched from there in the afternoon when they returned.

'One day, Das, you will find the police following up on our complaints if you fail to pay attention to them. And then who can tell what they will do to your pet?' That was the large and intemperate Mr Singh, who could not tolerate even a mosquito to approach his curly-headed and darling baba.

Mr Das mopped his brow and sweated copiously in fear and shame. 'That will not happen,' he insisted. 'I can promise you Diamond will do nothing you can report to the police—'

'If he tears my child limb from limb, you think the police will not act, Das?' flared up the parent in a voice of doom.

The neighbours stopped short of actually making a report. It was – had been – a friendly, peaceful neighbourhood, after all, built for government officials of a certain cadre: all the men had their work in common, many were colleagues in the same ministries, and it would not do to have any enmity or public airing of personal quarrels. It was quite bad enough when their wives quarrelled or children or servants carried gossip from one household to another, but such things could not be allowed to get out of control. Propriety, decorum, standards of behaviour: these had to be maintained. If they failed, what would become of Bharti Nagar, of society?

Also, some of them were moved to a kind of pity. It was clear to them – as to Mr Das's friends in the Lodi Gardens – that he had taken leave of his senses where Diamond was concerned. When Diamond, in chase of a bitch in heat in the neighbouring locality, disappeared for five days one dreadful summer, and Mr Das was observed walking the dusty streets in the livid heat of June, hatless, abject, crying, 'Diamond! Diamond! Diamond!' over garden walls and down empty alleys, in the filthy outskirts of the marketplace, and even along the reeking canal where disease lurked and no sensible person strayed, they could only feel sorry for him. Even the children who had earlier taken up against Diamond – for very good reason, it should be added – came up to Mr Das as he stumbled along on his search mission, and offered, 'We'll help you, Uncle. We'll search for Diamond too, Uncle.' Unfortunately, when this band of juvenile detectives caught up with Diamond in the alley behind the Ambassador Hotel, they caught him in flagrante delicto and witnessed Mr Das's strenuous exertions to separate his pet from its partner, a poor, pale, pathetic creature who bore all the sorry marks of a rape victim. The children went home and reported it all to their families, in graphic detail. The parents' disapproval was so thick, and so stormy, it was weeks before the air cleared over Bharti Nagar. But it was nothing compared to the drama of Mrs Das's reaction: sari corner held over her nose, hand over her mouth, she stood up holding a rolled newspaper in her hand as weapon and refused to let the beast into the house till Mr Das had taken him around to the tap in the courtyard at the back, and washed, soaped, shampooed, rinsed, powdered, groomed and combed the creature into a semblance of a domestic pet.

Mr Das bought stronger chains and collars for Diamond, took greater care to tie him up in the courtyard and lock every door, but when the season came – and only Diamond could sniff it in the air, no one else could predict it – there was no holding him back. His strength was as the strength of a demon, and he broke free, ripping off his collar, wrenching his chain, leaping over walls, and disappeared. In a way, the neighbours were relieved – no longer was the night air rent by that hideous howling as of wolves on the trail of their prey, and also there was the secret hope that this time the brute would not be found and not return. They hardened their hearts against the pitiful sight of Mr Das limping through the dust in search of his Diamond, like some forlorn lover whose beloved has scorned him and departed with another, but who has not abandoned his bitter, desperate hope.

The Lodi Gardens clique, at the end of their brisk early morning walks round the park, seated themselves in a row on the bench in the shade of the big neem tree, and discussed Mr Das's disintegration.

'The other day I had occasion to visit him at his office. I intended to invite him to a meeting of the Bharti Nagar Durga Puja Association – and found him talking on the phone, and it was clear he was apologizing, whether for the lateness of some work done, or for mistakes made, I could not make out, but it was a nasty scene,' said C. P. Biswas.

'His superior is that nasty fellow, Krishnaswamy, and he is nasty to everyone in the department.'

'Maybe so, but when I questioned Das about it, he only held his head – and did not even answer my questions. He kept saying "Diamond is missing, I can't find Diamond." Now I did not say it, but the words that came to my mouth were: "Good riddance, Das, my congratulations."'

The apologist for Das clucked reprovingly, and commiseratingly, 'Tch, tch.'

But one day, at dawn, Mr Das reappeared, holding a thinner, sorrier Diamond at the end of a leash while his own face beamed as ruddily as the sun rising above the dome of the Lodi tomb. He waved at his colleagues sitting in the shade. Diamond slouched at his heels: his last escapade had clearly left him exhausted, even jaded.

'Ha!' remarked C. P. Biswas, crossing his arms over his chest. 'The prodigal has returned, I see. And is he repenting his misbehaviour?'

'Oh, he is so sorry, so sorry – he is making up for it in his own sweet way.' Mr Das beamed, bending to fondle the dog's drooping head. 'He cannot help himself, you know, but afterwards he feels so sorry, and then he is *so* good!'

'Yes, I see that,' C. P. Biswas said out of the corner of his mouth, 'and how long is that to last?'

But Mr Das preferred not to hear, instead busying himself by making the collar more comfortable around Diamond's neck. 'Now I must take him back and give him his bath before I go to work.'

'Good idea,' said C. P. Biswas, tucking his lips tightly over his yellow teeth.

Diamond, who had been badly bitten and probably thrashed or stoned in the course of his latest affair, seemed to have quietened down a bit; at least there was a fairly long spell of obedience, lethargy, comparative meekness. Mr Das felt somewhat concerned about his health, but seeing him slip vitamin pills down the dog's throat, Mrs Das grimaced. 'Now what? He is *too* quiet for you? You need to give him strength to go back to his badmashi?'

That, sadly, was what happened. By the time the cool evenings and the early dark of November came around, Diamond was clearly champing at the bit: his howls echoed through sleepy Bharti Nagar, and neighbours pulled their quilts over their heads and huddled into their pillows, trying to block out the abominable noise. Mrs Das complained of the way he rattled his chain as he paced up and down the enclosed courtyard, and once again the garbage collectors, the postmen, the electric and telephone linesmen were menaced and threatened. Only Mr Das worried, 'He's gone off his food. Look, he's left his dinner uneaten again.'

Inevitably the day came when he returned from work and was faced by an angrily triumphant Mrs Das bursting to tell him the news. 'Didn't I tell you that dog was planning badmashi again? When the gate was opened to let the gas man bring in the cylinder, your beloved pet knocked him down, jumped over his head and vanished!'

The nights were chilly. With a woollen cap pulled down over his ears, and his tight short jacket buttoned up, Mr Das did his rounds in the dark, calling hoarsely till his throat rasped. He felt he was coming down with the flu, but he would not give up, he would not leave Diamond to the dire fate Mrs Das daily prophesied for him. A kind of mist enveloped the city streets – whether it was due to the dust, the exhaust of tired, snarled traffic or the cold, one could not tell, but the trees and hedges loomed like phantoms, the street-lamps were hazy, he imagined he saw Diamond when there was no dog there, and he was filled with a foreboding he would not confess to Mrs Das who waited for him at home with cough mixture, hot water and another muffler. 'Give him up,' she counselled grimly. 'Give him up before this search kills you.'

But when tragedy struck, it did so in broad daylight, in the bright sunshine of a winter Sunday, and so there were many witnesses, many who saw the horrific event clearly, so clearly it could not be brushed aside as a nightmare. Mr Das was on the road back from Khan Market where he had gone to buy vegetables for Mrs Das, when the dog-catcher's van passed down the road with its howling, yelping catch of hounds peering out through the barred window. Of course Mr Das's head jerked back, his chin trembled with alertness, with apprehension, his eyes snapped with rage when he saw his pet enclosed there, wailing as he was being carried to his doom.

'Diamond! They will kill my Diamond!' passersby heard him shriek in a voice unrecognizably high and sharp, and they saw the small man in his tight brown coat, his woollen cap and muffler, dash down his market bag into the dust, and chase the van with a speed no one would have thought possible. He sprang at its retreating back, hanging there from the bars for a horrid moment, and, as the van first braked, then jerked forward again, fell, fell backwards, onto his back, so that his head struck the stones in the street, and he lay there, entirely still, making no sound or movement at all.

Behind the bars of the window receding into the distance, Diamond glittered like a dead coal, or a black star, in daylight's blaze.

Underground

In that small town, clustered around and above the bay, every third house was a boarding house, while hotels were strung out along the promenade, stolidly gloomy all through the year except in summer when wet bathing suits hung out over every window-sill and sunburnt children raced screaming across the strip of melting asphalt and onto the shining sands, magnetized by the glittering, slithering metal of summer seas. Sand dunes, dune grass, shells, streams trickling across the beach, creating gulleys, valleys and estuaries in exquisite miniature and shades of purple, sienna and puce. Boat sails, surf boards, waves, foam, debris and light. Fish and chips, ice-cream cones, bouncy castles, spades, striped windbreakers. 'Where can I pee-pee? I have to pee-pee!' 'Spot, come away! Come away, Spot!' 'I've cut my foot! Ooh, look, boo-ooh!' And a hinterland of blackberry bushes, rabbit warrens, golf links, hedged meadows, whitewashed, slate-roofed farmhouses – and the motorway flowing all summer with a droning, steady stream of holidaymakers baking in their beetle-backed cars.

The White House Hotel alone appeared to take no part in this summer bacchanal. Summer and winter, spring and autumn, it remained the same: an immaculate whitewashed cottage built of Cornish stone, with a slate roof, red geraniums in green windowboxes, and wrought-iron gates shut to the road. Not exactly the kind of place you hoped to find when you came to the seaside – it was not far from the sea, true, but had no view of it. Instead, it looked out onto the long, low hills, their green downs speckled with the white fluffballs of grazing sheep, in their hollows the kind of woods that sheltered streams, bluebells, yellow flags and dragonflies. Pretty enough, but not providing that sense of being at the seaside which was what you came to this little town for, a hellish drive in August.

Jack Higgins turned to his wife who had fallen silent and begun to take on a somewhat overbaked look. They had been imprisoned for far too long in that small, overheated car. 'What d'you think, Meg? Will it do?'

She shrugged her roasted shoulders under the thin straps of her yellow checked sun dress (it had looked very much crisper that morning when he had slipped his hands under those straps, heard them snap against her skin). 'It'll have to, won't it. There's no room anywhere else.'

That was true: they had already tried the hotels along the promenade, the houses clustered around the bay with their B & B signs. Every one had turned them away with the message: No Vacancy. It had taken them an hour to explore the possibilities and accept the inevitable.

'Can't we stop for a drink?' she had asked at regular intervals, like a querulous child, and as time wound on, it had turned to 'What about supper then? If we stopped for a bite, we could go further—'

But he had had enough of driving for the day. They had come a long way: it had been the hottest day of summer so far, and he would not tolerate another hour in that roasting oven of a car if he could help it. What he wanted was not a drink or a bite but a cool, shadowed room, a wash, a change and a rest. He knew that was what she needed too, even if she would not admit it.

So he compromised. He had pulled up outside a shop in town, hung about with rubber balls, flip-flops, spades and pails, and went in to enquire: in a town as small as this, surely everyone would know where there might still be a vacancy.

He was right: the woman selling fudge and postcards at the counter, once she had finished with the family demanding her attention and sent them off happily licking their lollies (four different flavours for four different children), asked, 'And what can I do for *you*, sir?' then launched into a description of every boarding house, bed-and-breakfast establishment and hotel in the vicinity. Jack could not see the point of so much information since every one, she assured him, was full. 'On a Sunday in August as hot as this, you get trippers by the *millions*,' she boasted, and watched him wilt and mop his neck with smiling satisfaction.

'So there's nothing? D'you think we might do better down the coast?' he queried bleakly, and found himself eyeing, with envy, a ginger-haired boy who materialized at his side, licking a lime-green ice.

Quite unexpectedly, and also eyeing the ginger-haired child and his dripping ice, though not with envy, she said, 'You might try the White House up the road that way. That's usually empty.'

'How far—?'

'Just round the corner, up from here, five minutes,' she said, and wiped her counter clean, defying the boy to touch it. He turned away but his place was taken by a group of young girls in tight, revealing jeans and doll-sized T-shirts. She gave them a testy look, her head waggling.

He wanted to ask her why she had not told him earlier of the one place that might be vacant, and how it was that a hotel so close to the coast could have a vacancy, but after opening his mouth he closed it again – two young girls with painted mouths and eyes were combing through a case containing lipsticks, and the woman loomed across to guard it.

He went out into the sizzling blaze of light reflected off the sea and sand to his car and wife, twisting the key chain around his finger.

Much as he yearned for the quiet and shade of exactly such a place in exactly such a green glade, he hesitated before turning into the driveway lined with neatly clipped conifers and evergreens. Slipping into the car park where the only other vehicle was a green Land-Rover, he turned off the engine rather thoughtfully before slipping out. 'Coming?' he asked his wife, bending in. 'Go and ask,' she told him sulkily, and it was clear this was not the kind of place *she* had had in mind.

Something made Jack run his hand over his hair, almost nervously smoothing it down, then glance down at his midriff to make sure his shirt was tucked in, before he crossed the car park and climbed the white stone steps between pots full of fuchsias to the front door. As he put his hand out to press the shining brass doorbell, he glanced upwards: something had caught his eye – the slight movement of a white muslin curtain upstairs. Someone had been holding it aside, watching him, and now let it drop.

Bob McTaggart turned away from the window, knowing he had been seen. He would have to go downstairs and open the door. He padded softly down the corridor, his footfall silenced by the grey carpeting. On either side of the corridor, doors stood shut. He glanced at each, at the number painted in blue on the central white panel, between the frosted glass ones: 4, 5, 6, 7. At the end of the corridor, on the landing, there was a small table with a bowl of dried flowers on it, and above it a mirror. He stood and stared at the reflection of the flowers in the mirror which had a blue frame decorated with sea shells. On its slippery surface, behind the solid form of the vase and the splayed stars of the papery flowers, there was a grey shape – his. He could only stare at the middle of it for so long, then he had to glance up, meet his own eye. Almost at once he glanced away, and went quickly down the stairs, to the corridor below. This was carpeted in blue, and its doors stood shut, too: 1, 2, 3. He passed them as if he were swimming by, with slow strokes of his legs, up to the front door. He felt the familiar response to the doorbell rising up his chest which was constricted, making air passage hard. He wanted to shout – and he was afraid he might – 'No! Go away! Go!' when he opened the door.

He stood with his hand on the doorknob – wooden, smooth,

sensible – fighting back those words as he had done the first time they had had guests come looking for a room. He had just brought Helen back from the clinic that day, where she had had her check-up. He had been putting her to bed, filling a hot-water bottle, fetching her an extra blanket – warm as the night was, she was shivering – when a car turned in at the gate: it was a family of holidaymakers, the first ones of their first season as managers of the White House Hotel. Exactly what they had prepared for and waited for, and now there they were: the children hugging their bedtime dolls and blankets, the parents large and hopeful on the doorstep, impossible to turn away. He had been obliged to get a key from the office, open one of the shut doors into a pristine room for which Helen had chosen the curtains, the counterpane, the ruffles. The children bounded onto the bed, trying out its springs. The father wondered if anyone would give him a hand with the luggage, and the mother asked for a meal. He was flustered, he needed Helen, and she was lying in their room, on the other side of the living room, waiting for the hot-water bottle and the blanket he had promised her. But he needed to calm these people first, stop their invading the house any further. He thought that if he fed them, they would go away, retreat into their room, shut the door and leave him alone.

In the kitchen he bumped into tables and counters while opening cupboards, taking out bread, eggs, ham, cans of baked beans. He cut his finger on the can, blood ran into the tomato sauce as in a manic comedy show. He wiped both onto the clean teatowels. He and Helen had meant to take cooking lessons together: they had seen an advertisement, and enrolled – but there hadn't been time, and now all he could do was toast some bread, put baked beans on the toast, eggs in hot water, and he was failing.

While the toast burnt, the baked beans bubbled, sizzled and then subsided into a black crust in the pot, eggs split and oozed their gelid whites into the boiling water, he was reminded of the night when he had been the invader, the stranger, in another scene of confusion, chaos – strangely attractive – the night *he* had arrived in some desert outpost in Iraq where he was to spend three months, installing pipelines.

His firm had only just won the contract and he was the first to be sent out. They had told him there was an hotel near the airport where he was to stay till they built accommodation for all the engineers who were to follow. The airport had turned out to be a strip of tarmac laid across the sand which was quickly reclaiming it even as the small plane taxied down towards the long low barracks – he looked out to see it scurrying in busy wisps to overlay it. A windsock flapped in the hot white wind like a domestic flag. A man in orange overalls stood waving his two small flags at the pilot, a chequered scarf draped around his head and mouth. With a marvellous dramatic note, the sun, as orange as his clothing, but spherical and not oblong, was setting in a haze that surrounded him forebodingly.

In the barracks the Iraqi liaison officer met him with gold-toothed enthusiasm and insisted on carrying his bag, expressing surprise at its lightness and singleness, he could not tell with what sincerity. Tossing it into the jeep that waited outside, he had taken Bob McTaggart across what seemed an immense parking lot, already overlaid by the blowing sand, to another barracks, half-buried under the grains that had whirled through the air.

That was the hotel – hostel – whatever one might call it. It was clear it had few guests, if any. In fact, the doors stood open and its lobby was deserted as though, newly constructed as it might be, it was already abandoned. The manager, who was eventually summoned from some region beyond, led him down a corridor to his room. On either side there were metal doors, shut, numbers painted on them: 1, 2, 3 and so on. McTaggart pleaded travel fatigue as an excuse to decline the liaison officer's invitation to an evening's entertainment, then looked through the door opened for him and saw that although there was a wooden bedstead in the room allotted him, it was hardly prepared to receive a guest: the mattress had no sheets to cover it, only a blanket that looked like army surplus. A single unshaded light bulb hung from a cord to which flies had adhered themselves as though it were a candystick. On the discoloured wall a gecko clucked its displeasure at this intrusion. In the bathroom there was a plastic bucket and a tap but no drop of water. Yet the cistern above the toilet was stained with rust. At least it stank of hygiene – lysol, or phenyle, in quantities.

As darkness closed in, mosquitoes sailed in through the windows unimpeded because, although they were covered with wire gauze, the frames had wide cracks. He spent the evening lying on the mattress, trying to read the thriller he had bought at the airport for the trip. Then suddenly the generator stopped grinding – he had not even been aware that there was a generator till it did so – and the light went out, darkness whipped across like a blindfold. He wondered how he would get through that night: it promised to be very, very long.

Then, in no time at all – or so it seemed – the dark thinned into grey and the uncurtained window framed a new day, pale with sand. He was cold. He sat up and lifted the blanket about his shoulders. His mouth was dry, his throat scratched, and he felt he could not do without some hot water. He must get some hot water. None came from the tap so he went out into the corridor, huddled in his blanket, searching for the manager to help. The barracks – hotel, hostel – was as empty as the night before. McTaggart blundered into what was clearly meant to be a dining room – it had tables covered with tablecloths on which flies clustered and crowded, and chairs with red Rexine seats. The only sign that meals had ever been served here were the plastic salt cellars, the bottles of ketchup, and the stains on the once-white cloths to which the flies adhered.

Seeing a swing door at the far end, he went out through it and found himself on a veranda looking across at a cluster of outhouses. They had to be inhabited: he saw a curl of smoke rise from a small fire. Standing there in the half-light, wrapped in his blanket, he could make out figures huddled around it. Eventually the fire flared up – it was just made of a few sticks in a tin bucket – and he saw by its light a woman who had slipped off her bodice from one shoulder and was nursing an infant at her breast. Beside her a man squatted with his head thrown back and his teeth bared in laughter as he clapped his hands: a small girl was dancing before them, in a red dress too long for her so that its waist hugged her knees and its hem swung at her feet, while her curls tumbled about her face and she struck her bare feet on the earth, swaying her small hips to the rhythm of her father's clapping.

He stared at them: the woman with her bosom bared for the infant wrapped in her shawl, the man's teeth and moustache and lips and eyes that glittered with laughter and love, and the small girl, her legs, feet and curls swinging to inaudible music. Shrouded in the dust and dimness of day before dawn, intermittently and sporadically illuminated by the small flames shooting up from the bucket, they had about them a quality so fragile, so immaterial and implausible that it could have been a mirage, a dream – a dream he might have had, in fact, of how life should be, how it might be, if it were different, and closer to what he so passionately, in such a rush of overheated blood, wished it were.

'Hello!' he shouted.

The child ceased to dance, the woman hastily lowered her blouse, the man rose from his haunches in a flurry. Even the fire seemed to waver and go out. McTaggart, shocked at the dramatic effect his voice had had, wondered why he had shouted, why he had broken the fine glass pane of the mirage, and he wished he could withdraw, but the man was hurrying through the whirling dust towards him while the others in the tableau were receding into it. It was the manager, also huddled in a blanket, his face enquiring, and bewildered by the appearance of this intruder.

Suddenly angered, McTaggart demanded hot water, tea – chai, chai, he repeated, and heard his voice raised, loudly, like a caricature, a cartoon of a British colonial. And the manager's face, it became the other side of the colonial coin, confused, agitated, helpless in the face of these impossible demands, this infringement on his own life.

He remembered that moment now, that bubble of light in which those small figures had floated in the half-dark of dawn, his desire for it and his anger at it, the way he had shattered it with his voice, made all the fragments scatter and fly.

How strange, how very strange to find that he had changed places with them, so many years later, so far away, so inexplicably. He felt a sudden spasm grip his abdomen. He heaved with surprised laughter as he held his bleeding finger under the tap. He needed to tell Helen. Abandoning the ruined meal, he went into her room, and burst out, 'Helen, it's the damnedest thing – did I ever tell you – about that first time I ever went to—' and then saw her twisted to one side of her bed, her face contorted as she held back tears, and he stood stricken in the doorway.

Behind him, in the kitchen, the woman had appeared with a bottle of milk she wanted to warm for her baby, and shouted out, 'Hey, the toast's burning! Mister?'

The two notes of the doorbell sounded through the house again – two small brass apples falling and rolling. Having seen the movement at the window, Jack Higgins had decided to persist. The late afternoon sun slanted out of the western sky and sliced through the back of his neck. He mopped it, waiting with impatience and growing annoyance: he was going to get a room here, he insisted on having it, a cool room where he could wash and change and stretch out to rest, return Meg to a good temper before setting out to walk on the beach, find a pint of lager and some supper. He was not going to return to the car, to the road and the traffic, the heat and the lunacy of an August Sunday by the sea. His ear caught a sound – the brass bell-sounds had rolled up to an object, he heard a click – and he braced himself for the question he needed to ask, and the answer.

'Hello?' Bob McTaggart said, opening the door and wrinkling

his eyes at the glare of the August sun, the red burn of Jack's face, the push of his belly against the wilted shirt, ready to enter.

'Have you a room for the night, for my wife and myself? We want to stop a night before we go on down the coast tomorrow,' Jack said quickly, even forcing himself to smile. The man in the door looked far from welcoming. In fact he looked as if he did not expect guests at his hotel or invite them and was astonished by the sight of one. Odd. Odd bod. Maybe that was why the woman in the shop below had seemed to recommend him with such reluctance. He narrowed his eyes, waiting for the answer.

Bob McTaggart shook his head very slightly. 'I'm sorry, I have no room. Try the hotel up the road,' he said, and shut the door quietly.

There had never been time for those cooking lessons. The changes had all taken place so rapidly. Iraq, Nigeria, oil wells, installations, they had really occupied only a brief and negligible piece of his life, and receded as if blown back by the nuclear force of the news of her illness. When the smoke cleared, she had appeared out of it, pale and staggering, a victim, needing his attention, his entire, total attention. After the surgery, bringing her here to recover, he had felt the seams of his life, at first so drastically emptied by the news, filling out with his need of her, the comfort of her existence.

Perhaps that was why they had never made a success out of the White House Hotel: they hadn't really cared, couldn't really bother. They should have: they needed something to work out, to provide, when he threw up his job and brought her to the seaside, somehow believing they could flee the curse that had fallen upon them in the city. Like desperate refugees from the plague, they had also been pilgrims, voyaging in the belief that somewhere lay safety.

Could any place have seemed more of a haven, safe from wrath, than this sparkling inlet of sea, its tiny cottages like white pebbles clustered on the green clifftop, its innocent shops that sold ice cream and lollipops to holidaymakers, its fish and chip shops that filled twice a day unfailingly with the odour of their deep-fried fare? No sign of nightmare anywhere – no glare of lights, blank walls, beds like stretchers or pallets of torture, no gigantic machinery to swallow her out of sight, then return her drained of colour as of blood, exhausted, racked by nausea, only to have some nurse or doctor smile brightly across her corpse-like body and say, 'There you are! She's back!' as if summoning up a mother before her wailing child. He had not wailed, and Helen herself had said nothing, merely let him hold her hand and later, when she could, squeezed it.

At the end of that 'course of treatment', as it was called, he had made the decision, consulting her, of course, every step of the way. A new beginning in a new place. Somewhere quiet where they could pay attention to each other. What he meant was: pay attention solely to her, no distraction of going to work, catching trains, planes, going abroad. And after a few weeks in Mrs Bedford's B & B – Helen had not been able to resist that name, it made up for the lines of washing, the dishes in the sink, the sand on the floor – they had found the White House Hotel for sale. Although warned about its inauspicious lack of a sea view, they had bought it in the conviction that it would provide that shelter where they could be together and not be parted for a day or an hour. Its green hummocks of lawn, hedge, thickets and shade, its calm, its quiet, made it a kind of burrow for them to be safe in. In those early days when he needed to go and consult electricians and painters, or collect tiles or mirrors or carpeting, she had laughed at his reluctance to leave her. 'D'you think something would happen to me while you were away, *here*?' An unlikely setting for a nightmare, she had meant, but he had wanted to guard her, be certain that the illness could not approach her again, as if it were a crab scuttling sideways out of a crack between the rocks towards her.

He had not guarded her: he had failed to halt its approach, its invasion. There had been her pathetic attempts to hide it from him, to postpone the visit to the doctor and the clinic that confirmed its re-emergence; of course that had not lasted. Then she had tried to persuade him that people sometimes lived years in this condition – went into hospital, came back, had remissions; it was no more, she said, than a chronic cough, or asthma. She had gone on insisting that, while she shrivelled up on her bed into something smaller, more gaunt and emaciated by the day. Towards the end, not even a drive to the clifftop to look out at the sea was possible: they might as well not have been at the seaside.

Only one pleasure had been left and every evening he had carried her out onto the patio where their chairs stood side by side (those for hotel guests had simply been stacked and set aside along the wall). Settling her onto the wicker chaise longue, he had gone back to the kitchen for the bag of scraps, brought it out and sunk down beside her, holding her hand and not speaking. The blackbirds sang till it was dark. Down in the glen, the choughs circled over the elms till finally they sank down out of sight. Sometimes a fox cried. The sound of cars swishing by on the road dwindled and ceased. Sometimes there was a moon and sometimes a wisp of mist. They stayed very still, waiting, and then from the dark under the hedges around the lawn, the figures emerged, slipping along low on the grass, surreptitiously – dark, furry, with black bands drawn over their eyes as if convinced that these would provide camouflage. First the largest, heaviest, the one they felt to be the father, the patriarch of the set, and after him some that were smaller, more slender. Bob would empty out the bag of scraps a few feet away from the patio, on the grass, and they came sniffing delicately, hesitantly; but when they found the food there was a sudden tumble, a seething, a pushing aside and climbing over before they became engrossed in the eating, seeming to disregard the figures on the patio. Bob and Helen were not deceived; they knew they were being watched as keenly as they themselves watched, and sometimes one of them gave a shiver at the closeness of these dark, furtive creatures, the close sharing of the silent evening with the badgers.

Once Bob had almost spoken. Seeing two of them who had remained lower down in the garden, by the hedge, apparently playing games with each other, he had been on the verge of saying, 'What do you bet we'll see a whole brood of young ones in the spring?' and in time remembered the crassness, the cruelty of alluding to time, to the future, and he had bitten back the words.

There had been young ones in spring. The parents had brought them out to feed, moving disappointedly around the edge of the patio, sniffing. Bob had stood by the window indoors – it was cold, the nights frost-edged – and watched without moving. He could not bring himself to go to the kitchen and fetch them scraps. He had let them go hungry. Let them go and find the bugs and worms they live on, he'd thought, why should I feed them? What for?

Now he turned away from the door and walked down the tunnel of the corridor, its doors shut on either side. Going into the living room, he picked up and folded the newspaper that was lying on the table where he had thrown it earlier – *Cornish Panther Found to be Domestic Cat* read one headline – and tapped his cold, full pipe against an ashtray, then carried it into the kitchen to dispose of the ashes in the rubbish bin. The ticking of the clock was loud here, demanding to be looked at; he had always meant to change it for another, silent one. It was an authoritarian clock: telling him what to do, how to live. He probably couldn't do without it. He opened a cupboard, took out a loaf of bread, a tin of sardines. He placed slices of bread in the toaster, he fetched a can opener and opened the tin of sardines. Then he put all the ingredients together on a plate: they made a meal. He pulled up a chair to the kitchen table and sat down to eat. His eyes wandered restlessly across the table while he ate but there was nothing to meet his look: the blank face of the plate, the gleam of stove and refrigerator, all stationary, all featureless. He got up, went into the living room, fetched the newspaper and brought it back to the table, folding it neatly beside the plate so he could read while he ate: *Cornish Panther Found to be Domestic Cat.* He stared at the headline and the blurred grey photograph, stirring the crumbs on his plate for a long time. But eventually he had to rise from the table, wash the plate and stack it. Then he washed the sardine can before dropping it into the rubbish bin. He stood at the sink, vaguely aware that he had left something undone, and only after a long moment remembered he should have eaten some greens, that Helen would not have prepared a meal without some green ingredient. He considered washing some lettuce and eating that as an afterthought, but the prospect was so daunting he abandoned it.

Picking up the newspaper, he padded out to the living room again. Sinking into the chintz-covered armchair he waited for time to pass, looking out through the open door onto the patio where the garden sloped down into the glen. The summer evenings stretched so long, the daylight seemed never to fade, even after the sun was gone. For a while he wondered what he might do: mow the lawn, clip the hedges, trim the evergreens. Go into town and pick up some groceries. Or drive further out to a farm where he might get fresh eggs: that would be an outing, the kind of outing Helen enjoyed – small, trivial, undemanding. Just the sight of poppies blowing in the fields along the way, or the skylarks rising up above the meadows into the sky to trill, would give her enough pleasure to make it worthwhile. Then the fresh eggs would mean so much to her. 'We'll have a nice omelette for our supper,' she would say with the greatest satisfaction. To be satisfied with something so minor, so meaningless: how? He ought to have asked her, to have learnt himself. It was not enough to have observed and envied her that innocence. With shame he remembered how, in his earlier life, it had irritated him to come back from Iraq, from Jordan, to have seen all that he had seen, and then come home to find her so placid, so *limited* he had thought then – and now it seemed more than he could ever accomplish. The poppies might have been beetroots, the eggs might as well have come in a box from the supermarket for all he was concerned. How had they brought that peach-coloured fuzz of pleasure to her face, a suddenly light, girlish motion of delight in acceptance?

He had tried, when summer came around again. Collecting carrot tops, greens, scraps, whatever he had, he had gone out in the evenings and scattered it out on the grass with abrupt, bitter gestures. You might as well have it, then, was what he wanted to say. They'd come creeping up, glancing at him nervously, snatching at the pieces, scurrying off with them. Did they notice that Helen was not there, his mate? He disliked them for not noticing, not caring. But the habit remained. It was something to do.

So now he gathered a meal for them, and scattered it on the grass, then settled down on the patio with his pipe, to watch the blueness well out of the hollows of the hills and slowly swallow the brightness of the daytime meadows. The hedges along the sides of the lawn swelled with darkness. A blackbird sang and sang as if to pierce right through the walls of his heart, then stitch them shut again. But the song became gradually less intense, less fervent, watered down, and finally disappeared. The choughs had already settled and even their grumbling and scolding had subsided. He sank back, his pipe unlit, wondering if his visitors would come tonight. He was tired – tired of doing nothing at all all day – and wanted to go up to bed, read a few more pages of the detective novel he'd bought in town, go to sleep. But he did not rise, he stayed there, one of those moments when movement became totally impossible having come upon him. He could scarcely breathe, the effort was beyond him, and he felt a weakness flooding through him like dark, or rain. He felt himself dissolve, become one with the silent evening, having no existence apart from it.

Then the white bands of their fur started up out of the dark, and their movements stirred upon the still lawn. The big one was leading, as ever, slipping closer to the patio by the minute, till it came close enough for him to look the creature in the eye. 'Hey,

Brock,' he breathed out, the breath he had been holding back for so long that it hurt, as if his saviour had arrived. The creature paid no attention, its snout busy with a crust, but the slimmer, smaller one was slipping along through the dark and approached now. She came close enough to snatch at a bit of crust but, before she did, she too glanced in his direction, so secretively that the look could scarcely be discerned, and 'Hey, Helen,' he whispered, 'here, Helen.'

Having thrashed about for an hour, trying to sleep, Jack Higgins let out a groan of resignation, flung his arm over his head and pillow to touch Meg's head: the narrow bed made for a proximity that was far from comfortable on such a still, sticky night. Besides, the sounds of the revellers on the promenade below, screaming with laughter and curses, kicking beer cans along the pavement, made it seem like trying to get to sleep in a tube station. The window had to be left open to let in air and a street-lamp directly across from their window blasted the dark with its glare.

'Remember that odd bod in the White Hotel?' he asked Meg, who was yawning in frequent small gulps beside him.

'What was so odd about him?' she enquired, scratching at her neck and tossing her head about on the pillow.

'Bet that whole place was empty,' Jack murmured, 'and he wouldn't let us have a room. Now I wonder why.'

Meg did not seem to care. She jerked up her knees as if in anger. 'If that's so, he's got to be daft,' she said flatly, and resumed her scratching and yawning.

'Daft's right,' Jack Higgins sighed, thinking regretfully of that small green backwater, the shade of the tall elms across the lawn, touching the slates of the roof even in the blaze of afternoon. 'Daft as a—' and searching for the right word, he drifted into sleep.

The Man Who Saw Himself Drown

Paying off the taxi in the portico in front of the hotel, he went up the steps, nodded to the doorman, picked up his key at the desk where the receptionist was talking dreamily on the telephone, evidently to a friend not a customer, and took the small elevator up to the second floor. Letting himself into his room, he saw it had been cleaned during the day so that it looked uninhabited: everything was put in its place, out of sight, and the bedcover had been stretched over the bed and smoothed immaculately. He tossed his briefcase into the armchair – there, now the room knew someone had entered it and made it his own – and went into the bathroom to wash. It was what he had looked forward to all through the long drive from the business centre to the hotel. In the creaking old taxi with its seats slick with usage, going through streets where people and traffic pressed in from both sides, and from front and behind too, so that he felt they were being carried forward by it. All the grime and soot of the city had seeped in at the windows and under his clothes, filling in every crevice and fissure of his body. Now he luxuriated in soaping his hands and face and then washing off the suds and splashing his ears and neck as well. 'Ahh,' he sighed, wiping himself with a clean, rough towel. Ahh, now he was himself again.

He went back into the room, drew aside the curtains and opened the door which led to a veranda. Here there were wicker chairs and potted palms lined up against the white wall, and he chose one under a slowly revolving fan. Lowering himself into it, he uttered another 'Ahh'. But immediately he realized that he lacked something and had to get up and go back to the room to ring the reception desk and ask for a bottle of beer to be sent up. Then he went out onto the veranda again and settled down to wait.

He spent the evening on that veranda, drinking the cold beer that was brought to him on a tray. Gradually it grew dark. Small bats began to skim through the veranda and out into the garden that lay below, the crowns of trees filling it first with shadows, then with darkness. Small electric lights were strung from one to the next; these came on like buds opening all at once. He could see some of the hotel guests sitting in their light with drinks. Music was being played, but softly, unobtrusively, as he liked it.

When his business associate telephoned to invite him out to dinner, he made an excuse: he was very tired, he wanted to go to bed early in order to be rested and ready for the meeting tomorrow. Actually, he could not stand the thought of spending the evening in the company of the man who had been annoying him and irritating him all day. Although it might have helped to discuss their business privately over a meal before going to the meeting tomorrow, he could summon no interest in it at all: it seemed no more important to him than anything he had been doing for the last twenty-five years. He would go through the motions tomorrow but he could not pretend that he thought it important enough for him to give up an evening like this. He sipped his beer, ate the sandwiches and potato chips they had brought him when he decided not to go out to dinner, and contentedly watched the lights bob and sway in the pool of darkness below the veranda.

What he found he could not do was go to bed and fall asleep early, after an evening so relaxing and calm. He was not sleepy at all, in spite of the long, frustrating day at work. He was, instead, totally relaxed but wide awake. So he decided to go for a stroll, although the evening was warm and humid, telling himself a little fresh air would help to make him sleepy. Besides, he might as well take a look at some other part of the city before returning home tomorrow night.

The hotel was in the residential district, not the business quarter of the city. In fact, it had once been a private residence – a large villa, with a garden – and essentially had remained itself. So the street outside was as streets are in such an area: lined with trees, the lamps dim, few passersby and little traffic. The houses showed their lights through screens of trees, and over high walls. He whistled as he walked down those streets because he felt so calm and at peace.

Then he came to a great avenue where many lines of traffic moved. Here neon lights flashed, the cars' headlights beamed, and there was both noise and confusion. He waited on the pavement for the traffic lights to change, then crossed the avenue and found himself on the edge of a great park in which dark trees loomed as well as the pale bulbous shapes of the monuments for which this city was known. He had seen them by daylight, driving past, but they had seemed tourist sights then, both intimidating and slightly disappointing. Now at night, in the dark, they appeared more intimate, closer to him and his life. Again, he felt a happy calm and whistled, although he was also growing a little tired and his feet moved slowly over the dry grass. Sometimes someone would appear out of the shadows at his side, hiss at him, 'Psst! Psst!' and make suggestions or threats. He strode past them, refusing to stop and listen or be turned back by fear.

In this way he came to another avenue, also wide but with less traffic. The big lamps blazed on what was mostly empty tarmac. He crossed it easily and found it was lined on one side with boats, and that he had come to the bank of the tidal river that flowed through this city and that the tide was running high. A breeze sprang up, salt and sticky because it came from the sea but also murky and swampy because it was the delta. The sails of some big, flat-bottomed boats flapped with heavy, dull thuds against their masts. Small lamps burnt on decks, here and there, the wind making their reflections shiver in long snakes across the water.

He walked along and now his calm was ruffled by a sensation of adventure, of both fear and delight. Seeing the water glint, the waves heave, the boats lift and sink, he had a mad idea: what if he stepped onto the deck of one, untied its ropes and let the boat carry him up the river! It was ridiculous, at his age, to have this boyish, this childish urge, and he almost laughed out loud. He even clambered up onto the bank, looked at the distance between it and the deck, trying to gauge the length of a jump. His body impelled him forward but at the same time he threw himself backward to avoid the jump and the fall. He lost his balance for a moment, then righted himself, looking around to see if anyone had observed him. No, there was no one and he walked on, rapidly.

But he had to slow down and halt soon enough because a little further up, where there were broad steps leading down to the water, a group of people had gathered. From their attitudes and gestures, he could see they were agitated – they were crowding around something that one or two of them were dragging out of the water onto the bank. Water gushed from the object they lifted and from the men who raised it, and everyone was drenched. But they crowded around and called out in high, excited voices.

He didn't want to see, or hear. It was evidently a drama, and a moment ago drama was what he had longed for, but now he shrank back, ready to turn – he did not want to be drawn in. A shrinking and dwindling of his former urge overtook him, and he wished miserably that he had stayed back at the hotel, on the veranda, safely drinking beer.

But he had been seen. One of the people, a young man, called out, 'Police? Police? Will you go for the police?' Another, of a practical nature, shouted, 'Do you have a car? Can you take—?'

First he shook his head. Then he said 'No!' very loudly, 'No, no,' and thought of turning around and hurrying away. Just then the men who had lifted the drenched, streaming object from the river pressed past him as they laid it on the bank. He found himself, along with the others, in a circle around it, standing over it and peering down.

The body lying in the mud on the bank was of course sodden, and water ran from it in streams, but it could not have been in the water long, it was intact, and what I saw was a man five-feet ten-inches tall, with straight black hair that the river had swept off his face, a face that was square and brown, that had a cleft in its chin, a somewhat flat nose, and a mouth that parted slightly to show his teeth. Although it was dark, I could make out that the man wore a short-sleeved white shirt and the pants were of khaki material – that is, not very dark but not white either. He had taken off his shoes for some reason but still wore socks. The socks might have been green or black, I could not tell in the dark and the wet.

I stared at him, taking in every detail. Then I stared again, harder, and more details came into focus: the Tissot watch with the metal strap, the ball-point pen still attached to the shirt pocket. The face with the hair swept away from it, the flattened cheekbones, the cleft in the chin, the eyebrows black and heavy, the teeth uneven, crowding each other here, parted from each other there, and the glint of a filling. Every detail, in every detail, he was myself: I was looking at myself – after having spent half an hour, or an hour, underwater, sodden with river and mud – but it was I, in every detail, I. It was as though I was lying full-length, suspended in mid-air, and gazing down at my reflection below, soaked and muddy, but myself, I, after an accident in the river.

I do not know for how long I stared. But gradually I became aware that I was alone in standing stock-still, staring, that the others were all talking, hurrying away and hurrying back, bending over the man, touching him, and talking to each other in rough, rapid voices. Police, doctor, telephone, call . . . I heard these words, and then I saw them bend down and lift him up, three or four men putting their arms under and around the corpse, and together they hurried down the bank towards the lighted road. I did not follow them but stood on the bank and watched as they carried it away, shouting to each other in the dark.

It was only when they managed to stop a vehicle – or perhaps they had summoned it and it stopped deliberately – and lifted the body into it that I became seized by agitation. Just as I had felt a few moments ago when I contemplated leaping onto the deck of a boat, now one part of me felt impelled to run after them, and plead to be allowed to go with the body – my body – and another part of me held back, pulled back with violence in fact, and once again I stumbled because I had made a clumsy, lurching movement, although whether forwards or backwards, I really cannot say. I think I may even have fallen on my knees at that moment; later I discovered the knees of my khaki pants were muddy, and that my hands were also dirty. By then I had walked away, in another direction. As I hurried along the lighted highway, I was in great confusion, wondering if I should have followed the body to the morgue and claimed it, or whether I was right to flee from the scene.

I did find my way back to the hotel – I remembered the address clearly – and I did spend the night in the safety of my room and my bed. Next morning I might have dismissed the whole event as a nightmare – a delusion caused by the unfamiliar scene, the darkness, the solitude – but when I was brought my tea in in the morning, and a newspaper, I tried to divert my mind from the horror of the night by reading the news while I drank tea and ate toast.

I found myself skimming the pages, regardless of what news was printed there, searching for a particular item that would bear my name. When I found none, I repeated the whole procedure in case I had missed it the first time. I repeated the act more and more frenziedly, as if I had to confirm what I had seen. I sent away the maid who came to clean the room. I did not answer the telephone which rang and rang at regular intervals. I stayed in my room all day, too afraid to leave it. I could not say what it was I feared, but I found myself trembling. When I was exhausted, I slept, but never deeply – I kept waking, each time in a panic.

I am not sure how long I stayed in the hotel in this state, whether it was two days or three. It certainly was not longer before the newspaper that was brought to me, and that I went through in such a state of panic that I nearly choked, finally revealed the news I had all along expected – and feared – to find: there was my name printed halfway down the column on page 7 in the local news. Of course my name is not so singular that I imagine no one else could possess it – there must be many men who have both the very common first name and the last. But it went on to give my exact particulars – the firm for which I worked, my designation, the reason why I was in this city – and ended by saying I had been found in the river at midnight, drowned. That I 'left behind' a wife and two children in the city of X. That no foul play was suspected.

No foul play? Then what was this that was happening? I had been declared dead. I was here in the hotel room, washed, shaved, ready for work, and I was informed that I did not exist, that I had drowned in the river.

For some reason, at that instant I found this comic, grotesquely comic. I think I laughed – I felt the ripping sound erupt from my throat, I assume it was laughter. How does a man react to such news – the news that he is no more?

Again I was in such a state of agitation that I could not proceed. I was to attend a meeting that morning: that was my reason for being in the city. But if I was dead, if my death was reported, how then could I proceed with my life and keep appointments and attend meetings and continue as though nothing had happened? My colleagues and associates would be thunderstruck to see me, even horrified. How could I submit them to such an experience? Or myself submit to it?

While I pondered over the best course of action to take, I kept to the hotel room. The telephone did not ring. Then it struck me that someone might very well come down from the office to collect my belongings, perhaps to go through them in search of some telling evidence such as a suicide note (if 'no foul play' is suspected then suicide usually is), and this threw me into such agitation that I decided to flee the room. For a while I considered packing and taking my suitcase with me, but then I thought the matter over and decided it would make my disappearance even more suspicious. If I left my belongings where they were, at least the death by drowning would remain plausible. So I hurried away without a single piece of luggage.

I have always been a conscientious person and it was very hard for me to slip out of the hotel without paying the bill, but when I went down the stairs to the hall, I was afraid the receptionist might have read the paper and seen my name in it. If so, he would be terribly shocked at seeing me. On the other hand, since he had not come up to examine my room or clear it, it would seem he had not. However, if I were to stop and pay the bill, he would inform my business associates of the fact when they came, as inevitably they would. The only course open was for me to leave, and leave the bill unpaid. This caused me a considerable amount of disquiet which I had to suppress as I hurried out of the lobby and into the driveway. There was a taxi idling there and I could have stepped into it and so hastened my disappearance but I stopped myself with the thought: Where would I go?

Now I was truly perplexed. My previous life had ended, but did that mean I now had to construct a new one?

This is a hope, a fantasy many of us entertain in the course of our lives. What happiness, we think, to end the dull, wretched, routine-ridden, unfulfilling life we lead, and to begin on another – filled with all that our heart desires. Yes, but try to do that and you will find you are suddenly faced with hundreds of questions, no answers, doubts and no certainties. There is really no experience so perplexing. A new life – but what is it to be? And how to begin it?

I confess that I blundered around for the next few days – I no longer know how many – trying first one route, then another. Of course I considered escape; I knew it would be best to flee to another city, some part of the country where I knew no one, and no one would have heard of me or of my 'death'. But I found I simply could not embark on flight. A part of me was consumed by the desire to see what would happen now that I had 'died'. I even entertained the idea of going to my own funeral. It fascinated me to think I could stand beside a funeral pyre and watch my own body, my closest, most intimately known and familiar body, reduced to ash. In fact, it was the image that hovered before my eyes both in sleep and in waking. The only reason I did not follow this compulsion was the thought that I would be forced to see my family, who would naturally also be present, that my young son would come towards me with a torch to light the pyre, that I would have to witness his pain and my wife's sorrow . . . I knew I would not be able to control myself and remain 'dead' to them. Once when I was driving home, and had just turned in at the gate, I saw my son, then a small child, falling out of a swing that hung from a great tree, tumbling down into the dust. I leapt out of the car before it had even stopped moving – I simply sprang from it, abandoning it, in my rush to go to him and lift him in my arms and make sure he was not harmed. He was, slightly, and he was also to have several injuries later when he started playing cricket at school and bicycling and swimming, but that moment when he was so small and I saw him hurtling through the air into the dust like a bird was the moment that I felt our bond most intensely. Now that I was 'dead', were those bonds broken? Or would I become aware of them as soon as I was in another situation where they were tried?

I did not trust myself to have the nerves or the self-control required for such a bizarre experience, and so I stayed away, but all the time in a kind of anguish that made me clench and unclench my fists and often wipe the tears that streamed down my face. I could not even tell the exact cause of my anguish – was it for myself, the old self that had died, or was it for those I had been parted from and could not go to comfort?

I began to see that all of life was divided in two or into an infinite number of fragments, that nothing was whole, not even the strongest or purest feeling. As for the way before me, it multiplied before my eyes, the simplest question leading to a hundred possible answers.

This led me to blunder around in a state of still greater indecision. When the time came to an end that my body may have lain in a morgue, or possibly in my home in preparation for the funeral, and I knew – I cannot explain how, but I did with a certainty feel it within me – that I had been cremated and was no more, I was relieved. At least I ceased to see the scene of the cremation before my eyes in all its horrific detail – the smoke, the oils, the odours, the cries, the heat – and was able to put it behind me.

Yet I found I could not take the next step. I still felt caught, wrapped up in my life, my 'former' life as I needed now to think of it. It did not leave me free to think of what the next step might be. I was so absorbed in it that I can hardly provide any details of my existence at that time. I slept wherever I ended up – on a bench in the park, on a doorstep or a piece of sacking, or upon a sheet of newspaper. I ate whatever I could find; sometimes hunger made me see black and reel, sometimes I ate and was promptly sick. I know children followed me, laughing, down one street; on another, dogs barked and snapped their teeth at me ferociously and had watchmen come running out to chase me away. Somehow I escaped from them all, and mostly was left alone. Of course I must quickly have begun to look like a beggar, in just the one set of clothes in which I had walked away, and with next to nothing in my pockets.

It was in this state that I finally climbed onto a train – without a ticket for I could no longer afford one – and returned to the city where I had once had my home. By then I was reduced to a sorry state by being out in the sun and the rain, unwashed, mostly unfed. I felt, and possibly even looked, much as a lost dog does when it finally finds its way home, whipped, injured, frightened and hungry. Like that lost dog, I thought I would creep in at the gate of my house – I was still capable of such possessive thoughts – and go up the drive to the veranda, and I was certain, or at least ardently hoped, that my family would come out and find me, and treat me as they might a recovered pet, lavishing their attention and care upon me.

Somehow I did creep back to that gate, I did stand there by the hedge. I did look over it and see that the house was still standing, its verandas and doors and windows and roof, just as in the days when I had lived there myself. Even the tree by the portico – strange that I had never thought to learn its name – though it no longer had a swing dangling from its branches, was still large-leafed and shady, even if its fruit had never been edible except to the birds whose droppings spattered the driveway with white splashes and undigested seed.

So welcoming, so sheltering, yet I stayed out in the road, not even daring to touch the gate and unlatch it. The reason was that I saw many cars and people and much activity in that driveway and that portico. People were coming out of the house, carrying boxes, trunks, crates and cartons, and heaving them into a truck that stood waiting. After what must have been many hours, the truck rolled down the drive towards the gate. I made myself small against the hedge and watched as it drove away with the furniture and belongings with which I had filled my house. There was a moment when I thought of leaping onto the truck and going with my belongings to wherever they were being taken, but my body was much too weak for such acrobatic feats. Instead I huddled by the gate and watched as my wife – my wife! I called her that to myself, and yet the words already sounded strange now that I was no longer certain I possessed her and wondered how I could ever have imagined I did – came out of the house, dressed in white as a widow, with her parents on either side of her. They were all dressed in the colour of mourning. This distressed me greatly. I wished to run out and plead with them to change to bright colours once more. Had they forgotten how much I liked bright colours, had bought my wife clothes in every colour of the rainbow, and insisted my daughter wear reds and yellows and oranges? But here came the children behind them, carrying small boxes and baskets that contained, I felt sure, their most precious belongings. All of them came down the stairs to the portico where a grey car waited that I recognized as my father-in-law's. I watched them climb into it, and then there was a pause. Were they looking back at the house, saying goodbye to it? Or did they stop to think of me, whom they had last seen here? Then the car started up, quickly, with decorum, and smoothly rolled down the drive and came towards the gate.

Once again I pressed myself instinctively into the hedge. The last days that I had been through in the city had taught me to shrink, to make myself invisible, and so I did instead of springing out and standing there before them, in the middle of the road, and crying, 'Look, I am here! I have returned!' Neither the words nor the gestures came to me; it was as if they had been strangled inside me. How could I say them when they no longer rang true?

So the car passed by me, I crouched in the hedge, and none of those seated in the vehicle so much as turned their heads to glance at me. If only they had, surely those words, those gestures would have been wrung from me? Surely I would have cried out, at least to say, 'Please! Oh, please?'

As it happened, they did not. Not one of them turned to look back at the house they were leaving after so many years of occupation. Did they not feel any pang on departing? Their faces were all fixed, staring ahead as if into the future. Was that what concerned them – the future? Were they, perhaps, looking forward to it, eager for it?

And when I saw that, when I saw that they had a future, one that they looked forward to, or at least moved towards with resolution, I admit that I also felt, mixed with the bitterness of disappointment, a certain relief. It was as though I had at last shed them. My wife, my children, my house, they were all gone from me, and curiously, I did not feel bereft so much as lightened of my load.

The car disappeared down the road. Someone in a watchman's uniform came and locked the gate. The click of the latch reminded me the house was not mine, had in fact never been mine; it had belonged to the company for which I worked but no longer did. It was apparent they had asked my family to vacate it and move. And they had, to my wife's parents' home in another town. She belonged there, she was returning to it. She had been mine, my wife, for a stretch of time that now was over.

After a long time of sitting in a state of sorrow and exhaustion, I left my house and, not wanting to walk on the streets where I might meet neighbours or friends, I went by small back-streets that normally only servants and peddlers used, and came to the river that ran around the outskirts of the city. This was no wide, grand river as I had seen in the city where I died, but only a muddy, slimy trickle that ran through a wide sandy bed in which washermen spread out the clothes they washed, and alongside which stood a few straw-roofed shacks housing I had no idea whom. By then it was evening and I stayed on the bank and watched as the washermen folded up the washing, loaded it on the backs of small donkeys and led them away. Small fires were lit in the straw-roofed shacks which began to smoke in a dark, smothering drift. A child with a pot came down to the stones beside the river and filled it, then turned and wandered away.

By then it was growing dark and I felt it was safe for me to make my way down unobserved. I took off the shoes that somehow I had retained till now and left them in the grasses by the side of the road, then walked down and across the sand, which felt gritty to my feet, and came to the water. It looked more like a drain than a natural stream but I was in such need that I bent with cupped hands and scooped up some water to first wash my face, then splash some on my head and finally even to drink.

I could not have drowned myself in such a trickle if I had wanted to. That thought led me to wonder, as I stood up on the stones and stared into the murky opaqueness of the water, if that was what I wished: to drown this self that had remained, to drown the double of the self that had already died.

But that self, my other self, the self that had had a job and a wife and children and a home, that self was already gone. I wondered what it meant, that death of my mysterious double. It seemed to me that I had died with it; I was so convinced of this that I was not able to resume my life. But was that the only possible interpretation? Once again I felt my mind splinter into fragments that whirled wildly in some great vacuum, and one fragment that I seized upon as another possibility was this: could that death have meant that my double had died on my behalf, that his life was finished, freeing me, my new self, my second self, to go on with another life, a new life?

I searched in myself for an instinct, an urge that would provide the answer. Was it to be death, or life? I remembered how I had once stood on a river bank – in how different a condition, how different a state! – and considered leaping onto a boat and letting it carry me down the river and out to sea, but now I felt no impulse at all, not even one that needed to be confronted and stifled.

It seemed to me that by dying my double had not gifted me with possibility, only robbed me of all desire for one: by arriving at death, life had been closed to me. At his cremation, that was also reduced to ash.

Then I was filled with such despair that I sank onto my knees in the mud.

At daybreak the child with the pot returned to the river for water. What he saw made him stop and stare, first from the slope of the bank, then from closer up, the stones in the shallows. When he made out it was a man's body that lay in that trickle, face down, he dropped the pot on the stones in fright. Its clattering rang out so loud and clear, a flock of crows settling on the sands in curiosity took off in noisy flight.

The Artist's Life

When Polly returned from summer camp, there was still some time to go before school reopened. She took to slamming out of the house after breakfast and wandering barefoot into the backyard, disappearing behind the garage and the bean vines to where the old car tyre still hung on a rope from the maple tree. For years forgotten, its solaces were now to be rediscovered – the twirling herself round and round and then, when she had wound herself up to the point of strangulation, letting go and allowing herself to unwind in an accelerating spin; the dragging of a toe through the scrubby grass as she pushed herself moodily backwards and forwards; the contortions of her limbs into and around and about the reassuringly fissured and pulpy rubber to act out the contortions of the inarticulate mind. Then there was the great canopy of the maple drooping down over her and around her in its protective tent of green, and the sighings, stirrings and scamperings that went on softly and unobtrusively within it, and the shade, almost chill, it threw across the sticky yellow heat of the last August days. She hung, trailed, twirled and rocked within it, her eyes narrowed under a dusty fringe.

With those narrowed eyes she was gazing back into the remarkable fortnight of the summer camp. It made her push out her lower lip, clench her teeth as she remembered the bliss, so unexpected, so unlooked for, that came her way as if in search of her, Polly, its chosen recipient.

That summer, in the tedious summer camp beside the dully glittering, reed-edged lake in the north, Polly had been chosen the hand-maiden of Art. A red-haired young woman who wore

213

long, tie-dyed cotton shifts, and smiled cat-like through green eyes and moist lips, had chosen her.

Of course Polly had been introduced to Art as an infant. Of course the local school provided her – indiscriminately, as it did all children – with paint and clay and crayons, and she had made, as all children make, representations of her home and family – triangular-shaped father and mother holding hands, box-shaped brother in outsized shorts standing apart – as well as of daisies in a vase, and even a lopsided teacup or two, each of them intensely satisfying for a day or two, then desperately unsatisfying thereafter.

But what Miss Abigail at the camp introduced her to was Real Art: in her whispery, bubbly, disquieting voice she had urged them to 'paint your dreams – show me what you dreamt last night'. She had spaced the words, leaving great gaps for them to fill, and then sighed a replete sigh, as one might when overcome by swirls of incense or opium, when Polly presented a particularly lurid or mysterious painting – headless, shrouded figures in shades of purple appearing on the surface of a lake with large, many-pointed stars shining down on them out of a streaky sky, or purple pigeons swooping down out of a pink sky to light upon lilac roofs (Polly was very attached to the colour purple, and perhaps it was only a coincidence but that was the colour that dominated Miss Abigail's tie-dyed shifts too). For the sake of that narrowing of green cat's eyes, that slow exhalation of breath that spoke such volumes, and simply for the sake of staying close to that enchantingly incense-scented young woman with her flowing red hair and flowing purple dresses, Polly dedicated the summer to paint, letting others canoe, shoot arrows, roast marshmallows or run around working up a sweat like the damned and the demented.

She came home reluctantly, dazed into an uncharacteristic silence, with her paintings rolled up into an impressively long roll – Miss Abigail had insisted she always use large sheets of thick paper for her art. The family had been faintly surprised by what she spread out on the dining table for them; they turned to her with quizzical looks and remarks like 'Very nice, dear,' and 'Now what is *that* supposed to be?' making her roll them up again in offended exasperation, and carry them up to the attic where she spread them out along with all her painting equipment. She was determined to find herself a tie-dyed skirt, wear her hair loose, not in tight painful pigtails any more, and spend the rest of the summer drawing long strokes of purple and lilac paint across sheets of paper, humming the melancholy tunes Miss Abigail had hummed at the camp. 'And then my lover,' she moaned under her breath, 'left me a-lone . . .'

Unfortunately it was very, very hot under the attic roof, and in that thrumming heat of late August she would find her head spinning after a while. So much so that she was compelled to stretch out on a sheet of canvas and fall into a kind of stupor, struggling to keep her eyes open. Spiders descended from the rafters and spun their wavering webs, or dangled like aerial acrobats over her head. Seeing one unroll its lifeline and drop, cautiously and investigatively, closer and closer to the nest of her hair, she swatted at it, and upset a mug of water over a painting of a volcano spewing blood-red and orange paint. The water and paint seeped through several layers of paper, staining not only one but several other paintings as well.

That was when she descended the stairs, arms crossed over her chest, chin sunk, looking down at her bare feet, oppressed by the burden of being an artist. 'What's the matter, Polly?' her mother asked, 'Got a headache?' and her brother jumped out from behind a door, with a 'Yah-boo!' that made her drop her arms, jerk up her head, then stick out her tongue and scream 'You – *pig!*' or was it, her mother wondered, aghast, 'You – *pigs?*'

It was then that the maple's drooping August skirts and the rotting rubber tyre hanging from its branch became the only option for her during the remaining days of summer. It was then that she discovered she could sail through the green leaves and the yellow air and be the artist without having to go through the sticky manoeuvres required by actual painting. Truth be told, she had no distinct memory of any of Miss Abigail's paintings, only of her loose hair, the long skirts, the whispering voice. She became convinced that art was not so much a matter of painting as of *being* an artist. Her eyes blurred, seeing not the dusty leaves or the scolding squirrels, the grass with its sandy or weedy patches giving it an undesirable patchwork effect, or her brother's face with its ginger freckles leering at her through the bean vines that sagged off the garage roof, but great watery sunsets, wild frenzies of blossoming plants, suns colliding with stars, wisps of carelessly cavorting hair, and 'Paint what-e-ever you drream,' she sang to herself, stubbing one toe into the dirt and making the tyre swing upwards.

Unfortunately, the old heavy circle of ridged rubber could not be made to swoop upwards. At best, it dangled in its incurably pedestrian way, refusing to lift her into the higher realms where she wished to go. Those unpredictable roseate dreams were cruelly limited, encroached upon by the undeniable reality of the house, yard, suburb – enemies, all, of Art.

Although the suburb was as neat and trim as a picture (a *childish* picture, not the kind Polly had embarked on with Miss Abigail to inspire her) – white frame houses with black or green trim, standing in meticulously mowed lawns, neatly raked driveways, garages that housed two cars and had roll-up metal doors – there were those necessary but unsightly bits and pieces, too, that owners had managed to conceal with varying degrees of success: garbage cans with lids weighed down with rocks to prevent raccoons from tipping them over and spilling the rotting contents, washing lines hung not only with pretty skirts and coloured shirts but also with more unsightly items of apparel, and stacks of wood that had not been touched for many seasons and were slowly rotting where they stood. There was even an occasional sick tree begging for a visit from a tree doctor by dramatically holding up one blighted arm or exposing a wounded flank.

One of the most unsightly bits of the neighbourhood stood, shamefully, in their own yard, in the corner where the driveway curved away from the house and disappeared behind the lilac bushes that no one ever trimmed, so that it really was not visible to anyone else but to them, and then only if they happened to go past the garage and around the lilacs to the end of the drive. Normally it was only their father who went there, in winter when he was obliged by contract to clear the driveway of snow, because at the end of the drive stood a two-roomed wooden cabin with a condemned porch and a sagging roof that had been let out to their tenant, Miss Mabel Dodd.

Of course the tenant herself was visible, when she drove off to work in the gauzy grey steam of early morning, in her beaten-up old maroon Dodge with the grey paint showing through and flaking off as it creaked past the lilacs, fell into and lifted itself out of the deep ruts outside their kitchen window, scraped by the low-hanging branches of a thicket of lugubrious larch and spruce trees, and then cautiously edged onto Route 2, pointing towards Amherst. It was usually already dark when she made her way back at the end of the day, the headlights of the Dodge dragging through the leaves and grasses, leaving behind shadows. The cabin itself could not be seen from the house. The tenant spoke to none of them unless absolutely necessary and greetings were not: the mother had discovered that when she tried to greet her on their occasional, inevitable meetings in the driveway and there would be no reply. The father claimed he had actually had some conversations with Miss Dodd regarding particularly heavy snowfalls and problems with heating, but the children had not witnessed them and suspected him of imagining a relationship that did not exist, even so minimally. He would do that, pretend to be sociable when he was not.

When she first took up occupancy, the children fantasized about her, made up stories about her secret life as a witch. The

first Hallowe'en, they had even gone around wrapped in bed-
sheets and with baskets on their heads, to chant 'Trick-or-treat?'
under her windows. She had simply not answered the door. The
children persisted: the car stood outside, after all. They pressed
their ears to the front door, listening for a sound – and heard
creaks, cracks. They peered through the grimy windows to see if
they could spy a shadow or a light, and Polly, peering through a
slit in the sheet of grey plastic that hung over the window, thought
she did see something pale, wedged into a tall-backed chair in the
corner; it was certainly not a light. It had the substance of flesh,
but without any variation, entirely pallid from top to toe – or at
least as much of it as Polly could see. And a faint swirl of smoke
wound around it, slowly floating in the dark. When the other
children began to push at Polly and ask, 'Can you see? Can you
see anything?' she turned and elbowed past them, then leapt off
the porch, swearing, 'It's a ghost!' All of them echoed, 'It's – a –
ghost!' and Polly could not explain that the ghost had not
been light and afloat as it should have been, but solid and fleshy
and dull.

It was easy to forget that Miss Dodd lived there at all. For
long stretches, they did forget. They built themselves a tree house
one summer and sat on its uneven planks, dangling their legs and
looking out over the sagging, crumbling roof of shingles that
seemed a natural outgrowth of the earth. It was a long time since
the walls had been painted and it was impossible to tell what colour they had been. Now they were the colour of dried blood, a
boring brown. There was nothing that could be called a garden
or a yard around it; in fact, it was a wilderness of ivy and scrub
and some peculiarly vigorous ferns.

Polly was still humming 'Pa-aint just what you-u dre-eam—'
when she slipped out of the rubber tyre and slouched across
the grass to where the jungle spread in order to examine those
ferns; her painter's eye saw some promise in their furled and
unfurled shapes and tightly wound, or else exuberantly unwound,

clusters. There was something serpentine about them, something you might come across in a dream. She was barefoot, and
cautious, as if she expected them to hiss and sway, and when she
heard sounds behind her, she snapped her head around to look.
But it was only Tom following, lifting up his knees and plonking
down his feet like an intrepid explorer, a switch held in his fist in
readiness.

Since the tenant was always out at that time of day, they could
explore at leisure, and what they found surprised them: at the
bottom of the mouldering backstairs that ended in a tumble of
rhododendrons were a stone head, bald, blind, rising out of the
ivy, its shoulders submerged in all the dark groundcover, and
other bits of statuary – petrified hands and limbs pushing out of
the soft mould like gravestones, or lying scattered under the
branches of the spruce trees. They might have been the remains
of a battle, or else ploughed up out of a graveyard.

Polly and Tom said nothing to each other, but breathed hard
and noisily as they turned over and kicked at various bits of
stone and clay and plaster – mostly human shapes, thick and
clumsy, and some abstract ones that could not be called squares
or circles or anything at all, just contortions, blunted ones. There
was something disquieting about these ugly, abandoned pieces
that appeared to have been flung out of the windows of the cabin,
only one, the bald head, evidently planted. The children,
unnerved, were silent, as if they had walked into an invisible spider web in a forest or come upon bones in the wilds.

Polly thought of the yellow stack of *National Geographic* magazines piled up beside the sofa in the den, with photographs of
steaming jungles, vast ruins, ancient idols tumbled from their ped-
estals and lying prone on the forest floor. She caught a wisp of her
hair between her teeth and chewed on it. 'Miss Abigail at the camp
was a sculptress,' she said. 'She made a ballerina out of plaster. She
said she'd help me if I wanted to try. It was real pretty. Not like
this stuff—' and she kicked at it, but not hard, being barefoot.

'But that ole Miss Dodd didn't *make* this stuff, did she?' Tom said, striking out with his switch at a flattened nose. 'Bet she got it from somewhere – some witch doctor, maybe. Maybe she does voodoo,' he growled; he'd looked through the *National Geographics* too.

'Voo-doo!' Polly echoed him, in an even deeper voice. They began making spitting sounds of condemnation. There was an unpleasant smell about the place too. As they came around the back of the cabin, they saw the cause of it: under the kitchen window lay a pile of refuse, household garbage, kitchen waste, simply tossed out and lying in a heap, some brown, some black, some wet, some solid.

'Ugh! Did you *see* that?'

'Gross!'

'Diss-gust-ing!'

'We better tell Dad!'

That evening they did and he allowed some wrinkles to work their way through his forehead, but only said, 'Guess the rac- coons'll eat it up,' and went back to staring at the TV screen in the den: a sign he did not mean to get up and get involved.

For a while their mother did her best to make him do some- thing about it. 'Think of the flies,' she urged. 'It's a health hazard.'

'Christ,' he said, turning red – he'd been looking forward all week to this match. 'I've put two garbage cans outside her door – what more am I supposed to do? Clean her yard for her? With the rent she's paying us, it's not worth it.' The ball game was com- ing to an end in a frenzy of waving flags and blowing whistles. Frustrated, he got up. 'And that cabin isn't worth more than the rent she's paying – we're lucky she wants it,' he added. That was that, he implied, switching off the television.

But their mother would not let it drop: the thought of flies, and disease, was something she would not tolerate in her own back- yard. Finally she brought out an unopened box of garbage bags and handed them to him, ordering him to take them across to

her. 'If she won't come out, leave them on her porch. She'll have
to get the message.'

He went off grumbling and they waited for him to come back
and report. He returned with a hurried gait, his head lowered,
and still clutching the garbage bags.

'Didn't you give them to her? She's there – her car's there – I
saw it,' began the mother, but he flung them onto the table, muttering something about, 'You can't just go bursting in on people
like that,' and disappeared into the den.

'What do you mean?' the mother demanded, following him.
She stood in the doorway, questioningly. The children could not
see him, he had sunk onto the sofa, and it was difficult to hear
what he said since he had switched on the television again, but
they were almost certain – later, when they discussed it, they
found their certainties matched – that he'd said, 'What was I
supposed to *do*? She *was* there, she opened the door – nekkid as
the day that she was born. Stark nekkid. Not a stitch. What was
I to do – hand over the garbage bags for her to dress in?' The
mother quickly shut the door to the den. Polly and Tom stared at
each other till sputters of laughter began to erupt from them.
Tom's sputters turned to spit. Then Polly's did. They dribbled
their laughter till it ran.

By what had to be an odd coincidence, the next Sunday morning
they looked up from their breakfast of pancakes and maple
syrup, and saw the maroon Dodge come bumping slowly over the
ruts past their kitchen window, then turn around the lilacs and
disappear: their tenant had already been out that sleepy summer
Sunday morning and was already back, this time bringing with
her a visitor. She had never been known to have a visitor before.
That he was a black youth whose upright, only slightly inclined
head they had briefly glimpsed was equally extraordinary – in
their neighbourhood.

After breakfast, the children edged out into the backyard
before they could be caught up in any busy activity their parents

might think up for them. They made for the maple tree and took turns at swinging in the tyre seat, then climbed into the branches to see if anything remained of their tree house. That was what they told each other – 'D'you think there's anything left of it?' 'Can't see.' 'Let's go look.'

There was still the platform although the roof and walls had blown down in the previous winter's storms and snowfalls, and from it they could look across the yard and over the lilacs to the cabin. What they saw there was the black youth, in oversized jeans and a military-looking shirt hanging out below his hips, wearing a baseball cap turned backwards, sweeping up the porch with a broom, then coming down the rotten steps to sweep that area. Then he returned to the house and they saw his head at the kitchen window, bent over what must have been the sink and taps.

It was mysterious, and unsettling. Had she heard them, somehow, discuss the filthy state of her house? How? She would have had to be a witch, hovering in the air above them, invisibly. And who was the youth? A guest? But no one had a black boy for a guest. Had she employed him as a cleaner? What was going on? Was he going to stay?

The last question was soon answered: before noon they saw the car going up the driveway and edging onto Route 2, the tenant with her great flabby jaw sunk upon her chest as she drove, and the youth on the front seat beside her, also in a sunken posture. There was no explanation for this unusual visit, this departure from habit – none at all.

And it was repeated the next Sunday, so that it seemed to be a new habit. Quite failing to keep their curiosity to themselves, the children disengaged themselves from the rubber tyre and the maple tree – Polly had also quietly abandoned the paint pots in the attic – and found games to play on the gravel of the driveway in front of the battered old cabin. Hopscotch – something they hadn't played in years. The black youth, coming down the steps with a broom and a rag, unexpectedly stuck out his tongue, then grinned at them. He started to sweep the dust and cobwebs off the walls and from under the eaves where they hung in swags, then started to wipe the windows, so long obscured by dirt as to make them opaque. Turning around suddenly, he caught them gaping at him. 'Dirty, ain't it?' he said conversationally. 'Ugly, too.'

They did not know how to reply. Ugly it was, and dirty too, but it was theirs. Was it a comment on them, and their lives, and status? Certainly the facts were undeniable and they said, uneasily, 'Yeah,' and 'Guess so.'

'Y'know what,' he added, 't'owner's ugly, too. An' dirty as hell.'

They retreated, shocked. The boy and his efforts at cleaning up the slovenly shack became even more mysterious. He was not a guest, then. So what was he – to their sullen, black-browed tenant?

'Oh, a cleaner, I guess,' their mother said when they told her of this exchange. 'She must have hired a cleaner. High time, too. Never thought she'd do it.'

'D'you think she heard us? She'd have to be a witch!'

But their father only said, 'Good, place getting cleaned up at last,' with as much satisfaction as if it were his own achievement.

Instead, a shocking event took place that did not result in cleanliness at all. School had reopened by then, and the children had forgotten such trivial moments of their summer. Tom was launched on his project of getting into the swimming team but finding it far from easy, and Polly was struggling to maintain her identity as an artist (she had taken her roll of paintings to show the school art teacher who had looked at them down her nose and said, 'Yes, well, we're going to be doing pencil sketches and still lifes this term'). The routine of catching the school bus, going off every morning, bringing back homework, was settling into its usual monotony. It was early fall, the leaves grey and tinged with yellow, like the beard of an old man, when one morning Miss Mabel Dodd arrived at their back door and stood, in her heavy boots, her battered jacket, her hands in her pockets, and her chin sunk into her collar, addressing their father. Their mother, when summoned, went at once to see what it was about. So did the children, at risk of missing the school bus, and there in the drive stood the tenant's car, at which she was gesturing. It was scrawled all over with what was obviously excrement, since it stank, and in excrement someone had written the word PIG across the front and rear window. Some of it had been smeared over the hood, and over the trunk. When they tore their eyes away from this mound of desecration, they went out, walked around the lilacs and saw the cabin with bags of garbage strewn all around it, across the steps and over the porch. Miss Mabel Dodd stood with them, huddled into her jacket – worn, they saw, over a pair of faded flannel pyjamas – surveying it with them. Here finally was something she wished to share.

After a moment, the mother, audibly gulping, said, 'I'll call the police,' and fled.

It was a great pity, but the children missed the police visit – the parents would not, absolutely would not, allow them to miss school. And when they returned, the police had come and gone. The car was gone, too. Nothing to console them but their mother's explanation – as if it could.

'They thought it might be the boy she hired as a cleaner in the summer. Maybe she didn't pay him enough. Maybe she said something bad to him, something mean.'

'But who was he? Will they catch him? Will they put him in gaol?'

'Oh, I don't think he can get away – he was one of the boys she taught – in that school for delinquents, in Holyoke.'

'She *taught*—?'

They might have known – mathematics, spelling, history, all those rigours took over teachers like terminal illnesses; it was what made them so dried-up, so impervious to life. They should have known all along. Only the word 'delinquent' added a novel element to that grim pattern – and Holyoke, the gutted red-brick tenements, the emptied streets, the boarded-up shops, the groups huddled in corners of playgrounds where no one ever played, that they passed by on their way to Hartford, to Springfield and beyond . . .

'Yes,' said their mother, cutting bread for peanut butter sandwiches without missing a stroke. The slices fell into pairs, like the leaves of books, on the wooden board, then were thickly smeared with the oily paste, rising to a mound in the centre, thinning at the peripheries, before she slapped the leaves together, two by two, and drew a knife through each pair, pressing down, then releasing each triangle to puff up and rise, ready for sets of teeth to bite into, as luxuriously as sinking into soft beds of warmth and sweetness. 'She's taught art there for twenty years, the police told me. Those kids, they must be real hard to deal with – most of them from broken homes, or orphanages, and some of them with spells in prison. Imagine teaching them *art*! Imagine *her* teaching them art! Poor kids,' she said, laying out the sandwiches on a plate in a layered, fanned pattern before them. 'Can you *imagine?*'

Polly's mouth opened to form a protest. Her lips formed the letter 'O' or else 'NO'. She wanted to protest, she was not sure against what, but against something that had been presented to her, interposed between her and what she wanted and believed in – something objectionable, inadmissible, an imperfection. How was she to protest, to deny? Her lips stretched to form the word 'How?' but then she broke down and what burst from her was a surprising, 'Oh, Ma-ma.'

Her mother looked at her, questioningly. What was she protesting? Polly had no idea. All she knew was disillusion. It made her stretch out and grab a sandwich, then bury her teeth into it, despairingly.

Five Hours to Simla or Faisla

Then, miraculously, out of the pelt of yellow fur that was the dust growing across the great northern Indian plain, a wavering grey line emerged. It might have been a cloud bank looming, but it was not – the sun blazed, the earth shrivelled, the heat burned away every trace of such beneficence. Yet the grey darkened, turned bluish, took on substance.

'Look – mountains!'

'Where?'

'No! I can't see any mountains.'

'Are you blind? Look, look up – not down, fool!'

A scuffle broke out between the boys on the sticky grime of the Rexine-covered front seat and was quietened by a tap on their heads from their mother at the back. 'Yes, yes, mountains. The Himalayas. We'll be there soon.'

'Hunh.' A sceptical grunt from the driver of the tired, dust-coated grey Ambassador car. 'At least five more hours to Simla.' He ran his hand over the back of his neck where all the dirt of the road seemed to have found its way under the wilting cotton collar.

'Sim-la! Sim-la!' the boys set up a chant, their knees jouncing up and down in unison.

Smack, the driver's left hand landed on the closest pair, bringing out an instant flush of red and sudden, sullen silence.

'Be quiet!' the mother hissed from the back seat, unnecessarily.

The Ambassador gave a sudden lurch, throwing everyone forwards. The baby, whose mouth had been glued to the nipple of a rubber bottle like a fly to syrup, came unstuck and let out a wail of indignation. Even the mother let out a small involuntary cry. Her daughter, who had been asleep on the back seat, her legs across her mother's lap, crowding the baby and its bottle, now stirred.

'Accident!' howled the small boy who had been smacked, triumphantly.

But no, it was not. His father had stopped, with the usual infuriating control exercised by robotic adults, just short of the bicycle rickshaw ahead. The bicycle rickshaw had, equally robotically, avoided riding forwards into the bullock cart carrying a party of farmers' families to market. Then there was a bus, loaded with baggage and spilling over with passengers, and that too had shuddered to a halt with a grinding of brakes. Ahead of it was a truck, wrapped and folded in canvas sheets that blocked all else from sight. The mountains had disappeared and so had the road.

Also the first cacophony of screeching brakes and grinding gears. There followed the comparatively static hum of engines, and drivers waited in exasperation for the next lurch forwards. For the moment there was a lull, unusual on that highway. Then the waiting very quickly began to fray at the edges. The sun was beating on the metal of the vehicles and the road lay flattened across the parched plain without a tree to screen them from the sun or dust. First one car horn began to honk, then a bicycle rickshaw began to clang its bell, then a truck blared its musical horn maddeningly, and then the lesser ones began to go pom-pom, pom-pom, almost in harmony, and suddenly, out of the centre of all that noise, a long piercing wail emerged, almost from under their feet or out of their own mouths.

The two boys, the girl, the baby, all sat up, shocked, more so when they saw it was their father who was the perpetrator of this outrage. Clenching the wheel with both hands, his head was lowered onto it and the blare of the horn seemed to issue out of his fury.

The mother exclaimed.

He raised his head and banged on the wheel, struck it.

'How will we get to Simla before dark?' he howled.

The mother exclaimed again, shocked, 'But we'll be moving again, in a minute.'

As if to contradict her, the driver of the mountainous truck stalled at the top of the line swung himself out of the cabin into the road. He'd turned off his engine and stood in the deeply rutted dust, fumbling in his shirt pocket for cigarettes.

Other drivers got out of and off their vehicles – the bullock cart driver lowered himself from the creaking cart, the bicycle rickshaw driver descended, the bus driver got out and stalked, in his sweat-drenched khakis, towards the truck driver standing at the head of the line, and they all demanded, 'What's going on? Breakdown?'

The truck driver watched them approach but he was lighting his cigarette and didn't answer till it was lit and between his fingers. Then he waved an arm – and his movements were leisurely, elegant, quite unlike what his driving had been, on the highway in front of them, maniacal – and said, 'Stone throw. Somebody threw a stone. Hit my windshield. Cracked it.'

The father in the Ambassador had also joined them in the road. Hand on his hips, he demanded, 'So?'

'So?' said the truck driver, narrowing his eyes. They were grey in a tanned face, heavily outlined and elongated with kohl, and his hair was tied up in a bandana with a long loose end that dangled upon his shoulder. 'So we won't be moving again till the person who did it is caught and brought to a faisla.'

Immediately a babble broke out. All the drivers flung out their hands and arms in angry, demanding gestures, their voices rose in questioning, in cajoling, in argument. The truck driver stood looking at them, watching them, his face expressionless. Now and then he lifted the cigarette to his mouth and drew a deep puff. Then abruptly he swung around, clambered back into the cabin of his truck and started the engine with a roar, at which the others fell back, their attitudes slackening in relief. But then he wheeled it around and parked it squarely across the highway so no traffic could get past in either direction. The highway at that point had narrowed to a small culvert across a dry stream-bed full of stones. Now he clambered out again, then up the bank of the culvert on which he sat himself down, his legs wide apart in their loose and not too clean pyjamas, and sat there regarding the traffic piling up in both directions as though he might be regarding sheep filing into a pen.

The knot of drivers in the road began to grow, joined by many of the passengers demanding to know the cause of this impasse.

'Dadd-ee! Dadd-ee!' the small boys yelled, hanging out of the door their father had left open and all but falling out into the dust. 'What's happened, Dadd-ee?'

'Shut the door!' their mother ordered sharply, but too late. A yellow pai dog came crawling out of the shallow ditch that ran alongside the road and, spying an open door, came slinking up to it, thin hairless tail between its legs, eyes showing their whites, hoping for bread but quite prepared for a blow instead.

The boys drew back on seeing its exploring snout, the upper lip lifted back from the teeth in readiness for a taste of bread. 'Mad dog!' shouted one. 'Mad dog!' bellowed the other.

'Shh!' hissed their mother.

Since no one in the car dared drive away a creature so danger-ous, someone else did: a stone struck its ribs and with a yelp it ducked under the car and crept there to hide. But already the next beggar was at the door, throwing himself in with much the same mixture of leering enquiry and cringing readiness to withdraw. In place of one of his legs was a crutch worn down to almost a peg. 'Bread,' he whined, stretching out a bandaged hand. 'Paisa, paisa. Mother, mother,' he pleaded, seeing the mother cower back in her seat with the baby. The children cowered back too.

They knew that if they remained thus for long enough, and made no move towards purse or coin, he would leave: he couldn't afford to waste too much time on them when there were so many potential donors lined so conveniently up and down the highway. The mother stared glassily ahead through the windscreen at the heat beating off the metal bonnet. The children could not tear their eyes away from the beggar – his sores, his bandages, his crippled leg, the flies gathering . . .

When he moved on, the mother raised a corner of her sari to her mouth and nose. From behind it she hissed again, 'Shut-the-door!'

Unsticking their damp legs from the moistly adhesive seat, the boys scrambled to do so. As they leant out to grab the door, however, and the good feel of the blazing sun and the open air struck at their faces and arms, they turned around to plead, 'Can we get out? Can we go and see what's happening?'

So ardent was their need that they were about to fall out of the open door when they saw their father detaching himself from the knot of passengers and drivers standing in the road and making his way back to them. The boys hastily edged back, and he stood leaning in at the door. The family studied his face for signs; they were all adept at this, practising it daily over the breakfast table at home, and again when he came back from work. But this situation was a new one, a baffling one: they could not read it, or his position on it.

'What's happening?' the mother asked at last, faintly.

'Damn truck driver,' he swore through dark lips. 'Some boy threw a rock at it – probably some goatherd in the field – and cracked the windscreen. He's parked the truck across the road, won't let anyone pass. Says he won't move till the police come and get him compensation. Stupid damn fool – what compensation is a goatherd going to pay even if they find him?'

The mother leant her head back. What had reason to do with men's tempers? she might have asked. Instead she sighed. 'Is there a policeman?'

'What – here? In this forsaken desert?' her husband retorted. Withdrawing his head, he stood taking in harsh breaths of overheated, dust-laden air as if he were drawing in all the stupid-ity around him. He could see passengers climbing down from the bus and the bullock cart, clambering across the ditch into the fields, and fanning out – some to lower their trousers, others to lift their saris in the inadequate shelter provided by thorn bushes. If the glare was not playing tricks with his eyes, he thought he saw a puff of dust in the distance that might be raised by goats' hooves.

'Take me to see, Dadd-ee, take me to see,' the boys had begun to clamour, and to their astonishment he stood aside and let them climb out and even led them back to the truck that stood stalled imperviously across the culvert.

The mother opened and shut her mouth silently. Her daughter stood up and hung over the front seat to watch their disappearing figures. In despair, she cried, 'They're gone!'

'Sit down! Where can they go?'

'I want to go too, Mumm-ee, I want to go too-oo.'

'Be quiet. There's nowhere to go.'

The girl began to wail. It was usually a good strategy in a family with loud voices but this time her sense of aggrievement was genuine: her head ached from the long sleep in the car, from the heat beating on its metal top, from the lack of air, from the glare and from hunger. 'I'm hung-ree,' she wept.

'We were going to eat when we reached Solan,' her mother reminded her. 'There's such a nice-nice restaurant at the railway station in Solan. Such nice-nice omelettes they make there.'

'I want an omelette!' wailed the child.

'Wait till we get to Solan.'

'When will we reach it? *When*?'

'Oh, I don't know. Late. Sit down and open that basket at the back. You'll find something to eat there.'

But now that omelettes at Solan had been mentioned the basket packed at home with Gluco biscuits and potato chips held no attraction for the girl. She stopped wailing but sulked instead, sucking her thumb, a habit she was supposed to have given up but which resurfaced for comfort when necessary.

She did not need to draw upon her thumb juices for long. The news of the traffic jam on the highway had spread like ripples from a stone thrown. From somewhere, it seemed from nowhere for there was no village bazaar, marketplace or stalls visible in that dusty dereliction, wooden barrows came trundling along towards the waiting traffic, bearing freshly cut lengths of sugar-cane and a machine to extract their juice into thick dirty grey glasses; bananas already more black than yellow from the sun that baked them, peanuts in their shells roasting in pans set on embers. Men, women and children were climbing over the ditch like phantoms, materialising out of the dust, with baskets on their heads filled not only with sustenance but with amusement as well – a trayload of paper toys painted indigo blue and violent pink. Small bamboo pipes that released rude noises and a dyed feather on a spool, both together. Kites, puppets, clay carts, wooden toys and tin whistles. The vendors milled around the buses, cars and rickshaws, and were soon standing at their car window, both vocally and manually proffering goods for sale.

The baby let drop the narcotic rubber nipple, delighted. His eyes grew big and shone at the flowering outside. The little girl was perplexed, wondering what to take from so much abundance till the perfect choice presented itself in a rainbow of colour: green, pink and violet, her favourites. It was a barrow of soft drinks, and nothing on this day of gritty dust, yellow sun and frustrating delay could be more enticing than those bottles filled with syrups in dazzling floral colours. She set up a scream of desire.

'Are you mad?' her mother said promptly. 'You think I'll let you drink a bottle full of typhoid and cholera germs?'

The girl gasped with disbelief at being denied. Her mouth opened wide to issue a protest but her mother went on, 'After you have your typhoid-and-cholera injection, you may. You want a nice big typhoid-and-cholera injection first?'

The child's mouth was still open in contemplation of the impossible choice when her brothers came plodding back through the dust, each carrying a pith and bamboo toy – a clown that bounced up and down on a stick and a bird that whirled upon a pin. Behind them the father slouched morosely. He had his hands deep in his pockets and his face was lined with a frown deeply embedded with dust.

'We'll be here for hours,' he informed his wife through the car window. 'A rickshaw driver has gone off to the nearest thana to find a policeman who can put sense into that damn truck driver's thick head.' Despondently he threw himself into the driver's seat and sprawled there. 'Must be a hundred and twenty degrees,' he sighed.

'Pinky, where is the water bottle? Pass the water bottle to Daddy,' commanded the mother solicitously.

He drank from the plastic bottle, tilting his head back and letting the water spill into his mouth. But it was so warm it was hardly refreshing and he spat out the last mouthful from the car window into the dust. A scavenging chicken alongside the tyre skipped away with a squawk.

All along the road with its stalled traffic, drivers and passengers were searching for shade, for news, for some sign of release. Every now and then someone brought information on how long the line of stalled traffic now was. Two miles in each direction was the latest estimate, at least two miles – and the estimate was made not without a certain pride.

Up on the bank of the culvert the man who had caused it all sat sprawling, his legs wide apart. He had taken off his bandana, revealing a twist of cotton wool dipped in fragrant oil that was tucked behind his ear. He had bought himself a length of sugar cane and sat chewing it, ripping off the tough outer fibre then drawing the sweet syrup out of its soft inner fibre and spitting out, with relish and with expertise, the white fibre sucked dry. He seemed deliberately to spit in the direction of those who stood watching in growing frustration.

'Get hold of that fellow! *Force* him to move his truck,' somebody suddenly shouted out, having reached the limit of his endurance. 'If he doesn't, he'll get the thrashing of his life.'

'Calm down, sardarji,' another placated him with a light laugh to help put things back in perspective. 'Cool down. It's hot but you'll get your cold beer when you get to Solan.'

'When will that be? When my beard's gone grey?'

'Grey hair is nothing to be ashamed of,' philosophized an elder who had a good deal of it to show. 'Grey hair shows patience, forbearance, a long life. That is how to live long – patiently, with forbearance.'

'And when one has work to do, what then?' the Sikh demanded, rolling up his hands into fists. The metal ring on his wrist glinted.

'Work goes better after a little rest,' the elder replied, and demonstrated by lowering himself onto his haunches and squatting there on the roadside like an old bird on its perch or a man waiting to be shaved by a wayside barber. And, like an answer to a call, a barber did miraculously appear, an itinerant barber who carried the tools of his trade in a tin box on his head. No one could imagine from where he had emerged, or how far he had travelled in search of custom. Now he squatted and began to unpack a mirror, scissors, soap, blades, even a small rusty cigarette tin full of water. An audience stood watching his expert moves and flourishes and the evident pleasure these gave the elder.

Suddenly the truck driver on the bank waved a hand and called, 'Hey, come up here when you've finished. I could do with a shave too – and my ears need cleaning.'

There was a gasp at his insolence, and then indignant protests.

'Are you planning to get married over here? Are we not to move till your bride arrives and the wedding is over?' shouted someone.

This had the wrong effect: it made the crowd laugh. Even the truck driver laughed. He was somehow becoming a part of the conspiracy. How had this happened?

In the road, the men stood locked in bafflement. In the vehicles, the tired passengers waited. 'Oo-oof,' sighed the mother.

The baby, asleep as if stunned by the heat, felt heavy as lead in her arms. 'My head is paining, and it's time to have tea.'

'Mama wants tea, Mama wants tea!' chanted the daughter, kicking at the front seat.

'Stop it!' her father snapped at her. 'Where is the kitchen? Where is the cook? Am I to get them out of the sky? Or is there a well filled with tea?'

The children all burst out laughing at the idea of drawing tea from a well, but while they giggled helplessly, a chaiwallah did appear, a tray with glasses on his head, a kettle dangling from his hand, searching for the passenger who had called for tea.

There was no mention of cholera or typhoid now. He was summoned, glasses were filled with milky, sweet, frothing tea and handed out, the parents slurped thirstily and the children stared, demanding sips, then flinching from the scalding liquid.

Heartened, the father began to thrash around in the car, punch the horn, stamp ineffectually on the accelerator. 'Damn fool,' he swore. 'How can this happen? How can this be allowed? Only in this bloody country. Where else can one man hold up four miles of traffic—'

Handing back an empty glass, the mother suggested, 'Why don't you go and see if the policeman's arrived?'

'Am I to go up and down looking for a policeman? Should I walk to Solan to find one?' the man fumed. His tirade rolled on like thunder out of the white blaze of afternoon. The children listened, watched. Was it getting darker? Was a thunder cloud approaching? Was it less bright? Perhaps it was evening. Perhaps it would be night soon.

'What will we do when it grows dark?' the girl whimpered. 'Where will we sleep?'

'Here, in the car!' shouted the boys. 'Here, on the road!' Their toys were long since broken and discarded. They needed some distraction. The sister could easily be moved to tears by mention of night, jackals, ghosts that haunt highways at night, robbers who carry silk handkerchieves to strangle their victims . . .

Suddenly, simultaneously, two events occurred. In the ditch that ran beside the car the yellow pai dog began a snarling, yelping fight with a marauder upon her territory, and at the same time one of the drivers, hitching up his pyjamas and straightening his turban, came running back towards the stalled traffic, shouting, 'They're moving! The policeman's come! They'll move now! There'll be a faisla!'

Instantly the picture changed from one of discouragement, despair and possibly approaching darkness to animation, excitement, hope. All those loitering in the road leapt back into their vehicles, getting rid of empty bottles, paper bags, cigarette butts, the remains of whatever refreshment the roadway had afforded them, and in a moment the air was filled with the roar of revving engines as with applause.

The father too was pressing down on the accelerator, beating upon the steering wheel, and the children settling into position, all screaming, 'Sim-la! Sim-la!' in unison. The pai dogs scrambled out of the way and carried their quarrel over into the stony field.

But not a single vehicle moved an inch. None could. The obstructive truck had not been shifted out of the way. The driver still sprawled upon the bank, propped up on one elbow now, demanding of the policeman who had arrived, 'So? Have you brought me compensation? No? Why not? I told you I would not move till I received compensation. So where is it? Hah? What is the faisla? Hah?'

The roar of engines faltered, hiccupped, fell silent. After a while, car doors slammed as drivers and passengers climbed out again. Groups formed to discuss the latest development. What was to be done now? The elder's philosophical patience was no longer entertained. No one bandied jokes with the villain on the bank any more. Expressions turned grim.

Suddenly the mother wailed, 'We'll be here all night,' and the baby woke up crying: he had had enough of being confined in the suffocating heat, he wanted air, wanted escape. All the children began to whine. The mother drew herself together. 'We'll have to get something to eat,' she decided and called over to her husband standing in the road, 'Can't we get some food for the children?'

He threw her an irritated look over his shoulder. Together with the men in the road, he was going back to the culvert to see what could be done. There was an urgency about their talk now, their suggestions. Dusk had begun to creep across the fields like a thicker, greyer layer of dust. Some of the vendors lit kerosene lamps on their barrows, so small and faint that they did nothing but accentuate the darkness. Some of them were disappearing over the fields, along paths visible only to them, having sold their goods and possibly having a long way to travel. All that could be seen clearly in the growing dark were the lighted pinpricks of their cigarettes.

What the small girl had most feared did now happen – the long, mournful howl of a jackal lifted itself out of the stones and thorn bushes and unfurled through the dusk towards them. While she sat mute with fear her brothers let out howls of delight and began to imitate the invisible creature with joy and exuberance.

The mother was shushing them all fiercely when they heard the sound they had given up hope of hearing: the sound of a moving vehicle. It came roaring up the road from behind them – not at all where they had expected – overtaking them in a cloud of choking dust. Policemen in khaki, armed with steel-tipped canes, leant out of it, their moustaches bristling, their teeth gleaming, eyes flashing and ferocious as tigers. And the huddled crowd stranded on the roadside fell aside like sheep: it might have been they who were at fault.

But the police truck overtook them all, sending them hurriedly into the ditch for safety, and drew up at the culvert. Here the police jumped out, landing with great thuds on the asphalt, and striking their canes hard upon it for good measure. The truck's headlights lit up the bank with its pallid wash.

Caught in that illumination, the truck driver sprawling there rose calmly to his feet, dusted the seat of his pyjamas and wound up the bandana round his head, while everyone watched open-mouthed. Placing his hands on his hips, he called to the police, 'Get them all moving now, get them all moving!' And, as if satisfied with his role of leader, the commander, he leapt lightly into the driver's seat of his truck, turned the key, started the engine and manoeuvred the vehicle into an onward position and, while his audience held its disbelieving breath, set off towards the north.

After a moment they saw that he had switched on his lights; the tail-lights could be seen dwindling in the dark. He had also turned on his radio and a song could be heard like the wail of a jackal in the night:

Father, I am leaving your roof,
To my bridegroom's home I go . . .

The police, looking baffled, swung around, flourishing their canes. 'Get on! Chalo!' they bellowed. 'Chalo, chalo, get on, all of you,' and they did.

Tepoztlán Tomorrow

Luis was let in at the big door by the old workman who had married one of the maids. He greeted Luis with becoming joy and affection, then led him through the courtyard which was quiet now, the maids having finished their work and gone. Luis had to duck his head to make his way through the rubber trees, the bougainvillea, the shrubs of jasmine and hibiscus and plumbago that had tangled themselves into a jungle, leaving barely enough room to pass. The evening air was heavy with the scent of jasmine and lemon blossom. As he remembered, every branch was hung with a cage – he had memories that were still sharply etched of daylong screeches and screams that would ring through the courtyard and every room around it: the maids, doing the laundry at the water trough in the centre of the courtyard, crying, 'Pa-pa-ga-*yo?*' and being answered by twenty screeches of 'Pa-pa-ga-yo!' hour upon hour. But at this hour all the cages were covered with cloth and there was silence. A thought struck him: were they still alive? Perhaps they had all died: he imagined their skeletons clinging to the perches inside the shrouded cages, all beaks, claws and bones, dust and dried droppings below. 'Papa-ga-*yo?* Pa-pa-ga-yo!' he whistled softly.

The house, to him, was a larger cage, shrouded and still. It seemed equally dead. There was one light on, deep inside; the other rooms were all shadowy, except for the shrine of the Virgin of Guadalupe in her gown of dusty net and tinsel, illuminated by the glow of a red light bulb suspended over her head.

The old man was hobbling along the dark passages as if he could see perfectly in the dark. Perhaps he was blind, and accustomed to it. Luis bumped into a sharp-edged table and suddenly all the picture frames on it clattered in warning, and a voice called out, 'Quién es?'

As Luis approached the innermost rooms – actually the ones that fronted the street, but they could not be approached from it – the scent of lemons and jasmine in the courtyard and the heavy perfume of incense burning perpetually at the shrine receded and were replaced by an overpowering odour he remembered as being the distinctive smell of the house on Avenida Matamoros: that of mosquito repellent.

And there they were, Doña Celia on her square, upright, wooden-backed and wooden-seated throne, strategically placed so that she could look out of the window into the street and also, just by turning her head, into the house all the way down its central passage into the courtyard; and Nadyn beside her, poking with a hairpin at a Raidolito coil which was smoking ferociously and yet not enough to keep the evening's mosquitoes at bay.

Whereas Nadyn appeared stunned by the sudden appearance of a young man out of the dusk, and stepped back almost in fright, Doña Celia recognized him without a moment's hesitation. 'Ah, Teresa's son, eh? Luis, eh?'

Of course they were expecting him – his mother had telephoned, he too had spoken to them on the phone, all the while imagining it ringing through the empty house and the fluster it would cause in those silent rooms – but he was late, very late.

Doña Celia reminded him of this immediately. 'You are late,' she accused him. 'We have waited all day. What kept you, eh?'

He tried to explain, laughing falsely: he had hoped to get his father's car and drive up; he had waited, it hadn't turned up; he had made his way to the bus terminal but met friends on the way who insisted he stop, who delayed him. It was true, he admitted, taking off his hat and wiping his face, true that he had only managed to get away and catch a bus hours after he had said he would. That was how it was, he laughed.

Doña Celia's long face swung in the dark like a cow's. She

shifted on her chair, wrapping her shawl about her throat – a shawl, on such a still, warm evening indoors; that too he remembered. All her movements expressed her displeasure. 'Well, we have eaten. Finally, we ate, Nedy and I. But Nedy will show you to the kitchen and you can help yourself before you go to bed.'

'Oh, is it bedtime?' he blinked. Already?

This was taken as an impertinence. She was not going to reply. A young nephew to speak to his aunt so, and tell her what should and should not be the hour for bed? Her face set into its deeply cut folds. Luis could hardly believe this sour old lady could be the sister of his laughing, plump, brightly dressed mother. A much older sister, it was true, and the daughter of their father's first marriage, more like a mother to her younger sister by a second marriage, but still, there was not the faintest resemblance. Perhaps it was the difference between the old family home in Tepoztlán which the old lady had never left, her own husband having entered it when they married, and left her there when he died, while Luis's mother had married into a family that lived in Mexico City.

Following Nadyn into the kitchen for a bowl of sopa da tortilla she said she had kept warm for him, he sighed. Yes, Mexico City was very far, in a sense, not geographical, from Tepoztlán.

The bowl of soup Nadyn promised him turned out to be only one course of a succession of dishes she kept placing on the table and watching him eat his way through out of politeness, not hunger. She placed her elbows on the table, her chin on her cupped hands, and let her eyes wander. Why did she not put the light on? he thought querulously, peering into the dishes in the gloom, not even certain what he was eating although Nadyn assured him each time 'Your favourite.' 'It is?' he asked doubtfully, lifting a spoon and stirring. 'Of *course*,' she replied, '*we* remember.'

What else do you remember? And what do you do besides remember? he wanted to ask her, bad-temperedly and unfairly, since she was telling him, in some detail, all the events of their lives in the time he had been away in the USA, quite as if she were sure he had heard nothing about them, living as he did in exile. As she mentioned this uncle, that cousin, or the other nephew or niece, he drooped over his plate gloomily, wondering if he dared light a cigarette and indicate he would not eat any more.

But now she was bringing out the pièce de résistance of the meal, carefully preserved in an ancient icebox that stood grumbling in its corner, and even in the gloom the colour of the jelly that wobbled in its dish was such that it made him cringe. 'Your favourite,' she challenged him as she set it, trembling, before him. How could he tell her that he had long since outgrown green and red jelly puddings?

'Only if you share it with me,' he said, inspiration having suddenly struck. By the brevity of her hesitation, and the eagerness with which she brought across a glass dish for herself, he remembered how Nadyn had always been the one with the sweet tooth.

'So, Nedy,' he decided to tease her, passing over all but one spoonful of the jelly to her, 'que pasa, con Pedro? – is he still around?'

She collapsed against the table, as if she had been struck. He had been unfair: he should have let her finish her jelly before bringing up the matter which he knew to be unpleasant, had a long history of being unpleasant. Now she would not be able to enjoy her pudding.

But somehow she managed to combine two emotions and two activities – and he watched with fascination as the woman with the long grey face and the two pigtails who sat across from him in her grey dress managed to spoon the sweet into her mouth avidly, relishing each chill, slippery mouthful as an armadillo might enjoy slipping slugs down its throat, and at the same time emitting an endless flow of complaint and grumbling, all bitter as ash, raw as salt. There was such a long, long history, after all, of Doña Celia's opposition to Pedro as a suitor, and her objections:

that he was muy sucio, dirty, not fit to enter their house, and just because he ran a business in town. A business? queried Luis, was it not a truck? Oh yes, a truck was a part of it, how else was Pedro to deliver those tanques de gas if not by truck, but did Luis know how the people of Tepoztlán now relied on those tanques for heating and cooking, how good, how thriving a business it was? It was not that Pedro was not doing well, or that he did not work hard. Then what was it? Luis enquired. Here she threw up her hands, then clutched her head, then clasped her arms about her, and went off on another tack: that of Doña Celia's stubbornness, her adamant attitude, her rejection of Pedro's family – for how could she object to Pedro? No one could object to Pedro, it was his family – and here Nadyn became dejected, her mouth and shoulders and hands all drooped. She tinkled a spoon in the empty glass dish, making a forlorn sound: even Nadyn could not speak for Pedro's family. She had visited it, after all, and had to admit – and had told Pedro, too – that it was not the kind of home she had grown up in, that anyone could see. Pedro's home and Pedro's family could not be described as anything but sucios, not even by Nadyn. And she had not been given such a welcome by them either: they were not used to cultivated and aristocratic women such as the women of their own family, said Nadyn with a shrug, and their way of living – well, it was little better than pigs'. After all they had only recently made the move to Tepoztlán from the hills where they had raised pigs, turkeys, and scratched maize from the fields, but how could Pedro help that? He had worked hard to rise above that himself: only Mama would not see that, being of the old school – old-fashioned and stubborn.

Luis felt his eyelids weighted as if by lead with the repetitiveness of Nadyn's complaints. He could postpone the cigarette no longer. 'One day she will,' he sighed, without the least conviction, knowing as well as Nadyn that only over Doña Celia's dead body would Pedro cross the threshold of their home. His eyelids twitched with a sudden spasm of sympathy. People like Doña

Celia took a long, long time to die – he did not need to tell Nadyn that: she knew.

He took his cigarette out into the courtyard to smoke. This was only partly in order not to offend his aunt's and his cousin's nostrils – they were used to the heavy coils of smoke of Raidolito and of incense but not of tobacco – but also because he could not help feeling absurdly hurt that Nadyn had not asked him a single question. Instead she had taken for granted that he would want to hear *her* news, *their* news, without the faintest suspicion that he might have some of his own. It made him feel ridiculously childish – no one ever imagines a child could have anything of interest to say. So it was with a somewhat sulky air that he strolled out into the dense jungle of the courtyard, thinking to sit down on a bench beside the water trough in the ferny centre and brood silently upon his own affairs before going in to bed. For a while it was as he remembered: the scents, the sound of water dripping, the howling of dogs in the lanes of Tepoztlán in voices more human than canine, so full of despair, desire and woe, and in the distance the wail of similar human laments on a radio, broken into by the raucous gaiety of a mariachi band playing on another, and overhead the night sky so deep and so dark that it was like being upside down and peering into a well. But very soon not only did the cigarette dwindle to its end and the bench grow distinctly cold under him, but what he remembered and what he reaffirmed began to have a profoundly depressing effect on his spirits. He saw the light go off inside the house, only the red glow around the Virgin of Guadalupe left throbbing, and then it became too much for him and he got to his feet and withdrew as if afraid this might be the stage, the setting for his life as well.

When he woke, much too late – the sun was already smashing in through the windows he had left unshuttered – it was to find the mood of Doña Celia's house unchanged. The courtyard was still uninhabited, there was no longer a team of maids and manservants to labour there, and although someone had drawn the covers off the cages, a number of them did turn out to be empty while the few that were inhabited contained only very aged, disgruntled birds that glared at him out of a single eye as he made his way past them to the main wing of the house for his breakfast, and did not bother to squawk a greeting or whistle back. In the house things were as usual. Nadyn appeared to have her arms deep in tubs or basins or buckets of housework, and Doña Celia, whom he went to greet, was seated as always upon her comfortless throne and, even if it was a summer's day and the sun beating up from the white dust in the street outside, she was wrapped in her shawl, holding it about her throat as if to keep every sort of danger at bay – draughts, chills, unsuitable suitors for her daughter's hand, whatever. Kissing her cheek, Luis actually found it chill to his lips – chill and mouldy, as if disintegrating.

But, while he sat over his café con leche and his pan dulce, he learned about the changes that had occurred during his absence. The house was no longer the barricaded fortress, the safe retreat it had been for previous generations of Cruzes: the fortress was threatened on every side. Doña Celia filled in the news into his left ear, Nadyn into the right, since he had noticed nothing for himself. In a way Doña Celia had herself brought it all about – and Nadyn was full of sharp little barbs to remind her – but having already sold off orchards and farmland lower down in the valley, she had finally resorted to disposing of bits and pieces of their own compound. Did Luis remember the row of sheds at the far end of the courtyard? Yes, he did and he also knew they had been bought up by an entrepreneur who had rented them to shopkeepers so that now there was a tiendita in one, a video parlour in another, a lavandería in a third . . . What was wrong with that? he asked, irritated. Not only was it old history but it brought in an income off which the two of them lived, so what was their complaint? First they brought change to Tepoztlán and then they complained of it. He pushed aside the basket of rolls

Nadyn kept nudging towards him, and swept his hand over the dish of mermelada about which a very large, fat fly hovered.

But now they were coming towards the true horror they had to face, its pit, its bottom: that end of the courtyard, round the corner from the row of rooms now kept shut, they had had a piece of land planted with avocados and lemons, did he remember? Well, they had sold it to a man who had come to them with cash in hand, and a suitably respectful manner of speech, telling them he wished to build a house for his family which had only recently moved to Tepoztlán. Being who they were – a shawl was fingered, a brooch nervously touched – they had not thought to question him regarding his profession or the size of his family. After all, if they had sold their land to him, they had no right to do so (and of course they couldn't wait to sell it and have the money in their pockets, Luis thought viciously; had they not always been money-grubbing, was not the whole family so?) and now they had for a neighbour a man who was a garbage collector by profession—

'What? *What* by profession?'

Luis's reaction satisfied them deeply: it set them off on an even higher pitch of complaint. The man owned a truck that he parked in front of *their* front door, often right under their windows so they could smell its contents, and even when the maid went out and persuaded him to move it down the street a bit, it left behind a trail of stray bits and leavings of garbage scattered all over *their* threshold. What was more, behind the high wall he had built around his piece of property before he had even erected a shack upon it, they suspected he stacked and sorted his garbage—

'What do you mean? He doesn't go and dispose of it, he stores it?'

'Yes, yes,' screamed Doña Celia and Nadyn together, in agitation: they were convinced, they had evidence, the maid had climbed up a ladder and peered over the wall and seen there all the empty bottles of agua purificada, the beer cans, the flattened cardboard cartons, that his family sat sorting into bundles for resale. And the family! By the rising crescendo of their voices, Luis knew he was in for a long saga. He began to squirm, to indicate that he was done with his breakfast, but they paid him no attention whatsoever, they were carried along by the tide of their indignation regarding the family because the man had not informed them that he had no fewer than seven children, boys and girls of all sizes, all in rags, and all day that was what they occupied themselves with, rag-picking, while their father drove around the town in his truck, loudly ringing a bell and collecting garbage to bring home to *their* doorstep. That was what the Avenida de Matamoros had come to, and there was no way of ignoring it: not only did the most noxious smell rise from the foetid garbage pile that was his compound, but day and night the place rang with the abominable music from the radio and TV – had Luis not heard it last night? *They* had been kept awake, always were. The man had not yet got around to building his family a house – well, yes, he had built some walls and a roof, but not a door or a window, not fit for habitation, yet a radio and TV had been set up in it to entertain the family while it sat sorting garbage. All day that ungodly music thundered through their compound – Doña Celia drew her shawl about her and shivered with fury. But the shawl was worn thin, no one cared how she shivered, such was the sorry state of affairs that Luis could see for himself.

He thought of rising from the table on the pretext of going and examining this den, this pit, this abomination, for himself but the two women were already onto the next disclosure of iniquity. Could Luis imagine such a thing: the garbage collector's wife, she put a table outside their door, *their front door*, every evening, and thereon boiled a tubful of corncobs and stood there, impudently as you please, slathering them with mayonnaise and chillies, selling them to passersby, as if Doña Celia were growing maize in her garden and posting her maid out there to sell it!

'I am sure that has not occurred to anyone who knows you,

Aunt,' Luis said kindly, seeing her distress and beginning to feel a little amused in spite of himself.

'Yes, and what of all those who do *not* know me? Do you think Tepoztlán is the place it once was? Haven't you seen how it has been overtaken by hordes of newcomers, from Cuernavaca, from Mexico City, from God knows where . . .?'

'It's now got a good road and good transport – it's more lively now,' Luis reminded them, although it was clear liveliness was not to them a quality: they would have preferred it a morgue.

'Yes, yes, lively – we all know about lively. Men come to our street corner to drink. All afternoon you hear them drink and gamble there under the bamboos, and by evening you may see them lying stretched out in the road, dead drunk – *so* lively has it grown,' Doña Celia said bitterly.

'Why, is there a bar now at the corner?' Luis asked with interest.

'A bar! I should think not! I am sure it is that vile woman – that pigsty owner's wife – who supplies them with liquor. Home-brewed. Oh, we would go to the police, inform them – but do you know what we can expect of the police of Tepoztlán? If people go to them with an honest complaint, and ask for justice, they are first asked "And how much will you pay us?" Do you think Nedy and I should submit to—'

Luis could not help laughing at the idea of his aunt and cousin visiting that most disreputable department in the town hall by the zocalo where policemen sat playing cards in the sun and their families cooked meals over open fires. 'No, of course not, Aunt – but perhaps Cousin Heriberto could go along—'

'Heriberto!' Doña Celia threw up her hands. 'That one! If you only knew—'

'I thought I'd go and visit him.' Luis scrambled quickly to his feet. 'Is he still at the old place?'

'*His* old place? You don't *know* what he did with it?'

Luis began to back out of the room. 'And – and Don Beto – I need to see him – about my thesis – ask his advice—'

The two women, still seated at the table, still seething and quite capable of continuing through the afternoon, found their audience disappearing at such speed that they were cut short in midstream. 'Thesis!' Doña Celia snapped as he turned and ran. 'I should like to know what thesis! Does he think he can deceive *us* as he does his parents!' And Nadyn shook her head exactly as her mother did, at the foolishness of such a notion.

Making his way out of the house, Luis ran into Teresa returning from the mercado, her market bag bulging with the produce for the day's cooking. 'Ah, eh,' she greeted him delightedly – how was it that his aunt and cousin could not muster such a display? he wondered – and showed him the vegetables she had bought to prepare for him, and the corn to make the pozole, his favourite, she knew, then gestured at the lane outside, making a face and warning him, 'Basura, basura everywhere.'

It was as she said – the basura collector's truck was parked outside the door, and bits of plastic bolsas and newspaper and vegetable peel blew off it and littered the cobblestones. He carefully stepped over them and, at the corner, where the great clump of bamboos leant over Doña Celia's garden wall, there were the men she'd spoken of, leaning against the adobe, their sombreros pulled low over their foreheads, and every one with a beer bottle in his hand while empties littered the earth around them. Luis could not help feeling amused to find the town had crept up this far and was even daring to assail his aunt's fortress. Perhaps one day she would be brought face to face with the modern world. The confrontation would be worth witnessing.

He rounded the corner and crossed Avenida Galeana, then started to climb the humps and hillocks of Calle de Cima towards Barrio Santa Cruz, keeping his eyes on the ground and picking his way from one cobblestone to another, avoiding the trickles and runnels of drainwater in between. The sun struck at the back of his neck and he wished he had bought a hat from the woman with a stall at the corner on Avenida de Tepoztlán, but it was too late to go back for it now.

Up at the top, he paused by the church with the faded, mottled pink stucco walls and tower that looked like something made by a potter, then left out for decades in the rain and damp. He had arrived at Calle Sor Juana Inés de la Cruz. He stood there catching his breath and remembered the times he had run up so lightly and eagerly, on his way to converse with the one man he held in esteem, the man whom he thought of as his mentor, and who had persuaded him to postpone entering his father's firm and go to university instead. He hesitated now because he was not sure if Don Beto would admire the way he was proceeding – Luis knew there was little cause for admiration – or even if he was still interested. It was such a long time since Luis had gone away to university in the States, and it was true he had been neglectful of writing letters to the old man or visiting him but, at the same time, if Don Beto-were as he remembered him, then seeing him would surely give his work the impetus it required: lately it had foundered and stalled, leaving him wondering if he was really made for an academic career, if he hadn't better give up and enter Papa's firm. After all, his entire circle of friends appeared to have done just that, falling out of university one after the other, disappearing, then re-emerging as elegant young dandies, owners of sleek cars. Their social lives revolved on a higher plane to which Luis was invited whenever he visited from Texas but on which he felt like an interloper. It was one such invitation that had driven him back to Tepoztlán and to Don Beto: Marisol dressed in skin-tight pink silk and black lace, giggling, 'Paz? Octavio Paz and Hindoo philosophy? Oh, Eduardo, you didn't tell me your friend is a Hin-doo!' and making enormous eyes, while Eduardo called loudly from the bar, 'Luis? He was always a philosopher! Better give up trying to lure him, Marisol.'

He was resting in the shade of the church wall and thinking

of that evening when he heard his name called and looked up to see his childhood friend Arturo parting the vines of a flowering squash plant on the hillside and peering at him. 'Luis, hola! Hola, Luis! What are you doing here? Thought you were in Houston or somewhere.'

Luis blinked up at him and answered as lightly as he could: he was not at all certain he liked encountering this apparition from a past life – schooldays, days when his family had all lived together here in the old house, before his father had taken them away to Mexico City. He and Arturo had played basketball together after school, in the court on Avenida Tepoztlán, looking out over the valley. Arturo had sisters he had been fond of, quite sentimentally, taking care never to betray those feelings when they were together. They had given him a present when he left, declaring he was sure to forget them otherwise. Actually, he'd lost it even before he got to Texas. He had not forgotten them, however, even if he had not particularly remembered. Now he shaded his eyes from the sun, chatting with Arturo, trying to say as little as possible about the university or Texas: it did not seem right when Arturo had gone nowhere, was probably helping his mama run the little abarrote down the street – what else was a young man with little school learning to do in Tepoztlán? But Arturo seemed not to share his embarrassment at all; standing there on the hillside with his hands on his hips, he called down to Luis, 'You chose a good day to visit. Come along to the zocalo this afternoon – you'll see some fun.'

'What kind of fun?' Luis asked warily. His family had never approved of the fun boys could be expected to think up in Tepoztlán.

'Ah, it's a show we've put together, to show those bandits from the city what we think of them and their plan for a golf club—'

'A golf club?' It was the last thing Luis expected to hear. 'A club de golf, here in Tepoztlán?'

'That's right. It's a pretty place, no? Green hills, streams, nature – so why not come and spoil it all, make a playground for the rich so they can come up on weekends to play, and who cares if the green hills and the pure streams all vanish? Plenty of boys doing nothing who could caddy for them, too. But we're going to teach them a thing or two – we're putting up a real fight. Come along for the show – you'll meet the old gang.'

Luis wondered who the others were who had stayed back and were now members of this curious group he had never heard of, and even Doña Celia had not mentioned in her zeal to bring him up to date. He raised his hand in a wave, promising to come along 'after I've been to see Don Beto. He still lives up this way, doesn't he?'

Arturo beamed down at him. 'Oh yes, where would he go? He'll die here under Tepozteco – he's willing to die for the movement, you know. Just ask him about it.'

It was not at all what Luis expected to talk about to the old scholar, but the conversation with Arturo left him uncertain of what he might and might not find. Don Beto's house was exactly as he remembered it, built into the hillside under the forests and crags on which the small pyramid of the Aztec god Tepoztecatl stood perched, and invisible from the road and the wrought-iron gate. The rusty, cracked bell still hung from the branch of a mango tree, its rope draped casually over the gate for visitors to pull. Beyond, he could see the ruins of the former house, the one Don Beto had grown up in, at the back of the grassed-over cobbles of the courtyard, only one step and a broken arch left standing with a ruined wall for a backdrop. A canvas hung on that wall, incongruously – a painting of underwater blues and greens with piscine shapes faint in its wash. A piece of clay moulded into a curious shell shape lay on the step.

It certainly seemed like a gateway to the past, and Luis gave the rope a tug. Immediately a dog sounded a warning howl but did not make an appearance. Eventually Don Beto's daughter, Marta, came hurrying down the path between the avocado and citrus trees that grew at the back. She did not recognize Luis at first, and pushed a strand of grey hair out of her eyes to peer at the figure on the other side of the gate, but when he greeted her she opened the gate, shook his hand, remembering, smiling. What did she remember of him, Luis wondered.

'You didn't recognize me,' he complained.

'Oh, we are growing old, old – our memories are going,' she laughed, making an excuse.

'But still painting,' he said, gesturing towards the canvas on the wall and the shell sculpture on the step as they passed around to the back of the ruin and faced the house that Don Beto had moved into after his wife's death, nothing more than a small cube of concrete, weathered and mildewed, but a veranda in front where flowers grew in rusty old jalapeño cans.

She preceded him into the house from which she fetched her father out onto the veranda. (Was this town peopled by ageing daughters taking care of their aged parents? Luis wondered.) Don Beto was more bent than before, like a woodland goblin, with a face like a knot in an ancient tree, and he had a stick like a twisted root to help him move. Both his daughter and Luis tried to help him settle into a chair but he waved them away and perched on a bench, insisting that Luis have the chair instead. This produced in Luis a discomfort that lasted throughout his visit. Don Beto, unlike everybody else he had met so far, questioned him closely on his life at the university in Houston, on how work was progressing on his thesis, showing the same intense interest in what Luis was doing as he had always had. Luis had corresponded with him over the years and Don Beto had recommended books and writers to him all along but, to Luis's disappointment, he appeared not to have any suggestions to make now. For such a young man to be paid such attention by an old scholar had been a heady experience and it had led Luis to believe he could and should go to university and pursue a scholarly life himself, but now he sensed a certain remoteness in Don Beto, as though this pursuit was not a joint one as Luis had fondly imagined. It made him feel the loneliness of academic labour, the hardness of such a pursuit.

Marta brought them té de manzanilla in pretty cups, and a plate of pastries. Then, as they sat crumbling the pastries with their fingers and watching out of the corners of their eyes a minute hummingbird hover over a plate-sized hibiscus in a pot, Don Beto changed the subject abruptly, and made a wholly unexpected suggestion: perhaps Luis should turn his mind, temporarily of course, to another kind of writing. Polemical. Why not use his pen and his gifts to address the matter that concerned all of them so urgently? And what was that matter? Ah, had he not heard of the club de golf that a consortium of wealthy developers wished to create here, having robbed the country of enough and now having to find ways to spend that wealth, here in this unlikely, unsuitable setting of Tepoztlán, drawn as everyone was to its mountains, its sweet water, its flora and fauna, its allure . . . He gestured passionately; the hummingbird fled.

Stillness
not on the branch in the air
Not in the air
in the moment
hummingbird

'Is this true?' asked Luis. 'I did hear – from Arturo—'
'You have heard? You *have?*' Don Beto questioned, and seemed astonished that Luis had heard and yet not spoken of it, or acted. 'Of this scandal? Then you must inform the world of it, you must turn your pen into a sword and fight . . .' The old man lifted his hand from the knob of his walking stick and held it up in the air, steady with command.

Luis left his crumbled pastry uneaten on his plate. Don Beto was filling his ears with facts and statistics now, his voice rising to a high pencil-squeak of indignation as he detailed the losses such a project would create, the losses to what made Tepoztlán such a treasure – no, not in the eyes of the world that saw it as poor and backward, a place that should think itself lucky to be chosen for 'development', with the money such a club would bring in – but to what those who lived here knew to be its wealth . . . and as he spoke of the environment and its endangered condition, it was as if all the old interests they had shared had been swept aside to make room for what was evidently now the old man's consuming passion. Once when Don Beto paused, Luis ventured to ask, 'And are you writing poetry, Don Beto? Have you written any verse recently?' only to see Don Beto set his mouth firmly and dismiss it with a wave. 'I write what my young friends need, in language that people can read and understand. Not poetry, no,' abandoning what he had spent a lifetime on, and towards which he had directed Luis.

Still bemused by Don Beto's – the unworldly, retiring, scholarly Don Beto – actually having suggested he go in for journalism instead of poetry, and all in the name of opposing a golf club, Luis wandered down to the zocalo in the sun-struck heat of the afternoon, wondering if he would find anyone there at all.

In spite of Doña Celia's complaints, he found the town exactly as he remembered it. Visitors from Cuernavaca and Mexico City were still pouring in for the Sunday market as they had always done, in their holiday clothes, to fill the restaurants from which music loudly rollicked. In the zocalo, he was sure the old couple selling pottery, their own faces as brown and seamed and cracked as if fashioned from clay, were the same he had always seen seated on a mat under the rubber tree; there were the same elderly people eagerly buying herbs and roots and seeds from the herbalist to cure them of gout, insomnia, obesity and fits, impotence and urinary problems; chillies hung in dark, leathery bunches that still set him sneezing; the florist continued to decorate his potted cacti with tiny paper flowers, and in the food stalls pans sizzled and steamed and large curs prowled around the customers' feet in the hope of scraps.

Luis remembered all that but somehow, after his visit to Don Beto, he was not content simply to plunge back into it and wallow in nostalgia. Instead, he drifted towards the big marquee of blue plastic that had been set up in between the town hall and the bandstand, the recording and amplifying systems that were being unloaded and attached, and the crowds gathering around it, some chewing on corncobs and others licking helados. On the steps of the post office he could see some of the young men he had known. Arturo was there, in the same striped T-shirt he had worn in the morning but with the addition of a baseball cap. Reluctant to go up to him, Luis lingered to read the legends on the banners flying everywhere – El Pueblo contra el Fascismo! Tierra de la Muerte! – and study the lurid murals that had been painted on the town hall walls: a rubicund golfer with a tail protruding from his golf pants and hooves in place of shoes, his caddy a grinning imp with pointed ears and a forked tail, together facing a group of peasants huddled in blankets, dark, weary and watchful. In another, over the shoe stall with its rows of huaraches, rufescent golfers sported golf clubs and grinningly molested frightened young women whose blouses had been torn off their breasts. Every one of the rubber and laurel trees in the little park around the bandstand, and every pillar of the post office, had smaller, printed posters pasted on them. Several depicted frogs, squirrels, butterflies and birds, each saying 'No' to the golf club in a different language: Niet! Nein! Na! Non!

Now the first strains of an amplified guitar rang out. People dropped the huaraches and sombreros they were examining, got up from around the roasted corncob stalls, came out of the ice-cream parlours and cafés, and began to gather under the marquee. Luis strolled across as casually as he could, but when he saw who was playing the guitar and teaching the audience the lines he had composed 'for Tepoztlán', his assumed composure fell apart: it was Alejandro, who had been in school with him and Arturo, and had been known for his passion for fireworks, whose ambition it had been to launch a fire balloon which, once aloft, would release a burst of rockets. Now he was standing in front of a microphone in jeans and a black tank shirt, his head shaved on all sides, leaving one cornrow to grow along the centre where it stood in jagged peaks, dyed a fiery red. When he called out a line:

'Leave me my streams, leave me my hills,'

the crowd echoed him:

'Leave me my streams, leave me my hills,'

and then joined him in the refrain:

'Leave me my paradise, Tepoztlán.'

Luis fell back, allowing a party of curious tourists to edge up in front of him, in the hope they would conceal him from Alejandro. But of course Alejandro was not looking at him – he was plucking his guitar with his eyes closed and his head thrown back as he sang:

'Who dares to come and steal
My paradise, Tepoztlán?'

Someone was going around selling tapes of, presumably, Alejandro's songs. A young woman in a flowered skirt circled the crowds with a straw hat outstretched, collecting donations. She smiled into Luis's face: hers was like a ripe peach, so round and sweet. He dug into his pockets and brought out a crumpled note for her.

Now Alejandro was waving at the crowd and turning to run back up the post office steps and vanish among his friends there while another figure leapt into their midst: a lithe young man dressed entirely in black but with his pants cut off at the knees and his shirt open on his chest. In his hands he held an empty rum bottle and with it he performed a dance of a kind Luis had never seen in the clubs and parties to which he had been. He could hardly maintain his composure as he watched the man crouch, roll on the ground, leap, fall, clutch the bottle and fling it away, all with such abandon and fury that it had Luis flinching.

There was a comic interlude to follow: a fool-faced vendor of eggs strolled through the audience and tried to sell them, a clown-faced policeman accosted him with a rubber truncheon and dragged him off to a frowning judge with a cotton-wool beard who made a fool of himself by asking the vendor totally absurd and irrelevant questions till the egg vendor, exasperated, seized the policeman's truncheon and brought it down on the judge's head. The crowd roared. Luis felt he should now edge away and disappear. There was no need to be an onlooker at a market sideshow along with vegetable sellers and tortilla eaters.

But the dancer had returned to the ring and Luis, looking back, saw his feline body stalk across the space with the kind of authority that rivets an onlooker. Besides, Luis caught sight of another figure strutting across the ring from the other direction, towards him and past him – a girl in blue jeans and a white T-shirt, ordinary laced black shoes, her hair cut short to her shoulders, no make-up or costume, but with a dancer's controlled grace and carefully considered movements that invested the faintest turn of her head or twist of the wrist with significance. Luis was held by that grace and authority, and as he stared it dawned on him who she was: Arturo's kid sister, one of the two little girls who had smiled at him when he visited, sometimes played basketball in the garden with the boys, and for whom he had developed boyishly sentimental feelings he never confessed to anyone, scarcely even to himself. Ester and Isabel – he remembered their names now: which one was she? He glanced across at Arturo who was standing at the top of the stairs, watching, his arms folded about him, and his expression – watchful, proprietorial, concerned – confirmed his impression: this was Isabel, or perhaps Ester, grown into this astonishing young sylph, dancing with the man in black as he had never seen anyone dance in the city, at clubs or parties. Where had she learnt to dance like that – in that man's embrace, or rejected by him and on her own, then with a second dancer who entered the arena and prowled around, waiting for his chance and taking it? Here was Ester – or Isabel – and now she was grown-up, and dancing amongst grown-ups, performing, acting out those rites of attraction, infatuation, rejection and recovery that Luis had not only not experienced yet but not witnessed anyone in his circle of family and friends experience with such ardour, abandon and intensity.

The trio met in the centre of the ring and performed their dance together, then parted, stalking off in different directions, and Alejandro was returning, holding his guitar above his head, when Luis broke away and pushed his way out past the onlookers.

He hurried past the lurid murals, the huarache sellers and the comic-book stalls under the trees by the bandstand and out onto Avenida de la Revolución 1910 without thinking. It was the wrong direction, he realized, and he would have to walk down its length before he could take the turn that led him back to Matamoros – Matamoros where Doña Celia kept the old house as it had always been, and the world at bay.

The entire street was jammed with the gaieties of the Sunday market, shoppers strolling in the sun, picking through stalls of silver trinkets, scarves and blouses, paper flowers and painted mirrors. The ice cream and sorbet stall, festooned with pink and blue pompoms, was so busy it was hard to get past it. The middle of the street was taken up by the young, sipping margaritas from clay mugs, or large families enjoying helados. The women wore high heels and low-cut blouses, dark glasses and jewellery, the young girls had tinted hair, painted nails and laughing mouths and young men pressed against them, admiring.

These were the people from Cuernavaca and Mexico City to whose parties Luis went when he was at home; these were the girls with whom he danced, the young men with whom he played tennis. If there were a golf club here, then these were the people who would play on its course. His family would urge him to join them: he belonged, they belonged, to the same society. He did not belong to the people under the marquee – they would have been strangers to his family, and they would have looked upon him as an onlooker, and an outsider.

Then what made him push his way out of their company and stumble through the gate to the convento and seek out its calm, cool cloisters? He had always liked to come here, for its quiet and shade and vast views of the mountains and valleys from its deep windows. It had always been an oasis to which he could withdraw, for contemplation.

In the court, the sun stone, immobile;
above, the sun of fire and of time turns;
movement is sun and the sun is stone.

Now he walked down the shaded veranda under a ceiling painted with crimson roses not quite faded into the stone, and entered the courtyard where water dropped quietly from a fountain set amongst grass paths and potted bougainvillea. But above it hung a strange, unfamiliar shape fashioned out of wicker and fastened by ropes to the belfry. What was it? He climbed the stairs to the upper galleries for a closer look at the wicker basket – or was it a trap? – and found the galleries hung with art exhibits and remembered that that was the use to which the convento was nowadays put. If this could be called an art exhibit: the exhibition clearly had to do with Tepoztlán's environment – the subject could not be avoided, it confronted him wherever he went. Here were photographs of its flowers and birds, here were installations of sand scattered with ugly litter – Coke cans, plastic bolsas – and paintings of devastated landscapes, pitted and marred by modern, urban blight, photographs of the aged, their weathered faces looking out of doorways and windows, watching.

Luis caught his breath. Was there no escape from Tepoztlán's issues and involvements, its demands and accusations? And whose side was he on? Everything, everyone he encountered seemed to ask him to decide, to declare.

It was late afternoon when he finally turned into Avenida Matamoros, and early clouds had begun to descend from the mountains. The bamboo grove threw long shadows across the white dust and in it sprawled men he'd seen earlier, heavily asleep. He had to avoid stumbling on their limp figures and empty bottles. He turned in at the gate and shut it quickly behind him.

In the shadowy drawing room Doña Celia was seated stiffly as an idol but on seeing him began at once to complain about how the town had gone to pieces and wanted to know if he had noticed the deterioration. Who, what is it that has deteriorated but you, you old ghost? he wanted to ask and to say that everyone else was moving on, on, but instead he muttered his impressions as non-committally as possible. Nadyn, who was poking at a Raidolito with a hairpin and blinking against its fumes, interrupted to ask if he had met any of his old friends. What were they doing now? she wanted to know as if confident he would reply 'Nothing' at which she could pull a face, but he turned it into 'I don't know', disappointing her.

'There's nothing to know. The young today – pah!' snorted Doña Celia, drawing her shawl about her throat with a malevolent glare.

It was a relief when Teresa announced dinner and they rose to go and sit at a table where she had placed a pot of pozole and stood waiting for Luis to take his first spoonful. 'Good?' she queried. 'As good as before, eh?'

Nadyn looked up and frowned at her but Doña Celia herself was giving the soup her approval, slurping it up with indiscreet sounds that expressed relish – in spite of everything, expressed relish.

Luis had to wait till Teresa was gone before saying to his aunt, 'I will be leaving in the morning. Please don't let me disturb you – so early – I'll let myself out—'

What? Doña Celia's expression managed to say, after another quick, delicious swallow. Slowly her look of pleasure was overtaken by the habitual displeasure. So soon? He had only just come. 'And are you not staying for Cousin Heriberto's birthday celebration? It is to be a very big celebration, you know. He is eighty years old this week.' All his children were coming, from Monterrey, from Toluca – even Luis's parents had spoken of coming. Why then—

His thesis. His classes. The university— But not in the summer, surely? Research had to be continued, you see, no rest for the weary. He flushed as he stumbled over his excuses and Nadyn watched with a tightening of her lips – she of course saw through them instantly. Her pride at never having made them herself gave her mouth a bitter twist.

'We're too old for you, not up to date, eh?' she said. 'Ah, the gringo—'

He wanted to protest but the words disintegrated in his mouth, useless. He lowered his eyes to the bowl of soup, Teresa's excellent pozole. He felt ashamed of not doing it the honour it deserved.

The Rooftop Dwellers

Paying off the autorickshaw driver, she stepped down cautiously, clutching her handbag to her. The colony was much further out than she had expected – they had travelled through bazaars and commerical centres and suburbs she had not known existed – but the name given on the gate matched the one in her purse. She went up to it and rattled the latch to announce her arrival. Immediately a dog began to yap and she could tell by its shrillness that it was one of those small dogs that readily sink their tiny teeth into one's ankle or rip through the edge of one's sari. There were also screams from several children. Yet no one came to open the gate for her and finally she let herself in, hoping the dog was chained or indoors. Certainly there was no one in the tiny garden which consisted of a patch of lawn and a tap in front of the yellow stucco villa. All the commotion appeared to be going on indoors and she walked up to the front door – actually at the side of the house – and rang the bell, clearing her throat like a saleswoman preparing to sell a line in knitting patterns or homemade jams.

She was finally admitted by a very small servant boy in striped cotton pyjamas and a torn grey vest, and taken to meet the family. They were seated on a large bed in the centre of a room with walls painted an electric blue, all watching a show on a gigantic television set. It was an extremely loud, extremely dramatic scene showing a confrontation between a ranting hero, a weeping heroine and a benignly smiling saint, and the whole family was watching open-mouthed, reluctant to turn their attention away from it. But when their dog darted out from under the bed at her, she screamed and the servant boy flapped his duster and cried, 'No, Candy! Get down, Candy!' they had no alternative but to turn to her, resentfully.

'You have come just at *Mahabharata* time,' the woman crosslegged on the bed reproached her.

'Sit down, sit down, beti. You can watch it with us,' the man said more agreeably, waving at an open corner on the bed, and since they had all transferred their attention back to the screen, she was forced to perch on it, fearfully holding her ankles up in the air so as not to be nipped by Candy, who had been driven back under the bed and hid there, growling. The two children stared at her for a bit, impassively, then went back to picking their noses and following the episode of the *Mahabharata* that the whole city of Delhi watched, along with the rest of the country, on Sunday evenings – everyone, except for her.

There had been too much happening in her life to leave room for watching television and keeping up with the soap operas and mythological sagas. In any case, there was no television set in the women's hostel where she had a room. There was nothing in it except what was absolutely essential: the dining room on the ground floor with its long tables, its benches, its metal plates and utensils, and the kitchen with its hatch through which the food appeared in metal pots; and upstairs the rows of rooms, eight feet by ten, each equipped with a wooden bedframe, and a shelf nailed to the wall. She had had to purchase a plastic bucket to take to the bathroom at the end of the corridor so she could bathe under the standing tap – not high enough to work as a shower – and had arranged her toilet articles on the shelf and left her clothes in her tin trunk which she covered with a pink tablecloth and sat on when she did not want to sit on her bed, or when one of the other women in the hostel came to visit her and climbed onto her bed to have a chat.

The minimalism of these living arrangements was both a novelty and a shock to her. She came from a home where the accommodation of objects, their comfortable clutter and convenience, could be taken for granted. Nothing had been expensive or elaborate but there had been plenty of whatever there was, accumulated over many years: rugs, chairs, cushions, clothes, dishes, in rooms, verandas, odd corners and spaces. So for the first two weeks she felt she was trapped in a cell; whenever she shut the door, she was swallowed by the cell, its prisoner. If she left the door ajar, every girl going past would look in, scream, 'Oh, Moy-na!' and come in to talk, tell her of the latest atrocity committed by the matron or of the unbelievably rotten food being served downstairs, and also of their jobs, their bosses, their colleagues, and homes and families. Some were divorcees, some widows, and some supported large families, all of which led to an endless fund of stories to be told. In order to get any sleep, she would have to shut the door and pretend not to be in. Then she began to wonder if she was in herself.

But such was her determination to make her new life as a working woman in the metropolis succeed, and such was her unexpected, unforeseen capacity for adjustment, that after a month or so the minimalism became no longer privation and a challenge but simply a way of life. She even found herself stopping at her neighbours' open doors on her way back from the office, to say, 'D'you know what they're cooking for our dinner downstairs?' and laughing when the others groaned, invariably, 'Pumpkin!' because that was all there ever was, or else to give the warning, 'Matron's *mad*! I heard her screaming at Leila – she found out about her iron. Hide yours, quick!' It became a habit, instead of a subject of complaint, to carry her bucket down to the bathroom when she wanted to bathe, and bring it back to her room so it wouldn't be stolen: thefts were common, unfortunately. Even the tap, and water, began to seem like luxuries, bonuses not to be taken for granted in that hostel.

After a breakfast of tea, bread and fried eggs, she went out to stand at the bus stop with the other women, all of whom caught the Ladies' Special that came around at nine o'clock and carried them to their work places as telephone operators, typists, desk receptionists, nurses, teachers, airline hostesses and bank tellers, without the menace of crazed young men groping at them or pressing into them as if magnetized, or even delivering vicious pinches before leaping off the bus and running for their lives. Some women had had to develop defensive strategies. Lily, known to be 'bold', instructed others to carry a sharp pin concealed in their fists and use that to prod anyone who came too close. 'I've made big men cry,' she boasted proudly, but most women in the hostel preferred to pay the extra rupee or two to travel on the Ladies' Special instead of the regular DTS. Like tap water, it was a luxury, a bonus, which had their gratitude.

Moyna's descriptions of these strategies of living earned her the admiration of her family and friends back at home to whom she described them, but trouble began for her just as she was settling into this new, challenging way of life. She came across the hostel cook kicking viciously at the skeletal yellow kitten that had crept in from outside in the hope of one of life's unexpected bonuses – a drop of milk left in someone's tumbler, or a scrap from the garbage bin. Instinctively she lowered her hand and called it to her – she came from a home that was shelter to an assortment of cats, dogs, birds, some maimed, some pregnant, some dying. She shared her bread and fried egg with the kitten, and soon it started weaving in and out of her sari folds, then followed her up the stairs and darted into her room. This was novelty indeed: having someone to share the cell with her. It was curious how instantly the room ceased to be a prison. The kitten settled onto the pink tablecloth on the trunk and began to lick itself clean, delicately raising one leg at a time into the air and making a thorough toilet, as if it were preparing to be fit for such luxurious accommodation. Later, that night, she woke to find it had sprung from the trunk to her bed. Knowing it probably had fleas, she tried to kick it off, but it clung on and started to purr, as if to persuade her of its accomplishments. Purring, it lay against her leg and lulled her back to sleep.

One day the matron was inspecting during the day, when they were all away, for such forbidden items as irons and hot plates, and came out holding the kitten by the scruff of his neck. Moyna pleaded innocence and swore she did not know how he had got into her room. But when she was caught red-handed, emptying the milk jug into a saucer for Mao under the table, the matron slapped her with the eviction notice. Had Moyna not read the rule: No Pets Allowed?

Instinctively, she knew not to mention Mao to this family. Somehow that would have to be sorted out, if she took the room they had to offer. But, glancing round at their faces in the flickering light from the television set, she began to feel uncertain if she would take it. At her office, Tara, who was experienced in these matters, had told her, 'You don't have to take the first room you see, Moyna. You can look around and choose.' But Moyna had already 'looked around' and while, by comparison with the cell in the women's hostel, all the rooms had seemed princely, shamingly it was she who had been turned down by one prospective landlord or landlady after the other. She had been scrutinized with such suspicion, questioned with such hostility, that she realized that no matter what they stated in their advertisements, they had nothing but fear and loathing for the single working woman, and the greatest dread of allowing one into their safe, decent homes. Moyna wondered how she could convey such an impression of sin and wantonness. She dressed in a clean, starched cotton sari every day, and even though her hair was cut short, it was simply pinned back behind her ears, not curled or dyed. And surely her job in the office of a literary journal was innocent enough? But they narrowed their eyes, saw her as too young, too pretty, too unattached, too much an instrument of danger, and dismissed her as a candidate for their barsatis. These rooms had once been built on Delhi's flat rooftops so that families who slept out on their roofs on summer nights could draw in their beds in case of a sudden dust storm or thunder shower. But now that Delhi was far too unsafe for sleeping alfresco, these barsatis were being rented out to working spinsters or bachelors at a delightful profit.

Suddenly convinced that she would not, after all, want to occupy this unwelcoming family's barsati, Moyna lowered her feet to the floor gingerly and tried to rise and murmur an excuse. 'I have to be at the hostel before nine,' she said when the episode of the *Mahabharata* ended with a great display of fiery arrows being shot into the sky and a whirling disc beheading the villain. The landlord gestured to the children to turn off the set and, turning to Moyna, he shouted to the servant boy to bring her a drink. 'What will you have, beti? Chai, lassi, lemonade?'

'No, thank you, no, thank you,' she murmured, seeing the landlady's steely eyes on her, willing her to refuse, but the servant boy came out with a thick glass of tepid water for her anyway. While she sipped it, the inquisition began, interrupted frequently by the children who alternately demanded their dinner or another show on television and by the dog who emerged from under the bed and sniffed at her suspiciously. Moyna kept her eyes lowered to watch for Candy and perhaps they saw that as becoming modesty or demureness because, to her surprise, the landlady said, 'You want to see the room? Ramu, Ramu – eh, Ramu! Get the key to the barsati and open it up.'

And there, on the flat rooftop of the plain yellow stucco villa in a colony Moyna had never heard of before on the outskirts of New Delhi, there to her astonishment was a palace, a veritable palace amongst barsatis. The rooftop, which covered the entire area of the villa, seemed to her immense, larger than any space she had occupied since her arrival in Delhi, and it was clear, empty space under an empty sky, with a view of all the other rooftops stretching out on every side, giving Moyna, as she stood there, a sense of being the empress of all she surveyed. Of course it would bake under her feet in the heat of summer but – and this was the crowning glory – a pipal tree that grew in the small walled courtyard at the back of the house rose up over the barsati itself, sheltering it from the sun with a canopy of silvery, rustling leaves, spreading out its branches and murmuring, Moyna felt certain, a gracious welcome.

After that auspicious view, what could it matter if the barsati itself was merely a square walled cube, that it had not been cleaned in so long that its single window had turned opaque with dust, and spider webs hung in swags from every corner, that the bed was nothing but a string-cot, the cheapest kind of charpai? What did it matter that the single cupboard against the wall had doors that did not seem to meet but sagged on their hinges and could never be locked, that the 'kitchen' was only a blackened kerosene stove atop a wooden table that also served as desk and dining table, that the 'bathroom' was a closet-sized attached enclosure, open to the sky, with a very stained and yellowed squatter-type toilet and a single stand-pipe? Already Moyna's mind was racing with visions of what she could transform the place into. Why, its very bareness gave her the freedom to indulge her wildest dreams and fancies.

Then her look fell upon the servant boy who stood waiting by the door that opened onto the staircase, twirling the key round his finger and smirking, and she became aware that she herself had a smile across her face and that her hands were clasped to her throat in a most foolish fashion. Immediately she dropped them, adjusted her expression to one of severity, and followed him down the stairs.

The landlord and landlady, now risen from the bed and waiting for her on the veranda, looking as alike as twins with their corpulence, their drooping chins and expressions of benign self-satisfaction, appeared confident of her answer: it was only what could be expected after seeing what they were offering. She would of course sign a year's lease which could be terminated whenever they chose, pay three months' deposit, plus the first month's rent right now, immediately, 'and we will welcome you to our house as our own beti,' they assured her magnanimously.

'From now on, you need worry about nothing. Your parents need have no worries about you. We will be your parents.'

Tara came over from the office with her husband Ritwick to help her to move in. Moyna had only one tin trunk, a bedding roll and now her kitten in a basket, but they insisted she would not be able to move on her own, and Ritwick growled that he wanted to meet the Bhallas 'to make sure'. The Bhallas were seated on a wicker sofa in the veranda when they arrived, and watched them carry every item up the stairs with openly inquisitive stares. It seemed to Moyna that it was not Ritwick who was sizing them up so much as that they were sizing *him* up. Certainly they questioned him closely, when Moyna introduced him to them, regarding his parentage, ancestral home, present occupation and relation to Tara and Moyna before allowing him to set one foot on the stairs. But once they arrived on the rooftop, Ritwick looked into every crack and crevice with a suspicion to equal theirs. Then he asked, 'Where's the water tank?'

'What water tank?'

'*Your* water tank. Where is your water supply coming from?'

'I don't know. Where *does* it come from? The pipes, I suppose.'

He strode to the bathroom and turned on the tap. It spun around weakly, gurgled in a complaining tone, and sputtered into silence. There was no water. Moyna stood in the doorway, stricken. 'Water shortage,' she explained. 'You know Delhi has a water shortage, Ritwick.'

'Not if you have a storage tank. Everyone has a storage tank – or several. The Bhallas will have one downstairs, but you need a booster pump and your own tank up here so water can be pumped up from the one below.'

'Oh.'

He looked at her with the kind of exasperation her own brothers turned on her when she failed to understand what they were doing under the bonnet of the car or with electric gadgets at home. She came from a family so competent that she had never needed to be competent herself.

'Did you ask the Bhallas about it?'

'About what?'

'The storage tank. The booster pump.'

'No,' she admitted.

He strode off towards the staircase with every show of determination to enquire immediately. She ran after him, crying, 'Oh, Ritwick, I'll ask them – I'll ask them – later, when I go down.'

Tara came out of the barsati. 'D'you have curtains?'

'What for?'

'Because if you wipe the windowpanes clean, your neighbours can look right in.'

'No, they can't! There's the tree – don't you see my beautiful tree? It's like a screen.'

'Come in and see.'

Tara had wiped the windowpanes clean, and a young man with a face like a pat of butter and with a small moustache twitching over his pursed lips was standing on his rooftop and gazing at them with unconcealed curiosity and, it could easily be made out since the distance was small, some admiration.

'Oh, Tara, why did you go and clean that?' Moyna cried. 'No, I don't have a curtain. Where would I get a curtain from?'

'Get me a bedsheet then,' Tara commanded, 'and help me put it up at once.'

'But the tree—' Moyna tried again, and went out to see why it had not lowered a branch where it was needed. The tree shaded the entire barsati (and Ritwick admitted it would keep off the sun which would otherwise make a tandoori oven of it) but it was tall and provided no screen against the other rooftops and the rooftop dwellers who suddenly all seemed to be standing outside their barsati doors, surveying this newcomer to their level of elevation. Moyna suddenly realized she had joined a community.

'When I came yesterday, I saw no one,' she mumbled, abashed.

'Well, you can introduce yourself to all of them now,' Ritwick said, 'and just hope none of them are thieves or murderers because if they are –' he looked grim and gestured – 'all they need is one jump from their ledge to yours.'

'Don't, Ritwick,' Tara said sharply. 'Why are you trying to frighten poor Moyna?'

'All I'm saying is Moyna'd better stay indoors and keep her door locked.'

'But I was going to drag my bed out and sleep under the stars!'

'Are you crazy?' both Tara and Ritwick said together, and Tara added, 'D'you want your picture in the evening news, with a headline: "Single Woman Robbed and Murdered in Barsati"?' They looked at her sternly to see if their words had had the requisite effect, and Tara added, 'Now let's go to the market and get you all the things you need. Like one great big lock and key.'

When they returned from the market with cleaning fluids, brooms, scrubbing materials, provisions for 'the kitchen' – and the lock and key – Ritwick confronted the landlady who had in the meantime shampooed her hair and now sat on the veranda, to dry it in the sun.

'Excuse me,' he said, not very politely. 'Can you please show Moyna where the switch is for the booster pump?'

'What switch? What booster pump?' She parted her hair and peered out from under it with some hostility.

'Is there no booster pump to send water up to the barsati?'

'Water up to the barsati?' she repeated, as if he were mad. 'Why? Why? What is wrong?'

'There's no water in the tap. She'll need water, won't she?'

'She will get water,' declared Mrs Bhalla, drawing herself up and tossing her head so that the grey strands flew, 'when municipality is sending water. Municipality water is coming at five o'clock every morning and five o'clock every evening. The barsati will be getting water whenever municipality sends.'

'At five in the morning and five in the evening?' shouted Ritwick. 'You need a storage tank so water will collect.'

'Collect? Why she cannot collect in a bucket?' Mrs Bhalla shouted back. 'She has no bucket?' she added insultingly.

Tara and Moyna were standing with their purchases in their arms, ready to bolt upstairs, but Ritwick yelled, 'Yes, she *has* bucket, but how can she collect at five in the morning and five in the evening?'

'What is wrong?' Mrs Bhalla screamed back. 'We are all collecting – why she cannot collect also?'

'Because she will be sleeping at five in the morning and at work at five in the evening!'

Mrs Bhalla turned away from him and looked at her tenant with an expression that made clear what she thought of any young woman who would be asleep at five in the morning and 'at work' at five in the evening. She clearly had an equally low opinion of sleep and work, at least where her young tenant was concerned. Ritwick was shouting, 'Storage tank – booster pump—' when Moyna fled upstairs, dropping matchboxes and kitchen dusters along the way. When Tara followed her up, she found her sitting on her bed in tears, howling, 'And I've signed the lease for one year and paid for three months in advance!'

Moyna's way of life changed completely. It had to be adjusted to that of the Bhallas. She left her tap turned on when she went to bed – which she did earlier and earlier – so she could be woken by the sound of water gushing into the plastic bucket at five in the morning and get up to fill every pot, pan and kettle she had acquired before turning it off. All around her she could hear her fellow rooftop dwellers performing the same exercise – as well as bathing and washing clothes in the starlight before the water ran out. She went back to bed and lay there, panting, trying to get back to sleep, but by six o'clock all the birds that roosted in the pipal tree were awake and screaming and running on their little clawed feet across the corrugated iron roof, then lining up along the ledge of the rooftop to flutter their wings, crow, squawk and chirp their ode to dawn. It was just as well that they made it impossible for her to fall asleep again because at six she had to go downstairs and walk to the market where Mother Dairy would have opened its booth and all the colony residents would be lining up with their milk cans to have them filled. She stood there with all the servant boys and maidservants, sleepy-eyed, for the the sake of having her milk pail filled for Mao, and then carried it back carefully through the dust, in her slippers, trying not to spill any.

No Ladies' Special serviced this colony, and Tara had warned her against attempting to travel to work on an ordinary DTC bus. 'You don't know what men in Delhi do to women,' she said darkly. 'This isn't Bombay or Calcutta, you know.'

Moyna had heard this warning in the women's hostel but asked, 'What d'you mean?'

'In Calcutta all men call women Mother or Sister and never touch them. In Bombay, if any man did, the woman would give him a tight slap and drag him by his hair to the police station. But in Delhi – these Jats . . .' She shuddered, adding, 'Don't you even *try*.'

So Moyna walked back to the marketplace after breakfast, to the autorickshaw stand in front of Mother Dairy, and spent a sizeable part of her income on taking one to work. She clearly made a woebegone figure while waiting, and a kindly Sikh who rode his autorickshaw as if it were a sturdy ox, his slippered feet planted on either side of the gearbox, the end of his turban flying, and a garland of tinsel twinkling over the dashboard where he had pasted a photograph of his two children and an oleograph of Guru Gobind Singh, took pity on her. 'Beti, every day you go to work at the same time, to the same place. I will take you, for a monthly rate. It will be cheaper for you.' So Gurmail Singh became her private chauffeur, so to speak, and Moyna rode to work bouncing on the narrow backseat, her sari held over her nose to keep out the dust and oil and diesel fumes from all the office-bound traffic through which he expertly threaded his way.

Quite often he was waiting for her outside the office at six o'clock to take her home. 'I live in that colony myself, so it is no trouble to me,' he told her. 'If I have no other customer, I can take you, why not?' In a short while she got to know his entire family – his mother who cooked the best dal in the land, and the finest corn bread and mustard greens, his daughter who was the smartest student in her class – class two, he told Moyna – and his son who had only just started going to school but was unfortunately not showing the same keen interest in his studies as his sister. 'I tell him, "Do you want to go back to the village and herd buffaloes?" But he doesn't care, his heart is only in play. When it is schooltime, he cries. And his mother cries with him.'

'Gurmail Singh thinks it is the school that is bad. Bluebells, it's called,' Moyna reported at the office. 'He wants to get him into a good convent school, like St Mary's, but you need pull for that.' She sighed, lacking any.

'Moyna, can't you talk about anything but the Bhallas and Gurmail Singh and his family?' Tara asked one day, stubbing out her cigarette in an ashtray on her desk.

Moyna was startled: she had not realized she was growing so obsessive about these people, so prominent in her life, so uninteresting to her colleagues. But didn't Tara talk about Ritwick's position in the university, and about her own son and his trials at school, or the hardships of having to live with her widowed mother-in-law for lack of their own house? 'What d'you want to talk about then?' she asked, a little hurt.

'Look, we have to bring out the magazine, don't we?' Tara said, smoking furiously. 'And it isn't getting easier, it just gets harder all the time to get people to read a journal about *books*. Bose Sahib hardly comes to see what is going on here—' she complained.

'What is going on?' asked Raj Kumar, the peon, bringing them two mugs of coffee from the shop downstairs. 'I am here, running everything for you. Why do you need Bose Sahib?'

'Oh, Raj Kumar,' Tara sighed, putting out her cigarette and accepting the rich, frothing coffee from him. 'What will you do to make *Books* sell?'

Tara was the first person Ajoy Bose had employed when he started his literary review, *Books*, after coming to Delhi as a member of parliament from Calcutta. He had missed the literary life of that city so acutely, and had been so appalled by the absence of any equivalent in New Delhi, that he had decided to publish a small journal of book reviews to inform readers on what was being published, what might be read, a service no other magazine seemed to provide, obsessed as they all were with politics or the cinema, the only two subjects that appeared to bring people in the capital to life. Having first met Ritwick at the Jawaharlal Nehru University during a conference on Karl Marx and Twentieth Century Bengali Literature, and through him Tara, he had engaged her as the Managing Editor. The office was installed in two rooms above a coffee and sweet shop in Bengali Market. It was Tara's first paid job – she had been working in non-government organizations simply to escape from home and her mother-in-law – and she was extremely proud of these two modest rooms that she had furnished with cane mats and bamboo screens. Bose Sahib had magnanimously installed a desert cooler and a water cooler to keep life bearable in the summer heat. Together they had interviewed Raj Kumar, and found him literate enough to run their errands at the post office and bank. Then Tara had interviewed all the candidates who had applied for the post of assistant, and chosen Moyna. Moyna had no work experience at all, having only just taken her degree, in English literature, at a provincial university. She managed somehow to convey her need to escape from family and home, and Tara felt both maternal and proprietorial towards her, while Moyna immensely admired her style, the way she smoked cigarettes and drank her coffee black and spoke to both Raj Kumar and Bose Sahib as equals, and she hoped ardently to emulate her, one day.

Of course the only reason she had been allowed by her family to come to Delhi and take the job was that it was of a literary nature, and her father had known Bose Sahib at the university. They approved of all she told them in her weekly letters and, Moyna often thought while opening parcels of books that had arrived from the publishers or upon receiving stacks of printed copies of their journal fresh from the press, how proud they would be if they could see her, their youngest, and how incredulous . . .

Now here was Tara claiming that sales were so poor as to be shameful, and that if no one came to its rescue, the journal would fold. 'Just look at our list of subscribers,' Tara said disgustedly, tossing it over the desk to Moyna. 'It's the same list Bose Sahib drew up when we began – we haven't added one new subscriber in the last year!'

'Oh, Tara, my father is now a subscriber,' Moyna reminded her nervously, but Tara glared at her so she felt compelled to study the list seriously. It was actually quite interesting: apart from the names of a few of Bose Sahib's fellow members of parliament, and a scattering of college libraries, the rest of the list was made up of a circle so far-flung as to read like a list of the rural districts of India. She could not restrain a certain admiration. 'Srimati Shakuntala Pradhan in PO Barmana, Dist. Bilaspur, HP, and Sri Rajat Khanna in Dist. Birbhum, 24 Parganas, W. Bengal . . . Tara, just think of all the places the journal *does* get to! We ought to have a map on the wall—'

Raj Kumar, who was listening while washing out the coffee mugs in the corner with the water cooler which stood in a perennial puddle, called out heartily, 'Yes, and I am posting it from Gole Market Post Office to the whole of Bharat! Without me, no one is getting *Books*!'

Moyna turned to throw him a look of mutual congratulation but Tara said, 'Shut up, Raj Kumar. If we can't find new names for our list, we'll lose the special rate the post office gives journals.'

'Send to bogus names, then, and bogus addresses!' Raj Kumar returned smartly.

Now Tara turned to stare at him. 'How do you know so much about such bogus tricks?'

He did not quite give her a wink but, as he polished the mugs with a filthy rag, he began to hum the latest hit tune from the Bombay cinema which was the great love of his life and the bane of the two women's.

'The next time Bose Sahib comes, we'll really have to have a serious discussion,' Tara said. The truth was that her son Bunty had received such a bad report from school that it was clear he would need tutoring in maths as well as Hindi, and that would mean paying two private tutors on top of the school fees which were by no means negligible – and the matter of Ritwick's promotion had still not been brought up for consideration. She lit another cigarette nervously.

Bose only came to visit them when parliament opened for its summer session. He, too, had much on his mind – in his case, of a political nature – and *Books* was not a priority for him. But when he was met on the appointed day at the door by two such anxious young women, and saw the coffee and the Gluco biscuits spread out on Tara's desk in preparation for his announced visit, he realized this was not to be a casual visit but a business conference. He cleared his throat and sat down to listen to their problems with all the air of an MP faced with his constituents.

'So, we have to have a sales drive, eh?' he said after listening to Tara spell out the present precarious state of the journal.

'Yes, but before we have that, we have to have an overhaul,' Tara told him authoritatively. 'For instance, Bose Sahib, the name *Books* just has to go. I told you straightaway it is the most boring, unattractive name you could think up—'

'What do you mean? What do you mean?' he spluttered, tobacco flakes spilling from his fingers as he tamped them into his pipe. 'What can be more *attractive* than *Books*? What can be less *boring* than *Books*?' He seemed appalled by her philistinism.

'Oh, that's just for *you*.' Tara was not in the least put out by the accusation in his mild face or his eyes blinking behind the thick glasses in their black frames. 'What about people browsing in a shop, seeing all these magazines with pin-ups and headlines? Are they going to *glance* at a journal with a plain yellow cover like a school notebook, with just the word *Books* on it?'

'Why not? Why not?' he spluttered, still agitated.

'Perhaps we could choose a new title?' Moyna suggested, rubbing her fingers along the scratches on the desk, nervously.

The two women had already discussed the matter between them, and now spilled out their suggestions: *The Book Bag, The Book Shelf*... well, perhaps those weren't so much more exciting than plain *Books* but what about, what about – *Pen and Ink? The Pen Nib? Pen and Paper? Press and Paper?*

It seemed to make Bose Sahib think that new blood was required on the staff because his reaction to their session was to send them, a month later, a new employee he had taken on, a young man newly graduated from the University of Hoshiarpur who would aid Tara and Moyna in all their office chores. He would deal with the media, see the paper through the press, supervise its distribution, visit bookshops and persuade them to display the journal more prominently, and allow Tara and Moyna to take on extra work such as hunting for new subscribers and advertisers.

Tara and Moyna were not at all sure if they liked the new arrangement or if they really wanted anyone else on the staff. As for Raj Kumar, he was absolutely sure he did not. No warm reception had been planned for the graduate from Hoshiarpur University (in the opinion of Tara and Moyna, there could be no institution of learning on a lower rung of the ladder) but when young Mohan appeared, they had been disarmed. By his woebegone looks and low voice they learnt he no more wanted to be there than they wanted to have him there, that he had merely been talked into it by his professor, an old friend of Bose Sahib's. He himself was very sad to leave Hoshiarpur where his mother and four sisters provided him with a life of comfort. The very thought of those comforts made his eyes dewy when he told Tara and Moyna of the food he ate at home, the grilled chops, the egg curries, the biryanis and home-made pickles. Moreover, if it was necessary to begin a life of labour so young – he had only graduated three months ago and hardly felt prepared for the working life – then he had hoped for something else.

'What *would* you have liked to do, Mohan?' Moyna asked him sympathetically (she was not at all certain if she was cut out for a career at *Books* either).

'Travel and Tourism,' he announced without hesitation. 'One friend of mine, he is in Travel and Tourism and he is having a fine time – going to airport, receiving foreign tourists, taking them to five-star hotels in rented cars, with chauffeurs – and receiving tips. Fine time he is having, and much money also, in tips.'

Moyna felt so sorry for the sad contrast provided by *Books* that she asked Raj Kumar to fetch some samosas for them to have with their tea. Mohan slurped his up from a saucer, and when Raj Kumar returned with the samosas in an oily newspaper packet, he snapped up two without hesitation. Moyna wondered if he was living in a barsati: she thought she saw signs that he did. Wiping his fingers on Raj Kumar's all-purpose duster, Mohan remarked, 'Not so good as my sister makes.'

Tara thought Moyna could go out in search of advertisements, but when Moyna looked terror-struck and helpless, and cried, 'Oh, but I don't even know Delhi, Tara,' she got up, saying resignedly, 'All right, we'll do the rounds together, just this once,' and gave Raj Kumar and Mohan a string of instructions before leaving the office. Putting on her dark glasses, slinging her handbag over her shoulder, and hailing an autorickshaw that was idling outside the coffee shop, Tara looked distinctly cheerful at the prospect.

Moyna could not see what there was to be cheerful about: the publishing houses they visited were all in the back lanes of Darya Ganj and Kashmere Gate, far from salubrious to her way of thinking, particularly on a steaming afternoon in late summer, and the publishers they met all seemed oppressed by the weather, slumped in their offices listlessly, under slowly revolving fans – if the electricity had not broken down altogether, in which case they would be plunged in gloom, in dim candlelight – and they seemed far from interested in increasing sales of their wares by advertising in *Books*. 'We have been advertising,' one reminded them brusquely, 'for more than two years, and we are seeing no increase in sales. Who is reading *Books*? Nobody is reading.' Tara looked extremely offended and swept out with great dignity after reminding him that he had yet to pay for the advertisements he had placed. Moyna followed her, quietly impressed if uncertain as to whether she could bring off a confrontation so satisfactorily.

They had a little better luck with the bookshops in Connaught Place and Khan Market which were not nearly so depressing and were often run by pleasant proprietors who sent out for Campa Cola and Fanta for them, and at times even agreed to place a few advertisements of their bestselling thrillers. The bookshop for the publications of the USSR – mostly cheerful and cheap translations of Russian folk tales and fables in bright colours for children – proved particularly supportive. A charming Russian gentleman gave them a free calendar and a brochure listing the film, dance and music programmes at Tolstoy Bhavan. Encouraged, Tara suggested they visit the British Council next. 'But do they publish books?' Moyna asked. She was dusty, hot and very tired by now. Tara thought that irrelevant – they could advertise their library, couldn't they?

Actually, they could not, and did not, but the young man they spoke to, who had been summoned out of his office to deal with them, was so apologetic about the refusal that they gave him a copy of the latest edition of *Books* gratis. He looked overcome, pushing back a lock of his fair hair from his forehead and gazing at the magazine as if it were a work of art. 'Oh,' he said, several times, 'how perfectly splendid. Perfectly splendid, really.' Tara straightened her shoulders and gave Moyna a significant look before rising to her feet and making her departure. Moyna followed her reluctantly: the lobby of the British Council library had the best air-conditioning they had run into all day. After that – and the discreet lighting, the carpeting, the soft rustle of newspapers, the attractive look of detective novels and romantic fiction on the shelves – they returned to their office in Bengali Market with a sense of resignation. They did not really expect any results.

But there was Tara at the top of the stairs to the rooftop, pounding on the door and shouting, 'Moyna! Moyna, open up, Moyna!'

Moyna had just been preparing for a bath. It was not entirely uncommon for Tara and Ritwick to drop in on her unannounced if they had managed to persuade Ritwick's mother to mind their little son for a bit, and since she had still not managed to get a telephone installed, there was no way they could warn her. 'Wait a minute,' she called, and slipped back into her clothes before going barefoot across the roof to open the door to them.

Tara was standing there, laughing and in great spirits, not with Ritwick at all but, to Moyna's unconcealed astonishment, with the fair young man from the British Council, who stood a few steps lower down, looking more embarrassed even than before, and clutching in his hands a bottle filled with some dark liquid. Moyna stared.

'Oh, open the door, Moyna, and let us in. I know you don't have a phone so how could I warn you? Adrian rang me up about an advertisement and I asked him to come over, but you know how the Dragon Lady is in such a temper with me these days, so I brought him here instead.'

'Oh,' said Moyna doubtfully, thinking of her own Dragon Lady downstairs.

'*Won't* you let us in?'

Moyna stood aside and then led them towards her barsati. She really could not have company in there – Tara ought to know that. Feeling both vexed and embarrassed, she stood in front of the door now, frowning, and finally said, 'I'll bring out some chairs,' and left them waiting again. To her annoyance, Adrian followed her in to help pull out some chairs, first placing the bottle on the table and saying, 'I brought you some – um – wine. I thought – um – we could have a drink together. Um.'

'And I told him you would at least have peanuts—' Tara shouted from outside.

What could she mean – peanuts? What peanuts? Moyna frowned. After the chairs, there was the bother with glasses. What made Tara think she might have wine glasses? All she could find were two tumblers and a mug – and certainly there were no peanuts. In fact, she had just finished the last bit of bread with her dinner, there was not so much as a piece of toast to offer. But once they were seated on the rooftop, with the wine poured out, and had had a sip of that, Moyna looked up to see that the sky still had a pink flush to it, that it was not entirely dark, that the first stars were beginning to emerge from the day's dust and grime and glare, that the pipal tree was beginning to rustle like a shower of rain in the first breath of air that evening, and suddenly she felt her spirits break free and lift. Here she was, entertaining friends on 'her terrace' on a starry evening, just as she had imagined an adult working woman in the metropolis might do, just as she had imagined she would do – and now it was happening. She looked at Adrian, his six narrow feet of height somehow folded onto a small upright chair, and said with incredulity, 'This is nice!' He thought she meant the wine and hurried to refill her glass, blinking happily behind his spectacles.

It was not only she who thought it was nice. Tara seemed liberated by coming away from her mother-in-law's house where she had to live because of Ritwick's stalled promotion at the university. Adrian seemed enchanted by everything his eye encountered on the rooftop – the parrots streaking in to settle in the branches of the pipal tree for the night, the neighbourliness of the other roof dwellers, several of whom had lined up along their ledges to watch (discreetly or not so discreetly) Moyna's first social gathering. Mao the cat jumped upon Adrian's knee and sat there as if on a tall perch with his eyes narrowed to slits, and by the time the bottle of wine was emptied, they had begun to talk much more loudly and laugh more than they were aware. Tara had an endless fund of mother-in-law stories, as Moyna already knew, but Adrian was gratifyingly astounded by them. When Tara told them of the first time Ritwick had brought her to meet his mother and how the first thing she said to Tara was, 'Arré, why are you wearing this pale colour? It does not suit you at all, it makes your complexion muddy,' or of how she would insist Tara wear her wedding jewellery to work 'otherwise people will think you are a widow', Adrian became wide-eyed and gulped, 'She *said* that? You mean she has licence to say what she *likes* to you?' Tara, greatly encouraged, began to exaggerate – as Moyna could tell – and her stories grew wilder and funnier, reducing even Adrian to laughter. The neighbours spied on them, scandalized, hidden now by night's darkness, but they were unaware how their voices carried downstairs as well, and what a degree of grim disapproval was mounting there. When they descended the stairs, Moyna accompanying them with the key to unlock the front gate for them, they found Mr and Mrs Bhalla pacing up and down the small driveway, grey-faced with censure. They had let Candy out from under their bed and now she flew at them, yipping with small snaps of her teeth, till she was curtly called back by Mr Bhalla.

Their looks made Moyna wonder if it was really so late, had they been kept awake? She put on an apologetic look but Tara, on the contrary, threw back her head and said loudly, 'OK, Moyna, good night – see you tomorrow!' and swept out of the gate. Adrian followed her hastily, carefully keeping out of range of Candy's snapping jaws.

Moyna was certain she would have to face the Bhallas' wrath as she turned around, but they drew back and stared at her in silence as she walked up the stairs and vanished.

Although they did not bring it up directly, after that whenever Moyna encountered them, on her way to work or back, they never failed to refer obliquely to that evening. 'You are having more guests tonight?' they would ask when they saw her returning with the shopping she had done along the way. 'No? You seem to be having many friends,' they went on, prodding her to say more. She shook her head, hurrying. 'No? Then why not come and watch TV tonight? *Ramayana* is showing at seven p.m. Very fine film, *Ramayana*. You should join us,' they commanded, as if testing her true colours. She shook her head, making her excuses. 'Oh, then you are going out? With your friends?' they deliberately misunderstood, taunting her. The children, Sweetie and Pinky, giggled behind their fingers.

'Tara, please don't bring Adrian again,' Moyna begged. 'I don't know what my landlord thinks about me. He seems to think I'm some *hostess* or *entertainer*, the way he and his wife go on.'

'Oh, tell them to go to hell,' Tara snapped. 'As if renting their bloody barsati means you can't have any social life.'

'Social life with girls would be all right, but not with *men*, and not with *foreign* men.'

'Really, Moyna,' Tara stared at her and shrugged, 'when are you going to grow up?' Her mother-in-law had clearly had a lot to say about Tara's going out without Ritwick the other evening; Tara showed all the signs of having had a fine row.

'I *am* grown up! I live in a barsati! I don't want to be thrown out of it, that's all.'

Mohan looked up from the omelette he was eating. He had no cooking facilities where he roomed, and the first thing he did on entering the office in the morning was to send Raj Kumar to fetch him a bun omelette which he seemed to greatly enjoy. Wiping up the last streak of grease with the remains of the bun, he said, 'Barsati living is no good for girls. Why not women's hostel?'

*

She need not have worried about Adrian visiting her again: the look the landlord had given him, plus Candy's warning nips, proved quite enough of a disincentive. The next male to create a problem for Moyna was Mao, now a strapping young tom ready to test his charms in the wider world. No longer willing to stay where she put him, he liked to strut about the barsati roof, or leap up onto the ledge and slowly perform his toilet there where he could be seen, occasionally lifting his head to snarl at a sparrow that mocked and taunted him from a safe distance in the pipal tree, or blink when he became aware of someone watching, possibly admiring him. Moyna feared she would not be able to keep him concealed for long. Already the Bhalla children, Sweetie and Pinky, suspecting his existence, would come up the stairs and peep under the door to catch a glimpse of him, cry, 'Tiger! Tiger!' if they did, and come running pell-mell down the stairs again. They had clearly said something to their mother who would watch Moyna return from the market clutching a wet paper bag reeking of fish and call out, 'Oh, I see you are fond of eating fish!' and had also noted that Moyna took in an unlikely quantity of milk. 'So much milk you are drinking,' she had commented early one morning, seeing Moyna return with her filled pail. 'Very good habit – drinking milk,' she added, contriving to make Moyna understand that this was an indirect comment on the evil of drinking wine. 'Or you are making curd? Kheer pudding, then? No? You don't know how to make kheer pudding?'

The next signal Mao gave was an audible one: a strange, unexpected, long drawn-out wail in the night that woke Moyna and made her shoot out of bed, ready to leap to the door. Mao himself was nowhere to be seen; he generally slipped in and out of the window which had a missing pane that Mr Bhalla had never thought to replace and now proved a convenience. Looking through it, Moyna saw, as in a dream, a feline bacchanalia in full swing on the rooftop. How had all these female felines found their way to the barsati – and to Mao? Moyna rushed out in her nightgown to make sure the door was locked. It was. Was there a drainpipe they might have climbed? There couldn't be or Mao would have discovered it long ago. As she stood wondering, the cats crept into a corner discreetly screened by a box or two, and as she watched, the pipal tree gave a shiver. The pipal tree – of course! She stared at its massive trunk, pale in the moonlight, and the sinuous branches and twigs silvery and ashiver, and spied another insomniac – her neighbour, a few feet away, his moony face cupped in his hands as he leant upon the ledge and gazed yearningly at her. He was close enough to speak to her but, instead, he first sighed and then began to hum. It sounded like the tune of a disgusting song to Moyna's ears, a lewd, suggestive song, an outrageous affront of a song:

'O, a girl is like a flame,
O, a girl can start a fire—'

Moyna darted back into her room and slammed the door. Its echoes rang out and for a while there was a shocked silence. But, a little later, the cats crept out to caterwaul again and all Moyna could do was wrap a pillow round her head and moan.

Although she did her best to avoid the Bhallas next morning – and usually when she left for work they were in the dining room, from which tantalizing whiffs of fried dough, curried eggs and creamy tea floated out – today Mrs Bhalla was lying in wait, having her scalp massaged at that very hour. She looked up from under the tent of greying hair spread out on her shoulders and fixed her eye on the rapidly fleeing Moyna. 'Come here!' she cried. 'I'm late!' shouted Moyna from the gate. 'What is that animal on your roof?' shrieked Mrs Bhalla, throwing off the ministering fingers of the old crone she had engaged for the service. 'Animal?' called Moyna from the other side of the gate, 'What animal?' and jumped across the ditch to the dusty road where Gurmail Singh waited for her, his autorickshaw put-putting reassuringly.

*

Catastrophe struck from an unexpected quarter. Returning from work the same day, Moyna climbed slowly up the stairs with a bag of fish she had stopped to buy, unlocked the door to the rooftop and went in, sighing with relief at having gained the open barsati, at seeing the pipal tree dark against the mauve and pink evening sky, wondering if there was enough water in the bucket for a wash. She let herself into her room and set about putting away her sling bag, her market bag, slipping out of her slippers, shedding the day like a worn garment, sweaty and dusty. Mao was not around but he rarely was now that he had discovered the route of the pipal tree: there was nothing she could do but hope Candy would not be waiting at the foot of it. She decided to switch on some music instead, reached out – and saw the blank space beside her bed where she kept her radio and tape recorder. It was not there.

Her first foolish reaction was to blame Mao. Could he have taken it? Then she whirled around, thinking she might have placed it elsewhere last night, or this morning, and forgotten. It was not on the kitchen table, and there was no other surface where it could be. Looking around for some corner where it might have hidden itself, she began to notice other objects were missing: her alarm clock, the little box containing the tapes, even the tin-framed mirror she had hung on the wall. What else? Flinging open the cupboard that would not lock, she began to cry as she groped on the shelves, trying to count her saris. Wiping her face with her hand, she banged it shut and ran down the stairs to the Bhallas.

They were all seated crosslegged on the bed, chins cupped in their hands, deeply absorbed in the latest episode of their favourite American soap opera (the mythological epics were aired only on Sundays, to guarantee maximum viewership). Sweetie and Pinky refused to turn their attention away from *I Love Lucy* but the elder Bhallas sensed Moyna's hysteria, turned off the TV, listened to her tearful outburst, then burst themselves, with fulsome indignation. What was she insinuating? Was she accusing *them?* Did she think *they* would go up to her barsati and haul away her miserable goods – *they*, with all these goods of their own around them . . .

Now Moyna had to deny their accusation, assure them she had never harboured such an idea, only wanted to know if they had any idea *who* it could be. *Who?* they thundered, how would they know *who?* What with Moyna's unsavoury circle of friends coming and going at all hours of the day and night, how could they tell which one had found his way to her barsati? Had they seen anyone? she begged. *Seen* anyone? Seen *who?* they roared. At this point, she wailed, 'Please call the police!' which incensed them further. They nearly exploded – even Candy, Sweetie and Pinky shrank back. Police? On their property? What was Moyna suggesting? Was she out of her mind? If the police visited their house, their immaculate, impeccable house of decency, purity and family values, what would their neighbours think, or say? Never had such a thing happened in their home, their locality, their community – till *she* had come along and brought into their midst this evil, this sin . . .

Moyna retreated. She shut the door upon the Bhallas, who were standing at the foot of the stairs and shaking their fists and shouting loud enough for all the neighbours to hear. Then she sat down on a chair under the tree, feeling as if all her strength were gone; she could not even stand. Mao reappeared, wrapping himself around and around her legs, finally leaping onto her lap and kneading it with his paws, loudly purring. She held him, sure he was telling her something, saying comforting, consoling things, and sat there till it was dark, listening to him and the pipal tree that shivered and rustled, the birds subsiding into its branches, eventually falling silent. More than any other sensation, it was homesickness she felt: she was trying to suppress the most child-ish urge to run and hide her head in her mother's lap, feel her mother stroking her hair. She was also suppressing the urge to write a long letter home, describing everything as it really was. She told herself it would be unforgivable to cause her parents concern. As it was, they had never felt comfortable about her living alone in the big city; every letter from them voiced their anxiety, begging her to keep her doors securely locked, never go out after dark and take good care of her health. She also knew she was trying to hold onto her pride, as she sat there, stroking and stroking Mao.

Still, Moyna knew she had to do something, and planned to tell Tara immediately. But next morning Tara had arranged to hold a 'conference', as she liked to call such a gathering, with their usual cast of reviewers. Most of them were Ritwick's friends and colleagues from the Jawaharlal Nehru University, with a sprinkling of 'outsiders' from Delhi University and the lesser colleges. This was not a regular meeting but somehow, by some kind of natural osmosis that no one quite understood, the hard core of their critics who reviewed regularly for *Books* happened to have a free morning and came to meet Tara and Moyna at the Coffee House in Connaught Place where they took up a long table in one corner. This was the occasion, greatly enjoyed by all, when the young lecturers and readers pleaded for the books they were desperate to have, the latest academic treatises published by the university presses at Oxford and Cambridge, Harvard and Yale, at impossible prices, and Tara and Moyna magnanimously dispensed them with the understanding that the reviewers could expect little reward other than the prized books themselves. In return, the eager young men in their handspun shirts, shaggy beards and dusty sandals plied them with small earthen mugs of coffee and all the delicacies the Coffee House had to offer – dosa, idli, vada, whatever they liked – and which harried waiters flapping dishcloths and tin trays around brought to them in regular relays. There were also some professional critics, usually older men, some really quite old, worn and grey from years of piecing together a living by writing, who looked over the books with a more practised and cynical eye and quickly reached for whatever would take the least time to read and fetch the most at the second-hand bookshops on the pavement outside.

But the customary bonhomie of the occasion which recalled their carefree student days – O careless youth! – was unexpectedly disrupted that morning by Moyna's state of agitation which she could not conceal, leading to an open confession under questioning from Tara. Theft, landlords, police – all were appalled and looked at Moyna in horror.

'Bloody lumpen proletariat!' raged the young man who always contrived to sit directly across from Moyna in order to gaze at her when he was not looking out for a book he could attack and demolish. 'Should be taught a lesson. Think they rule the world, huh? Have to be shown—'

'By whom? The polizia? Those stooges—'

This enraged the young gallant. 'If not, I'll make them. Come on, Moyna, I'll go to the police if the landlord won't—'

Moyna grew alarmed. She had here all the reaction she could have asked for but was not at all sure if she wanted to go any further, that is, go to the police about it. She had come to the office that morning hoping Tara or Raj Kumar or Mohan might offer to go with her, or at least offer sympathy and advice. Then she had found Tara bustling about, arranging to leave the office to Raj Kumar and go to the Coffee House with Moyna and a pile of books, while Raj Kumar settled down to telephone all his friends and Mohan was poring over a postcard from his sisters about a prospective bride they had found for him. She had had to hold back the matter till it had burst from her when someone merely asked, 'How's life, Moyna?' which in turn had led to this show of outrage and gallantry.

A few minutes later Ritwick dropped in on the conference, hoping to pick up a book on medieval trade routes through the Arabian Sea that Tara had promised to keep for him. On hearing of Moyna's calamity, he insisted on accompanying her and Karan to the police station. 'Is there a justice system or is there not?' he demanded, glaring at all around the table with its coffee cups, its trays and plates of greasy fried food. 'I need to know!'

At the police station, the officer in charge sat at his desk looking uncomfortable in a khaki uniform that did not fit and had to be nudged, tugged and scratched into place constantly. Several lesser officials stood around with their nightsticks, and stared at Moyna with open mouths while the two men did all the talking. Moyna was glad not to have to speak but she did have to sign the yellow charge sheet that the officer filled out with slow deliberation, then handed to her. When she had done that, he rose from his chair and commanded his underlings to follow him to the Bhalla household.

At the gate, Moyna's courage failed. She looked around wildly in the hope of seeing Gurmail Singh with his autorickshaw ready to put-put her away from the scene, but of course he was not there and Ritwick and Karan between them silently compelled her to open the gate and lead the party in.

Only Mrs Bhalla was at home at that hour; the servant boy vanished from sight as soon as the police made their appearance. Nevertheless, the scene was awful. Or so it seemed to Moyna although, in retrospect, perhaps not as awful as it might have been. It was true that Mrs Bhalla stood at the foot of the stairs, screaming imprecations against tenants who made false accusations and brought disgrace to the homes that sheltered them, but the police merely marched past her and up the stairs, stalked around the barsati, twisting their moustaches like comic-book or cartoon cops, pointing out the sights to each other with an amused, even bemused air – Mao stretched out on the bed, blinking lazily at the intruders, the neighbours peering over the walls and ledges with open curiosity, Moyna's toilet goods arranged on the windowsill – and examined the full height and length of the pipal tree, then climbed down the stairs, and vanished. 'Complaint has been filed,' they told the indignant Ritwick and Karan. 'Investigation has been completed.'

*

When Moyna queued up at the Mother Dairy with her milk can next morning, she found herself standing next to a young woman she had often noticed there but never spoken to: she seemed to be a foreigner, with light brown hair pulled back and tied in a long pigtail down her back, wearing the cheapest of cotton saris and rubber slippers. Now the young woman spoke to her, unexpectedly. 'I have heard,' she said haltingly, 'you have had – theft?' Moyna nodded, and hardly dared reply, knowing everyone in the line was listening. Many did turn around at the word 'theft'. 'I too,' said the young woman sympathetically. 'I see you on roof. I, too,' she said, and after they had had their milk cans filled, they walked back together along the dusty verge of the road, and Simona told Moyna how she had employed a boy who had regularly burgled her barsati of anything she bought for it. 'But didn't you dismiss him?' Moyna asked, thinking that even she would have had the wits to do that. 'Of course,' Simona replied, 'after first time! But he had key for my barsati, came back and thieved again, and again. Now I have nothing left, nothing,' she added, with a joyful smile. 'And the police—?' 'Oh, they caught him – again, and again. But always they had to let him go because he said he was twelve years old! Too young for gaol.' Simona shrugged. 'Still he is twelve. He does not grow any older. So he can be thief for longer.'

This gave Moyna so much food for thought that she walked along in silence, and almost forgot to ask Simona her name or address. When she did, it turned out that Simona was one of her neighbours, only too discreet to hang over her ledge and spy on Moyna like the others. Now she promised to wave and call when she saw Moyna out on her rooftop. 'You have most beautiful tree,' she said on parting, and Moyna glowed till it struck her it could be the reason why she stayed on with the Bhallas, and if that would not be considered foolishness by anyone but Simona.

The next day Tara and Ritwick came to visit. They stalked around the rooftop, peering through every possible loophole through which the burglar might re-enter. The trouble was that he probably had a key to the door and could let himself in whenever Moyna left: it was unlikely he risked climbing the great tree in the backyard.

'This place is just not secure, Moyna. You've got to ask your landlord to make it secure. Fence in the entire outer wall—'

'Ask Mr Bhalla?' Moyna croaked.

Lately whenever Moyna passed through the Bhalla home she felt she needed protective clothing. Mr Bhalla's jowls seemed set in a permanent scowl like a thunder cloud (the fact that he rarely shaved and his jaws were always blue added to the illusion) while Mrs Bhalla would plant herself in a central location, her eyes following Moyna down to the gate or up the stairs as if she suspected Moyna herself of the theft. Her mutterings implied as much – 'These girls, these days, think they can go to work, live alone – huh! Can't even take care of their own belongings!' Did she actually say these words, or was Moyna imagining them? She felt them creep over her back, across her neck, like spiders settling there.

As for their servant boy, after her conversation with Simona, Moyna was certain she sensed an extra insouciance to his manner. He had always watched her with open, unconcealed curiosity, but now she felt he gave his hips an insulting swing, twitched his filthy kitchen duster over his shoulder with a flick, and pursed his lips to whistle a bar from some Bombay film tune although that was surely not fitting in a servant boy, even if employed in a household like the Bhallas'. When she passed the open kitchen door one day and he cocked an eyebrow at her and sang:

'With blouse cut low, with hair cut short,
This memsahib so fine—'

she decided to complain to the Bhallas, but discovered she had chosen a bad moment: that very morning, while she was at work, Mao had slithered down the tree trunk to the Bhallas' compound and been pounced upon by Candy, with Sweetie and Pinky in hot pursuit. Mao had somehow escaped from all three, but Moyna's secret of owning what the Bhallas insultingly called a 'billa', a tom, had been uncovered. Rising to her feet, Mrs Bhalla launched into a tirade about lying tenants who neglected to inform their landlords of their pets that would never have been permitted into their own pristine homes. Moyna, already incensed by the servant boy's behaviour and now by his employers', stood her ground stoutly and replied, 'Then do you want me to leave?' half hoping the reply would free her of them. But Mrs Bhalla retreated promptly – she knew to a whisker's breadth how far she could go as a landlady – claiming she could hear the telephone ringing. That evening she sent Pinky and Sweetie upstairs to ask if Moyna would like to come down and watch a rerun of the old film classic *Awaara* with them. Moyna told them she had a cold.

It was not untrue. The change of season had affected Moyna as it had practically every other citizen of Delhi. Still listless from the heat during the day, at night she found herself shivering under her cotton quilt in the barsati: the windowpane had never been replaced and allowed a chill blast of wintry air in.

She was sniffling over her desk at the office one morning with her head in her hands, trying to correct proofs, only half-listening to Tara complain of her mother-in-law's unreasonable and ungenerous reaction to Tara and Ritwick's staying out at the cinema late last night, when a visitor appeared at the door, demanding to see the editor. Tara's tirade was cut short, she hastily tossed her nail file into a drawer, pulled a page of proofs from Moyna's desk, and lifted an editorial expression to a man whose face appeared to be made entirely out of bristling hair and gleaming teeth, although he did wear thick, black-framed glasses and a silk scarf as well, tucked into the v-neck of a purple sweater.

'What can I do for you?' Tara had barely asked when she began to regret it.

The visitor was the author of a collection of short stories in Hindi that had been reviewed by Karan in the last issue. He had a copy of it rolled up in his hand. He spread it out before them, asking if they, as editors, had paid attention to what they were printing in a journal that at one time had had a distinguished reputation but now was nothing but a rag in the filthy hands of reviewers like the one who signed himself KK. Did they know who he was talking about?

Moyna got up and came across to glance at the review together with Tara, out of a sense of loyalty to her and an awareness of threat, as the author of the short stories jabbed his finger at one line, then another – 'so devoid of imagination that Sri Awasthi has had to borrow from sources such as *The Sound of Music* and—' 'in language that would get a sixth-standard student in trouble with his teacher—' 'situations so absurd that he can hardly expect his readers to take them any more seriously than the nightly soap opera on TV—' 'characters cut out of cardboard and pasted onto the page with Sri Awasthi's stunning lack of subtlety—'

Tara recovered her poise before Moyna could. Snatching the journal out of the visitor's hands, she held it out of his reach. 'We choose our reviewers for their standing in the academic world. Every one of them is an authority on—'

'Authority? What authority? This dog – he claims he is an authority on Hindi literature?' ranted the man, snatching the journal back from Tara. 'It is a scandal – such a standard of reviewing is a scandal. It must not go unnoticed – or unpunished. Where is this man? I would like to see him. I should like to know—'

'If you have any complaint, you can make it in writing,' Tara told him. She was, Moyna could see, as good a fighter as she had always claimed.

'Make it in writing? If I make it, will you publish it? If I put in writing what I think of your journal, your name will be—'

'Mr Awasthi,' Tara said, using his name as if she remembered it with difficulty, and managing to mispronounce it, 'there is no need to be so insulting.'

'If that is so, then why have I been insulted? I am a member of Sahitya Akademi. I am author of forty volumes of short stories, one of autobiography, seven books of travel, and also of essays. I am award-winning. I am invited by universities in foreign countries. My name is known in all Hindi-speaking areas—'

Mohan suddenly strode in; he had been standing in the doorway with Raj Kumar but now entered the room to stand beside Tara and Moyna. He was enjoying this; it was the first drama to take place in the office. Plucking the journal out of Mr Awasthi's hands, he tossed it on the desk with a contemptuous gesture. 'The editor is not responsible for the reviewer's views,' he announced, which it had not occurred to the two women to say.

This was not very original but Mr Awasthi's face turned a dangerously purple colour, not unlike the sweater he wore. But now Mohan had him by the elbow and was guiding him out of the door. Tara and Moyna fell back into their chairs, pushing their hair away from their flushed faces. Tara, lighting a cigarette with shaking hands, said, 'Did you *hear* Mohan? Did you *see* how he got him out?'

That visit proved to be a prelude to an entire winter in which the battle raged. Mr Awasthi's rebuttal was printed in the next issue, followed by Karan's still more scurrilous response – he worked in an attack on the Hindi-speaking 'cow belt' which proved a starting point for a whole new series of entertaining insults – and their days at the office were enlivened by visits from either one or other, each intent on getting the 'editor's ear' (in the case of Karan, it was mostly the Assistant Editor's ear he tried to get). Even Bose Sahib wrote from Calcutta and implored Tara to close the correspondence on the matter (he thought mention of the 'cow belt' particularly deplorable and unparliamentary). He added some disquieting remarks that Tara relayed to Moyna gloomily. 'He says the journal is still in the red, and he may not be able to go on publishing it if it fails to make money. Never thought Bose Sahib would consider *Books* as if it were a commercial enterprise. Ritwick says it is clear capitalism has killed Marxism in Calcutta if even Bose Sahib talks like an industrialist.'

'Oh Tara,' Moyna said in dismay. It was not just that Bose Sahib was something of an icon in their circle but it also shook her confidence in her ability to be a career woman in Delhi. What would happen if she lost her job? What if she did not find another employer? Would she lose her barsati? And return to her parents' home? Back where she started from? She began to sniffle.

Her cold, which had been growing worse for weeks, burgeoned into full-scale flu. After going downstairs to send Gurmail Singh away in his autorickshaw, she went back to bed, pulling the quilt over her ears. Mao, sympathetic or, perhaps, delighted at this development, crept in beside her. She drifted in and out of sleep, and her sleep was always crowded with thoughts of office life. Behind closed lids, she continued to see the journal's columns before her, requiring her to proofread:

Sir—Sri Ritwick Misra has reviewed Sri Nirad Chaudhuri's biography of Max Müller without proving his credentials for doing so. Has Sri Misra any knowledge of Max Müller's native tongue? Has Sri Chaudhuri? If not, can we believe all the necessary documents have been studied without which no scholar can trust, etc., Yrs truly, B. Chattopadhyay, Asansol, W. Bengal.

Sir—May I compliment you on your discovery of a true genius, i.e Srimati Devika Bijlinai, whose poem, *Lover, lover*, is a work of poetic excellence. I hope you will continue to publish the work of this lovable poetess. Kindly convey my humble respects to her. Also publish photograph of same in next issue. Yrs truly, A. Reddy, Begumpet, Hyderabad, A.P.

It was in this state that Raj Kumar found her when he came in with a message from Tara saying, 'Why won't you get yourself a phone, Moyna, and tell us when you're not coming to work? Just when the new issue is ready to go to press—' and ending 'Shall I bring over a doctor this evening?'

Moyna was not sure what to do with Raj Kumar but was grateful for his obvious concern and felt she could not send him straight back to the office. 'Can I make you a cup of tea, Raj Kumar?' she asked hoarsely. 'I'll have some, too.'

Raj Kumar perched on the edge of her straight-backed chair. He planted his hands on his knees, and studied every object in the room with the same deep interest while Moyna boiled water in a pan and got out the earthen mugs to make tea.

'No TV?' he asked finally.

She shook her head and put a few biscuits on a plate to offer him. He ate one with great solemnity, as if considering its qualities, then asked, 'Who is doing the cooking?' She admitted she did her own, wondering who he imagined would perform such chores for her. 'Ah, that is why you are never bringing lunch from home,' he said, with pity. She agreed it was. He of course had a wife to fill a tiffin container's three or four compartments to bursting with freshly cooked, still warm food. He asked for more details of her domestic existence. As Moyna told him of her regimen of rising to store water at five, then queueing for milk at six, and the shopping she did at the market on her way home with the essential stop at the fish shop for Mao's diet, Raj Kumar's eyes widened. He was too polite to say anything but when he had finished his tea and biscuits and rose to go, he said in a voice of true concern, 'Please lock door safely. Not safe to live alone like this.' She assured him she would.

At the door he turned to say, 'Also, you should purchase TV set,' with great earnestness. 'TV set is good company,' he explained, 'like friend.'

Going back to bed after shutting and locking the door behind him, she did feel friendless – but not convinced that she wanted a TV in place of one. And no sooner had she closed her eyes than the lines of print began to unroll again:

Sir—It is a great disappointment that you continue to harbour a reviewer such as KK who has a clear bias against one of the great languages of our motherland. Because he is reviewing for an English-language journal in the capital, does he think he has the right to spurn the literature composed in the vernacular? This attitude is as despicable as the sight of seeing mother's milk rejected for sake of foreign liquor. Yrs truly, C. Bhanot, Pataliputra Colony, Bihar.

Sir—The monthly arrival of *Books* is greatly looked forward to by my immediate family. I regret that you choose to include in it such filth as Srimati Devika Bijliani's poem, *Lover, lover*. This is not what we expect to find in decent family magazine. Kindly refrain from publishing offensive matter of sexual nature and return to former family status. Yrs truly, D. Ramanathan, Trivandrum, Kerala.

Simona, not having seen Moyna in the milk queue for days, came to visit. She brought with her a gift that touched Moyna deeply – fish tails and heads wrapped in newspaper for Mao's dinner. Simona explained, 'I saw you are not getting milk so I know that cat is not getting fish.' She sat crosslegged on Moyna's bed, tucking her cotton sari around her shoulders, and told Moyna that she herself had been sick – 'for many, many days. Months, perhaps. Hep-a-ti-tis. You have hep-a-titis?' 'Oh no,' Moyna denied it vigorously, 'only flu,' and was afraid to think now that she might lie alone in the barsati for so long, sick, away from home. 'And you are so far from home,' she said to Simona with sudden sympathy, and wondered what could keep the young woman here, ageing before her eyes into a pale, drawn invalid. But Simona put on her rapt expression, one that often overtook her even in the most inconvenient places – passing the garbage heap behind the marketplace, for instance, or seeing a beggar approach – and told Moyna joyfully, 'This is my home. It is where my guru lives, you see.' Moyna cowered under her quilt: she did not feel strong enough for such revelations. 'Please make yourself tea,' she croaked, and broke into a paroxysm of coughs.

Having received a letter in which Moyna mentioned that she had flu, Moyna's mother arrived. Moyna was actually on her way to recovery by then and many of the remedies her mother brought with her, the special teas and balms and syrups, were no longer needed, but evidently much else was. Putting her hand into the containers on Moyna's kitchen shelf, her mother was shocked to find less than a handful of rice, of lentils. 'You are starving!' she exclaimed, as horrified at herself as her daughter, 'and we did not know!' 'Do I look as if I'm starving?' Moyna asked, but she could not stop her mother from shopping and cooking and storing food in a storm of energy and activity in the barsati, which was now bathed in mild sunlight and at its most livable in Delhi's pleasant winter.

Mrs Bhalla downstairs roused herself too, and began to cook and send treats upstairs, either with the servant boy or with Pinky or Sweetie, little jars of pickles she had put up, or metal trays with sweets she had made, dissolving in pools of oil and reeking of rose water, or covered pots containing specialities known only to Mrs Bhalla and the village that was once her home.

'How kind she is,' Moyna's mother exclaimed, accepting these gifts. 'How lucky you are to have found such a landlady, Moyna.'

Nothing Moyna told her could completely alter her mother's impression. 'She's just trying to fool you,' she cried. 'She *wants* you to think she's a nice person.'

She glowered at Mrs Bhalla whenever she passed her on the

veranda, but Mrs Bhalla now called out to her with great sweetness, 'How is your mother, Moyna? Please ask her to come and visit me.'

'I don't know why you both like each other so much,' Moyna said darkly, on conveying this message.

'We are both mothers, that is why,' her mother replied with what Moyna now found an indigestible sweetness. It was this motherliness she had missed and longed for but now she found it superfluous. Her barsati no longer looked as it had in the days of penury, austerity and minimalism. Her mother had bought curtains, cushions, filled every available space with kitchen gadgets, foods, whatever comfort she could think of. Now Moyna found she was no longer used to comfort, that it annoyed and irritated her. Picking up Mao and a book, she would retreat to the rooftop while her mother bustled about in the crowded room, clattering and humming and enjoying herself. She leant over the ledge and stared moodily into the quaking leaves of the pipal tree and the hazy winter light that filtered through. Downstairs, in the Bhallas' brightly lit kitchen, she could see the Bhallas' servant boy, rolling out chapatis for their dinner. He had music on to entertain him while he worked, and Moyna listened too. She was enjoying its somewhat melancholy and dirge-like tone when she started in recognition: was that not Joan Baez singing? And was it not one of her own tapes? She stiffened and bent over the ledge, trying to look past the pipal leaves to get a clearer picture of what was on the kitchen counter below. But she did not really need to look, she could hear clearly enough, and it made her roll her hands into fists and pound on the ledge with frustration.

While her instinct was to run and tell her mother, then run down and inform Mrs Bhalla and demand her belongings back, she found herself silent. Letting her mother pile a spinach curry and lentils on her plate at dinner, she kept quiet: she knew it would be unwise to tell her mother that she lived amongst thieves. How then could she declare to her that she intended to remain here with them, not return to family and home, comfort and care?

'What are you thinking, Moyna?' her mother asked impatiently. 'Why don't you eat?'

Fortunately, her mother could not stay long. Unfortunately, when Moyna returned with relief to her own routine, she found Tara at the office consumed by the same housemaking fervour. This was not at all customary where Tara was concerned. Tara had taken the job at *Books* to escape from housewifeliness, as her mother-in-law so cannily suspected – and now she confounded Moyna by talking incessantly of real estate, bank loans, co-ops . . . true, not housekeeping matters exactly, but just as boring to Moyna who had plunged into the next issue which had yet another blistering attack by Karan on the Hindi author's newest offering. Tara was hardly around to see to it; she was either on the telephone, earnestly discussing finances with Ritwick, or, with her handbag slung over her shoulder and her dark glasses on, was off to visit yet another co-op.

'Why are you doing this?' Moyna protested. 'You *have* a nice house to live in. I mean,' she added hastily, seeing Tara's expression, 'I know it's the Dragon Lady's, but still, it *is* nice and you don't pay for it—' She refrained from mentioning the free babysitting service it provided.

'You don't understand. You're too young. At our age, we need our own place,' Tara explained loftily.

In her concern for this nest for the future, Tara seemed strangely unaffected by the letter they received from Bose Sahib, announcing his decision to close the magazine. He was planning to start another, he added, this time about development projects in rural areas – were Tara and Moyna interested in working for it? Tara would not even consider it: she was settling into this nest she had found, she was not going to go touring the hinterland, she would turn down the offer. Moyna was pale with dismay and disbelief; she begged Tara not to speak so loudly, to come down to the sweet shop below where they could discuss it over a cup of tea without Mohan and Raj Kumar overhearing. 'It will be such a shock to them,' she explained to Tara. But Tara did not see any cause for shock: 'Mohan is looking for a job in hotels anyway, or a travel agency,' she said. 'What?' asked Moyna. Why had she not been told the world of *Books* was coming unravelled around her? Had she been so immersed in the wretched business of barsati living to ignore far more important matters? What about all the book reviewers and their supply of foreign books being cut short? She sat at the small tin-topped table with Tara, not able to swallow her tea, and pleaded with her to reconsider. 'But why?' Tara asked, her eyes looking into the distance where her dream house waited for her like a mirage in the desert outside Delhi. 'I'm not married to *Books*, or to Bose Sahib. Let them go to hell. I'm not going to go around looking at weaving centres and dairy farms for Bose Sahib!'

Moyna bit her lip. It was certainly not what she had come to Delhi for, nor was it what she had expected to do with her life. But she had grown used to the two-roomed office with its bamboo shutters, Raj Kumar sitting in a corner and tying up book parcels, Mohan enjoying his bun omelette and samosas at his desk. She had even grown used, if that was what resignation could be called, to the barsati, although when the year's lease was up, she would be free to rent another: there were almost as many barsatis in Delhi as there were top-floor flats. She turned the teaspoon over and over in her hands, considering all the possibilities, weighing the pros and cons, till Tara snatched it out of her hand. 'Stop fidgeting, Moyna. Just *decide*,' she snapped, tossing back her hair with all the authority of someone who had done just that.

It was too difficult, too weighty a decision to be made in a moment, over a cup of tea. Moyna went back and forth between the office and the barsati, sick with anxiety. Only occasionally and momentarily could she forget the problem: when Gurmail Singh told her with pride that his daughter had passed the entrance test to the Loreto Convent, ensuring a fine future for her and leaving him only to worry about his less promising son; or when she received an invitation to a film show at the British Council to be followed by a reception, placing her on a rung above those who went there only for the air conditioning and the newspapers. Then she would fall to brooding again and sit crosslegged on her bed, stroking Mao and turning the matter over in her mind.

It was when she was in such a state that a letter arrived from her mother. She opened it listlessly, knowing in advance what it would contain – advice on how to run her household, how to cook a specially strengthening stew, an offer of monetary help, pleas to return home, her father's message that she should consider studying for a higher degree before embarking on a career – and she glanced at it cursorily: her mother did not understand even now the attraction of living, alone, in Delhi, and could think of it only as a poor substitute for living at home.

But at the bottom of this letter, her mother had added, craftily:

> Our neighbours have invited us to a welcome party next week; their son Arun is returning from the United States. He has taken a degree in geology and is expected to find a suitable job in the field. I am sure he would be pleased to meet you again. If you are planning a visit soon, we shall ask him over for a meal. I know his family is very keen . . .

Mao gave a leap off the bed as Moyna flung herself backwards, at the same time throwing the letter into the air with a shout of laughter. She rolled her head about on the pillow, spluttering, 'Oh, Mama – re-a-ll-y, Mama!' Mao had not seen such behaviour in a long time. He sat by the door and watched her, his paws primly together, his tail wrapped around him, disapproving. It was clear he thought she had gone crazy. Even he, with his fine senses, could not know that the letter made up Moyna's mind for her. She was free, she was determined, she had made her decision, and she sat up, laughing.

In the kitchen below, the Bhallas' servant boy turned up the music and sang along with it.

The Landing

The moving company's truck, emptied of its load, now turned around in the driveway, using the single immense hemlock tree as the pole on which to turn, and went lumbering down the dirt road on to the highway below, and slowly withdrew.

Then the silence began to ring in her ears. Louder and louder till it practically shrieked.

So she thought it best to turn too, and go into the house to see what distraction it could provide from that insistent ring.

It was, after all, very new to her even though it was very old: 1743 was the date carved into the beam over the entrance. But she had entered it newly and now had to learn every plank and brick and beam in it, one by one, till all became familiar and she could move about without hesitation.

She paced the length of it and then the breadth, going from room to room. In one, the floor sloped, in others the boards creaked, and the height of the ceiling changed from high to low. Some were well lit, others shadowy. They all belonged to her now, and she had to show them she was mistress. She said to herself, 'Hmm, I will put my desk here' and 'I will need some shelves there' but there was something hollow, not quite convinced about these intentions. That was because she was growing increasingly aware that there was an opposition to these intentions that was also growing, and that she was not in command of the house so much as it was of her. By entering it, she had subjected herself to it.

When she recognized that, she shook a little, a small shiver running down her neck and through her shoulders.

She had bought the house and established herself in it – but now it was projecting a powerful suggestion that it was not so amenable to her purchase as she had imagined. She had not asked for its consent, after all, and it struck her that the house was withholding it.

Of course this was absurd. How could the house, an inanimate object, possibly contain feelings or make them apparent?

Reason would not support such an intuition, however strong.

The house *was* inanimate, surely; a thing of stone, brick, board and beam. Mortar and lath. Sheetrock and slate.

But there was also the air entering it through the windows. She had gone around opening them while the men from the moving company unloaded their boxes and brought them in.

And it was these windows that let the air in – let it in, let it out, in, then out. It was not the house breathing, she told herself. That was an illusion, she said, and continued to prowl through the house she now owned.

Having learnt the dimensions of one floor, she grasped the banisters and went up the stairs. They were wide and hollowed out at the centre, as one might expect: through the years, many had climbed them and climbed down. Generations. The banisters provided safety and reassurance: these stairs could take more.

It was the landing that invited pause. It was somehow, inexplicably, more than simply a place to stop and catch one's breath before proceeding. Evidently bare and empty, yet strongly suggestive of more. She stopped to study the whitewashed walls and wondered if there weren't traces of openings that no longer existed and were covered over with plaster. Some heavy timber beams entered those walls, then vanished. They suggested that once they had led to, and supported, another space, perhaps a room that had once led off the landing.

If so, it no longer existed – all was bricked up, plastered over and painted.

What was it concealing?

She was certain that the landing, comfortably large as it was, was reduced from a formerly large space. She could not have said why but had the clear impression of another, yet undetected chamber that had for some reason been closed off. Why?

Baffled, she continued up the stairs to the upper floor. This too she carefully paced, measuring it with her stride. Here the ceiling was lower, the windows smaller, as were the rooms. All in all, they gave an impression of greater intimacy and friendliness than the rooms downstairs. What linked them to those places was of course the staircase – and the landing.

When she thought of how the landing separated and demarcated them, the image that came to her was of a landing stage on a river, or lake, where such a structure marked a point of transition between earth and water, one element and what was distinctly another.

Then there was the other landing, the long strip of tarmac trembling in an excess of light and heat, on which planes landed and from which they took off: she thought of such a strip in the middle of a forest, or plantation, or grassland – a kind of scar or scab marking the point of departure and arrival.

This had never before been suggested to her by a house.

Perplexed, she went back downstairs – and found all the windows shut. She had not heard them bang in the wind, and they were securely fastened.

Perhaps she had not opened them, after all, only thought she did. Surely that was the explanation. It was not a good idea, she knew, to start imagining ghosts in the house, or intruders.

Still, she went upstairs to check and found the windows that she was sure she had not touched, now all open. Breathing the air in, breathing it out. Perhaps they had been open all along.

It was both irritating and intimidating to find that her memory had begun to play tricks on her. Entering the old house – 1743, was it not carved in the beam over the door? – she herself had suddenly aged, with a failing memory, she told herself, and shook her head at the absurdity of it all.

But perhaps it was just being entirely alone, in that ringing silence, that made her imagine things. Hallucinate. She would have to take care.

As she might have foreseen, it was all even harder at night. Once darkness fell, she could not look around and reassure herself of what was there and what was not. She could have switched on lights and done so of course, for in place of the lanterns that must once have hung from the hooks in the ceiling there were now electric lights. But she never turned on more than one light at a time, and if she went from one room to the next, she turned off one light as soon as she turned on another. To have all the lights on at once and have every room blazing would have been a sign, a blatant show of panic. To light just one at a time was like taking a candle from room to room. As she might have, would have, done in 1743.

In that way, she lit the way up the stairs to bed. On the landing she paused again, to see if the beams still gave that effect of going through the walls to another space, and if a bricked-up opening could still be deciphered under the pale layer of plaster and whitewash. But there was no light on the landing itself, only one at the bottom of the stairs and another at the top, and it was too dimly lit for her to see such traces. The walls and the stairs were mute, giving away nothing.

She had a bed upstairs – she had bought a few pieces of furniture along with the house: this four-poster bed and a chest of drawers upstairs, a kitchen table downstairs, all too large and heavy, obviously, for the previous owners to have removed and taken with them. Now she made up the bed for the night, and changed into a nightgown she had brought up in a valise. She put out the light and climbed into the bed, actually glad for the darkness so that she could not make out any details – whether the closet doors were open or shut, the ceiling low or high – and perhaps they would no longer trouble her but allow the erasure of sleep.

She fell deeply into oblivion as if falling into a pit that had opened suddenly under her: she was tired. But soon, suddenly, awoke. In that pitch darkness she had a strong, throbbing sense – like a pulse beating in her temple – that someone was standing at the foot of her bed, watching her. She could distinctly hear it breathing, heavily and unevenly. It made no motion at all and she herself felt paralysed, incapable of any. It took a sudden lightning flash of will – Off! On! – to leap up and switch on a light.

The space revealed around her bed was empty of course. There was no one there. What she had taken for somebody was one post of the four-poster bed, at the foot. That was what had stood there, watching her. And it was her own breath, struggling to heave itself out of her sleep, that she had heard and taken for another's.

So she sat back on the edge of the bed, weak with foolishness. Then lay back and waited for day.

When it appeared, almost imperceptibly, as a silent dissolving of darkness, she went barefoot down the stairs to the landing. Here the presence – or intimation – of what had existed before and no longer did had become strongest. It no longer was, but had left a grey and insubstantial after-image.

It could not be verified because there was no evidence of a door or window that might once have opened on to an additional space. Yet here, at what was arguably the heart, or centre, of the house, was the most powerful sense of what had once been the heart and centre and still marked a transition that had been made – from earth to water, land to space, night to day, life to death. That was what left behind an after-image, as a boat leaves a wake in water, a plane a trail of vapour in the sky.

She passed her hands over the surface of the walls to see if she could detect what her eyes could not: traces. Apart from her certainty that there was a chamber to which the presence that had watched her sleep had withdrawn, there was no other clue.

Perplexed and frustrated, she went back up the stairs with nothing but a sense of absence and bereavement.

*

When she went in to work, colleagues asked her, carelessly, as if not really interested in her replies, if she was 'settling in'. She kept her replies suitably brief and cryptic. Yes. She was. Settling in.

Once she went to the water cooler for a drink because she had had such an urge to shout: 'No! I'm not! Settling in!' and to ask some of them – some of the nicer ones in the department – to come and see for themselves. And an aged man who was something of a ghost of the department – he had been there for so long that he had almost been forgotten – came out of the hall to collect his hat and coat, looked at her briefly from under ashy eyebrows, and asked, 'Well, and how are you liking the house on the hill?' She wondered if he had ever lived there himself but she had never spoken to him before and could hardly start questioning him or inviting him to tea so that he could see for himself. That was what she might have done but he was already shuffling off down the hall, head sunk between his shoulders like an aged turtle. The house might have suited him, she thought as she collected her own coat from the stand; perhaps he would have been more attuned to its message and vibrations and been able to decipher them.

On returning to the house, she took a few moments to pace the grounds, looking at the walls, eaves and roofs from outside, studying them to see if there were traces of an extension that might have existed. That could have provided an explanation of sorts of her suspicion that there had been one and that, like an amputated limb, it lived on, making itself apparent in her discomfort, her distress at its absence.

But all she saw was a tile coming loose, a ring of mossy green damp rising along the foundation and a spattering of bird droppings across a windowpane, but no clue that might give her direction for further search.

She turned to go in and suddenly a scattering of black rooks fell out of the hemlock tree with an astonishing volume of sound – flapping of wings, ruffling of feathers, indignant caws – and sat on the ground beneath the tree, trying to get back their balance, then stalked off across the drive into the shrubs, complaining of her intrusion.

She watched them till they were gone and only the rustling in the shrubs betrayed their passage. Gradually her own alarm subsided, and she went in and unpacked the groceries she had bought on to the kitchen table and made herself a meal, determined to keep herself occupied. It was the empty stretch of time and the empty space that night and darkness hollowed out of the visible world that let out the presence that came to watch her, audibly breathing, when she lay on the four-poster bed. She knew that, but it manifested what was otherwise invisible.

She was not afraid. Oh no. It was only that, while she had imagined the house she had bought and moved into to be vacant, it proved not to be so. There was this presence occupying it – and eluding her.

It became a nightly ritual to get up and pad on bare feet down the stairs to the landing, both to escape it and to confront it there. It was the landing, she knew, that the presence inhabited and that it slipped through its walls as if they were porous, curtains rather than walls – in and out, in and out, like breath.

There was another chamber, she knew it, but when she touched the walls, they were just that – solid, not porous, cool and smooth to her touch like a blank face turning upon her, saying, 'Did you want something?'

Because she so much wanted that meeting, that confrontation, she began to try to entice it into the open – by setting a place for it at the table, by leaving a light on in a room she had left, or by placing a chair across from the one she occupied.

She did not talk to it, not yet. She held back that final communication. Not because it was too difficult, but because it would have been too easy. To talk to it would have been to acknowledge it out loud – and she would not do that, it would too closely resemble defeat.

But when the voices of the rooks startled her out of sleep at daybreak, she wondered if it was actually trying to talk to her in those harsh, jagged syllables. Perhaps it was making the attempt to break through that final barrier that she could not bring herself to make.

She started staying at work later and later, pretending she had paperwork to deal with after everyone else had gone. But the sense that it was waiting for her would grow steadily more powerful and more irresistible. Besides, she would be tired and want her tea and want to be home, by herself. Eventually she would give in, drive back and stride to the front door in a rush – to find it shut but unlocked, making her question herself: surely she had locked it on leaving? Or else find it double locked when she was certain she had not done that: why should she? Always the door yielded reluctantly to her push as if the air, the emptiness behind it, were pushing back to keep her out.

This was too much – it was *her* house, after all. So she set down her bag and spoke to it, finally. 'I'm leaving.'

She did, at great expense and in great discomfort and, worst of all, a sense of acting foolishly. It made her angry to have bought and moved into that house and angry at now moving out. Her colleagues at work expressed surprise but also sympathy. The old man who, she now felt, had something malevolent in his lidded eyes, twinkled darkly at her, 'Too lonely up there, eh?' and she very nearly snapped back, 'On the contrary, not lonely enough,' but caught herself in time.

The wretchedness of the transition was increased by the fact that the alternative accommodation she found was a set of small rooms above a row of shops in town. She chose it because there was simply no room here for any presence other than hers. She filled it completely with her furnishings and belongings. She could barely turn around among them. When the heat of summer drammed down on the low roof over her head and beat at the vinyl panel on the outside, it became suffocating.

Lying awake on the narrow couch – actually just a metal fold-up contraption – she thought of the big house on the hill, and the presence in it prowling from room to room, looking for her, waiting for her. If she returned, would it emerge from its secret chamber and ask her into it at last, in welcome?

She turned on to her side and closed her eyes, imagining that welcome. She felt neither triumphant nor relieved at having escaped its embrace; she only felt bereft at having abandoned all possibility of it.

Just under her window, on the street, a lamp glowed with ferocious zeal; some insects revolved around it in a rumbling drone while others hurled themselves at it with piercing detonations. If she drew her curtains to shut out the demon light, the room became so oppressive that she could not breathe.

She stood leaning out of the window, her palms pressed upon the sill, and waited for someone, some presence to appear, even if only a cat prowling by night. But there was no one there at all. Till a car appeared, raucous with music and drunken voices. It slowed and someone flung a bottle that smashed against the wall just under her window. The shards burst outwards into the light, then showered down. There was laughter, a shouted expletive. That was the message, for her. It left her trembling.

Eventually, she returned to the house, as she knew she would, her small car laboriously climbing the hill, seeming to remember the potholes and exposed rocks and roots, then arriving with a sudden, inexpert swerve. She tried hard to think of what she would say to the present owners if they saw her and came out to see what she wanted. Perhaps she could ask for some object she had left behind the house by the woodpile, or some garden tools propped up against the shed. Yes, she could do that.

What she had forgotten were the rooks, the way they yelled in alarm when she appeared under their hemlock tree, tumbled out of it as if they were going to launch themselves into the sky but fell to the ground instead and waddled away in their ungainly, lumbering way, darkly muttering.

Other than them there was no one around, although the new occupants' car was parked in the open garage.

She stood there uncertainly, letting her eyes rove, waiting to see if anyone would come out and talk to her. No one did. No one ever did. She had missed the meeting on the landing.

She returned to her car, turned it around the hemlock tree and slowly withdrew.

The Museum of Final Journeys

We had driven for never-ending miles along what seemed to be more a mudbank than a road between fields of virulent green – jute? rice? what was it this benighted hinterland produced? I ought to have known, but my head was pounded into too much of a daze by the heat and the sun and the fatigue to take in what my driver was telling me in answer to my listless questions.

The sun was setting into a sullen murk of ashes and embers along the horizon when he turned the jeep into the circular driveway in front of a low, white bungalow. This was the circuit house where I was to stay until I had found a place of my own. As a very junior officer, a mere subdivisional officer in the august government service, it was all I could expect, a temporary place for one of its minor servants. There was nothing around but fields and dirt roads and dust, no lights or signs of a town to be seen. Noting my disappointment and hesitation at the first sight of my new residence – where had we come to? – the driver climbed out first, lifted my bags from the back of the jeep and led the way up the broad steps to a long veranda which had doors fitted with wire screens one could not see through. He clapped his hands and shouted, 'Koi hai?' I had not imagined anyone still used that imperious announcement from the days of the Raj: Anyone there? But perhaps, in this setting, itself a leftover from the empire, not so incongruous at all. Besides, there was no bell and one cannot knock on a screen door.

I didn't think anyone had heard. Certainly no light went on and no footsteps were to be heard, but in a bit someone came around the house from the back where there must have been huts or quarters for servants.

'I've brought the new officer-sahib,' the driver announced officiously (he wore a uniform of sorts, khaki, with lettering in red over the shirt pocket that gave him the right). 'Open a room for him. And switch on some lights, will you?'

'No lights,' the man replied with dignity. He wore no uniform, only some loose clothing, and his feet were bare, but he held his back straight and somehow established his authority. 'Power cut.'

'Get a lantern then,' the driver barked. He clearly enjoyed giving orders.

I didn't, and was relieved when the chowkidar – for clearly he was the watchman for all his lack of a uniform – took over my bags and the driver turned to leave. It was night now, and when I saw the headlights of the jeep sweep over the dark foliage that crowded against the house and lined the driveway, then turn around so that the tail-lights could be seen to dwindle and disappear, I felt my heart sinking. I did not want to stay in this desolate place, I wanted to run after the jeep, throw myself in and return to a familiar scene. I was used to city life, to the cacophony of traffic, the clamour and din and discordancy of human voices, the pushing and shoving of humanity, all that was absent here.

While I stood waiting on the veranda for a lamp to be lit so I could be shown to my room, I listened to the dry, grating crackle of palm leaves over the roof, the voices of frogs issuing low warnings from some invisible pond or swamp nearby, and these sounds were even more disquieting than the silence.

A lighted lantern was finally brought out and I followed its ghostly glow in, past large, looming pieces of furniture, to the room the chowkidar opened for me. It released a dank odour of mildew as of a trunk opened after a long stretch of time and a death or two, and I thought this was surely not a chapter of my life; it was only a chapter in one of those novels I used to read in my student days, something by Robert Louis Stevenson or Arthur Conan Doyle or Wilkie Collins (I had been a great reader then and secretly hoped to become a writer). I remembered, too, the hated voice of the gym master at school shouting 'Stiffen up now, boys, stiffen up!' and I nearly laughed – a bitter laugh.

All the actions that one performs automatically and habitually in the real world, the lighted world – of bathing, dressing, eating a meal – here had to be performed in a state of almost gelid slow motion. I carried the lantern into the bathroom with me – it created grotesquely hovering shadows rather than light, and made the slimy walls and floor glisten dangerously – and made do with a rudimentary bucket of water and a tin mug. To put on a clean set of clothes when I could scarcely make out what I had picked from my suitcase (packed with an idiotic lack of good sense: a tie? when would I ever wear a tie in this pit?) and then to find my way to the dining room and sit down to a meal placed before me that I could scarcely identify – was it lentils, or a mush of vegetables, and was this whitish puddle rice or what? – all were manoeuvres to be carried out with slow deliberation, so much so that they seemed barely worthwhile, just habits belonging to another world and time carried on weakly. The high-pitched whining of mosquitoes sounded all around me and I slapped angrily at their invisible presences.

Then, with a small explosion, the electricity came on and lights flared with an intensity that made me flinch. An abrupt shift took place. The circuit house dining room, the metal bowls and dishes set on the table, the heavy pieces of furniture, the yellow curry stains on the tablecloth all revealed themselves with painful clarity while the whine of mosquitoes faded with disappointment. Now large, winged ants insinuated their way through the wire screens and hurled themselves at the electric bulb suspended over my head; some floated down into my plate where they drowned in the gravy, wings detaching themselves from the small, floundering worms of their bodies.

I pushed back my chair and rose so precipitately, the chowki-dar came forward to see what was wrong. I saw no point in telling him that everything was. Instructing him abruptly to bring me tea at six next morning, I returned to my room. It felt like a mercy to turn off the impudent light dangling on a cord over my bed and prepare to throw myself into it for the night.

I had not taken the mosquito net that swaddled the bed into account. First I had to fumble around for an opening to crawl in, then tuck it back to keep out the mosquitoes. At this I failed, and those that found themselves trapped in the netting with me, furiously bit at every exposed surface they could find. What was more, the netting prevented any breath of air reaching me from the sluggishly revolving fan overhead.

Throughout the night voices rang back and forth in my head: would I be able to go through with this training in a remote outpost that was supposed to prepare me for great deeds in public service? Should I quit now before I became known as a failure and a disgrace? Could I appeal to anyone for help, some mentor, or possibly my father, retired now from this very service, his honour and his pride intact like an iron rod he had swallowed?

Across the jungle, or the swamp or whatever it was that surrounded this isolated house, pai dogs in hamlets and homesteads scattered far apart echoed the voices in my head, some questioning and plaintive, others fierce and challenging.

If I had not been 'stiffened up' in school and by my father, I might have shed a tear or two into my flat grey pillow. I came close to it but morning rescued me.

I resolved to look for another, more amenable place to live during my posting here, but soon had to admit that the chance of finding such a place was very unlikely. The town, if you could call it that, was not one where people built houses with the intention of selling or renting them for profit; its citizens built for the purpose of housing their families till they fell apart. Many of the houses were embarked on that inexorable process, larger and larger families crowding into smaller and smaller spaces while roofs collapsed and walls crumbled. Families did not move even when forced onto verandas or into outhouses. The whole town appeared a shambles.

It must have had its days of prosperity in the past when the jute that grew thick and strong in the surrounding fields gave rise to a flourishing business, but that was now overtaken by chemical fibres, plastics and polyesters. Their products – the bags, washing lines, buckets and basins that hung from shopfronts – littered the dusty streets where their strident colours soon faded.

Every morning I went to court, a crumbling structure of red brick that stood in a field where cattle grazed and washermen spread their washing, and there I sat at a desk on a slightly raised platform to hear the cases brought before me. These had chiefly to do with disputes over property. You would not have thought the local property was anything to be fought over but the citizens of this district were devoted to litigation with an ardour not evident in any other area of life. A wall that had caved in or two coconut trees that had not borne fruit for as long as anyone could remember, even these aroused the passion of ownership. I began to see it as the one local industry. I took back files with me to read in the evenings on the veranda of the circuit house while the power cuts held off.

In my office in the administrative buildings, I attended to more urgent matters like power and water supplies and their frequent breakdowns, roads, traffic, police – very important that, the police force – communications, security, trade and industry. (The litigators, and especially their lawyers, were always willing to have their cases postponed from one hearing to the next.) My secretary brought in the files to me, tied with red tape – I was amused to see these existed, literally – and ushered in visitors with their requests, demands and complaints. I would order tea for them, but try as I would, I could never have tea, sugar and milk served in separate pots as my mother would have: these would always arrive already mixed in the cups, and for some reason this irritated me greatly and I never ceased to complain about it.

I must have complained in my letters to my mother, too, because she worried that I was not being looked after as I would be at home. She even made efforts to find a bride for me, convinced that a wife was what I needed, a woman who would order my life and make it comfortable and pleasant for me. I was lonely enough not to discourage her, even though the idea of some stranger entering my life in such an intimate fashion did somewhat alarm me. No such thing came to pass, however. When my father discovered she was interviewing the unmarried daughters and nieces of her friends and acquaintances, dangling my position in the Civil Service and my prospects for promotions to high and important posts in the future as incentives, he put a stop to all such machinations: there was to be no marriage till my training was over and confirmation in the service achieved.

In a very short time the routine of my working life became oppressive. When I entered the service it was with the thought that it would be an endless adventure, and each day would bring fresh challenges and demand new solutions. My father and my senior colleagues had all assured me it would be so. They talked of their own adventures – shooting man-eaters that had terrorised the locals and 'lifted' their cattle, confronting dacoits who had been robbing travellers on highways, hunting down 'criminal elements' that dealt in smuggling goods or illicit liquor, and, most threatening of all, instigators of political insurgencies. To me these remained rumours, legends, and I came to suspect that my leg had been pulled. *My* most strenuous activity seemed to be wielding the fly-swatter and mopping my face in the thick damp heat that clung like wet clothing in the most debilitating way.

There was the occasional visitor to the circuit house: another officer on a tour of duty would stop for a night on his way to inspect the waterworks or the sewage plant or the government-run clinic or school or whatever he happened to be in charge of, and leave the next day, having provided me with one evening of company. Since all we had to talk about was the business at hand, these visits did not provide me with the much needed diversion.

The only release to be had was to find an excuse to go 'on tour', summon my jeep and driver and make for the further reaches of the district. At its northern rim was tea country and the sight of that trim landscape of tea bushes and shade trees on softly rolling hills that rose eventually into the blue mountain range – alas, not my territory – was as reviving as a drink of cool water to me.

Seated in the ample cane furniture on the broad veranda of one fortunate tea-estate manager's bungalow over a whisky and soda, I could not help a sigh of relief tinged with melancholy that this salubrious place was not mine and I would soon have to return to my sorry posting below.

My host enquired how I was faring. When I told him – I admit with an openly pathetic plea for sympathy – he said, 'I know the town. I have to visit it from time to time. It doesn't even have a club, does it?'

'No! If only there were a club where I could play tennis after work . . .' I gave another sigh, drawn out of me by his evident sympathy.

'No social life either?'

'There's no one I could have a conversation with about *anything* but work. There's no library or anyone who reads. I'm running out of books too.'

My host got up to pour me another peg at the bar constructed of bamboo at the other end of the spacious veranda. My eyes followed him, admiring the polished floor, the pots of ferns that lined the steps and the orchids that hung in baskets above them.

When he returned to his seat, he handed me my drink and said, 'In the old days there used to be wealthy Calcutta families who owned land around here and who would come to visit it from time to time, throw parties and organise hunts. Of course, those times are over and their estates must have gone to rack and ruin by now.'

We talked a bit longer about this and that till I had to leave, and as I walked past the open door on my way to the steps and stood waiting for my jeep to be driven round to the front, my eye fell on a small object on the hall table – two small Chinese figures in flowered tunics and black slippers carrying a kind of palanquin between them. It was both unusual and pretty and I looked at it more closely: the details were exquisite and there was a gloss to it such as you see on the finest china. My host saw me lingering to study it and said, 'Oh, it's one of those objects one sometimes comes across in these parts that belonged to the old houses I was telling you about. One of them even had a museum once: perhaps this came from there. My wife picked it up, she has an eye for such things. I told her she had paid too much – it's only a wind-up toy, you know, and has lost its key.'

'A wind-up toy!' I exclaimed. 'It looks too precious for that. Is it very old?'

'I couldn't tell you, I don't know a thing about it. It's a pity my wife is in Shillong – our daughters are at school there – she would have been able to tell you more.'

'Beautiful,' I said, and reluctantly took my leave.

I can't say I gave that beautiful object or its provenance any more thought. Inevitably, I grew more involved in my work and had to see through various projects I had started on as well as the daily routine of attending court to hear cases that grew drearily familiar, and going through the bottomless stack of files in my office. I even stopped asking for milk and sugar to be brought separately for my tea and resigned myself to drinking the thick, murky liquid I was served.

I became so settled in a state of apathy – it was like an infection I had caught from those around me – that I felt quite irritated when the chowkidar at the circuit house roused me from it one evening as I sat slumped in the reclining chair under the revolving fan in my room, waiting for darkness to fall and for him to call me to my dinner.

Instead he said, 'Someone to see you, sahib.'

'Who?' I snapped, and added, 'Tell him to come and see me in my office tomorrow. I don't see visitors here.'

'That is right, sahib,' the chowkidar acknowledged, 'but he has come from far and says it is a matter he needs to discuss privately.'

'What matter?' I snapped again (I had acquired this habitual manner of speech to those in an inferior position – servants, petitioners, supplicants; I found it was expected of me, it went with the job).

Of course the chowkidar could not know or tell. He stood there expecting some action from me, so, with a show of petulance, I threw down the newspaper folded to the crossword puzzle that I had been pretending to solve, and went out to the veranda where the visitor stood waiting: an elderly, rather bowed man with wisps of white hair showing under his cap like feathers, enormous spectacles with thick lenses and heavy frames attached to him by string, and dressed in a faded black cloth coat and close white trousers, perhaps the outfit he had adopted as a clerk (he had the obsequious manner of one) before his superannuation.

Some remnant of my upbringing surfaced through my adopted manner of irritable superiority (from behind my father's looming shadow, my mother occasionally emerged to stand watching me, hopefully, trustingly). I gestured to him to be seated and called to the chowkidar to bring us water. Just that, pani.

The clerical creature folded his hands and asked me not to bother. 'I am deeply sorry to disturb your rest,' he said in a voice just slightly above the whine of a mosquito, perhaps closer to the sound of a small cricket.

I found my habitual annoyance beginning to creep back and said abruptly, 'What can I do for you?'

'Sir, I have come from the Mukherjee estate thirty-five miles from here,' the poor man brought out as if embarrassed to make a statement that might sound boastful. Why should it? I wondered, and waited. 'I have served the family for fifty years,' he went on, barely above a whisper, and kept touching, nervously, his small white beard like a goat's – a goatee.

'I don't know the place,' I told him.

'Sir, it was once the largest estate in the district,' he said imploringly, seeing that I needed to be persuaded. 'The family owned fields of jute and rice and even tea and cinchona in the north. Also coal mines. Many properties in the district belonged to them. They were rented out. It was my duty to keep account of it all. In those days I had many assistants, it was too much for me to handle alone. My father had served before me and I was employed by the family when I was still a boy. They trusted my family and they put it all in my hands.'

This was going to be a long story, I realized, if I was to allow him to unfold it at this pace. We might need to travel backwards to generations now long gone, pallid ghosts disappearing one after the other into the dark night of the past. When would we arrive in the daylight of the present? I wondered, sitting up with a jerk to accept a glass of water from the chowkidar and hoping by my brisk action to indicate that my time was valuable and it was running out.

But, like a mosquito that has got under one's net and can't be driven out, the ancient gnome went on murmuring, and the tale he had to tell was exactly the one I had feared: the usual saga of a descent from riches to rags, the property fragmenting as the sons of one generation quarrelled and insisted on ill-judged divisions, the gradual crumbling of wealth as tenant farmers failed to pay rent, and litigation that never led to solutions, only protracted the death throes. Then the house itself, the one the family had occupied while it multiplied, falling down piecemeal, the cost of repair and maintenance making its eventual disintegration inevitable.

The familiar story of the fabled zamindars of old. I could have recited any number of them to this poor, whispering ancient who seemed to think his was the only such story to be told.

But at some point – perhaps I had dozed off briefly, then woken – I began to hear what he was saying. It was the word 'museum' that had the effect of a mosquito bite after a long spell of droning.

'The museum at our house was started by Srimati Sarita Mukherjee who was married to my master in the year 19— when she was thirteen and he sixty years of age. She was the second wife of Sri Bhupen Mukherjee who inherited the property from his father Debabrata Mukherjee in 19—. He had no issue from his first marriage. Srimati Sarita Devi was of the Sinha family that resides in Serampore. The family was wealthy and accordingly she brought with her a substantial dowry. It was not so large in property as in gold and gems. The family was known for its love of art and literature and she had grown up in the company of educated men and women and had some education herself.

'It was not easy for her to adjust to the life on our estate, which is not only a great distance from her home but far from any other estate in our district. Sri Bhupen Mukherjee, being an only son, had no brothers or sisters-in-law who might have provided her with some company. Naturally she had many lonely years as the only lady in the house. Then, when she was nineteen years of age, a son was born to her. Sri Jiban Mukherjee gave us all joy as he was the natural heir and we had great hopes he would keep the estate intact and make it prosper. Sadly, Sri Bhupen Mukherjee did not live much longer and could take pride in his heir for only a few short years before he expired. So my duty became very clear to me: I had to make sure that the inheritance that came to the young boy would be substantial and he and his mother would lack for nothing.'

At this point I found my knee beginning to jog involuntarily up and down. I am sure it was because I was growing impatient to learn: did *she* create a museum? Did it exist?

'Then we had a number of bad years in a row when the rains did not come and the crops were ruined and our coal mines suffered one disaster after another and had to be abandoned. For several years the estate had no income at all, only losses. There was no money available for repairs and maintenance. We were forced to take loans simply to keep the place running and we fell into debt.

'Times did improve but whatever income there was had to be spent on paying off debts. It was sad to see Srimati Sarita Devi's face so careworn and her hair turn grey before her time. She was burdened with worry not only with regard to finances but also to her son Sri Jiban's upbringing and education of which she had sole responsibility after the death of his father.'

At this point the narrator paused. He seemed crushed by the sadness of what he had to relate. I found I had become involved with it in spite of myself and so had to allow him to unfold the tale at his own pace which was slow but persistent. Having run out of books to read, even so slight and familiar a story as I was hearing now had enough interest to keep me from seeing off this unwelcome insect of a visitor.

'I am sorry to say she had to sell her gold and jewellery bit by bit to pay for his education as the estate itself could not bear the expense. She saw to it that he was sent to the best school in Calcutta, one run by the Jesuit fathers, and thereafter to university in England as his father would have wished. We had great hopes that on his return with a degree in law, he would set up a successful practice as a barrister so that he could support his mother in the manner to which she was born.'

His voice had grown so low that it seemed to mimic the dusk into which the circuit house, its veranda and the surrounding wilderness had sunk, leaving us in darkness, and for a while I could barely hear him at all, but perhaps that was because the chowkidar had arrived with a mosquito coil which he lit to drive away the mosquitoes now beginning to swarm, then went indoors to pump a Flit gun vigorously for the same purpose, and finally turned on the lights. He also coughed repeatedly, in a blatantly false manner, to signal it was time for my visitor to leave so he could serve me my dinner, then retire. I could interpret all these signs after my protracted stay in the circuit house but my visitor ignored him and after a few long sighs resumed his narrative.

'Unfortunately, Sri Jiban, having lived abroad for several years, could not adjust to life on our estate or even to Calcutta. He had no interest in the affairs of the estate and left it all to his mother to take care of as before. We waited to see what his plans were for the future. Naturally he did not confide in me but one day I saw him packing his bags and heard him send for a tonga to take him to the nearest railway station. His mother wept as she saw him drive away and when I attempted to console her by saying he would surely return soon, she replied she did not think he would because he was planning a long sea voyage to countries in the East. I was astounded by this information because I did not see how he could fund such an ambitious voyage; nor could I see its purpose. I then learnt she had sold the last of her jewellery to finance his desire.'

I was now beginning to wonder why I was being made privy to the family's secrets. I would have risen to my feet to indicate the time I had given him was now up, but something about his posture, so crushed, his hands held tightly together as if in agony, and the way his old white head trembled on its thin stalk of a neck stopped me. Also, frankly, I wanted to know where the story would go.

To my surprise, he now lifted his head so I could see his expression more clearly by the light that fell on us from the lighted rooms within, and I saw that he looked quite serene, almost joyful.

'Then the boxes began to arrive. They came from Burma, from Thailand, from Indonesia, from Malaya, Cambodia, the Philippines and even China and Japan, containing such objects as had never been seen in our part of the world! People would come from their villages miles away to our gates to watch the bullock carts they had seen hauling these boxes to our door, and there was much talk about what they might contain.' He actually laughed at this point, a dry rustling in his throat like that made by a bird or insect in a bush, a kind of cackle you might call it. 'Our people are simple folk. They have no knowledge of the world and the countries our young master had visited but, seeing the size of the containers, they thought he was involved in trade and that he had made a fortune so he could send his mother treasures in the form of silks and jewels and other valuable goods.' He shook his head now at their foolishness and gullibility. 'They believed the young master would return a wealthy man and restore our estate,' and here his laugh ended in a small hiccup. 'We opened the containers as they came and were astonished by what we found. He had sent us few letters or messages and we could only conjecture where he had been and where he had found or purchased the goods revealed to us.'

'And—?'

'One room after the other was filled with these objects. We brought in carpenters to build glass cases and put up shelves to display them. Each container provided the contents for a different room, the rooms that had been empty for so long – we had been selling items of furniture and other belongings ever since we fell upon hard times – and now they were filled again. Visitors came to the house and were astonished by what they saw. One even wished to make a catalogue of these objects and publish it to make the collection known. Srimati Sarita Devi could not tell them anything about the objects or where her son had obtained them, but they gave her great solace because they allowed her to accompany him on his voyage. Only I was perturbed: I did not see the use of such things. They were objects of beauty and interest, but what was the use of collecting them? I could not see, but Srimati Sarita Devi did. She told me, "Bijan, we are creating a great museum. My son's collection is forming a museum that people will hear about all over our land and will come from far to see."'

Ah, so there *was* a museum! I found myself growing excited

to learn this had not been merely a rumour or a folk tale but actually existed. I even asked him if I could come and visit it.

At this he first closed his eyes as if in weariness, then opened them wide with a radiant gaze, and cried out, 'Sir, this is my dearest wish! Come, please come and visit us, advise me what to do! I am old now, as you see, and I do not know what will become of it once I am gone. Already people – visitors, perhaps even members of our own staff who have learnt there are no guards, no security – have been removing some small objects. I have myself seen these things appearing in markets here and there. The only way open to me to keep it intact is to request the government, the sarkar, take it over and maintain it. If you come and see it for yourself, you will see how great the need is for security and support. Without it—' He broke off, as if the alternative was unthinkable, and mopped his face with a cloth he withdrew from his pocket.

But was there no alternative? Did the errant son not return to his ancestral property? What of Srimati Sarita Devi, his mother? What were her wishes in the matter? I tried to probe tactfully.

'Sir,' the unhappy man confessed, 'she left us with no instructions.'

This seemed vague to me. Had she died and 'left for her heavenly abode' as they say in the classified columns of our newspapers? Or moved out of the museum/mausoleum and left it to him? He seemed strangely unwilling to say. He had come to the end of his narrative and had, he seemed to indicate, no more to say. 'The collection' was all that was left at the end of it.

My own enthusiasm came to an abrupt halt as if it had met with an obstruction, a speed break. I began to see only too well the tangle of legal problems ahead. Not at all what I had imagined, although I should have done so. I felt let down by the realization that it all came down to practicalities, legal and administrative. Just as if I hadn't had my fill of these. While others dreamt dreams and lived lives of imagination and adventure, my role was only to take care of the mess left by them.

My curiosity about the museum and my desire to see it were

quickly evaporating. But, if they afforded me a break from the daily routine of office and courtroom in this oppressively limited outpost, why not accept? I told him I would have my driver bring me, asked for directions, and found a suitable date. His gratitude made him practically bow before me – a display of obsequiousness that was more than I could bear. I turned my head and went in to my dinner, leaving him to find his own way out.

I should have known better than to expect some miraculous Xanadu. As my jeep bumped and bounced its way along the mudbank that passed for a road between flattened fields of stubble with only an occasional coconut tree or grove of bananas beside a stagnant pond to break the monotony of a landscape bleached of colour, my expectations dwindled and sobered. The last stretch ended at what no doubt had been an imposing gateway, but now consisted of two pillars of brick with parasitic trees growing out of the cracks, and only some rusty hinges left to show where the wrought-iron gates had hung.

Ahead of us lay what had probably been the driveway but was now a grassy field in which a few skeletal cows grazed, watched over by a cowherd with a staff. He stood with one foot resting against the knee of the other leg like a flamingo blackened by the sun. His face did register some astonishment at seeing a motor vehicle make its way over the hummocky grass, but other than that he made no acknowledgement of our intrusion. And the cows merely switched their tails and flicked their ears at our passing and a few cattle egrets took off from their flanks with lazy flaps of their wings.

Having traversed the length of the field we came to what had to be 'the palace' I had come to see. What did I expect? There was a broad flight of stairs with grass growing between the flagstones, and beyond it the mournful remains of what I had been assured was once the most substantial house in the district. At first sight I could make out no architectural features in the blackened, crumbling ruin.

Only time, and dissolution.

But here came my acquaintance, the clerk/caretaker, tumbling recklessly down the irregular stairs while adjusting the cap on his head and the buttons of his long black cloth coat as if these gave him his identity and status. Yet his manner on greeting me was gracious and courtly in a way that could only be called 'cultured' or even 'aristocratic', and I felt a twinge of shame at recalling how brusquely I had dismissed him. Although, when he launched into a flowery speech of gratitude at my coming, his joy at seeing me, the honour it accorded him and the house he served, I could not help cutting him short and being curt once again. I suggested we set about doing our tour.

He insisted, however, that I first rest a little and take some refreshment. On the broad veranda spread around the rooms like a lap on which they had settled, a table had been set with an embroidered cloth and a tarnished silver tray on which was a jug, covered with a square of net edged with beads, and some tall metal tumblers. A servant boy emerged from somewhere – a coal-hole, I conjectured – to pour out some coloured sherbet drink that I was not able to refuse.

'Bring the keys,' my host the clerk commanded, assuming the posture of one whose right it was to give orders. Before my eyes he became stiffly upright – still small of course but upright nevertheless – his mouth set in a firm line, his eyes sharp and watchful, his bearing almost arrogant. Here was a person, I saw, who was much more capable of commanding than I was. I observed him and the air with which he accepted the ring of keys from the servant boy as though they were the keys to a castle, his castle. Then, to my surprise, he held them behind his back with one hand, and with the other gestured to me to precede him through an open door. Were the keys only some part of a charade?

We entered the hall of the palace of the past between two marble – or highly polished ceramic – slave figures holding up lamps filled with dust and dead moths; they had onyx for eyes that bulged grotesquely out of their heads.

The room itself was empty except for a small marble-topped table on ornate legs, carved like dragons. Under it was what looked like a china chamber pot – but could that be? Perhaps I have imagined or misinterpreted it, and other details. On the faded, mottled walls portraits hung from long ropes and huge nails, tilting forward as if to peer down at us. They were photographs in the main but tinted by hand to look like paintings, a strange technique by which one art was imposed on another, leaving the surface oddly ambiguous. One was of a small man in a large turban who stood in front of a dead tiger with its mouth propped open in a snarl; another of a large man with whiskers that bristled like the tiger's, seated upon a gilt chair. Yet another image of perhaps the same man standing, his foot on a recently murdered elephant, a gun in his hand and a row of barely clad servants – beaters? – on either side.

And then one of a woman, scarcely more than a child, slender, her cheeks tinted pink and with strands of pearls around her neck from which hung one large gem tinted green. She wore an old-fashioned blouse with long puffed sleeves that ended in lace at the wrists, and a sari that fell in sculpted folds from her shoulders to her slippered feet, its silver trim draped over her head where her hair was parted in two wings over wide-set eyes. This was the only female portrait, and as we passed it, I heard the clerk sigh, 'Srimati Sarita Devi.' Or perhaps I imagined that because I wished it to be her, the child bride. Since he had not said 'The late Srimati' I still did not know if she was alive, somewhere in the recesses of this faded mansion, and if I would be taken to meet her, or if she was the late, departed Srimati S. My escort remained silent on the matter.

He was already showing me into an adjoining hall where the beasts slaughtered by this family had been embalmed and stuffed to look lifelike or had had their pelts removed and stretched out upon the walls under a forest of antlers and the mounted heads of glass-eyed stags. I tried to avoid looking up at them: I did not enjoy the sensation of being watched, accusingly I thought. 'The men in the family were great hunters,' my guide said, as if explanation were needed, and I could detect neither apology nor pride in his voice because he kept it as low as if we were in a mausoleum. I decided it was merely respectful so I too tried to look respectful but must have failed: my father had also been a hunter in his days and I had not liked to look on his trophies or hear about his exploits which sounded boastful and made my mother cringe. I probably looked merely blank as I stared at the scalloped and scaly skin of a crocodile or of a python, mottled and moth-like, one resembling broken rubble, the other faded netting. I turned to the clerk, who had his hands behind his back and his head uplifted to these specimens he was set here to guard, and indicated I wished to hurry on. But, before leaving this chamber of death, I had to pass a large, pot-like object by the door. From its folds and wrinkles and the massive flattened toenails, I discerned it to be the foot of an elephant. In case I missed the point of this dismemberment, some umbrellas had been placed in it, their cloth covering frayed and their tin ribs exposed.

Unfortunately the next chamber was one of stuffed birds and they did little to improve my spirits. If anything, the glass eyes set in grey sockets were even more accusing and I was certain that their faded, iridescent feathers were creeping with parasitic life.

The only living creatures visible in these chambers were the spiders that spun their webs to make shrouds for the birds and the geckoes that probably fed on the spiders. I saw one lizard flattened against the wall, immobile, a pulse beating under its nearly transparent skin to show it was just waiting for us to leave, for night to fall, so it could come to life again. In one doorway, a gecko caught by the slam of the door had left its fragile skeleton splayed against the plaster like a web spun by one of the spiders, to stay till it peeled.

'Is this,' I demanded, 'is *this* the young master's collection?' If there was sarcasm in my tone, it was intentional.

My guide, proving aware of it, quickly responded, 'No, no, no.

No, this was left to him by his ancestors. Now we will go to see *his* collection.' And, to my huge relief, we came out into a corridor completely bare of trophies, one side opening onto a courtyard where a marble goddess stood in the shallow basin of a waterless fountain. Her limbs were broken at the joints and lichen had crept up her sandalled feet to the hem of her robe. This stretch of corridor evidently led to the wing that held the items sent to the estate by the absconding master in containers that had created such a stir in the district and a legacy for the inheritors – if any.

And now my guide produced the ring of keys from behind his back because we had come to a door that was locked. Choosing one extraordinarily long key from the ring, he inserted it into the lock and turned it with a great sense of drama. I followed him in with some trepidation and impatience: how many more hunting trophies and murdered spoils was I to be shown? The heat of the day was gathering in these closed, unventilated rooms, and although it must have been noon by now, there was very little light here.

Except, I was astonished to find, what the collection itself radiated. The chamber we had entered was hung, draped, laid and overlaid with rugs in the splendid colours of royalty – plum, wine, mulberry and pomegranate – woven into intricate patterns. I hesitated to step on one, they were surely precious and, besides, had not been touched in ages by hand, still less by foot. Only a raja might recline on one, with his rani, while listening to the music of sitar and sarod, tabla and tanpura. I could imagine these invisible potentates and pashas lifting goblets in their ringed hands or, better still, the chased silver mouthpiece of a hookah. Lives lived in such a setting could only have been noble and luxurious – not of this poor, hardworked land around.

It was only when I lowered my eyes to examine them more closely that I noted what the imperial colours concealed: patches that were faded, threadbare, some even darned and mended, clumsily.

My guide watched my reactions as they flickered across my

face – I'm sure my expressions gave me away – and seemed gratified, a small smile lifting the corners of his compressed lips. But before I could bend and examine more closely these Persian, Turkish, Afghan, Moroccan and Kashmiri treasures, he ushered me into the next room.

And this was even more richly rewarding, for here hung the miniature paintings of Turkey, Persia, Moghul India, Rajasthan and Kangra. I was not enough of a connoisseur to identify them and it would have taken days, even a lifetime, to examine each separately and study the clues enclosed by the gilt margins. Here were jewel-like illustrations of floral and avian life, tiny figures mounted on curvaceous horses in pursuit of lions and gazelles, or kneeling before bearded saints in mountain caves. I glimpsed a pair of cranes performing a mating dance on a green hillock before passing on to a young maiden conversing with her pet parrot in a cage and another penning a letter to a distant beloved, and so to a sly young man spying from behind a tree on a bevy of young girls bathing in a river, clothed, but transparently. Here elephants with gilded howdahs on their backs carried noblemen up bare hills to crenellated forts on the summits, and now blue storm clouds appeared, driving white egrets before them; a dancing girl performed in a walled courtyard; a prince posed with a pink rose in his hand, another proudly exhibited a hawk upon his wrist. Hunting dogs streamed after deer in a forest, a hunter following them with a bow and arrow. A ship set sail. Lightning struck. Lines of exquisite script curled through the borders, naming their names, telling their tales.

I could not read them, partly from the unfamiliarity of the scripts, but also because the glass that separated these wonderful worlds from the spectator was filmed with dust. No hand had touched them since they were framed and hung. There were no visitors to admire them, just the old caretaker who seemed more proud than knowledgeable, and I who could say nothing but 'Ah!' and 'Ahh!'

*

If I had been shown just these two chambers, I should have felt satisfied and certain of the value of this collection, but we did not stop here. The caretaker, bowing slightly, was showing me through the door to another chamber, this one filled with fans and kimonos. Disembodied, they contrived somehow to beckon and flirt. It was easy to imagine the fine tapered fingers that must have wielded these fans of carved ivory and pleated silk painted with scenes of gardens and festivals, or the slender figures that had worn these silk gowns, opulent and elaborate with sweeping sleeves and trailing borders of indigo and verdigris, bronze and jade, amethyst and azure. They seemed to plead for their glass cases to be opened so they might step out of these frozen tableaux and assume the roles of queens and courtesans to which they were born.

But such exposure might have revealed them to be ghosts, a touch of air might have turned them to dust. The sleeves were empty, the hems ended in no slippers and no feet. Their fans stirred no air. It occurred to me that the little toylike object, which had caught my eye in my friend the tea-estate manager's house, might once have stood among these ghosts, their plaything, before it was spirited away by some light-fingered viewer. And so they had no vehicle, not even a miniature palanquin.

I found myself invaded by their poetic melancholy and would have liked to linger, fancying myself a privileged visitor to a past world, but the caretaker gave a warning cough to remind me of his presence and our purpose in being here; I turned round to see him holding open another door to another chamber.

And so I was marched through one filled with masks of wood, straw, leather and clay, painted and embellished with bone, shells, rings, strings and fur, masks that threatened or mocked or terrified, then one of textiles – printed, woven, dyed and bleached, gauze, muslin, silk and brocade – and after that one of footwear – fantastical, foolish, foppish – followed by one of headwear – caps and bonnets of velvet, straw, net and felt . . . What kind of traveller had this been who desired and acquired the stuff of other people's lands and lives? Why did he? And how had it all arrived here to make up this preposterous collection?

The guide, smiling enigmatically, would give me no clues. Now he was showing me cases filled with weapons of war – curved swords, stout daggers, hilts engraved with decorative patterns that concealed murderous intent – and now he was glancing to see my reaction to a display of porcelain and ceramic – delicate receptacles painted with scenes of arched bridges and willow groves, mountains and waterfalls, or abstract patterns of fierce intricacy in bold and brilliant colours.

I felt sated, wanted to protest, hardly able to take in any more wonders, any more miracles, but detected a certain ruthlessness to my guide's opening of door after door, ushering me on and on, much further than I wished to go. I had thought of him as aged and frail, but his pride and determination to impress me seemed to give him a strength and stamina I would not have imagined possible and it was I who was exhausted, overcome by the heat, stopping to mop my face, even stumbling, yet also curiously unwilling to admit defeat and leave what I had undertaken incomplete.

And there was a chamber we came across every now and then that I would have gladly lingered in, the chamber of scrolls and manuscripts, for instance, which I would have wished to examine more closely. Was this scroll Chinese, or Japanese or Korean? And what did it say, so elegantly, in letters like bees and dragonflies launched across the yellowed sheets, only half unrolled, with faded seals scattered here and there like pressed roses, the insignia of previous owners? Did states, lands, governments exist that produced documents of marriage, property or cases presented in court with such artistry – settlements of wills and disputes, perhaps decrees and laws and declarations of war and peace? What were they? I compared them in my mind to the tattered files that piled up in heaps on my desk, and marvelled. But only insects examined the ones here, eating their way through papery labyrinths, creating intricate tracks before vanishing, leaving behind networks of faint channels the colour of tea, or rust, and small heaps of grey excrement.

Whole worlds were encrypted here and I looked to my guide for elucidation but he only gave a slight shrug as if to say: what does it matter? The young master collected them and that was what made them precious.

And there was still more to see: cases that held all manner of writing materials with inks reduced to powder at the bottom of glass containers, pens and quills no one would ever use again, seals that no longer stamped; a chamber of clocks where no sand seeped through the hourglasses, water had long since evaporated from the clepsydras, bells were stilled, cuckoos silenced, dancing figures paralysed. Time halted, waiting for a magician to start it again.

The sense of futility was underlined by the sounds my footsteps made on the stone flooring. My guide's feet were shod in slippers that only shuffled. We might have been a pair of ghosts from the museum the owner had conjured up in a dream.

My curiosity was now so reduced that, like a fading spectre, it barely existed. I found myself hurrying after my guide, no longer stopping to admire or decipher, wishing only to bring the tour to an end.

But now we came to a halt in the dustiest and shabbiest chamber of all, as if here the voyager's travels were being rounded up and stored away. It held all the appurtenances of travel itself – leather suitcases with peeling labels of famous hotels still clinging to them, railway and shipping timetables decades out of date and obsolete, baskets held together with string, canvas bedrolls with splitting leather straps and rusty buckles, Gladstone bags as cracked and crushed as broken old men, bundles of bus, ferry and railway tickets preserved by an obsessive, entrance tickets to castles, museums, palaces and picture galleries, reminders of experiences that must once have seemed rich and rewarding. On the walls, peeling posters for lands where beaches were golden, palm trees loaded with coconuts, cruise liners afloat on high seas, flags fluttering – their original colours now barely perceptible. On a table in the centre, an antique globe, round as a teapot, with a map on it centuries out of date, showing continents that had shifted or disappeared and oceans that had spread or shrunk, and portraying marine life – spouting whales, flying fish, as well as mythical creatures like sirens and mermaids, all beckoning: come, come see!

Perhaps this had been the restless young man's source of inspiration. As for me, all desire I had ever felt for adventure had been drained away by seeing these traces that he had left of his, this gloomy storehouse of abandoned, disused, decaying objects. Their sad obsolescence cast a spell on me and I wanted only to break free and flee.

But my guide had one more thing he wanted to show me. Pointing at a long, shallow box that stood open along one wall, he said, 'This was the final box we received. It was empty and Srimati Sarita Devi knew it was the last. She said to me, "There will not be another."'

'And there wasn't?' I asked, wondering if I was meant to take this as some miraculous revelation of a mother's bond to her child or if it would lead to another tale.

'No, no more boxes.'

'And did he himself not return?'

He shook his head and, as if to avoid a show of emotion, turned aside and pushed open the last heavy door.

And suddenly we found ourselves expelled from the darkness and gloom and outside on the wide stairs open to the white blaze of day. I tried to adjust my eyes to the harsh contrast and to think of something to say, but my mouth was dry and stale, in need of a drink of water. I turned to my host to take my leave and was startled to find he did not at all intend to let me go. Instead, he was hurrying down the stairs to the dusty, uninviting field below, no longer the meek, obsequious clerk who had come to petition me at the circuit house, nor the proud curator of what he clearly deemed a valuable piece of property, but a small, determined man doggedly performing his duties to the last.

'Where are we going now?' I protested, unwillingly following him to the foot of the stairs.

He turned back, suddenly snapped open an umbrella – a large black dome lifted on its rusty spokes – that he must have picked out of the unlucky elephant's foot without my noticing and said, 'This way, please, this way. I have one last gift to show you,' and, holding the clumsy object over my head to provide me with shade, proceeded to cross the field. We came to what was evidently the end of the extensive compound where there was a brick wall – or the remains of one – rising above the top of which I could see a stand of susurrating bamboo bleached by the sun.

He led me through a doorway – it was actually a gap in the wall and doorless – and suddenly we were in the bamboo grove that I had glimpsed from without. Here, in a rustling, crackling bed of dry, sharp-tipped leaves shed by the bamboo stalks, and looming up in the striped shade like a grounded monsoon cloud, restlessly shifting from one padded foot to another as if fretting at its captivity, an elephant stood chained. Its trunk swung downward as if wilted by the heat and gave out long deep sighs that stirred the dust on the ground. Although the animal glanced at us from under lashes like bristles, with small, sharp, canny eyes, it gave no sign of curiosity or alarm. Weariness perhaps, that was all.

A man, bare-bodied, his waist wrapped in a brief, discoloured rag, rose from where he had been squatting in the shade by some buckets and troughs filled with leaves, and came forward to meet us with, I thought, the same weariness as his charge.

To my surprise, my small timid host went up to the great grey wall of the elephant's side and placed his hand on it, proprietori-ally. The creature stood listless, the merest twitch running through its flank as if it had been bothered by a fly. And there were flies. Also heaps of dung for them to feed on.

The two men spoke to each other in one of the local dialects unknown to me, the one in rags not even troubling to remove the stalk on which he was chewing from his mouth, and the clerk/curator giving him what sounded like instructions. The keeper of the elephant shrugged and said something laconic from the corner of his mouth and scratched the sparse hairs on his chest. He and his charge, the one minute and the other monumental, shared a surprising number of tics and mannerisms.

The clerk/curator turned to me and his elderly face with its white wisp of a beard looked tired and older still than it had earlier seemed.

'She was the last gift Sri Jiban sent his mother. She travelled to us over the border from Burma; it was a long journey by foot and this was her final destination. Her keeper brought us no letter and no explanation except that she was sent us by *him*, and we have had the care of her and the feeding of her ever since. And it is now many years. Srimati Sarita Devi saw to it as long as she had the strength and the means, then left her in my care. She gave me whatever remained in her hands, then departed for Varanasi where she has lived ever since. I did not hear from her again. Perhaps she is no more. She went there, you see, to die.'

I saw that he laid his hand on the great beast's flank with an immense gentleness; it might have been the touch a father bestows on an idiot son, a mad daughter or an invalid wife, gentle and despairing, because she also provided him with the purpose of his life.

'If she lives longer,' he murmured, 'and requires more feeding, I will have to start dismantling the museum, disposing of it piece by piece. It is her only inheritance.'

I had no idea what I should do or say, and stood there in the shade of the monstrous cloud, staring at the flies and the shifting padded feet and the dust they stirred up, away from the two small, spare men who, I now saw, were not only older and shorter than I, but also emaciated, probably lacking even the basic nutrition and necessities, while their ward lived on and on and fed and fed.

Then the clerk put his hands together and turned to me in pleading. 'Sir, please help us. Please appeal on our behalf to the government, the sarkar, to take the museum from us into its custody and provide for us, and for this last gift we were sent. I am ashamed, sir, but I can no longer care for her myself. Forgive me for begging you.'

I could not think of what to say, how to meet his request, his evident need. I mumbled something about it being late, about having to get back, about how I would think about what could be done and how I would let him know as soon, as soon as—

That year of my training in the service is long past. I have been for years now in senior positions, mostly in the capital. I have been transferred from one ministry to another, have dealt with finance, with law and order, with agriculture, with mines and minerals, with health care and education . . . you could call it a long and rewarding career of service. I might even say my father took some pride in it. I am of course no longer the lonely bachelor I was when I was first sent out to the districts and compelled to stay in that benighted circuit house; my mother was able to arrange a marriage for me to a wife who is in every way suited to me and my life, and I am a family man with grown sons and daughters. In fact, I rarely think back to that time now.

I am ashamed to say that once I was transferred to the capital I did not look back, I did not keep in touch with the keeper of the museum and I never found out what happened to it, or to him. What is that saying about ships passing in the night? Is there a landlocked version of it – caravans passing in the desert, or elephants in the forest?

Elephants – now those are creatures which make me uneasy still. Of course I rarely encounter one. Even when my children were young, I avoided zoos, circuses, any place an elephant might be sighted. I feared to have that sad, shrewd eye turned on me, taking my measure and finding it wanting.

Once I had a nightmare – it was while I was still in the

district and it was never repeated and never forgotten – in which such a beast devoured, blade by blade, leaf by leaf, an entire forest till it was laid waste, and then it raised its trunk and stepped forward to the tree where I was hiding, to expose – what? I don't know because such nightmares do not have endings. One flees them by waking.

And in wakefulness I would think of the immense creature as innocent and defenceless, who dwindles from neglect and finally lies down not to rise again. A death so huge as to be incomprehensible. This disturbs me and I turn away to distract myself from it. I know behind it is the question: Could I have done more? But it is not for us to do everything for everyone. In the end my reputation in the service was good, solid. What else could I have done?

In fact, by now I am not even sure the museum existed, or the man who created it or his mother who received it or the keeper who kept it. Or if it was a mirage I saw or a book I once read and only vaguely remembered, with none of the solidity, the actuality of objects and men and beasts.

Occasionally a scene from it will rise out of my subconscious just as I am drifting into sleep. Then it slips away.

Translator Translated

The two women had not met since they were in school together. And at that time they barely had anything to do with each other. That is how it is, of course, when one is a natural-born leader, excels in both sports and studies, is captain of any number of societies, a model for the subdued and discouraged mediocrities who cannot really aspire to imitating her and who feel a disturbing mix of envy and admiration – currents travelling in opposite directions and coiling into treacherous and unsettling whirlpools – and the other, meanwhile, belongs to the latter group, someone who stands out neither by her looks nor her brains and whom others later have a hard time remembering as having been present at all.

Yet, at the Founder's Day function held at their old school one year, they were both present in the small group of alumni who attended. Prema, now middle-aged, even prematurely aged one might say, found herself in the presence of someone she had admired for so long from afar. It would not have occurred to her to approach the tall, elegant woman with a lock of white hair gleaming like a bold statement amid the smooth black tresses that swung about her shoulders. The woman wore enormous dark glasses – they used to be called 'goggles' – which she removed only to read the programme, but she must have looked around her and taken in more because she half turned in her seat to Prema who sat behind her and said, quite naturally and unaffectedly, 'We were in the same class, weren't we? Do you remember?' And Prema had to make a pretence of being puzzled, confused and surprised, before remembering – as if she had ever forgotten.

Prema's astonishment at being recognized made her tongue-tied. As a schoolgirl she had never gone up and spoken to Tara – there had been no occasion to do so. Only once was a connection made, when she threw a ball right across the court with an unaccustomed, even anguished force, and Tara, leaping to catch it, twirled so that her short pleated skirt whipped about her hips, and effortlessly, balletically, lifted the ball into the net to eruptions of cheers. Now Prema could find nothing to say. If only there were, again, a ball to fling and to catch, so gloriously! Finally, 'It's been a long time,' she stammered, and wished she had dressed better and brought her new handbag with her instead of the cloth satchel into which she stuffed books, papers, everything – just the way only the most despised and unfashionable teachers did.

'Not when one is back here – it's changed so little,' Tara said easily. 'Miss Dutt is gone, of course. I wish I'd come sooner and seen her again.'

Miss Dutt, the dragon? She wished she had seen her again? Prema blinked: it just showed what different worlds they occupied. To Prema, Miss Dutt had never been anything but a scourge and a terror; she could still remember the withering stare she cast at Prema's battered shoes, unshined, slovenly and uncouth.

'One is too busy,' she said finally, awkwardly. 'Where is the time?'

She should not have said that; it made Tara ask, 'What have you been doing all these years?' which of course uncovered the hollowness of Prema's words. What *had* she been doing that she could talk of, compared with Tara's achievements of which everyone knew?

Prema had kept herself informed of Tara's career: how could one not when it had been so much mentioned in the media – one of the first interns to be taken on by a national paper, later a contributor to an international magazine, especially popular in their part of the world, eventually with her own syndicated column. It had been a bit surprising when she gave up her career in journalism and took up publishing instead, in those days not so glamorous as it seemed to have become now. She had founded the first feminist press in the country and made it, unexpectedly, an outstanding success. At least once a week a photograph of her attending a conference or speaking at a seminar appeared. And how could Tara possibly have kept herself informed of Prema's progress – or stasis? Naturally there was no mention of that to be found anywhere.

But now there was a flurry of activity up on the stage, behind the row of potted palms; while the microphone was shifted and adjusted, figures came and disappeared, the next item on the programme was revealed to be not quite ready, and Tara actually seemed willing to carry on this pointless conversation that Prema wished she had not begun.

And then a providential act took place. A small, grubby paperback slid out of the overstuffed, ungainly satchel that Prema was trying to keep from falling off her lap. And as Prema tried to stuff it back before any further objects followed it out, Tara, idly continuing the conversation since nothing else seemed to be happening, asked, 'What is that you're reading?'

Prema had to hold it out for her observation so as not to seem unduly secretive, confident that Tara could not read the script in which it was printed, so distant was it from life here in the capital. But, as she did so, the thought flitted across her mind like an unforeseen fly that Tara may be genuinely interested since she was a publisher and in a very specialised field. Prema realised that there was, after all, something about which they might converse.

'It is in Oriya,' she said, handing over the soiled copy and regretting how badly she had used it, dog-earing the pages, scribbling in the margins, even putting down cups of tea on its cover so that the lurid illustration of a forest fire, a burning hut and a fleeing woman was marked with brown rims. 'It is very good,' she hastened to assure Tara in spite of its appearance to the contrary. 'Very moving.'

'Who is it by? And do you read Oriya?'

Prema fussily adjusted the spectacles on the bridge of her nose in an embarrassment grotesquely enlarged by their lenses. 'It was my childhood language. And it is written by a woman who comes from the same area where my mother lived. She is very much respected there even if no one knows about her here.'

Tara continued to hold the book and turn its pages as if they could impart something to her. Onstage a row of schoolgirls in the school uniform of pleated skirts, white blouses, knitted ties, limp socks and once-white gym shoes had lined up to sing, but the book seemed to interest her more even if she could not read one letter in that script. When the song onstage ended – rising in a crescendo that could not possibly be maintained and wasn't – she handed the book back to Prema, saying, 'I wish I could read it. I am thinking of starting a new division of my publishing house. We've published texts in English, you see, but I want to branch into translations now, and publish writers well known in their own regions but unknown outside which is such a shame. What do you think?'

Inarticulate Prema could not at first reply but her spectacles glittered with the enthusiasm of her unspoken response until, just before the principal's speech began to be broadcast, the loudspeaker causing it to echo at fluctuating volume, she managed to say, fervently, 'That is a *wonderful* idea. That is what we *need*.'

Then the principal was well launched upon her speech, the microphone tamed, it seemed, by her authority, and there was no alternative but to be silent and listen. At the end of it, some of the women who had been in their class and recognized Tara – although clearly not Prema – swooped upon her with cries and exclamations and Prema picked up her satchel and retreated. It was time for tea.

When she got home on the bus and climbed the stairs to her rooftop apartment – left unswept as usual by the landlady's slatternly maid (she would have to complain again) – the day was sinking into its murky nicotine-tinged haze of dust with home-going traffic pouring through it like blue-black oil from a leak in the street below. The crows that spent the day swinging on the electric and telephone wires and squabbling were dropping into the scraggly branches of the lopped tree below with exhausted squawks. Would she allow herself to be dragged into the gloom by it all once again? Heaving the cloth satchel off her shoulder (which had become permanently lowered by its familiar weight), she determined she would not. Letting spill the book she had shown Tara – which had so miraculously caught Tara's eye – she ran her fingers lightly over its smeared and smudged cover because that was where Tara had thought to run hers, and then opened it out on the table where she worked, ate, wrote and arranged her books, papers and pens. Without even fetching herself a glass of water or sitting down to rest, she read the first few lines to herself and once again the syllables of that language evoked the distant world which linked her to the writer.

It was the place where her father had been posted, briefly, as a junior officer in government service, and where he had met and married her mother, his landlady's daughter – to the horror and consternation of his family, who had never imagined such a thing as an inter-caste marriage between its strict boundaries, and to the sorrow and foreboding of hers, equally strict within its own limits – then brought her back with him to the city. It was in her earliest years, steadily growing more distant, more remote in its wrappings of nostalgia, that Prema had heard her mother speak to her and sing to her in her language (only when her father was not present; he could not tolerate it once he was back where he belonged, in the capital). But after her mother's early death (hadn't her family foretold it, *exactly* this?) Prema had lost contact with what was literally her mother tongue. Then recovered it by choosing to study the language at an adult education evening class during a slack period in her life, after receiving her degree in English literature, a respectable but common qualification.

Not content to stop there, for some reason she could not

explain to her father or his family who considered it an aberration, unfathomable in someone given the opportunity to take up any line of study at any college she chose, she decided it was imperative that she visit the region where Oriya was a spoken, living language. Her teacher, a preternaturally mild and soft-spoken man, dangerously thin and withdrawn, had offered, on hearing her plan, a baffled smile which confirmed that no previous student of his had ever responded in this way to the evening classes he gave so timidly and tentatively, in an almost empty classroom made available in a local, underfunded school for such lost souls as herself. He seemed unsure whether to congratulate her or warn her.

She remembered with what trepidation she had made her travel arrangements – if one could use the term 'arrangement' for such a haphazard journey involving many changes from broad- to narrow-gauge railway, then country buses, finally a choice of horse-drawn tonga or bicycle rickshaw – and how warily she had faced her time in a women's hostel at a local college, no more than a scattering of brick barracks in a dusty field. There was a tea stall under a drooping neem tree where she kept herself alive on tea and biscuits through the many slow, stifling days she had to spend there before the language lifted itself off the pages of her textbook and assumed once again the mobility, the unselfconscious agility it had once had for her. Almost to her surprise, it slowly became recognizable in the speech of the tea-stall owner, the cycle-rickshaw driver and the women in the hostel with whom she shared a bathroom – a row of stalls along a perpetually wet and dripping hall – and whom she ran into after classes were over and there were empty evenings to while away.

Turning the pages of the limp little paperback, running her eyes over the script, she thought with a kind of guilty nostalgia of the homesickness she had suffered for the city, for its comforts and conveniences rather, and how she had found, once she could converse again in their language, that the other women were just as homesick for the villages and hamlets from which they had come for their 'higher education'. They named them to her – she had never even seen them on a map – and she asked questions continually, always picturing her mother, as a girl, living in such a place as they described.

One day, in class, her teacher named this very writer whose book lay open before her – Suvarna Devi – and spoke of her as the unsung heroine of Oriya letters. She told Prema, the most ardent student she had ever had, that it was worth learning the language simply to read the work of Suvarna Devi. 'She will not only reveal the sweetness of the language to you but open your eyes to what you don't even know exists here.' So Prema stopped in the bazaar on her way back to the hostel and found this very paperback amid the magazines, calendars and greeting cards with which the so-called bookshop was mainly stocked. She showed her find to the women at the hostel who expressed amazement that she had not known about this writer: they had been made to read her short stories in school – not always with reverence, it seemed. One of the women who stood out from the others because she wore her hair cropped in a place where all the other women had long pigtails or tightly wound and carefully pinned buns, and even wore trousers if she was not going to classes, said, 'Why do you want to waste your time reading Suvarna Devi? You won't get a job at a university if you do. You need to read Jane Austen, George Eliot and Simone de Beauvoir. No university will look at you if you haven't read *The Second Sex*. Forget Suvarna Devi, read the feminists, read Simone de Beauvoir.' This reduced many of the others to helpless laughter; they tried out the foreign name in many different ways, all of which sounded absurd.

Prema not only read the collection of Suvarna Devi's short stories but returned to the bookshop to see if they had any more of her work. They did not, but in the college library she came across a journal the writer had kept while living in the tribal areas to the south; it was bound in green Rexine and the library flap at the back showed that it had been issued to readers exactly twice in the last seven years. Prema borrowed it and took it back to read in the hostel and found that the journal entries, many of them of an anthropological nature, and the notes on village life in the forest, provided a backdrop for the fiction she had already read but were otherwise disappointingly dry. Prema had little interest in nature or the rituals and ceremonies of tribal society per se and found the notes lacking in the characters and events that had made the short stories so lively and engaging.

She asked her companions at the hostel if they knew anything of the life of this author, so oddly divided between literature and anthropology. 'Oh, she goes to those areas with her husband,' they told her. 'He is a doctor and runs clinics there. Who wants to read about *that*?' It suddenly occurred to Prema that the writer might live in this very town. She was told, casually, that yes, they believed she did. 'Where?' cried Prema. 'Can you tell me *where*?' Her mind leapt ahead to that prized objective of any serious student: a personal interview. Besides, such a meeting might create another link to her mother's world. And there was so little time left, she was due to return to Delhi in just a week. Someone told her in which part of the town Suvarna Devi's husband had his practice but no one could give her a specific address. They knew Suvarna Devi's work from their school syllabus but that did not make her a local celebrity: instead, it just made her one of them.

Prema went there on foot one day, after her class, to see if she could find it for herself. It was a neighbourhood rather like a suburb on the far outskirts of Delhi where the city petered out into the dusty plains, a jumble of small bungalows no longer new, many with signboards on their gates to denote their middleclass status: doctors, lawyers, advocates, specialists in gynaecology, homeopathy, ayurveda, urology, and also schools that gave evening classes in typing, shorthand and tailoring.

Not knowing the exact address and coming across the same surnames repeated over and over, Prema gave up, suddenly conscious of the dust gathering between her toes and invading the folds of her neck and elbows, sticky and gritty at the same time. She could not continue to trail up and down the maze of little streets with dogs barking at her through closed gates, men staring at her from bicycle and radio repair shops and concrete bus shelters under stunted, lopped trees. Defeated, she returned to the hostel.

It did not matter, she told herself as she packed for the long journey back to the capital; she had found the subject of her studies and that was all that mattered. How could she have returned *without* one?

Her thesis supervisor accepted the subject with the greatest reluctance: it was not part of the regular syllabus and it was hard to see how it could be made to fit in. But then Prema showed she could be stubborn when she chose: her subject was not the language itself but the author and how her work belonged to the greater world. She wrote the thesis and, rather to her supervisor's surprise, it was accepted.

She might have anticipated what followed. After so many years of thinking this would be the climax of her life, she discovered that instead everyone expected her to continue as if there had been no such climax. What next? she was asked continually, by family and friends, what next?

After a wait of too many unhappy and discouraging years – the first sighting of stray white hairs a defining moment – she finally accepted a junior position in a minor women's college in a bleak and distant quarter of the city. And even here her thesis counted for little. What an odd subject, they all thought, a writer in Oriya? Why, what had made her pursue such an unpromising course of study? Why had she not gone to Jawaharlal Nehru University and studied French, Russian or Chinese? What good was this provincial author in a provincial language to her or to anyone here? So Prema found herself in the department of English literature after all, teaching Jane Austen and George Eliot (though not Simone de Beauvoir).

This left a small, smouldering ember deep inside her soul (so she designated its location, no other would do), where it released an odour of heated rubber, threatening to destroy whatever pleasure or satisfaction she might court. It burnt two deep grooves across her forehead as if with a stick of charcoal, and two more from the corners of her nostrils to the edges of her mouth. Sometimes, when passing a shop window filled with spangled and sequinned saris that encouraged reflection, or catching a glimpse of herself in the small, chipped mirror over her bathroom sink, she was startled by the grimness of her expression. No wonder she was rarely invited out, or made part of any gathering for celebration or enjoyment. She turned away and trudged along to the bus stop with the satchel of books weighing down her left shoulder. She put in the necessary hours of work, meeting her colleagues in the staffroom during the lunch hour which they all utilised to complain of their workload and the perfidy of the principal and heads of departments, and the disrespectful, boisterous and unruly students. At the end of the day she trudged back even more depressed than when she had set out. That was when she wondered if her life was any different from that of the crows dividing their time between the telephone lines and the dying tree in her street with equally raucous disorder and dissent.

This was what had made her accept the invitation to attend the Founder's Day function at her old school. Her schooldays had not been a particularly happy period in her life either – she had already shown signs of a failed life there, it seemed, something that attracts no friends – but at least it was now so far in the past that she could look back on it forgivingly, almost benignly.

And, as it happened, it had turned out well. She had not only met her old school idol Tara, after so many years of following her brilliant career in the press, but Tara had recognized *her*, and by showing an interest in the book that had so providentially fallen out of her satchel, given her a nod.

A nod. Such a small gesture, almost inconspicuous, but it was what Prema had been waiting for, she now realized, a nod no one had been willing to give her before. It must have been the sign she needed because now, sitting over the empty plate from which she had eaten her dinner – some slices of bread with pickles – the book propped up beside the pickle jar, the sugar pot and the bottle of antacid pills, she began to have thoughts that ought to have come to her earlier: thoughts, plans, like a hand of cards dealt to her that were worth studying.

She began nodding to herself, unconsciously but encouragingly. In the street below, quieter now than an hour or two earlier, a car with a siren tore past, screeching its metallic nail across her eardrum. But Prema barely noticed, even though it set all the neighbourhood dogs howling.

Having made an appointment – costing her an anguish of indecision no one else would have understood – Prema was at Tara's office in Sri Aurobindo Market punctually at three o'clock on a Friday afternoon. She was somewhat disappointed to find Tara's office was not in a shiny new high-rise but in somewhat obscure quarters above a grimy copy shop with a small arrow on the wall pointing up the stairs, stairs just as unswept as in her own building, she noted. The office itself, she was relieved to find, was bright and neat, freshly painted, with a tall potted plant in the corner that appeared to be flourishing, and a row of shelves on which the latest publications of Tara's press were lined up, the newest of them facing out. These were so attractive – small in size but with covers of terracotta, lapis lazuli and moss green, each with a small miniature painting printed in the centre above the title and below the author's name – that Prema felt deeply ashamed of the state of the paperback she had brought with her to refresh Tara's memory. While the secretary dialled Tara's number to announce the visitor, Prema gazed at these delectable, desirable objects, recognizing some of the authors' names and wondering about the others. Then the door opened and there was Tara, dark glasses pushed back over her hair, which Prema now saw had a fashionable red glow of henna, and wearing a sari that was elegant in its extreme simplicity – fine white cotton, black-bordered, such as Prema would never have considered wearing. She looked a bit preoccupied but remembered having made the appointment – flattering in itself – and had Prema come into her office which was larger and untidier than the little reception room, with ceramic coffee mugs amid the books on her desk, and a lingering odour of cigarette smoke.

'It was wonderful to see you the other day,' Prema began, determinedly smiling to keep those depressing wrinkles away, but, on seeing Tara assume a somewhat impatient air, decided to hurry along to the purpose of her visit. Placing the book she had brought with her on the desk between them, she went on: 'When you said you were thinking of commissioning translations from indigenous languages – our many great languages – and bringing writers to the notice of those readers who don't know them – I thought of Suvarna Devi.' She had to stop for breath, she had spoken so fast and was almost panting. 'She is such a great writer and no one here even knows her name. It is very sad but I am sure if you publish a translation of her work, she will become as well-known as – as – Simone de Beauvoir,' she ended in an inspired burst.

Tara was listening, although she was playing with a pencil and occasionally glancing at her watch – she clearly had something on her mind, probably another engagement coming up – but after calling her secretary to send in a bottle of Fanta for Prema – such a hot day – she did begin to tell Prema her plan for this new division of her publishing house and what she hoped to publish under its imprint. 'Of course, I am no linguist myself,' she apologized, 'and I will have to depend on others – academics and critics – to tell me what they think worthwhile.'

And by the time the Fanta had been drunk (bringing on an embarrassing sequence of barely suppressed burps) and Prema, the academic and critic, was on her way out, it had been decided she would write a synopsis of the book, a brief biography and bibliography of Suvarna Devi's work, and a few pages – oh, five or ten – of her translation as a sample. Once she had sent that in, she would hear from Tara. Yes, definitely, within a month – or two at the most.

Then the secretary rang to announce the next visitor and Tara flew out of her chair to receive the young man who had come in with his arms flung wide, no longer merely polite but positively exuberant. Of course, he *was* young and attractive, Prema could see that before she left.

What actually saddened me when I left was not the sight of masculine youth and its attraction for Tara but the thought, now settling on me as I sat on the bus – it was a Ladies' Special which was why I had a seat – that Tara had not asked me a single question about my involvement with this language. I had been given no opportunity to explain how I came about it, what it meant to me and why, while teaching the usual, accepted course of English literature in a women's college, I had maintained my commitment to it. I could have told her so much, so much – but was given no chance and so I had to keep the information withheld, a secret. No one knew what a weight that exerted, one I longed to relieve.

But, getting off the bus and climbing the stairs to my room at the top, I found I could, in a quite miraculous way, unload myself of that weight. As soon as I took out the little paperback – its pages were coming loose from the binding, I noticed – and pulled a piece of paper to me and began to translate the first line, it was as if I had been given a magic key that would open the rest.

'It started to rain. It was getting dark.'

But no – immediately I could see how blunt that looked, how lacking in spirit. Where was the music, the lilt of the original?

'Rain began to fall. The village was in darkness.'

Yes, and yes. How easy to see that these words worked, the others did not. I hurried on, hurried while that sense lasted of what was right, what was wrong, an instinct sometimes elusive which had to be courted and kept alert. Selecting, recognizing, acknowledging. I was only the conduit, the medium between that language and this – but I was the one doing the selecting, the discriminating, and I was the only one who could; the writer herself could not. I was interpreting the text for her because I had the power – too strong a word perhaps, but the ability, yes. I was also the one who knew what she meant, what worlds her words evoked. They were not mine but they were my mother's. I barely remembered her or those earliest years spent in her lap; I only imagined I did. I was not sure if I had ever seen the shefali tree's night-blooming flowers in the morning, or the pond where blue lotuses bloomed and intoxicated bumblebees buzzed, or heard the sound of cattle lowing as they made their way homewards at twilight, but at some subconscious level, I found I knew them just as she did. Translating Suvarna Devi's words and text into English was not so different, I thought, from what she herself must have felt when writing them in her own language, which was, after all, a kind of translation too – from seeing and hearing and feeling into syntax. And I, who had inherited the language, understood it and understood her in a way no one else could have done, by instinct and empathy. The act of translation brought us together as if we were sisters – or even as if we were one, two compatible halves of one writer.

Of course there were instances – small stumbles – when I could not find the exact word or phrase. In Suvarna Devi's language, each word conjured a whole world; the English equivalent, I had to admit, did not. Cloud, thunder, rain. Forest and pool. Rooster and calf. How limited they sounded if they could not evoke the scene, its sounds and scents – images without shadows. Perhaps an adjective was needed. Or two, or three.

I tried them out. In the original, adjectives were barely used, but I needed them to make up for what was lost in the translation. Of course I could see that restraint was called for, I had to hold fast. Not too fast, though. A middle way. A golden mean.

I laughed out loud and struck my forehead with my hand to think of all the different strains and currents of my life and how they were coming into play. I had never felt such power, never *had* such power, such joy in power. Or such confusion.

I stopped only when I became aware it was night outside, the crows silent, the street lights burning, the traffic thinning, its roar subsiding into a tired growl. The television set in my landlady's flat was turned on, the evening soap opera at full volume – and I hadn't even noticed it earlier.

Pushing back my hair – as if I too had a pair of dark glasses perched up there, or a gleaming strand of distinguished white like Tara! – I got up, picked up my purse, went downstairs and crossed the street to the small shop where I sometimes bought essentials, a bar of soap or a packet of candles during a power breakdown. Tonight, though, I bought a packet of cigarettes – not the brand I had seen on Tara's desk and that I wanted but a cheaper one that the shopkeeper stocked. I had never bought cigarettes from him before and he gave me a strange look. He recognized me of course but I didn't care what he thought. This was something I was now discovering – that there were things about which I did not need to care. I recrossed the street with the packet in my purse, stepping aside just in time to avoid an autorickshaw that came careering round the corner, its driver singing at the top of his lungs with the joy of going home, free, at the end of a day's work. I almost could not restrain an impulse to join in before I went up the stairs to my room to see what the cigarettes could do for me, for my new career – Prema Joshi, translator.

Smoking one was another matter, I admit, and not very successful. I was glad no one was there to observe how I doubled over, coughing, and stubbed out the obnoxious weed, in disappointment.

The synopsis and the sample pages were quickly done. Perhaps a little too quickly, Prema worried, but found she really did not wish anything to slow or halt the momentum, and so she slipped them into a brown paper envelope and took them to be posted in the same flush of high excitement with which she had written them.

Tara had her secretary call Prema – that was a disappointment, Prema had not expected to have to deal with an intermediary – to tell her to go ahead with the translation. So the first step had been taken, and Prema drew a deep breath, poised now on the brink of this new career.

Her old career began to seem irksome. Her lectures became perfunctory; she no longer cared if they did not inspire her students with the same passion she felt for literature. *The Mill on the Floss, Emma, Persuasion* – what did they mean to these girls? She marked their papers impatiently, merely skimming them, not stopping to put right their grotesque errors and misrepresentations. She could not be bothered: every one of these girls would leave college to marry, bear children and, to everyone's huge relief, never read another book.

All that mattered now was to do as fine a translation as possible of Suvarna Devi's stories, so simple in their language and structure, but how forceful and powerful for all that!

The experience had aspects to it that Prema had not imagined when she set out. It reminded her, for instance, of how she had struggled to write stories herself when she was young – younger – and how she had sent them out to magazines only to have them returned with curt rejection slips, the hurt and bitterness with which she had mourned them as she put them away, and how discouragement had made her admit she was probably no writer after all.

Now she could laugh at those rejections and the way she had taken them to heart, letting their poison seep into her till the urge to write, the ambition to write, had quite died inside her.

She realized that all she had needed was this opportunity, this invitation held out to her – by Tara, of all people – to discover her true vocation. It was surely the right one since it had given her this new-found ease, and speed, and delight.

So the work was done sooner than she, and perhaps Tara, had expected, and it was with a certain sense of regret, and trepidation, that she typed it out, then had a typist she knew at a copy shop down the road retype it for neatness – 'Don't worry, auntie,' he said, 'it will look just like print' – and carried the bundle ceremoniously to Tara's office. Mailing it was of course possible and perhaps more professional but she couldn't resist the satisfaction of handing it over herself and seeing Tara's face register approval. The completion of this labour needed somehow to be marked and rewarded.

Unfortunately, Tara was away. Her secretary informed Prema that she was at a conference in Prague, would be back in a week. If she left the manuscript, it would be given to Tara on her return. Prema could expect to hear from her very soon.

She did not. Tara took her time, a very long time it seemed to Prema. In fact, Prema advanced from disappointment to impatience to annoyance at being treated in this manner and kept waiting as if she were only one of many people in a queue for Tara's attention. Had she no consideration for what an author – all right, a translator – might feel at being ignored, left in the dark, waiting, hoping?

She could feel the grooves across her forehead and from her nostrils to her mouth deepening by the day. She snapped at her students. She marked their papers with increasing severity. She knew they found her unfair, ill-tempered and dull. But why did they consider themselves worthy of her attention? They were not, not. She was a translator, an author.

Then, just like that, a change in the atmosphere, a sudden breeze to fill her sails, give her hope and move her forwards at last.

A telephone call from Tara – first her secretary, then Tara herself – to say she was pleased, she approved the translation and would publish it; it would appear in the first list of translations by her press.

It was true she did not exactly convey enthusiasm. She was certainly not effusive. In fact she did not even say she thought the translation 'good'. She said it was 'quite good'. Could there be a more tepid qualification?

That might have crushed Prema as much as an outright rejection but Tara followed that limp opinion by saying she would get in touch with Suvarna Devi to draw up a contract, and asked if Prema knew how she might do that.

So suddenly Prema had not only to see to the few notes and suggestions Tara made about the translation – just as the students were sitting their exams which meant their papers would soon be pouring in for her to mark – but she also had to busy herself with finding out about Suvarna Devi's whereabouts. *Why* had she not done that when she was actually there in her home town? And why did the publisher of her book, evidently a local one in the same town, not reply to her queries?

It all proved incredibly difficult and frustrating. Until she thought of writing to the principal of the women's college where she had spent that one summer. To that she received a reply with an address but also a warning that she was often away in the tribal regions with her husband who ran a string of clinics there (and where she obviously found the material for those heartbreaking stories that Prema found so moving).

Weeks went by without a response to Prema's letter in which she had introduced herself and informed her of Tara's publishing house and its new imprint. Would their proposal to publish her short stories meet with her approval?

There was a long stretch, a very long stretch, of waiting again and Prema found it hard to maintain her hope of a new career in the face of such silence. She tried to be patient, telling herself that the mail in those jungle outposts had to be slow and unreliable, but at the same time she felt that a matter of such importance *ought* to break through and elicit a reply.

Eventually it did – a letter written on several small sheets of yellow stationery, each sheet with a red rose printed in the top corner, the stationery of someone who was not accustomed to writing letters except on special occasions requiring a rose. Prema was both touched and a little apprehensive: it did not denote professionalism.

Still, she took it across to Tara in a state of some excitement and translated the few lines expressing thanks for the interest shown in her 'humble work'. Tara wondered how to draw up a contract with someone who might not be able to read it but Prema assured her it was quite possible that she did – after all, she *was* a published writer – and besides, her husband who was a doctor would surely be able to go over it with her. Tara was encouraged to proceed.

Happy times followed for Prema – feeling free to visit Tara's office, sharing her editorial notes with her, going over them together, discussing such matters as footnotes and glossaries, then seeing through the galleys and the proofs, picking the right illustration for the forest-green cover they chose, and the artistic lettering to go with it – roman of course but with Sanskritic embellishment.

Prema brimmed over and shone, gleamed as never before. Tara began to search for other titles to publish under the new imprint. Sometimes Prema was included when she discussed another literary gem she had discovered or consulted regarding a suitable translator. Prema became so light-hearted, she smiled and laughed even with her students who began to speculate as to whether she had a lover. The idea made them sputter with laughter, it was so ridiculous, and Prema occasionally caught them at it and felt a twist of suspicion.

Then, through her new contact with the publishing world, she learnt there was to be a conference of writers in the 'indigenous languages' who had no outlet to the larger market and a wider readership.

'Tara,' she found herself saying with a new-found confidence and optimism that made her push back the (invisible) white strand in her hair and the non-existent dark designer glasses, 'we must make sure Suvarna Devi is invited to attend!'

The publication of her book was hurried along so that it could be brought out in time for the conference. Prema could think of nothing else – college, students, exams, all receded page by page, face by face, into a blur in the distance. The central place in her mind was occupied by the beautiful little moss-green book with the Kangra painting of a forest glade on the cover and Suvarna Devi's name in elegantly Sanskritized roman letters. The young man who had burst into Tara's office at their first meeting was the 'genius' behind the design. Inside were the words: *Translated by Prema Joshi*, not in the same painterly script but in print nevertheless, black on white, irrefutable.

When she arrived at the convention hall which was hung with purple and orange bunting for the occasion, Prema went straight to the stall set up in the foyer for the books by authors who had come from all over India for the conference, almost trembling with the anticipation of seeing the book she – well, she together with Suvarna Devi – had created.

Surely this was the crowning moment of her life even if there were no golden bugles to proclaim it. She had prepared for it as nervously as if for a party. Taken out a sari she had bought to wear to the wedding of a young cousin but never worn since; it had a broad red border with a gold trim and was certainly an assertion in itself. But, on putting it on, draping it carefully fold by fold around her middle, she became bitterly critical of the foolishness of dressing up, and changed it for everyday garb. This made her late. She arrived at the convention hall in a fluster with no time to comb her hair, and rushed straight to the bookstall. Her eyesight blurred for an instant as it alighted on the book but that may have been because it was somewhat obscured by other titles in bigger letters, on brighter, glossier and, she thought, rather vulgar covers. After taking in this slight, Prema reached out surreptitiously and quickly reordered the books so that Suvarna Devi's lay on top, others beneath, then moved on: the conference was due to be inaugurated by the Minister of Education, and all were requested to be in their seats before he entered with his entourage.

The loudspeaker whined excruciatingly. Then sputtered, then brayed. Harassed men ran around trying to fix it, alternately shouting 'Stop, stop' and 'OK, go'. The minister slumped into his chair, looking disgusted. The 'honoured guests' who occupied the front rows sat very stiff and upright, waiting for things to be fixed and proceedings to start. Prema found herself embarrassed that things were not going more smoothly but of course this was how all such affairs began, and probably in the regions from which the writers came things were no different.

Eventually the minister made his speech. He read it slowly – as if he did not think the honoured guests, representing so many different languages, could possibly follow, or perhaps he just was and always had been a slow reader (the speech was, after all, written for him by someone else). Then a younger man, perhaps a junior minister, spoke, very rapidly so as to get the greatest number of words into the allotted time – which still seemed to most of the audience far too long. Everyone had come not to hear the bureaucrats but the authors after all, and most of them had travelled a great distance to come to the capital, bringing papers to read which they had written themselves. They were staying at various government hostels scattered about the city and had come together for the first time with much to say for themselves and to each other.

Prema, seated further back, stared at the backs of their heads, wondering which one belonged to Suvarna Devi, her protégée, as she thought of her fondly, protectively. But there were quite a few women among the delegates, none of whom Prema knew by sight. She had to wait till the official speeches were over, the minister escorted out into the foyer, to prowl among the delegates and try to guess who was hers – *her* trophy.

She had never seen a photograph of Suvarna Devi, had been told she was reclusive, that she rarely left her home town and environs, and that was all. So Prema searched the outer edges of the crowd which was made up of the more social and animated delegates of whom there were many. In fact, the roar of voices was rising rapidly into the great pink sandstone cupola above them till it was interrupted by an announcement: the conference would now continue.

If anyone was interested in the spectrum of languages in India, this was certainly the place to be – the place, the day and the time. One after the other the delegates stepped up to the podium to be met by the applause of their particular, and separate, readers, editors and publishers. Bengalis in the audience applauded the Bengali author, Gujaratis the Gujarati, Punjabis the Punjabi and so on. To begin with, the simultaneous translators tried valiantly to keep up with the babel, then faltered, then fell aside.

Providentially a lunch break was announced, when everyone could assemble in the foyer once again, to lift the lids off great serving dishes of stainless steel and dip into bubbling and aromatic concoctions, then go on to little glass dishes of syrupy sweets.

It was very late in the long day when finally Suvarna Devi's name was announced as the next speaker. By then many delegates had visibly succumbed to the soporific effects of the large meal and the warm afternoon.

Suvarna Devi too seemed tired by the proceedings that had gone before. That was Prema's first impression – how tired she seemed, how apart from the rest of the pleased, satisfied crowd. Wrapped about in her grey cotton sari and wearing a shawl that was clearly a sample of her region's weaving, incongruously bright, and steel-rimmed spectacles perched on her nose, in a small, hurried voice she spoke a few lines in the language she wrote in but which only a segment of the audience understood.

Of course Prema did. And Prema, after an initial disappointment at how unimpressive, how unprepossessing a figure her

writer cut on the stage during her five minutes of public fame –
she would have liked her to be more assured, more flamboyant,
more like Tara, she admitted – began to feel an unaccustomed
urge to take this elderly, unassuming woman under her wing,
protect her and support her as she might a sister or an elder. She
hardly paid attention to the speech, so involved was she in taking
in Suvarna Devi's presence, trying to connect it to her writing,
out of which she had constructed an image that was not quite
corroborated by the reality.

Then the proceedings for the day were over and everyone
poured out of the auditorium into the foyer. Prema went scurrying around agitatedly like a beetle ahead of a broom, trying to
find her author and have at least one private moment, or two,
with her. When she finally found her, she was in conversation
with Tara who had managed to locate her and welcome her
before Prema could do so. This was upsetting; Prema was upset.
Was she not the one to have a word with the author she had discovered and come to know so well during the arduous labour of
going over, line by line and word by word, the author's work in a
way no one else could claim to have done?

And there was the shy grey person she had hurried to protect
and chaperone, conversing with Tara who did not know a word
of the language she wrote in and would never have heard of it if it
had not been for Prema who now broke in with a cry: 'Suvarna
Devi! Oh, at last we meet!'

Suvarna Devi, a little startled, looked from her to Tara. It was
Tara who introduced them, formally, instead of the other way
round as Prema had imagined the introduction.

'Prema Joshi, your translator, and we hope you are pleased
with her—'

Hope? That was all Tara felt, *hope*? Prema found she could
barely speak for outrage. She hardly knew how to place herself,
how to draw away Suvarna Devi's attention and make Tara leave
them alone to discuss what they had in common, author and
translator, sisters in spirit.

It looked as if the moment would elude her and the author vanish with barely a word of recognition of who and what her translator represented. She had already folded her hands and bowed, turning away to leave, when Prema flew after her, confronted her and insisted they have a few moments together, to discuss – didn't she know there were matters to discuss?

Suvarna Devi seemed taken aback. Perhaps she had not realized how large a role Prema had played in getting her book accepted by Tara's firm, in making her book available to a larger audience by translating it into English. She seemed like a creature who had been startled out of her forest hiding, one of those well-camouflaged speckled birds that will dart under the bushes on being surprised, and now she was flustered, at a loss as to how to respond. But once Prema had made clear the need to meet again, in private, and talk, she asked Prema to come and see her – if she wished, if she could, if it was not too much trouble, in which case she would quite understand and write a letter instead – at her nephew's house where she was staying. And now she had to go . . . There he was, come to collect her in his car.

It was not what Prema would have planned – in place of a meeting with the author alone so they might have an intellectual discussion about books, translation and language. Suvarna Devi's family – the nephew, a young married man and a dentist, his wife, his little daughter and baby son, his wife's parents, all seated on the veranda of their small house in one of Delhi's outer colonies, having tea together, did everything they could to make Prema feel welcome. Suvarna Devi herself seemed entirely relaxed and happy in their midst, quite unlike her shy, apprehensive public persona the day before.

The nephew, a rotund and affable young man, seemed the most at ease, conversing with Prema in English, asking her about the college where she taught, in between popping a biscuit in the baby's rubbery mouth, then turning to some family gossip with Suvarna Devi in their own language. 'She has never been to visit us before,' he told Prema. 'This is a rare occasion for us. I used to live in her house when I was a schoolboy – there was no school in my village, you see – but since coming to Delhi I have only been back a few times. So now she has to give me all the news from there.' This made Prema feel uneasy and an intruder, in spite of being plied with cups of tea and plates of fried snacks by his wife and her parents. She wondered how long she could behave politely in the circumstances. (It was a long time since she had lived with a family, after all; not since her father had remarried.)

It was only when Suvarna Devi rose to her feet and accompanied Prema down the short drive to the gate where her autorickshaw stood waiting (its driver, asleep on the back seat, having to be woken) that she was able to put some of the questions she had come to ask, at least the most urgent ones.

'Now that the short stories have been published – I hope you liked the translation?' she felt compelled to say, rather desperately.

'Yes, yes, very much, very much,' cooed the woodland bird, soothingly.

That was disappointingly vague, but Prema pursued. 'What do you suggest we do next? Are you working on anything new?'

Suvarna Devi did not seem to have given that any thought. Just as clearly, she had had no discussion with Tara on the future of her writing. She seemed genuinely confused and only on lifting the latch of the gate to let Prema out, she admitted, 'Maybe I will write a novel next, I am thinking about it,' and gave an uncertain laugh at her own temerity.

'You are?' Prema cried with enthusiasm, partly sincere and partly affected to encourage the reluctant author. 'Please send it to me, as soon as you have anything to show. That way I could start work on it immediately. Tara will be so happy to hear of it. Just send me a chapter, or even a few pages at a time, it doesn't have to be the complete work.'

But the shy bird had withdrawn again. She looked almost afraid as she folded her hands to say goodbye, murmuring, 'I will,

I will try,' before she hurried back up the drive to the family on the broad, sheltered and hospitable veranda again.

Prema has barely got home – discarding her satchel, pouring herself a glass of water – when the telephone rings. It is Tara, to inform her that the Association of Publishers has called for a press conference as a coda to the writers' conference.

In a panic, Prema: 'A press conference? What is that?'

She will find out, Tara suggests tersely. 'Be there.'

It is too much, coming so hard on the heels of the conference and the meeting with Suvarna Devi, too much at once. She would like to have a little time to sort it all out before she goes on. She can barely eat or sleep that night, fretting till it is time to leave for the venue.

With almost no transition, it seems, there she is, tired from the sleepless night, on a podium with Tara and people she assumes are publishers and translators too, inquisitorial lights shining into her eyes, making her flinch and blink. For a while she is so discomfited that she can barely pay attention to what is being said or by whom. She is still fidgeting with her papers, her books, adjusting to what she finds is literally a spotlight when, far too soon, the dread moment of interrogation arrives.

A pudgy man in a sweat-stained shirt is standing up somewhere in the hall, holding a microphone and saying, 'I would like to address my question to Prema Joshi, translator of Suvarna Devi's stories.'

Sitting up, tight as tight with fright, out comes a croak: 'Ye-es?'

'What made you decide to translate these stories into a colonial language that was responsible for destroying the original language?'

Blank, blank, blank.

Then, blinking, and under an expectant stare from Tara, she stammers out the words, 'But the stories – the stories prove – don't they? – it is not destroyed. It exists.'

371

A flash from Tara's dark glasses, approving, encouraging. So Prema goes on: 'And isn't the translation – the publication of the translation – a way of preventing it from – ah, loss? And proving it exists to, to – the public?'

'What public are you addressing?' The pudgy man adopts a more belligerent tone now that he has found the person at whom he can direct it. 'The English-speaking world?' he asks rhetorically. 'The international public? Why? Doesn't it already have a readership here?'

'Isn't it – isn't it important,' Prema flusters on as if she were one of her own students being interrogated, 'to make it more widely known?'

'To whom is it important? To the writer? To the reader? To what readers? Here in Hindustan? Or in the West? Employing a Western language indicates your wish to win a Western audience, does it not?'

Tara, sitting forward, tapping impatiently on the tabletop: 'I would like to inform you that a press such as mine—'

Prema sits back in relief, letting Tara take over.

'—aims to reveal the writer to a wider public here in India too. Writing that so far has not been accessible to them. Because I, and my colleagues, believe it is our mission—'

'Ha!' the pudgy man explodes with sarcasm. Now that he is on his feet, with a captive microphone, nothing will make him give it up or sit down. 'Who needs to have this revealed to them? The *English* speakers in this country? Why? Why are you catering to *them*? Why not to the speakers of the many native languages of our country?'

Laughter and applause, both approving.

Tara, very upright and fierce: 'If there are publishers in those languages willing to commission translations, as I have done into English, where are they and why are they not coming forward? They are needed, certainly.' Looking around with raised eyebrows, arousing approving murmurs, she repeats, 'Where are they?'

Prema, in gratitude, turning to convey her appreciation to

Tara. Argument has erupted. Terms proliferate that indicate the large number of academics in the audience: Subaltern. Discourse. Reify. Validate.

Prema crouches low, fearing some of them will be flung at her. Wasn't 'subaltern' a military term? She feels like the lowliest of students in her class instead of its leader and hopes none of them is present to observe her shame. Where has she been all this time, reading Jane Austen with them, and George Eliot? What has she been doing, talking of Victorian England and its mores? What has stalled her and kept her from joining the current that is now surging past, leaving her helplessly clinging to the raft of *The Mill on the Floss*, the rock of *Pride and Prejudice*?

The chapters of the promised novel began to come in during the course of that summer, in large Manila envelopes that were always torn around the edges and had to be held together with string. They looked as if they had travelled a long and dusty road and suffered many misadventures along the way – and they probably had. At first I fell upon them as soon as I returned from work and found them lying upon the doormat, then immediately settled down to read them. But quite soon I found myself disappointed and dismayed by what I read.

Instead of the artless charm and the liveliness of the short stories, the novel seemed by contrast slow, almost sluggish, as it followed the fortunes of one family from grandparents to parents to children in a not very interesting town – in fact, very like the dusty, ramshackle one where I had first come across Suvarna Devi's work. I found myself growing increasingly impatient with the noble, suffering grandparents, the quarrelling parents, the drifting children, all of whom seemed to follow predictable paths under the effects of changing circumstances: an increase in wealth followed by a dispersal of property, higher education foundering in lost opportunities – and *too* many births, marriages and deaths. Stories recounted, time and time again, in different ways, all over the world.

Perhaps Suvarna Devi did not read very much herself, and was unaware of that? Or had her work actually deteriorated? Where was the passion and the drama of those early stories? Where was that keen observation that had given them their authenticity?

Instead of the ardent admiration I had felt once for the author, the excited joy with which I had set to work rendering my childhood language as faithfully as possible into English, I now looked on Suvarna Devi's work with a much colder eye. More professional perhaps.

I began to wonder if publishing such a disappointing novel would be good for Suvarna Devi's reputation, which I had worked hard to establish. And what would it do to my newly created career as a translator? That too had to be considered, did it not? Having linked myself to the author, didn't it require the best from both of us? And what about the reputation of Tara's press and this imprint she had introduced with Suvarna Devi's short-story collection as its first publication? All these factors had to be considered.

Prema took the manuscript across to Tara. Of course Tara could not read the language and would not be able to judge it till it was translated, but Prema felt compelled to warn her that this was not the masterpiece for which they had hoped. Yet she could not let Tara withdraw from the project and bring her new-found vocation to a halt. The warning would have to be delicately phrased, Tara's interest in it kept alive but no false hopes raised.

Fortunately or not, Tara was distracted and did not seem too concerned by what Prema had to tell her. 'I trust you, Prema,' she said, without too much emphasis. 'I know I can rely on you. Not like the translator of this Urdu novel I was pinning my hopes on. It's a major novel by a brilliant new writer, and the first chapters the translator sent in were wonderful. But now he's gone off to Beirut, never answers letters, just makes promises over the phone and never keeps them. I am *so* annoyed. I was going to give it special treatment.' She tapped the Urdu book on her desk with a pencil impatiently, then glanced at the manuscript Prema had brought in without much interest. '*You* are such a relief,' she sighed. 'I know I can trust you to do your job. It's OK to take your time, no need to hurry.'

Prema bridled, thinking: all this pandering to the Muslim minority, hadn't it gone too far? Really, Tara seemed not to have taken in any of Prema's cautiously worded assessment of Suvarna Devi's novel – as if it didn't matter.

So she picked up the manuscript and carried it away with an aggrieved determination to make of it something Tara *would* notice.

The next step was to make room for the task by taking leave from her college. The principal barely reacted and the students saw her off with undisguised joy: they had been told the substitute would be a Miss Batra, who was known to be younger and livelier, dressed in jeans, was seen to smoke, and intended to introduce them to contemporary American authors not yet admitted to the academic pantheon.

Through the suppurating heat of June and July, under a slowly revolving electric fan, and with perspiration streaming down her face in sheets, Prema settled to trying to rediscover the joy she had initially taken in translation. She suffered from a sense that she was struggling, like a drowning fly, to raise herself up from the dull, turgid prose before her and somehow recover the art of flying.

I knew this was the hardest task I had set myself, the greatest challenge (aside from my initial decision to make this language my field of study). I felt a pressure settle upon my head that was uncomfortable but somehow not suffocating. In fact, the challenge was like a terrific headache that might leave one dazed but also uplifted.

A faithful translation would clearly make for a flat, boring read. I saw that what was needed was for me to be inventive, take things into my own hands and create a style for the book. So, instead of a literal translation, I decided to take liberties with the text – to begin with, Suvarna Devi's modest syntax. And once I did that, I began to enjoy myself. What a difference it made when I turned 'red' to 'crimson', 'anger' to 'rage'. My pen began to fly. Using Suvarna Devi's text as a basis on which to build, I found I could touch it with small brush strokes of colour and variation. Wasn't this what the Impressionist painters had done in those early adventurous days, breaking up flat surfaces to refract light into many scattered molecules, and so reconstruct the surface and make it stir to life?

And together with this 'enhancement', as I named it, of the text, I could see that reduction and deletion were called for too. I had to be a teacher and a critic, underline words she had used again and again: how often could I let her use the same adjective for one character? There was no need to repeat 'gentle' and 'kind-hearted' every time the grandmother was mentioned: her words and acts alone could convey that. And it was not necessary to keep calling the daughter-in-law 'greedy' and 'bad-tempered' if there were incidents that showed her greed and insolence.

As with adjectives, I found verbs and adverbs, too, could go. The death of the grandfather, for instance, described by one character in chapter two, surely did not need to be repeated in chapter three by another character with the same 'wailing' and signs of 'grief'. It could be dramatized just once, not oftener: the effect would be to make the text tighter, stronger.

I admit that now and then, in tired moments when I sat back and became aware of how my neck ached and how the heat was solidifying and pressing on me, I did wonder if what I was doing was my brief – to render a faithful translation of Suvarna Devi's work. But then I would get up, fetch myself a glass of water from the big clay jar that rested on the ledge of the kitchen window and kept the water marginally cooler than what emerged from the tap, return to my table and take a sip. Then ideas would come to me like drops of moisture falling on the arid manuscript, reviving my interest.

Picking up my pen, I would remind myself that the best translations are the most inspired, when the translator becomes fully a co-author of the work so that it is a coming together of two creative spirits in a single venture. If the translator cannot rise to that, then the translation will be a failure.

It made me laugh, almost, to see how improved the text was with the changes I had made, and the paring away of repetition. Oh, I should have been an editor – Tara should have employed me in her publishing house – and Suvarna Devi ought to have had an editor before she had a translator. Now she had both. How could she be anything but pleased? My translation was an uncovering, a revealing of what had been buried, concealed in her work. In a way, you could say I was the writer, only I would not be given the recognition. Not by Tara who had not read the original, and not by Suvarna Devi who was unlikely to read the translation. She had said, in the speech she gave at the conference, that although she could read English, she could not write in it because its vocabulary did not 'cover' – that was her word – *her* experience of life. I had thought that a strange remark but now I found reassurance in it. It had been my role to prove that it *could*. Perhaps one day we would meet again and I would explain to her the different way of translation I had discovered: a transcreation? or even a collaboration?

All this was clear to me in the day, while I worked, but I have to confess that darkness, sleeplessness and anxiety made the nights a different matter. Lying on my back, trying to ignore the heat, the sounds and lights of passing traffic, I found that the thoughts and worries I could hold at bay in daylight approached me like ghosts, like monsters come to threaten me. They exerted a weight on my chest and sometimes I could hardly breathe. I would have to get up to try and escape them. I would go to the kitchen and pour myself a glass of water. I would drink it standing by the window and looking out on the deserted street. The streetlights would be shining. Sometimes a dog appeared to scavenge in a pile of garbage left outside a tea stall, now shuttered. Occasionally an empty bus passed by, probably returning, at this hour, to the depot. I tried to distract myself with these sights of the ordinary world, but in my mind it was the lines I had been translating and the lines that I had been writing that remained in the forefront. I longed for sleep to obliterate them but it eluded me. Perhaps everything would be normal again once I had sent off the manuscript, I thought, and looked forward to completing the work.

In the interval between handing over the manuscript to Tara and the appearance of the published book, Prema returned to teaching, much to her students' regret. They found her more harsh and ill-tempered than ever and were certain that if she had had a love affair, it must have come to a bitter end. In the staff room, Prema's colleagues asked her how her work had gone during her leave of absence; she answered curtly and seemed unwilling to speak of it. The college librarian asked her to be sure to give her a copy when it was published, and Prema only nodded.

When Tara telephoned to let her know the advance copies had arrived, she did go across to collect them, and Tara found her oddly subdued. Not elated as she might have been at the sight of the beautiful little volume with its cover of pale ochre like the clay of a village wall, a painted window frame in the centre for illustration, arresting in its simplicity.

'Don't you like it?' Tara asked, looking curiously at Prema's grey and drawn face. The arduous labour of translating it through the summer had aged and fatigued her, Tara thought.

'I do, I do,' Prema roused herself to say but, curiously, did not open a copy to look inside. Instead she asked, 'Have copies been sent to Suvarna Devi? And the critics?'

'Of course,' Tara assured her. 'Of course. Now we have just to wait to see what they say.'

Prema carried her copy home, laid it on the table, made herself tea, then sat down to open it finally. She could not help feeling moved by the sight of her name in it, under Suvarna Devi's. Then, with increasing tension, she let her eyes drift over the sentences, from one to the other. Together they had made this book, its text, its lilt and rhythm, its images and metaphors. Would Suvarna Devi approve? Then she came across a phrase she knew had not been there in the original, and the gaps where she had deleted what had seemed to her unnecessary repetitions: the death of the grandfather, the weeping and wailing. Would Suvarna Devi notice? If she did, what would she think? Would she acknowledge the improvement Prema had brought about, or would she oppose it? And the critics, would anyone notice? Would she hear from them?

What she could hear was the raucous cawing of the crows outside, balancing on the telephone wires, and they sounded to her more mocking and scolding than ever.

Then there was a long and difficult silence. Reviews of translations were always scant, Tara reminded her. It was this new breed of authors writing in the colonial tongue, English, who hogged all the attention, not only in England but even here in India, disgracefully. The one review that appeared, in a little-read but serious political journal, commended Tara's noble venture in commissioning translations and calling attention to so far 'unknown' writing (as though there were no readers of regional languages). The critic called Suvarna Devi's novel an 'important' one but made no reference to the translation.

'We'll have to wait till the regional press reviews come in,' Tara said and, seeing how anxious Prema looked when she came in to enquire, added kindly, 'I'm sure they will be good. It *is* a good translation after all.'

It was not Tara's way to be effusive and she did sound sincere. In fact, she was. So it was a shock when, a few days later, a letter arrived at her office from someone who informed Tara he was Suvarna Devi's nephew. He came at once to the point, which was that he had read the original text written by his aunt and bought a copy of the translation. On reading it, he had found innumerable discrepancies between the two. He went on to list them.

Frowning heavily, Tara wondered if he was pointing out serious flaws or if he was just nit-picking the way some readers were sure to do, more to prove their superior knowledge than for any other reason. But, she had to conclude on rereading the list several times, he appeared to have reason for complaint. According to him several pages had been cut out of the translation, the role of some of the characters – e.g. the grandfather – had been abbreviated, and the language itself diverged wildly from the original text. As a native speaker of the language, he felt a responsibility and wished the translator and the publisher to know that he objected strenuously to this 'cavalier attitude' to his aunt's work. He was debating whether to inform her; he did not wish to disturb or upset her, knowing how gentle and sensitive a person she was, but he demanded an explanation for the way she had been treated by Tara's press. What did Tara propose to do? Was she going to continue to bring out these 'spurious' equivalents for the English-speaking elite of what was so much more powerful and beautiful in the original? He advised her against putting out any more of them 'to hoodwink the public'.

Tara put off all meetings for the day and sent for her secretary in order to dictate two letters, one to the nephew to apologize for 'any errors and shortcomings in the translation' and another to the leading newspaper in his aunt's home town to assure them 'appropriate measures were being taken to ensure that in future only rigorously supervised and faithful translations' would be published by her press. cc Prema Joshi.

Eventually Tara's secretary forwarded a packet of letters to Prema sent by other readers with the same objections – not very many since those who read the original did not necessarily read the translation as well. Also a letter that arrived from Suvarna Devi, written on her yellow stationery with the red rose imprint, thanking her for sending the copies of her book which she said 'looked very nice', and making no mention of the translation. Nor was there any hint of suspicion or attack. Either her nephew had not informed her of his findings or she had chosen to overlook them; she did, after all, have other, possibly more compelling interests in life. Tara did not withdraw the book nor did she ever order a reprint.

The Association of Indian Publishers sent Prema, c/o Tara, an invitation to its next gathering of authors and translators. Prema declined, pleading illness.

So I haven't given up teaching. I continue to go through the same texts with my students. I know they are bored by me. I know they make fun of me behind my back. And I know the principal is waiting for me to retire so she can bring in someone new, someone who will arouse enthusiasm among the students. But, if I do that, what would I do with the rest of my life? That stretches out before me like an empty, unlit road.

Sometimes, on the bus going home from work, I look at the others seated beside me and across from me. Or, rather, since I don't like staring at people's faces, I look down at their feet, shod in slippers or sandals or dusty shoes of cracked leather, and the packages they are holding on their knees, and I think: that is how I must look to them – a tired woman going home from work with nothing to look forward to, nothing to smile about. Whyever did I imagine I was different, and could live differently from them? We are all in this together, this world of loss and defeat. All of us, every one of us, has had a moment when a window opened, when we caught a glimpse of the open, sunlit world beyond, but all of us, on this bus, have had that window close and remain closed.

It is not that I did not try to open that window again. I gave up, of course, the idea of translating another book, though it meant giving up the language I had acquired with such ardour. In the course of those sleepless nights I spent, a thought did come to me – that I might write a book of my own. It would be an original work, it would draw from no one else and no one else's work. I did feel I owed Suvarna Devi a debt for teaching me, but now it was for me to prove I could establish my own worth as a writer.

For a while I felt excited by that idea – as if the window had opened again, a little, and some light was slanting through it. I had had an idea that bifurcated into more ideas, and I followed these paths with a stirring of hope and delight. The one that drew me more powerfully than any other was the story of my parents' marriage. Their short-lived marriage and its sad end. By writing their stories, I could bring in all the different aspects of my life – the ones I inherited from my mother, her language and her background, and the ones I inherited from my father. I felt the story had promise and even sat down with a large new note-book I purchased from the store across the street, propped my feet up and started scribbling, trying out these themes.

I worked hard at it but whatever pleasure or hope I had had at the outset dissipated. There were scenes I could write in English but other scenes called out to be written in my mother's language. I was torn between the two and could settle on neither. I wrote scraps in one, then scraps in the other, but tore them all up and threw them away: who would read such a jumble?

I was sitting in the dark one evening, listening to the crows on the telephone lines and the lopped tree outside as they quarrelled over their roosting places for the night, hoarse with combat, when it occurred to me that only Suvarna Devi could write this story. Only she had the voice for it; I did not. I had been writing under her influence, with her voice; it was not mine. In adopting hers, I had lost mine.

Then, browsing through a bookshop as I often did on a Saturday morning, I looked up from a display of discounted books spread out on a table and saw a young man I recognized at once as Suvarna Devi's nephew. He had his little son with him, now a toddler, and was pointing out to him some colourful children's books.

For a second I felt panic and wondered if I could slip away unseen. But then I decided that would be cowardly, and I went round the table to face him.

I wondered if he would recognize me but it was clear that he did. I greeted him and asked after his wife and daughter, and then his aunt. He seemed perfectly pleased to see me again and told me they were all well. After that I hesitated, not sure whether to refer to her books, her writing. Perhaps he hesitated too, slightly, but then, smiling, informed me that not only was she well but 'working as hard as ever. Now she has started a school – a primary school for tribal children. She was always so interested in their education. She is working full-time with them and asked me to select some books to send them.' He beamed with pride, then became distracted by his son who had grabbed at some books and was pulling them off a shelf with delight.

So I said goodbye, asking him to convey my regards to his aunt, and in the hubbub of the shopkeeper coming to reprimand the child and the young father's flustered apologies, I left.

The Artist of Disappearance

Nobody climbed that hill any more. Not unless they wished to retreat. It was a good place for that: a retreat. Just the burnt-out remains of the house that had stood there. Only a few walls still standing, a makeshift roof of zinc sheets in place of the turrets and towers that had been there, the rest just blackened stones, ashes, rubble, charred beams, weeds crowding into gaping windows. An occasional newt slipping silently by.

But Ravi was there, sitting on the stone steps that led up to the veranda. It was what he had always done in the evenings when he returned to the house, to listen for the sound of a cowbell ringing faintly and intermittently downhill, then more clearly and metallically as the beast drew closer. Mingled with that tolling was the noise of goat hooves clicking smartly on the stony path, and the goats' small eager bleats as they anticipated the food that would be waiting for them. They were the first to arrive at the homestead below, hunger quickening their pace and dancing approach. Then the cow, eager too but with more body to trundle along a path too narrow for her bony breadth. She had to be encouraged by the flick of a switch that her owner wielded with one hand while with the other he steadied on top of his head the bundle of firewood he had gathered.

And when these shapes appeared in the clearing below, the dogs that had been slumbering the afternoon away scrambled to their feet with an air of importance to show they were alert to their duties, and let out sharp yelps of welcome to announce their arrival to the family that lived there.

The children began to chase the chickens into their pen for the night. The mother called for firewood to be brought in. Smoke unwound in a spool from the gaps in the thatch of the roof. The goats were directed into an enclosure, walled with thorns, by showing them a tin basin in which bits of broken bread had been soaked in warm water, and the cow was led into her shed, with its comfortable smells of dung and straw, to be milked.

Then there was a lull as the activity shifted indoors where a fire of sticks crackled, a pot boiled and the aroma of food was conjured. Around it the children gathered on their haunches, tin plates before them, waiting. The father lowered himself onto a stool, and the mother was finally ready to ladle out the meal she had prepared.

But the older of the two boys remained standing by the door, knowing his role in the day's duties. He took the enamel dish from his mother's hands: she had filled it with rice and dhal into which she threw a handful of green chillies. She gave him a tin lid to cover the plate and by a slight shift of her chin – which bore a small blue tattoo – she indicated he was to take it, take it up.

The boy nodded, then set off up the hill: he knew he should be quick so as not to let the food cool and congeal. Besides, he was eager to return for his share. So he climbed the hill as quickly as he could without tripping or spilling.

When the boy appeared with the covered dish, instead of merely nodding to indicate he should put it down, Ravi startled him by speaking instead. His voice was hoarse, he used it so seldom, and it was clear it cost him great effort to speak.

His voice rasping, he asked, 'Have they gone?'

The boy nodded, yes.

'You are sure?'

Yes, the boy nodded again.

Then Ravi took the dish from him, and even mumbled thanks, adding, 'Tell your father I will not be coming down tonight.'

Yes, the boy nodded, he would. Duty done, he turned and went flying downhill to his own meal, and gave three sharp whistles as he leapt from one stone to the next, to mark his freedom. The dogs came running up to meet him with their own eager, hungry barks.

Up at the burnt house, Ravi finished his meal and set the plate down on the step beside him, then took a biri out of his shirt pocket, lit it and leant back against one of the veranda posts which was still standing, and waited for the sounds of the household below to subside into silence and the light to withdraw from the valley and climb the hills till only their peaks were lit by the sun. Then they too faded into dusk but he continued to sit there, listening for the last calls of a lone cuckoo to die out and the rustle of the flying squirrel that lived under the eaves as it crept out and launched itself into the evening air where the bats were now swooping and plunging after insects.

He stubbed out the biri, then drew a matchbox out of his shirt pocket and began to play with it, thoughtfully; he might have been a monk with his prayer beads. When he looked up from it he found the woolly dusk had knitted him into the evening scene, inextricably. Silence had fallen on the homestead below and the light of its small fire had sunk and gone out.

He got to his feet and made his way to the bushes encroaching on the house. He lowered his trousers and there was a sound of urine trickling on the stones at his feet. Then he turned and retraced his steps. Picking up the empty dish, he carried it across the veranda to the one area that might still be called a room: it had walls, it was covered, and it held the string-cot that Bhola had fetched for him from the hut below, and the few remnants salvaged from the fire, lined up against the blackened wall. Ravi fumbled his way to a table, scarred by the knives and choppers of its kitchen past, on which a kerosene lantern stood. He lit it – there, another match gone – and surveyed the sorry items: an overstuffed chair on which he never sat, a hatstand which held neither a hat nor a walking stick – and saw they were all still there, mute and untouched, as if waiting for the day when they would be chopped up for firewood.

All else that the house had once contained – and there had been an abundance – was gone, just like the leather suitcases that used to be lined up in the hall – the hall! – waiting to be carried out, past the grandfather clock and the portraits of his ancestors, tinted photographs that leant away from the wall to look down as his father unhooked his favourite walking stick from the hatstand and the astrakhan cap that he liked to wear when travelling, then gave the soft, polite whistle with which he might summon his wife who was detained in her dressing room – her dressing room! – by some last-minute adjustment to her toilet.

While they waited for her to emerge, the father turned to look at the boy standing half hidden by the door to his room, one leg locked around the other, and gave him a playful wink as he set the astrakhan cap jauntily on his head. 'Like it? I bought it in Berlin, I'll have you know, on the Kurfürstendamm. Can you say that – "Kur-fürst-en-damm"? It had started to snow and I went into this very elegant shop and a most polite gentleman came out from the back to see what I wanted. I pointed it out to him and when I walked out, I had it on my head – just so!' and he gave another wink. 'I'll let you wear it one day – when you can say "Kur-fürst-en-damm",' he offered, and the child knew it was an offer that would evaporate along with all the others and looked away in embarrassment at how glibly his father lied.

Then his mother emerged, smelling powerfully of flowers – rose and lily of the valley – dressed in a sage-green sari with a narrow trim of embroidery. 'We must hurry or we'll miss the train,' she cried as if it were the others who had kept her waiting.

Hari Singh, who was waiting at the foot of the stairs, came up to lift one suitcase onto his head and grasp two others in his hands, then carried these out to the waiting automobile that would take them to the railhead in Dehra Dun. The chauffeur came up to carry down the rest.

At the foot of the stairs the parents remembered to turn

round and wave at the boy. 'We're off now!' the father announced. 'Be good!' he added, and the mother called out, 'We'll bring you back—' but forgot what she had promised to bring back and left it up in the air. This didn't matter because whatever expensive or elaborate toy it was, it would only be locked up for safe keeping once unpacked and briefly revealed for his tentative admiration.

He sidled down the stairs to the front door and watched the car proceed slowly down the gravelled drive, then disappear under the oak trees that closed behind it like dark stage curtains. For a while he could hear the engine grinding uphill to the motor road, then gave up trying to follow its progress. If it had been night he would have been able to see the lights as they slowly descended downhill to the valley, but it was still afternoon.

And then he could let out the breath he had been holding inside his chest till it swelled into a balloon, tight against his ribs. A balloon he held pinched between his thumb and forefinger and could now set free. Off it went with a whistle, twisting and turning and wriggling, till it descended, hollowed, into the limp rubber norm of normality.

Not only he but everyone, everything experienced that moment. Hari Singh, recovering, took his cloth cap off his head and was suddenly upright, divested of the posture and demeanour of servanthood. Coming back up the stairs to the veranda, he shouted, 'Come on, come on! Let us go and hunt tigers, you and I!'

Not that they would – Hari Singh was no more given to keeping his promises than were the boy's parents, but just to hear the invitation made, loudly and heartily, changed the air, the atmosphere, and Hari's son Bhola, who had been waiting behind the bushes, catapult in hand, appeared to see if Ravi would now come out to play.

Outdoors was freedom. Outdoors was the life to which he chose to belong – the life of the crickets springing out of the grass, the birds wheeling hundreds of feet below in the valley or soaring upwards above the mountains, and the animals invisible in the undergrowth, giving themselves away by an occasional rustle or eruption of cries or flurried calls; plants following their own green compulsions and purposes, almost imperceptibly, and the rocks and stones, seemingly inert but mysteriously part of the constant change and movement of the earth. One had only to be silent, aware, observe and perceive – and this was Ravi's one talent as far as anyone could see.

Outdoors, Ravi had watched as a snake shed itself of its old skin, emerging into a slithering new length, leaving behind on the path a shroud, transparent as gauze, fragile as glass. Once he had come upon a tree with long, cream-coloured cylinders for flowers, attracting armies of ants coming to raid their fabled sweetness and sap, armies that would not be deflected by the intervention of a stick, a twig, and would persist till they reached the treasure, and drowned.

Outdoors, the spiders spun their webs in tall grass, a spinning you would not observe unless you became soundless, motionless, almost breathless and invisible, as when he had seen a praying mantis on a leaf exactly the same shade of green as itself, holding in its careful claws a round, striped bee buzzing even as it was devoured, which halted when its eyes swivelled towards him and became aware it was being watched.

And there was always the unexpected – lifting a flat stone and finding underneath an unsuspected scorpion immediately aroused and prepared for attack, or coming across an eruption from the tobacco-dark leaf mould of a family of mushrooms with their ghostly pallor and caps, hats and bonnets, like refugees that had arrived in the night.

Or a troop of silver-haired, black-masked monkeys bounding through the trees to arrive with war whoops, or sporting like trapeze artists at a circus, then disappearing like actors from a stage that the forest provided.

And everywhere were the stones – flat blue splinters of slate, pebbles worn to an irresistible silkiness by the weather and that could be collected and arranged according to size and colour in an infinite number of patterns and designs, none of which were ever repeated or fixed.

Infinite – unless you were like Bhola who always brought with him a catapult and almost automatically raised it whenever he saw a dove or a squirrel that could be brought down with a shot. Ravi was not for such sport; a heap of dead feathers or fur were for him as unnatural as for the slain creature. Ravi was interested only in the variations and mutations of the living, their innumerable possibilities.

It was as if the curtains came down on all this, if not entirely obliterated it, when the monsoon rose up in thunderous clouds from the parched valley below to engulf the hills, invade them with an opaque mist in which a pine tree or a mountain top appeared only intermittently, and then unleashed a downpour that brought Ravi's rambling to a halt and confined him to the house for days at a time, deafened by the rain drumming on the rooftop and cascading down the gutters and through the spouts to rush downhill in torrents.

Everything in the house turned damp; the blue fur of mildew crept furtively over any object left standing for the briefest length of time: shoes, bags, boxes, it consumed them all. The sheets on the bed were clammy when he got between them at night, and the darkness rang with the strident cacophony of the big tree crickets that had been waiting for this, their season. From the pond down in the clearing below came the gleeful bellowing of bullfrogs. Lying awake, listening, Ravi wished he could slip out with Hari Singh's big flashlight and catch them in its beam, but perhaps the gleam emitted by the fireflies flitting among the trees by the thousands would be light enough. He shivered with cold and anticipation.

But Hari Singh locked him in carefully every night, and by day filled his ears with tales of the leopards that came out of the forest to prey on any poor goat or calf left outdoors and were known to carry away even the fierce bhutia dogs people kept to guard their homes and livestock. What chance had a small, thin boy like Ravi against such creatures? Hari Singh demanded as he served Ravi his dinner at one end of the dining table, standing by with a dishcloth over his shoulder. While Ravi picked at his food, Hari Singh talked of his glory days when Ravi's grandfather had taken him on hunting expeditions and allowed him to carry the guns with which he shot the bears, deer and panthers whose pelts, horns and glass-eyed heads watched Ravi make his way through his meal. Of course the boy ate very little, his mouth hanging open with wonder as he listened, and consequently Hari Singh gave up setting a place at the table with the requisite glass and silverware, and took to letting Ravi eat his meals at a small table out on the veranda where he would not be separated from the outdoor world that provided all the nourishment he wanted. When it rained he gave Ravi his food on a plate and set him on a stool in a corner of the kitchen by the sooty glow of the kitchen fire while he himself smoked a biri which he was strictly forbidden to do when the parents were present.

The only visitor to the house during the long summers when the parents were away was the teacher they had employed to supervise Ravi's homework, a Mr Benjamin who taught at one of the many boarding schools strung out along the ridge, and supplemented his income by giving private tuition on the side. The parents approved of him because he always wore a suit and tie and spoke in what approximated to 'good English', so they did not look too far into his qualifications for teaching their son mathematics whose strong subject it was not (nor was it Mr Benjamin's). Ravi wished the subject might be something else – ornithology, for instance, or geology, but Mr Benjamin regarded himself as far above such frivolous matters. He cleared his throat on arriving, hung up his walking stick and umbrella, scraped his shoes ferociously on the doormat to dislodge the dirt they had collected on the way to the house on the hilltop, wondering aloud what had possessed Ravi's parents to live so far from the civilized centre of

Mussoorie (though he knew perfectly well that Ravi's father had inherited the house from *his* father who had owned a brewery in these parts and used to come up from Bombay ostensibly to inspect the brewery but actually for the shikar and its trophies). Then Mr Benjamin would tell Ravi to open his books and get to work.

As the afternoon dragged sluggishly on, Ravi drooped lower and lower over the smudged and spotted copybook, chewing at his pencil till it splintered and had to be spat out, for which he received a smart whack on the head from Mr Benjamin's ruler. He could hear Hari Singh's children playing in the clearing below, their rooster crowing, their goats bleating, and he grew despondently aware of the afternoon light dying all the while.

But Mr Benjamin stayed till punctually at four o'clock Hari Singh brought him a cup of hot tea frothing with milk and thick with sugar. Ah-h, the tutor sighed, and let slip his professional manner enough to pour out a bit from the cup into the saucer and blow on it, then slurp it up blissfully. Ah-h, ah-h. It was not what he would do in front of his employers but of course Ravi was not that and all Ravi was thinking was that Hari Singh needed somehow to be persuaded to bring in the tea earlier. When Mr Benjamin came reluctantly to the end of this sweet pleasure, he gave Ravi a few more taps of the ruler to remind him he was only a miserable schoolboy and ought to be attending to his schoolwork instead of staring at him open-mouthed, then picked up his walking stick and umbrella and disappeared into the floating mists of the monsoon.

Why did his parents never take him with them when they travelled abroad? The boy never asked and they never explained. It seemed they believed the child belonged at home while they belonged to the wider world where of course they would not have the time for him (or a servant to see to his needs). One day, they said, he would be old enough to accompany them and it occurred to no one that there was no reason he could not accompany them now. (What was not said, never even mentioned, was that they were a childless couple, Ravi the child they had adopted – at the suggestion of a distant, philanthropic aunt – yet as far as anyone could see, they never made up a family.) And of course, in a way, their absence *was* his vacation, which came to an end when the parents returned.

Their return coincided with the beginning of the school year – the taking out and putting on of grey flannels and crimson blazer with a crest on the pocket proclaiming a Latin aspiration no one understood, the knotting of a noose-like tie under the shirt collar; each day a slower and more reluctant walk uphill to the prison of the school buildings grouped around a courtyard from which rose a roar that bubbled fiercely as a kettle on the boil till a gong was struck and the kettle was abruptly lifted off the fire. Rows of boys filed off to the regime of lessons administered by furious teachers who threw chalk at one or twisted another's ear, picking on the most miserable targets to punish in inventive and fiendish ways. This was considered the only way in which the Latin motto that no one understood might be upheld.

After that treatment – and Ravi was too ashamed to tell anyone or even admit to himself that he was the inquisitors' favourite target – he could not turn light-heartedly to the escapades of his fellow victims who lingered around the school gates after classes to watch the girls in their pleated skirts and green sweaters come out of the adjoining school, and attempt to lure them, sometimes, sometimes successfully, with the promise of an ice cream at Magnolia's or a film show at the Picture Palace. Ravi was too crushed by the school day to take the risk of any other failure, and heaved his school bag onto his back to slink home with the hope of going unnoticed – which he mostly was.

To be released from school meant only being released into the house where the parents now presided. If they did not use a ruler to crack across his head, or throw things at him in a rage, they had other ways to plunge their son into misery. The house, in their presence, had a set of rigid rules. The bell rang at intervals, punctually (punctuality being one cardinal mark of their Westernized ways), table manners had to be observed meticulously (another of those cardinal marks of which they possessed an arsenal), each infraction was pounced on and corrected (spare the rod etc. was the maxim by which they had been raised so they thought of themselves as permissive), and great lengths of time went by at the table as soup was followed by an entrée which was followed by a pudding which was followed by a savoury, some with enticing names – 'angels on horseback'! – which they never lived up to.

And then there was the entertaining they did which required his complete invisibility and silence while the parents played bridge and canasta and drank tea or cocktails. There was a certain pleasure to be had in hiding in the kitchen and watching Hari Singh arrange a tea tray or whip egg whites for a pudding and being slipped a sweet or a savoury titbit – but there were also the hours he had to sit more or less confined to a chair, swinging his legs till his own supper and bedtime could be seen to, also by Hari Singh.

It was better when his parents dressed up, sprayed themselves with exotic Parisian perfumes, got into their car and went out – but this did not happen nearly often enough for Ravi because his parents went abroad during what was known as 'the season' in Mussoorie, when British society came up to the hills to 'escape' from 'the plains' and brought their plays, balls, charades and garden parties with them.

Ravi's father sometimes said, wistfully, 'Why don't we spend the summer here for once, Tehmi? It's very jolly, I'm told,' but Tehmi had been brought up – in Bombay and at finishing school in Switzerland – to think summers had to be spent in Nice or Montreux where many of her family were now ensconced. Sometimes the father went on to complain, 'It's a damned expense, you know, Tehmi,' which made her screw her face into an expression of distaste at the mention of anything so unmentionable.

Fortunately for him, the father, these excursions were brought to an end when war broke out. Although the family liquor business flourished as never before, it was out of the question to risk a sea voyage when ships were being regularly torpedoed. And Mussoorie had never been as gay as now, nor its salubrious climate so needed for the health and recreation of the British soldiers on leave from the war fronts in Burma, Malaya and Singapore, and it was incumbent on the ladies of Mussoorie to provide them with the fun and relaxation that was their due.

The father was finally able to enjoy their exile in Mussoorie in what had been his father's 'hunting lodge' (once his brothers and uncles had discovered the disasters he could create in their business and the need to keep him away). He could now go to dances at Hackman's every night he liked, in his evening clothes with a silk scarf thrown over his shoulders and the astrakhan cap he had purchased in Berlin set rakishly on his head gleaming with pomade. He literally danced his way through one pair of shiny patent leather shoes after another. He would come home with a breath as fierce as a dragon's and putrid as a tiger's, singing his way to bed, and Ravi in the room next door cowered under his blankets to shut out the horror of it.

It was his mother who wilted in these years. She went with her husband to the parties and dances but it was clearly not her milieu and not her style. She set out, as exquisitely dressed as always, but drawing her light summer shawl about her as if she needed its protection, and with an expression on her face not radiant or expectant but rather as if she was about to swallow an unpleasant potion. She would not dance with the English officers and watched from among a group of likewise scandalized but dutiful wives, as her Hosni went blithely up to the English WAAFs and invited them to dance. Most of them were amused by this little man who did not seem to understand his place, and many accepted: he was an excellent dancer if a bit of a show-off.

And he had the comeuppance anyone might have predicted: a British army officer recently up from the battlefields and probably more deeply affected by what he had experienced than anyone knew, and royally drunk, objected to this little dark man dancing like an organ-grinder's monkey with his wife, and followed him out to where his car was waiting. In another age he might have challenged him to a duel but these were more brazen times and he simply lifted his baton and let the upstart have it on the head, the shoulders, the back, till Hosni's chauffeur was able to get him away, bundle him into their car and escape.

Ravi's mother did not return to what was known as Mussoorie society. The father, on recovering, lifted up his chin – sticking-plastered – and insisted on going out in a show of pride that might be considered nationalistic or merely pigheaded, but he did not go to Hackman's again, nor did he attempt to re-enter British society. He kept to the more familiar Indian scene – bridge games, sedate celebrations of anniversaries of one kind or another, and many hours in the club bar. His wife kept mostly to her room and even to her bed. It was not she who had been injured – not physically – but anyone who cared to analyse her condition would have said 'her spirit' had suffered a blow. All they actually said was that poor Tehmi's asthma had taken a turn for the worse.

Ravi was seldom invited into his mother's bedroom; her nerves would not stand it. But at this time a fourth person was admitted into their household and, like a fourth wheel attached to a wobbling carriage, provided some balance to what had become so seriously unbalanced.

No one would have thought Miss Dora Wilkinson capable of such a feat of engineering. She had been recruited from a home for indigent British ladies although she had few skills to show for herself. She was undeniably elderly and her once blonde hair and once blue eyes had faded to grey. Hosni turned away from interviewing her as a possible companion to his wife with a look of unconcealed disappointment, but for that very reason she was thought eminently suitable for the position: she would certainly not ask for leave to go to an afternoon dance. She could not even join her employers for a game of whist. But she did her best to provide a bit of nursing in the form of a dab of 4711 cologne or a cup of tea, and she could read aloud in a somewhat tremulous voice the sonnets of Elizabeth Barrett Browning and of Christina Rossetti. Her presence was immensely soothing to the mother for this and also for another reason, unspoken and perhaps unconscious: the woman's pale skin and light eyes and English diction made up in some inexplicable way for the treatment that her husband had suffered, the humiliation of it. Here was Miss Wilkinson bathing her brow with eau de cologne and helping her sip consommé from a cup of delicate china, and it was good to know, soothing to know, that such things could also be.

Her only fault, apart from her age, was that she had a cat. The cat was forbidden anywhere near the asthmatic's bedroom and expected to be kept confined to Miss Wilkinson's quarters. Ravi would shyly ask if he could enter in order to study the cat, his first experience of an animal as 'a pet'. He was not sure if he liked a 'pet' animal or if it merely seemed a curiosity, unrelated to the wild world where she belonged, but he liked to sit on a stool, his chin cupped in his hands, and gaze at her. She too seemed unsure if she approved of him and, folding her two front paws under her chin and narrowing her green eyes into slits to observe him discreetly, gave no hint that she was doing so other than to start if he made the slightest move. They were held by mutual fascination, nervous apprehension and an irresistible attraction.

Only Miss Wilkinson smiled and smiled, certain there had never been so harmonious a society. This earned Ravi her undying gratitude. She would ask him to do little favours for her (really for the awkward adolescent's sake as much as for hers), find her a feather for a bookmark or bring her some flowers for her vase. He would flush with pride at being asked and stumble off to pull some passion-fruit flowers off a vine over the veranda balustrade or pick out a blue magpie's tail feather he had found on the hillside, a prized possession of his. She received them with extravagant praise and thanks.

The father, almost as if he realized he had no further role to play, allowed the car to carry him, after an evening of bridge at the club, into the pouring rain that had washed away large tracts of the sharply curving road and down a landslide that had not shown in the beam of the headlights in the driving rain, halfway into the khud where it crashed into a pine tree with such force that the vehicle was almost split in two. The villagers who found him and the driver, and carried them to the hospital on the ridge, sent a message to the family that he was not seriously injured and would recover (about the driver they could make no such sanguine prognosis for he was already dead), but they proved wrong: he died that night of internal injuries just after asking for a brandy but before he could consume it.

The years that followed, Ravi did not count. He did not count them because he did not acknowledge them as his: they did not belong to his life because they did not belong to the forest and the hills. They belonged to the family in Bombay, to the business office, to his duties there, his relations to the family, and some years at a college studying 'management' (although they never made clear and he never understood what he was supposed to 'manage'). One might think these would yield a full volume of incident and event, but it was as if Ravi, encased in a block of grey cement, could see nothing, hear nothing and say nothing either.

He knew the family thought him freakishly backward, a wild creature from the mountains. His cousins sometimes sniggered as he passed them. An aunt would raise her finger to her head and wriggle it like a loose screw when she thought he was not looking.

Once they picnicked by the sea. It was the only time he recalled seeing the Indian Ocean. Of course this could not be true since Bombay is an island city and the sea lies all around it, but he had never been taken closer to it than in a passing automobile. On this occasion he actually broke free to clamber across some rocks exposed by the receding tide and gulped down lungfuls of soggy sea air as if he were gulping lungfuls of life-saving oxygen. Everywhere were pools left scattered among the streaming wet rocks, and he walked into them blindly, socks and shoes still on, dazed by this glittering aquatic world he had not known existed. He went down on his knees in the wet sand and stared into one such pool, his face dropping lower and lower, very nearly into it. He felt it could take an entire life to study the strange, extraordinary life that teemed in it – minute, multifarious and totally unlike any earthbound equivalent. But the family sent the servant boy they had brought along to facilitate the picnic to seize him by his sleeve, haul him to his feet and lead him back to where they sat, scandalized, on a mat spread out of range of the sea.

He might have been their prisoner and, like any prisoner, was despised and mistreated to the precise degree that mistreatment could go without detection. The room he was given had formerly been a storeroom and was still blocked by broken furniture and packed boxes. Its one window opened onto the garbage chute of the building. Neighbours tossed bags of refuse into the chute out of their kitchen and bathroom windows; its walls were streaked black, yellow and green and the odour rose to his window in thick coils. He became convinced he would die here and then be placed in a garbage bag and dropped into the miasma himself. There was no one to whom he could explain that in order to survive he needed to be at altitude, a Himalayan altitude, so he might breathe.

He might very well have suffocated if he had stayed longer. As it was he really did not know how long it was – months? years? – before news came that his mother had been moved into intensive care at the hospital, followed by news of her death. Thus, release – hers followed by his.

Perhaps he babbled and laughed like a madman on the journey back, perhaps not. But he remembered leaping onto the platform before the train had quite come to a halt at the station in Dehra Dun, nearly falling onto his knees, then fighting his way onto a bus to Mussoorie (his relatives in Bombay would not have believed his ferocity). For a while he continued, desperate: it did not look as if the bus could free itself of the city traffic, and then the country traffic – the other buses and huge, lumbering trucks loaded with rocks, logs, sacks and bundles and men perched on top, their mouths and noses wrapped in scarves against the dust and fumes of exhaust. Where was the silence that he remembered, or the solitude? he asked himself in a frenzy of impatience, till he realized that each turn in the twisting road was carrying him higher and higher and the air that blew in through the open windows was cooler, fresher, drier, air he could draw into his lungs in long draughts because it blew, he believed, from the snows themselves, half imagined, half perceived, a pale scribble against a pale sky.

Here the forest began. Here a monkey clan sat on a strip of wall, grooming each other and watching the passing buses for a handful of peanuts or a banana tossed out by the laughing passengers. Here a rivulet tumbled over rocks and a rough shelter built of stones and sticks straddled it. Here a pine tree leant precariously over a cliff, its trunk split in two by lightning. Here an orange grove grew in a green clearing, its fruit glowing bright. The dust and odour of the city and plains left behind, the bus rose higher into the mountains where these were replaced by the sharp sweetness of pine woods, the smoke of wood fires, the glass-like clarity of mountain air.

He covered the last stretch on foot, rediscovering the paths that led out of the town, downhill into the forest, and through it to where the house stood, its roof showing above the treetops. Birds sent out their long, fluting calls in spirals that he returned to them in long, fluting whistles through the silence.

Silence, but not solitude: Miss Wilkinson remained. It seemed cruel to send her back, after his mother's death, to the home for indigent British ladies which was by then close to collapse, with no funds now that the British were gone to repair or staff it, so that whoever still lived there and had not been sent or fetched away, lived in a ruin and increasingly resembled one themselves.

Ravi, finding her in a state of despair at the thought of being made to leave the family of cats she had stealthily acquired over time, assured her she need not, that she could stay and 'run the house' for him – as he thought to tell her in a moment of inspiration. It was clear that Miss Wilkinson could run nothing, not the house nor her own life. She had never confessed to anyone that her eyesight had been deteriorating over the years, the spectacles she wore less than useless, and for years she had been reciting not reading the poems of Christina Rossetti to her employer who did not miss the dropped line or forgotten word. When Ravi returned, he suspected her of being quite blind and only pretending not to be. The manner in which she fumbled and felt her way around the room gave her away and she no longer ventured out of it, though her cats slipped in and out freely, having the run of the place now. Hari Singh had retired and gone to live in his village in Tehri, leaving his son Bhola in charge, and it was Bhola who brought her meals cooked by his wife in the hut below, and provided her with a small paraffin stove on which to make herself tea if she wanted a cup when she could not sleep at night.

Ravi had not thought, after his time in Bombay, that he would ever want to live in proximity with anyone again. He would have revelled in clear space inhabited by no other than a line of ants creeping across the floor by day on their endless forages, the flying squirrel that lodged in the eaves launching itself into space at dusk to go hunting by night, and an occasional snake or scorpion that had lost its way and strayed into his. He was relieved to find that Miss Wilkinson, in her room upstairs next to his parents' empty one, was in no need of anyone either. Her wan aura was tinged by nothing more visible, or audible, than gratitude. She had never learnt Hindi and could exchange no words with Bhola when he brought her a bowl of porridge in the morning, her cup of lentil soup at night, but murmured her thanks in English. Only the occasional hiss or growl of one of her cats in combat or competition with another roused her to speak and then she would murmur, 'Oh, Pusskins, is that you again?

You naughty you, hmm? And where's old Billy then? You're not fighting poor Billy, are you?' and they would come up and rub themselves against her legs till she herself uttered a kind of low purr of delight.

When Ravi came in at dusk – it was at this time that he had developed the habit of staying outdoors all day, invisibly engaged in an art no one witnessed and he himself barely acknowledged – he would find himself going upstairs to her, surprised that he would seek out anyone's company. Hers was the one presence that did not make him turn and flee. She neither wanted nor asked anything of him. She would hear his step and look up, sightlessly, and the cats would rise to their feet or descend from their perches and come towards him, confident that he would make no loud, sudden movement but simply sink into an arm-chair beside Miss Wilkinson's where one might reach up to his knees to be stroked or else curl up and go back to sleep. Ravi, on enquiring after Miss Wilkinson's health that day, would reach out to the small row of books on a spindly bamboo stand between them and ask, 'Would you like me to read to you, Miss Wilkinson?'

She nodded but made no suggestion and he would choose something at random. No one else had discovered his talent for reading aloud in a low, modulated voice that scarcely broke the quiet. He found he could not adapt it to the dramatic pauses and the rising and falling tones of poetry which embarrassed him, so he read to her from the books he had brought across from his parents' room, the novels of Trollope and Sir Walter Scott, and she would listen, her head lowered, till she began to nod and her mouth to fall open, her breath coming and going audibly. Some-times he left her like that, replacing the book and leaving without waking her. Having her in the house was like having a very old pet cat that continued to doze through what was left of its life and did not disturb him beyond an underlying concern over its inevitable end.

*

No one could have imagined the end she would create for herself, unwittingly or not. Did she merely wake one morning and automatically fumble at the little paraffin stove to make herself tea? Or did she light it to invite an explosion, a conflagration of light in her dark world? Would this harmless, almost ectoplasmic creature choose to light it, then knock it over – she who took such care not to knock into anything – and so set the curtains alight? Was she aware of how one flame split into many within seconds, into an army of advancing swords of fire that charged through the room as if it were made of paper, then poured through the house in an ocean of smoke, sending sparks upwards into the roof beams and downwards along the banisters and stairs?

Probably Ravi became aware of it at almost the same moment she did, opened his door to find the smoke surging towards him, preceded by Miss Wilkinson's crazed, leaping cats, and had to fight against it up the stairs which was already a river of fire.

No one could explain how he made it to Miss Wilkinson's room or, on finding her on her knees attempting to crawl out, lifted her – she might have been a paper doll or a rag in his arms – and brought her down seconds before the stairs cracked and crashed in a great cascade of fire.

Bhola was at the front door, trying to break it down, and the villagers, who had been up early and seen the great bonfire billowing up over the oak trees like the millennial sun, were running forward when the two of them emerged, blackened and smouldering themselves. They were caught up and flung down in the dirt to put out the flames, and when the firemen finally arrived they were found seated on the grass, shrouded in ash. The fire had already reached its zenith, and the remains of the house within it a blackened skeleton knee-deep in soot and smoke, contorting and writhing in the heat. Miss Wilkinson was asking for her cats, for Pusskins and Billikins, reaching out her blackened, peeling fingers as if she might encounter them and draw them to her. 'Ravi, Ravi, where are they? Do you see them? Are they here?' 'Don't worry, Miss Wilkinson, don't worry, they'll be back,' he kept saying, for they had either perished in the flames or fled into the forest, he could not know. When an ambulance arrived and he helped to lift her into it, she began to wail, 'I can't go, Ravi, not without them, I can't,' but she did, she had to, and she went, wailing 'Pusskins, Billikins, my dears!' like a ghostly siren. Some of those present were to swear later that it was the cats who were heard wailing.

Ravi knew he could not, although he wished to, leave the scene himself. He knew he had to wait for the firemen to quench the flames and then enter the ruins with Bhola to see what could be salvaged. By then half the town seemed to have arrived. This was not really so: the house was too far out of town for news to have travelled that fast, but the people from nearby villages up and down the hillside had come running to see the blaze, uncommon at this time of year, just after the rains, although common enough in summer when the forest was dry as tinder and a bolt of lightning could set it on fire. And a fire is always a fine thing to see, a fine thing. So now they milled around, shouting, trying to help and also to catch a glimpse of the recluse who had occupied it. 'Look!' shouted a boy who led a tribe of urchins. 'He's there! I saw him!' 'That's not him, that's Bhola the chowkidar.' 'But look what I found – a spoon. Look, a spoon!' and the firemen had to chase them off to a safe distance from which to watch the undoing of the house.

So Ravi withdrew into the woods and did not return till everyone was gone and Bhola came looking for him with a large flashlight that cut swathes of light through the night forest, startling owls and nightjars. Then he voiced his wish to stay on in the house. He entered the ruin and found the walls of one room still nearly intact as well as its roof. After standing around in disbelief and disapproval for a while, Bhola finally went and fetched him a string-cot from his own hut below, and food when he saw Ravi had not given that a thought. He also brought him a kerosene lamp which seemed something of a travesty in that burnt house, and lit it, turning Ravi into a shadow that leapt and clawed at the walls.

He went once to see Miss Wilkinson in the hospital. But she was in the general ward – it was a small one and clean but inevitably there were other patients there and their visitors too. He found he could not sit and he could not speak with all of them watching and listening. The news of the fire had become common knowledge and there was much curiosity, as Ravi ought to have known. All along the road to the hospital people had come out to stand in the doorways and watch him go. He had felt he was being stalked by them and now he was hunted down and trapped.

Aware of his presence in spite of his silence, an unrecognizably shrunken and damaged Miss Wilkinson parted her parched lips to croak, 'You don't need to stay, Ravi. Don't stay.'

He could not bring himself to visit her again. It was agony to him knowing he ought to, that he was the only person who could and should, but he did not.

It cost him an almost unbearable effort to appear when he heard of her death. Instead of following the funeral cortège, which was made up of a priest who had visited the home for indigent ladies (from whose name the word 'British' had long been removed) and a few of the able-bodied still left there, he slipped around the hillside and waited for them at the foot of the British cemetery.

A grave had been dug out at the lower end where it stopped in a thicket of oak trees and mounds of moss. On the upper slope were tumbled gravestones, mostly covered in lichen, leaving few decipherable words, always the same ones – 'the beloved', 'the devoted' – and here and there a headless angel or a cross in pieces among the ferns. The air at the lower depth was always in the shade and perpetually chill and dank.

Standing to one side, concealed by a tree trunk with low branches – almost as if he were a criminal at the scene of a crime, said those who spied him – he watched the shuffling, mumbling ceremony, before Miss Wilkinson in her plain pine coffin was lowered into the earth. He hoped they had dug the earth deep, that jackals would not come in the night to dig it up, that the heavy rain that fell would not penetrate it, nor the frost in winter. He hoped she had been wrapped in a shawl for warmth, that a pillow had been placed under her head. It seemed the most cruel end to be placed in a pit in the ground and sealed into it so no light reached her and the world of cats and books, tea and touch was shut off. When he heard the earth being shovelled over the coffin, falling on it in clods, he fled.

The children in the villages said he had buried the cats the old lady was said to have had, some of them alive. Others claimed the cats had escaped into the forest and turned into bagad-billas whose glowing amber eyes could be encountered in the dark if you were out late. Some said the cats could be heard wailing as they prowled the ruins at night, and some that the house was haunted by the old lady. They said the recluse had the power to turn himself into a ghost in the night, a bhoot, so he could keep company with her ghost and the cats', then turn back into the wild-haired man in rags who would sometimes emerge from the house by day but immediately disappear if encountered, leaving behind a whiff of smoke. He had that power, they observed, to disappear as if by magic.

They tried to get Bhola to tell them some thrillingly blood-curdling stories about what went on in the ruin, but Bhola had grown as taciturn as his employer, and only grunted a refusal. As for the children he had after his marriage to Manju Rani of Tehri, they never heard such tales either; to them Ravi was the harmless man in the burnt house to whom they carried a plateful of food or a can of kerosene for his lamp and who thanked them without looking up.

He was encountered sometimes by a goatherd or men looking for firewood in the forest, an occasional villager with a bundle on his head and a switch in his hand, on a path leading downhill – never the path uphill to town. The wild raspberry bushes closed in on the path and one came to a great boulder that looked as if it might fall and block the descent completely in the next monsoon; there the path twisted away and continued down through the lantana bushes and blue-flowering ageratum of the lower hillside to a scattering of stone huts with sheaves of corn and pumpkins drying on their roofs and a stream running past that was straddled by a watermill where the great grinding stones could be heard milling the corn and wheat brought to it. Occasionally they saw Ravi on the path, but always above the level of the boulder, and murmured a greeting as they hurried after their goats or steadied the heavy load on their head, receiving only a grunt in reply.

But at that point, by the boulder, he ceased to be on the path. The boulder might have been a hulking black magician that waited for him to appear, then threw its shadow down on him like a cloak, and spirited him away.

The boulder presented a block to others but not to Ravi: he would slip around and let himself through the crease between it and the hillside, and so into the hollow below where only the merest trickle of water made its way from the lip of the cliff above, if the weather was not too dry. Then he had only to part the branches of the chestnut tree that drooped over the opening to the glade, curtain-like, and let them come together again to conceal him. The liquid flow of this path then entered into the hidden pool of the glade that no one else knew existed.

All signs of the outer world vanished: the distant halloos criss-crossing the terraced fields in the valley below, the barking of a dog in the village on the other side of the stream, the grinding of the stones of the watermill. Only a bird sang, with piercing sweetness, till it noted Ravi's appearance, and took off.

He then prowled around like an animal returning to its shelter: some ferns might have unfolded their tight knots of brown fur and transformed themselves into waving green fans; the family of pallid mushrooms of the day before might now be scattered and lie in shreds of fawn suede tinged with mauve. The leaves of the chestnut could be studied for signs of turning and he would watch and wait for the precise shade of dark honey that he wanted before he collected the leaves and filled the clearing he was making around the strange conical stone at the centre of the hollow. And the broken branch he had found on the way and dragged in with him, once dried and bleached to suggest a skeleton, could be added to the design. The berries he picked along the way could be worked into the creases of the rock so it might seem inlaid with strands of gleaming gems or as if it had sprung veins of precious ore.

He considered enlarging the design by bringing enough pebbles, or perhaps some sand from the stream-bed below, to see how they could be arranged to suggest a pool in which the rock formed an island.

Spider-like, Ravi set to work spinning the web of his vision over the hidden glade. And each day it had to be done before night fell.

It was already dark when the visitors drew up at the tea stall on the ridge, tired and hungry and not too good-tempered. Balram lit the Petromax and it roared to life, its blue flame flaring out and hissing like a demon, making them wince at its aggression.

The girl made a face of annoyance and shaded her eyes.

Chand laughed and shrugged as if it could not be helped, and poured out the beer Balram had brought them. 'Ready to eat?' he asked, because he was.

'You think they'll have anything to eat?'

'Ask.'

They called over to Balram who was making a show of wiping the counter. 'D'you serve food?'

Of course he served food. What did these city slickers up from the plains in their too-heavy jackets and too-new boots take him for, him and his establishment and his town? Resentfully he allowed he could give them samosas, bhajias, two-egg omelettes, three- and four-egg omelettes, as much as they wanted, and in double-quick time.

'Any roti?'

'Roti of course, the best you've ever had,' he told them, at once proud and rude.

'We'll have that, lots. And more beer.'

Sitting at a tin-topped table, they juggled their beer mugs, their plates of food, wolfing it all down ravenously in silence. It was the first meal they had had that day, travelling from the city in the dust of the vast plain, the jeep breaking down again and again in the most inconvenient places, far from any habitation, so that the two men had to take turns at trekking out, cursing and complaining, in search of motor workshops and spare parts to get them moving again. They had done the last stretch, winding steeply uphill, as darkness fell.

Had it really been such a good idea, coming up here to shoot a film on environmental degradation in the Himalayas? It had seemed so, but now they found themselves sinking into the familiar sense of defeat at the start of a project, the stage at which they began to doubt if it could be done.

'Wait till tomorrow, we haven't seen anything yet. We've been told about the quarries and the landslides, the tunnelling and the logging. There should be a lot.'

'Where will we find all this, in a holiday resort? We'd better get a guide,' Chand said, and called over to the tea-stall owner, manager, whoever he was. But how were they to explain what they wanted? Soil erosion, cattle grazing, deforestation: could he ever have heard these terms or given a thought to such matters in his world of a chai dukan and its beer and omelettes?

The man came over reluctantly, flinging his dishcloth over his shoulder. 'My name is Balram,' he told them, sensing he might have further dealings with this lot than just providing them with a meal. These people from the plains needed a lot of help when they came up here, especially if they came outside the tourist season. During the season you could count on them moving in a herd; they could be left to themselves, to promenade on the Mall, eyeing the flashy women, looking for bars, hotels, the kind of thing they were used to in the cities. But when they came out of season they came for other reasons.

He had seen the jeep they had driven up in, with its Delhi licence plate and a lot of what looked like expensive luggage, stuff they brought in with them, not wanting to let it out of their sight. Then there was this girl, wearing pants, dark glasses, her hair cut short. Balram was not at all sure he approved. Any daughter of his who went around like that would have got a tight slap from him. People came up from the plains, thought they could get away with that here. He had better show them they couldn't fool him. He saw a lot of that around here, knew a lot. He also had a very fine moustache – small, but kept well trimmed. He touched it for reassurance.

The two men had the decency to half rise from their chairs and shake his hand. Now he knew they really needed him, he relaxed. 'What can I do for you?'

'We have come here to do a few days' shooting,' the older man, who had been picking his teeth and still had a toothpick to chew on, began to explain. Seeing Balram's moustache twitch slightly in curiosity – what kind of shoot: boar, deer, panther, partridge? – he went on: 'To make a film.'

'Oh, a fill-um.' Balram was not nearly as impressed as they seemed to think he might be. Mussoorie had seen any number of films made, actors coming up from Bombay, plump and glossy with success, to dance down the Mall and pose against the mountainscape. Crowds would gather around, gape, shout out lewd comments and hoot with laughter, enjoying the tamasha. Traffic would get blocked, police would be called. 'So you are from Bombay, are you?'

'No, no,' Chand, the younger, the quicker, corrected. 'We make documentaries, for television.'

'Television, hunh?' Balram had been meaning to buy a set for his shop, and would have if the electric supply were more dependable. What was the use of a television without that? he'd said to his son who clamoured for one.

'And the documentary we have come to make is about these hills.'

Balram gave a snicker of laughter. 'Many directors come for that. Scenery, they all like scenery.'

'No, we're not interested in that. What we have heard is that the scenery is being spoilt, destroyed. Timber companies are cutting down the trees. Limestone quarries and phosphate mines are making the hills unstable. Soil erosion is taking place. Lots of landslides are occurring. That is what we have come to film.'

Balram could not think of anything more dull, and unnecessary. He fingered his moustache in what was clearly scepticism if not derision.

'So we need to go to spots where this is taking place.'

Now that he saw they needed help, Balram decided to be magnanimous. He waved his hand, offering it all to them as if it were nothing to him. 'You can go,' he gave his permission. 'You can see.'

But to them that sounded too vague and uncertain. They could see this was not his idea of a film. It was not scenic and had no commercial potential.

'Can you get us a guide who can take us to such sites?'

'Hmm.' It was a matter for thought and calculation, not to be dismissed in haste. Balram was a man to act judiciously, not rashly. Possibilities arose. He nodded. 'I will see.'

'But soon?' Chand, anyone could see, was a man in a hurry. Nothing could happen fast enough. When nothing happened, he jigged his legs up and down, in and out. 'We only have three – four days here.'

'Tell me where you are staying. I will bring you a guide.'

'We need to find a hotel.'

Now a light went on in Balram's face, in the form of a smooth glisten. This was more like it, his scene. He kept them on tenterhooks while he ran through suggestions, then dismissed them, and eventually chose. Hotel Honeymoon he could recommend confidently, he assured them, because it was where his cousin brother was manager. They would have every comfort there, and security. He had them write out the address and directions on a piece of paper. 'And tomorrow I will bring someone there, a guide.' He saw the horizons open out, thinking of all the relatives for whom he could do a favour, who would then be beholden to him, and began to smile. These city types, he could mould them like putty in his hands.

When they had carried out their bags and got into the jeep, he cleared their table, flicked it over with his dishcloth, now richly and satisfyingly blackened, and took the dishes behind the shack where a tap ran onto stones. He could close the place now with a sense of a day well spent.

The girl Shalini protested on seeing Hotel Honeymoon and did not want to dismount from the jeep, but they pointed out how late it was and how unlikely they were to find anything else at this hour. She went into her room sulkily, making Chand feel guilty, but not Bhatia. Bhatia had a strange sliding smile on his face and Chand could almost see the obscene thoughts behind it. He began removing his shoes, his clothes, reluctantly, while Bhatia stretched out on his cot under the light bulb that hung from the ceiling, flies adhering to its whole length.

On the other side of the partition wall – it was scarcely more than a screen – they could hear the girl undressing, item by item. Chand could see Bhatia imagining what those items were. He gave a snort of disgust, but could say nothing: the screen did not provide privacy of speech any more than of action. He threw himself onto his cot so that the strings creaked, and folded his arms across his chest: somehow he had to endure the night. 'Bloody Balram,' he muttered before he shut his eyes to its irritations.

In the morning Balram appeared at Hotel Honeymoon as the film crew were drinking tea and trying to eat greasy eggs with even greasier bread, hardly able to speak to one another for anger at the flea-bitten night they had endured. He brought along with him a boy. Who, what was he? An amalgam of virtues! Balram assured them: honesty, diligence, experience—

'What experience?' Bhatia interrupted, discarding the hopeless breakfast and choosing a cigarette in its place. 'At what? What has he done?'

Balram took a step back, spreading out his hands at this obviously unnecessary and offensive question. '*Everything*,' he stated with absolute conviction, and what more could be required than that?

'Such as?' The girl picked up Chand's scepticism although it was not for her to voice it. She was only the assistant, not the producer or the photographer. Still, she could not entirely suppress her opinion. It grew from the zeal she brought to the team of one whose first job it was out in the big world.

The boy stood by, his posture slack, his eyes downcast, studying his nails – some of them were flecked with crimson – as he permitted Balram to speak for him; surely it was too much to expect *him* to do so, this boy fed by his mother's hand just this morning, his hair oiled and combed by her, his clean shirt picked out for him. And now it was for Balram, his mother's brother, to do the rest and secure the job for him – if that was what they wished. What the job was had not been divulged to him, but he had heard the thrilling word – movie – in the dialogue between brother and sister last night. Movie – now he knew about movies. Once a week he bought a ticket at the Picture Palace and saw whatever it offered. The confidence that he could step into that, the world of movies, had been growing through the morning's preparations but now was somewhat reduced in the presence of these three common-looking people in their disappointing hotel. Besides, he was at a certain disadvantage here: this was the hotel where he had once washed dishes and from where he had been thrown out for unsatisfactory work. What else had they expected?

'Tell him, just tell him what you want,' Balram was saying in a loud voice as if to drown out all objections, even unspoken ones, 'and he will do.'

Having no alternative, it was with him in their jeep that they drove to the spot that Balram had picked for them as the site of the entrance to an illegal phosphate mine. The boy's name was Nakhu. He seemed in a state of disbelief that this was happening to him and whether it would be good or bad was not yet possible to tell. Could it, would it lead to his dancing on-screen with a bejewelled Bombay belle? Or would it only—

And abruptly the answer arrived: they had drawn up at the milestone Balram had suggested, under the overhang of a hill dense with shrub oak, at the edge of a precipice that dropped steeply downhill to what they could not see. It became immediately clear that the boy had not only never been here before but was incredulous that they seemed to think he had and that they expected him to dismount and let himself down a stony track that only a goat could have tackled, slipping and sliding downhill in an avalanche of rubble, taking all manner of risks with his nearly new jeans and his good shoes. He stood hesitating and teetering when Bhatia shouted, 'This is where Balram said we'd find the entrance to the mine. OK, so now take us there.'

Chand and Shalini, exchanging looks, decided to take over the lead, asking the others to follow as they stumbled and slid their way down to the promised scene of environmental degradation they might film.

The degradation did materialize, even without Nakhu's help. 'Look, look,' Shalini cried as they came upon a heap of fallen logs and charred stumps. 'Loggers have been here!'

'Then why go further?' Bhatia had already given up following them and was panting: all this exercise was not for him. 'Forget the phosphate mine, let's just film here and get it over with.'

Chand and Shalini exchanged disgusted looks. To them the effort was an essential part of their undertaking. If they had wanted to do something easy, they could have filmed in a studio, conducted interviews, put together a collage. But they had decided on filming actual sites, and sites would have to be found, perpetrators tracked down, caught red-handed if possible. Leaving Bhatia and Nakhu to follow, they continued down the slippery gravel, grasping at any bushes that seemed rooted, skirting agaves that sent out dangerously spiked spears, and got ahead – or, rather, further down the hillside.

It was dusty going and both were panting.

'Where *are* we going?' Shalini finally asked, stopping to wipe her face of perspiration. The dark glasses were proving a distinct encumbrance. 'How far did Balram say we had to go to get to the mine?'

Chand shook his head to show he didn't know but, on hearing the doubt in her voice, paused as well. It had occurred to him that the lower they went, the further they would have to climb on the way back. And even if they managed it, it was very doubtful that their equipment and equipment carriers would. 'That bloody Balram,' he swore. 'What sort of guide has he given us?'

'Where *is* he? And where is Bhatia?'

'With Nakhu.'

'Shall we wait?'

They stood and listened. Down below, concealed by the bushes, they could hear a stream running, a dog barking, someone hallooing, and up on the road they had left, a truck slowly grinding by.

'We should have asked a few more people for directions,' Shalini said.

Chand gave her a bitter look. He did not need her, his assistant, to give him advice. He was in charge of the project and it was time to take over. 'I'll go down to the river – they said there was a river – you take another direction, then double back. We'll meet at the jeep. Tell Bhatia to wait. Tell him not to risk bringing the equipment with him till we find the site.'

Shalini seemed about to protest, not sure if she wanted to be left alone, but reminded herself that Chand was her boss. He was the one who had given her this chance to show her mettle. So she nodded and struck off along a narrow track that cut into the side of the hill. Goat droppings on the stones showed it was used by others. It should be the way to somewhere.

After a while she realized what a relief it was to be on her own, not to feel the two men were keeping an eye on her, a critical, judging eye. She stopped to pick the berries of a wild raspberry bush, eating them with enjoyment even if they were tart and dry and bristly. Crushing them between her teeth, she found they revived a childhood memory of a holiday with pony rides, ice cream, a band playing in a gazebo on the Mall. Her family was not one that could often afford a holiday, it had been a rare one and memorable, but, until now, it had sunk so far back into her subconscious, she had forgotten it. Now she sniffed at the pine sap in the air with the pleasure of a renewed memory.

She almost forgot she was supposed to be looking for the entrance to the phosphate mine, or the evidence of illegal logging. She concentrated on making her way along the track, grasping at grasses here, an overhanging branch there, watching small yellow birds dart low over the lantana bushes that crowded against her legs. When her hand brushed a nettle that seemed to set it on fire, she had to stop and suck at the burn, standing under the overhang of a boulder that jutted out of the hillside, obstructing her way.

It seemed to be a natural barrier, the track was hardly likely to continue beyond it, but curiosity made her wonder if it did. The uncertainty had an edge not only of curiosity but also of fear – not exactly fear, but certainly a chill, an intimation of danger.

She would go round the rock only to see if the track continued, then turn back. As she held onto it, edging her way cautiously around, various possibilities entered her mind like brief passing shadows – of a snake in hiding, or a man with bad intentions. Or simply of getting lost. In a strange place. She was, after all, a city girl.

What she came upon was a kind of glade, so secluded it might have been undiscovered and untrodden by anyone. A wild place, half concealed from view by an enormous chestnut tree. It could have been the lair of a wild animal or perhaps even a secret hermitage.

Instead, as she peered past the overhanging branches of the tree, she saw something entirely different – a place surely ordered by human design, human hands, not nature. Nature could not have created those circles within circles of perfectly identical stones in rings of pigeon shades of grey and blue and mauve, or hoisted fallen branches into sculpted shapes, or filled the cracks in granite and slate with what seemed to be garlands of beads and petals. It looked like a bower – but of bird, beast or man? Any one of these was barely credible.

It seemed totally deserted, as composed and still as a work of art. Or nature. Or both, in uncommon harmony. The place thrummed with meaning. But what *was* the meaning? Was it a place of worship? But of what? There was no idol – unless that rock, that pattern of pebbles or that stripped branch constituted an idol. It actually seemed antithetical to any form or concept.

So what there was was a secret. Shalini gave a quiver at having found it and felt a sudden desire to give a shout, a halloo, about her find, when she became aware of someone who had been out of sight behind some rocks emerging into the glade. She caught a glimpse of a bowed head, a sleeve, a hand wielding – what? what?

She turned and ran.

When she heaved herself over the lip of the hill, hauling herself up by hands that were scratched and bleeding, and digging the toes of her boots into the gravelly earth, breathing hard from both fear and exertion, she found the jeep standing where they had left it – and desperately feared it might not be. Then, seeing Bhatia and Nakhu sitting there in sullen silence, her relief turned quickly to annoyance at the surly looks they directed at her.

'Where's Chand? We've been waiting for the two of you to

417

come and tell us if you had found anything. We've been waiting for *hours*.'

This was unfair, if true. Heatedly, she responded, 'We thought you were to follow us!'

'With all this stuff to carry? D'you think I could let it all go and get smashed? Or stolen from the jeep?'

This made sense of course and she pulled herself up into the jeep and sat there, unscrewing the top of a Thermos to gulp water and then wipe her face with her sleeve. Nakhu watched her inquisitively now that she had removed her dark glasses. She glared at him and put her glasses back on firmly, so.

It was a long wait till Chand finally returned to report on sites of illegal logging he had found, but there was no way they could carry their equipment down there: it was unfortunate that Nakhu was only partly and not completely a donkey.

'So let's just get back to town and find the office of the timber company or the mining business, and do interviews there,' Bhatia said with all the authority of reason, and neither Shalini nor Chand could put up a protest.

Bhatia told them of a tandoori restaurant he had seen near their hotel that looked promising and later that day, having washed and changed, they went there for dinner. But when he found the food was over-spiced and greasy, it was Bhatia who complained loudest and declared he would go to bed early, which left Shalini and Chand sitting in the hissing blaze of a Petromax to finish the last of the flat, warm beer they had been served, reluctant to go back to their flea-ridden rooms at the Honeymoon Hotel.

'So, we didn't get what we came for,' Chand sighed, seeing the expedition coming to the verge of collapse.

Shalini pushed her glasses up over the bridge of her nose. 'No,' she agreed, then ventured, 'Perhaps we can look at something else now that we're here.'

'What?' Chand's snort of contempt showed what he thought of the once-alluring, now decrepit and degraded mountains.

'I saw a strange place down below, on the way downhill,' Shalini admitted in a tone of unaccustomed uncertainty. 'I could show it to you.'

'Why?'

She would have to explain. It was a strange place she had stumbled on, made entirely *of* nature, yet not *by* nature. Someone had made it. Or was making it. Some kind of artist perhaps.

Now artists were a species for whom Chand had a grudging but profound respect. What they did was what he aspired to – or once had. Then, he had imagined his training in the year at film school in Pune would lead to it. Those had been the best times he had known. But he was also bitterly aware of how far he had strayed from any artistic ideals.

'And what kind of artist would *that* be?' he growled.

'I don't know. But you've heard of that man in Chandigarh, a road engineer or something, who collected all the scrap from his road projects and built a kind of sculpture garden of it? Kept it hidden because the land he built it on didn't belong to him? Then it was found and he became famous? What's his name, do you know?'

Chand threw her a surprised and wondering look in spite of himself.

Shalini took it for an aroused interest, and curiosity. 'We could go down tomorrow and look at it. Without Bhatia and Nakhu.'

That too appealed to Chand. He had had enough of those two, and he missed his girlfriend in Delhi, the easy-going, relaxed relationship he had with her, a divorcee in print journalism with whom he could have a drink at the Press Club any evening, and who seemed content with just that, someone to accompany her. He glanced at Shalini and decided he wouldn't mind an afternoon in her company, looking for this artist, this art – whatever it was.

Bhatia had no desire to accompany them on another bone-jolting ride in the jeep to nowhere. In fact, he begged them to leave him behind – his stomach was in turmoil, he was sure it was that tandoori chicken – he couldn't think of going anywhere. Instead, he would track down 'contacts' right there in town. At the photographer's studio, his first stop since he needed some film and some lenses, he found the town was already aware of their presence and project. The photographer, chewing upon a wad of betel leaves in his cheek, asked juicily, 'You are making a movie, I hear?'

Bhatia, tired of explaining the difference between movies and television, snapped, 'What did you hear about it?'

The photographer shrugged, laughed. 'Many come to make movies here,' he said, which was no longer an original remark. 'Everybody likes the scenery here.'

'We're not interested in scenery,' Bhatia assured him and then, thinking this man might prove a 'contact', expanded: 'We are looking into illegal mines, illegal logging, reasons why this scenery of yours is getting spoilt.'

His instinct proved right. Not only did the photographer plant his elbows on the glass counter and begin giving him the inside story of the corruption and skullduggery going on in the town, but several of the men who had been slouching in the doorway, watching the street for something interesting to happen – so little did in the off-season – edged deeper into the shop and began to add their own stories, and suggestions. Bhatia grew more and more comfortable: this was his scene, this was how he had always known the project would work. Accepting betel leaves, handing out cigarettes, he asked his new acquaintances if they could set up some interviews for him.

Chand drove the jeep back to the milestone where they had first stopped. But Shalini could not find the track she had taken the day before. Of course they had to go downhill but this time the track she mistakenly chose led through a thick growth of pine and instead of coming to the glade from around the boulder, they came upon it from above, not even aware of it till they almost plunged off a shelf of rock into it, it was so well concealed in the fold between the hills by ferns and the shadows of ferns.

Shalini put out her hand to alert Chand. He stood with his hands on his hips, staring, and what he saw – what he could make out through the screen of foliage and shadows – affected him enough to make him silent, take out cigarettes and matches from his pocket, then put them away again, unlit.

'Good?' Shalini whispered, trying not to grin.

Good, bad – hardly the words that applied. He was not even sure this garden – this design, whatever it was – was man-made. How could anything man-made surpass the Himalayas themselves, the flow of hills from the plains to the snows, mounting from light into cloud into sky? Or the eagles slowly circling on currents of air in the golden valleys below, or the sound of water gushing from invisible sources above?

What he saw here, however, contained these elements, the essence of them, in constricted, concentrated form, as one glittering bee or beetle or single note of birdsong might contain an entire season.

He let out a low whistle and turned to nod to Shalini. Yes.

They drove back along the loop that ringed the hilltop to the tea stall where they had stopped on their first night for omelettes.

Nakhu had clearly kept his uncle informed of the television crew's doings. Balram greeted them with an almost familial welcome, wiping a table clear of flies for them, suggesting, 'Chai? Coffee? Omelette?'

Shalini and Chand unburdened themselves of their backpacks, and exchanged looks: shall we ask? Chand did, carefully. 'There is a garden down that hill. Whose is it? Who made it? Do you know?'

There was nothing Balram did not know: that was the reputation he liked to maintain. But here he encountered some uncertainty. His fingers searched for an answer in his moustache. 'On that hill?' he asked eventually. 'The one with the burnt house at the top?'

'We didn't see one.'

Now he could tell them about the burnt house, its reputation, its mystery. But as he was telling it, it occurred to him that he could tell them nothing about the survivor of the fire except that there was one. And what they called a 'garden' might belong to him. 'Ask Bhola,' he said at last. 'Bhola is the caretaker. He will know.'

'Where will we find him? Where is this house?'

'Nakhu is with you. Nakhu will show you the way.'

They had almost left Nakhu out of their plans, he had been of so little use. But now they had to include him. And Bhatia.

Over dinner, they listened silently to Bhatia boast about his day's achievements. 'Got some good interviews. Lots of info. You should see the men running these businesses. You won't believe, such goondas. They talked, they don't care who knows. They've got everyone in their pockets. The whole town is making money. So we can wrap it up here, and on the way down to Dehra Dun, stop at some of these quarries – right out in the open – for background, and finish off.'

'Wait!' Shalini cried agitatedly since Chand did not.

'For what?' Bhatia turned an annoyed look at her.

She turned to Chand to explain, so he did. 'We think there might be something for us to film. Shalini showed me. It is a kind of garden. Very private, no one knows about it. But if we can find who made it – is making it – it could make a beautiful ending for the film, Bhatia. Someone who is different, someone who is not destroying the land but making something of it, something beautiful. You can see whoever it is really understands this landscape, appreciates it. We need to speak to him and see if he will let us film his garden.'

Bhatia lowered his head into the palm of his hand and ground it, groaning. Suddenly he was sick of the whole project. Everything about it was wrong, hopeless. And he needed to get home, to his wife's cooking, her care. He had had enough discomfort. Now he needed to leave.

'It's true,' Shalini broke in eagerly. 'It will make the perfect ending. First, all the bad things happening here. Then finish with something beautiful. Hopeful.'

'It's worth trying for, Bhatia,' Chand urged. It was, after all, the closest he had come in his career to art.

'And how are you going to produce this magician? Have you even *seen* him?'

'We will, we will,' they assured him, 'just give us some time,' and they sent for Nakhu. Nakhu was to lead them to the burnt house, and the magician.

Ravi was sitting on the veranda steps in the late-evening light, waiting for the homestead below to settle into its familiar pattern, smoke to rise from the thatched roof, his meal brought to him as usual, but it was Bhola who came up the path, empty-handed and strangely hesitant in manner. In addition, he cleared his throat to make Ravi aware he had something to say, and that he had been right to sense some unease in the air, something he had not been able to identify.

'There are some people here from Delhi,' Bhola began, 'they came to see me. People have been talking about them. They are here to make a fill-um.'

Ravi decided he needed to give himself time to adjust to this information. He offered a biri to Bhola although Bhola never took one from him, and lighted one himself.

'They are here to make a film,' he echoed, and wondered why he was being told this. Surely Bhola knew he had no interest at all in anything that was happening in town.

'And they wish to come and talk to you.'

It was too dark to see the expressions on each other's faces but not so dark that Bhola could not see Ravi's hand, holding the lighted biri, remain in mid-air and his entire posture freeze.

'No!' The answer finally broke from Ravi like something breaking deep inside him. 'No!'

Bhola felt compelled to offer understanding, and comfort. 'I will tell them. I will tell them you will not speak to them.'

'Yes,' Ravi said from between tightly compressed lips, a tightly constricted throat. 'Tell them. Tell them that.'

'I will tell that boy Nakhu they have engaged. I know Nakhu. Nakhu will tell them.'

Bhola meant the words to be reassuring but they did not seem to reassure Ravi. That was clear from the way he got to his feet and went blundering up the steps to his room. Bhola waited to see if he would light his lamp but he did not. The room stayed dark.

Ravi did not come out next morning. The house remained shut and silent. But at dusk, after he had brought home the goats and cow and a load of firewood for his wife, Bhola climbed the path and, on not seeing Ravi, went up the stairs and opened the door to his room. This was unprecedented: he never intruded on Ravi for any reason. But now he stood in the doorway, silently, looking in, so Ravi should be aware he was there.

'They found your garden,' Bhola told him, and he was as upset as he knew Ravi would be on hearing of the trespass. 'They filmed it, and tomorrow they want to come here. Nakhu is to bring them. They pay him.'

He could make out that Ravi was sitting at the table by the abrupt movement he made now, half rising from his chair.

'Come with me,' Bhola said and, going up to him, took him by his arm and directed him out of the room, down the steps. On the path he loosened his hold a bit but still held him by his sleeve as they followed each other down the uneven, stony track.

The dogs ran up to them in a band, clamouring. Bhola silenced them gruffly, and they turned round and led the way to the hut. Bhola's wife Manju was in the cowshed, milking the cow he had brought back from grazing. The air was thick with the smell of straw and the milk she squirted into the tin pail. The children had been whooping around, driving the chickens into their pen, but now they fell silent and stared.

Bhola took Ravi into the hut where the fire had just been lit to make the evening meal. In the semi-dark, he took down some clothes that were hanging on a line across one corner of the room and handed them to Ravi. 'Here,' he said, 'change into these. Even if you are seen, no one will think it is you. I will tell them you are my brother, visiting.' He left the room, leaving Ravi to follow his instructions, removing his khaki trousers and white shirt and pulling on Bhola's old, ragged pyjamas and a long shirt that came down to his knees. He removed his shoes and let his feet find their way into a pair of stiff, cracked leather sandals.

After a while Manju Rani came in with the milk pail and on seeing that she kept her face averted and acknowledged his presence only by drawing a fold of her headscarf a little lower over her forehead, Ravi went out into the yard among the animals. He looked for a corner where he would be out of the way. There was a log beside the cowshed and he went and sat there quietly to let the disturbance he had caused subside. The children stood and stared, not knowing what to make of all this: was he staying? Was he not going back up the hill?

When their mother called them, they went in, and Bhola came out to fetch Ravi. He indicated that Ravi was to sit beside them on the swept clay floor by the fire and passed him a tin plate that Manju Rani had filled with the potato curry she had made and some thick rotis that smelled of roasted wheat and were pleasantly charred. He ate, they all ate, no one spoke and there was no sound other than of eating and the occasional crackle of the fire. Its smoke thickened the darkness, making the darkness visible. No one was at ease.

Then Bhola led him out and showed him where he could wash at the pump, which he did, water splashing onto his sandals, making a puddle of mud around. Then he took him to an outhouse where stacks of firewood and implements were stored in the lower half and a ladder led to a shelf where there was hay and straw for the cow. Bhola had already been there and laid a rough wool blanket to make up a bed. Ravi, visibly relieved to find he was not expected to sleep with the family in the main hut, impulsively turned to thank Bhola, or in some way express his gratitude, but could not overcome his reserve, and simply nodded in acceptance of all he had been given. Bhola neither expected words nor required them and left him there.

Bhola's sons brought news to their father of the film crew's movements – down in Ravi's glade or up on the hill and around the burnt house. The children followed them around, fascinated, ready to hoot and guffaw, till they were called away roughly by Bhola who did not pass on any information to Ravi, telling him only 'It is better that you stay here. Till they are gone.' He found Ravi a Himachal cap such as he wore himself, with a band of red velvet on grey felt, to put on his head. It completed the disguise.

All day, while Bhola was gone with the beasts and the boys were supposedly at school but in truth up on the hill, Ravi had nowhere to go and nothing to do. He sat on the log by the cowshed, watching the chickens pick at grains and the insects they found among the stones, or rising up in sudden flurries of beating wings and frightened squawks at the shadow of an eagle crossing their earth, and Manju Rani going in and out about her chores, her head tied up in a long Himachal scarf and her eyes averted from him. Bhola had brought her back from Tehri as a bride; it had marked the end of his boyhood, of catapults and cricket games. After that he had been a householder, with responsibilities, and Manju Rani clearly had hers. Ravi never looked directly at her but was aware of her movements as she filled a bucket at the pump or clambered up the hillside to cut grasses for the goats with her curved scythe, tossing them into the basket strapped to her back. Her youngest child, a girl of about four, followed her around. Her feet were always bare, her nose was always running, her flowered frock filthy as was her hair, but her face was as round and pink as a rose in bloom. Mostly she clutched at her mother's kameez and followed her, but sometimes she broke away and came to study the man seated on the log, wondering at his stillness and silence in the midst of such continuous sound and movement. Her mother would call her sharply and she would run away, laughing.

It was a long time since Ravi had been around a woman. His

mother, his female relatives in Bombay, Miss Wilkinson the last. He had no way of making any connection with those in Bhola's family but he knew he did not want to: they in no way compensated for what he had lost – his space, his enclosure, the pattern and design he had created, was creating within it. Would those barbarians from the city have stepped on it? Touched it, broken and wrecked it? Their gaze alone was a desecration. Then there were all the natural changes that were wrought daily and nightly by a passing breeze, a fall of leaves, a dwindling and dying of what had been fresh and new the day before, or else the eruption of the renewed and unexpected – and he was not there to observe and mark and celebrate them. He knew he would never go there again. It would revert to wilderness. His longing to resume what was his real life was left smouldering inside him like a match blown at but not put out. Brooding, he sat studying his hands as if they were all that were left to him now that he had nothing to work on.

Then, after a glass of tea and some bread in Bhola's hut one morning, after everyone had gone their separate ways, he saw that Manju Rani had left an empty matchbox on the clay hearth. He picked it up and went outdoors with it in his hands. It was his way, to observe and study. Seating himself on the log in his corner, he slid the flimsy container open and studied its emptiness with his habitual concentration. It might have been a crib, a cradle – but to hold what? Looking around for something small enough to fit in it, he found a sliver of bark and a scrap of moss but they left room for more. In the ground at his feet he spied a fragment of quartz that could be added. He slid the box shut and put it in the deep pocket of his shirt. All day long he reached to touch it, finding there a source of contentment and wonder at what other collections might be made.

He began to look out for empty matchboxes. Each offered a world of possibilities for the minute objects and the patterns he could make of them, patterns that he could alter endlessly as pieces of coloured glass can be shifted in a kaleidoscope. Lying open, they revealed themselves like constellations in the night. Shut in a box, they became invisible. And he could carry them on him, keep them to himself; no one would know.

Up at the burnt house, the film crew prowled around with their camera, searching for the hermit. From the veranda they could look down at the clearing, at Bhola's hut, the chickens picking around it, Manju Rani going in and out with armfuls of grass, her child in a pink frock following, a man seated by the cowshed, idly, a dog asleep in the sun.

'There's no one there,' Bhatia pronounced authoritatively. 'He's gone.'

Crouching around the projector later in the back room at the photographer's, they viewed the film they had shot 'in the garden' as Shalini called it. It was a scene drained of life, with neither colour nor fragrance nor movement. Tree, rock, leaf, stone, together or separately, they remained lifeless, the backdrop of a stage on which nothing happened.

The spool unwound with a long, rasping whirr, and its last flashes and symbols vanished into the dark. They remained crouched, unwilling to turn on the light and face each other.

Finally Bhatia said, 'We can't use this. Who would want to watch it? We'll just have to throw it away. It's dead, a dead loss, a waste of time.'

Shalini turned to face him, her face full of protest, but Chand merely sighed, accepting defeat. She realized he would not fight.

As they went to their separate rooms at the Hotel Honeymoon with Bhatia loudly bellowing, 'We can leave in the morning! First thing! It's a wrap!' Shalini said to Chand, in a low voice, 'I *could* have made it better, if we'd only found the artist who made it to show us around and talk about it, *that* would have been the ending we needed.'

'But we didn't,' Chand said with a resigned shrug. 'Perhaps he doesn't exist.'

*

The jeep descended the tawny hills, curve by curve, in the wake of the dust raised by a long line of buses and trucks ahead. The air grew warmer with each turn. The pine trees grew fewer, the grasses drier.

The traffic moved sluggishly, then came to an abrupt halt. Chand braked sharply to avoid crashing into the truck in front. At the bend two or three men appeared, waving red flags. Their appearance was followed by a series of dull thuds that seemed to come from inside the hill, rocking the jeep on its wheels. White dust spouted into the air, spreading in balloons and descending in parachutes, so thick it caused everyone to cough and choke.

All traffic had halted, exhaling fumes that added to the dust cloud. Bhatia jumped out of his seat – now that they were on their way back, he seemed filled with energy and determination – and joined some drivers who had climbed out along the verge. As Shalini and Chand watched, still half blinded by the explosion, they heard him give a shout and saw him throw out his arm, pointing downwards like an explorer who had made a discovery.

With reluctance and resentment, the two got down to join him and follow the direction of his pointing finger. The shelf on which they stood seemed dangerously precarious: right under it they could see great gashes that had opened out into caverns of white limestone. Even as they stood staring, another explosion went off and more white dust came boiling up towards them while echoes of the dynamite blast continued to reverberate.

Once those died away, men were seen to detach themselves from the hillside on which they had been crouching, their hair and clothes cloaked in white dust that made them look like ghostly figures in a photographic negative. With pickaxes and shovels, they began to dig, hammer and excavate.

Shalini turned away, closing her eyes to the grit and dust, and Chand doubled over, coughing, but Bhatia was triumphant.

'That is what we need for a finish!' he shouted. 'Get the camera, let's shoot!'

A line of trucks went rumbling down a newly made track into the gully, and the ghost men below began to load them for the journey down to the plains.

A Note on the Author

Anita Desai was born and educated in India. Her published works include many award-winning short-story collections and novels, three of which have been shortlisted for the Booker Prize, most recently *Fasting, Feasting*. She is a Fellow of the Royal Society of Literature and of the American Academy of Arts and Letters.